The Land Of [...]

Mount S[...]

Crystal Gorge

The Wasteland

The Nest
Of Vlagh

Long Pass

The Falls
Of Vash

The Isle Of
Thurn

Lattash

The Isle
Of Akalla

The Isle
Of Arash

Aracia's Ice Zone

Castano

Kaldacin

Poress

Ranta

Ondos

Vatan

Venata

Chalan

Palka

Ermol

Septos

Bergalta

Forlen

Witor

Bolgan

Tashan

Udar

Avel

The Trogite Empire

THE ELDER GODS

By David and Leigh Eddings

THE BELGARIAD
Book One: Pawn of Prophecy
Book Two: Queen of Sorcery
Book Three: Magician's Gambit
Book Four: Castle of Wizardry
Book Five: Enchanters' End Game

THE MALLOREON
Book One: Guardian of the West
Book Two: King of the Murgos
Book Three: Demon Lord of Karanda
Book Four: Sorceress of Darshiva
Book Five: The Seeress of Kell

BELGARATH THE SORCERER
POLGARA THE SORCERESS
THE RIVAN CODEX

THE ELENIUM
Book One: The Diamond Throne
Book Two: The Ruby Knight
Book Three: The Sapphire Rose

THE TAMULI
Book One: Domes of Fire
Book Two: The Shining Ones
Book Three: The Hidden City

THE REDEMPTION OF ALTHALUS
HIGH HUNT
THE LOSERS
REGINA'S SONG

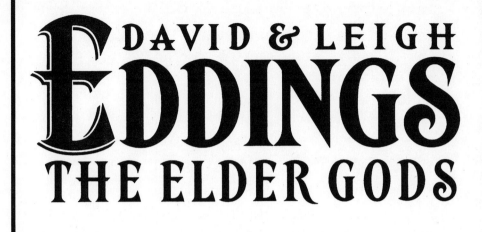

DAVID & LEIGH EDDINGS
THE ELDER GODS

BOOK ONE

OF

THE DREAMERS

ASPECT

WARNER BOOKS

An AOL Time Warner Company

Aspect® name and logo are registered trademarks of Warner Books, Inc.

Warner Books, Inc., 1271 Avenue of the Americas, New York, NY 10020
Visit our Web site at www.twbookmark.com.

An AOL Time Warner Company

Printed in the United States of America

First Printing: October 2003
10 9 8 7 6 5 4 3 2 1

Library of Congress Cataloging-in-Publication Data
Eddings, David.
    The Elder Gods / David and Leigh Eddings.
        p. cm. — (The Dreamers ; bk. 1)
    ISBN 0-446-53221-5
        1. Children—Fiction 2. Dreams—Fiction. I. Eddings, Leigh. II. Title.

PS3555.D38E44 2003
813'.54—dc21   2003048582

THE ELDER GODS

The Wasteland

The Village
Of
Old Bear

The Isle Of
Thurn

N

Lattash
(Tribe Of
White-Braid)

The House
Of Veltan

The
Domain
Of Zelana

The Isle
Of Arash

Preface*

The Land of Dhrall, if we are to believe the sometimes fanciful legends of the region, has existed in its present location since the beginning of time. Father Earth is unstable, and other continents move hither and yon across the face of Mother Sea, wandering, ever wandering, in search of new places in which to abide, but the Land of Dhrall, we are told, was firmly anchored to its present location by the will of the gods of Dhrall, and it shall remain ever so until the end of the world.

Now, from whence this world came—and why—is far beyond human comprehension, but the legends of Dhrall maintain that it is the work of ancient gods, and the making of it was a task so enormous that the gods, immortal and omnipotent though they be, ofttimes wearied of their labor.

Now, there were younger gods abroad in the land at this time, and great was their pity for their exhausted elders, and they urged their kin to rest while they themselves took up the burden of creation. And grateful beyond measure were the old

*Excerpted from "The Land of Dhrall," a study by the Comparative Theology Department of the University of Kaldacin.

1

ones, for they had labored well-nigh unto death. And so they slept while creation continued uninterrupted in the hands of the younger gods.

So it was that the elder gods slept for twenty-five eons and then they awoke, refreshed and ready to resume their eternal task; and when they awoke, their younger counterparts were well ready to relinquish the task and go to *their* rest.

And mountains rose up from out of the earth and were worn down by weather and time. And Mother Sea brought forth life in many forms, and some of the creatures of Mother Sea came up on the dry face of Father Earth in search of a dwelling place. And time and place altered them there upon the face of Father Earth, and many were those alterations. Forms not seen before emerged, and older forms died out as the creatures blindly groped for fulfillment.

Now, the gods of the Land of Dhrall chose not to interfere in the growth and development of the creatures of their Domains, for they wisely concluded that the creatures should follow their own course in response to the world around them. For truly, the world is in a constant state of flux, and a creature suitable for one era may well not survive in another, and the gods had come to realize that change must be a response to the world rather than some divine preconception.

And constant time continued her stately march toward an end that none could know, and the cycles of labor and rest among the gods continued even as Mother Sea and Father Earth watched but said nothing.

Now, the gods of the land of Dhrall have divided the land, and each, younger or elder, holds dominion over a certain portion of the land. There remains, however, a vast Wasteland in the center that is not part of any of the four Domains, be they East or West, North or South, for the Wasteland of Dhrall is barren and without beauty. There is life there, however, but the life-forms of the Wasteland are unlike those of the rest of the Land of Dhrall. The legends of Dhrall maintain that the life-forms of the Wasteland are the creations of That-Called-the-Vlagh.

The legends of Dhrall are uncertain as to the origins of the Vlagh. Some maintain that it is no more than a nightmare, which one of the early gods experienced during their first long sleep. Other legends contend that the Vlagh is vastly older than the gods, whose forms resemble those of humans, and that it was the lord of stinging insects and venomous reptiles, which have long since vanished from the faces of Mother Sea and Father Earth. All legends of Dhrall agree on one point, however. That-Called-the-Vlagh was too impatient to give the creatures which served it sufficient time to follow the slow, natural process of development and alteration favored by the true gods of Dhrall, but rather it chose to manipulate their development so that they might better serve it.

And it came to the Vlagh that its servants might be of greater value if they were not all the same, for a creature designed for one task and one only would be far more efficient than a more generalized creature.

To achieve that end, the Vlagh periodically enveloped itself in a woven cocoon in its dark nest in the center of the Wasteland, and when it emerged from its cocoon, it was a creature of an entirely different aspect than it had been before. Then it tested the capabilities of its new form to determine its ability to perform its specific task, noting its strengths and weaknesses. And then once again it enclosed itself in the cocoon, and when it emerged once more, the weaknesses were no longer there and the strengths had been enhanced.

Thus, by experimentation, That-Called-the-Vlagh altered and modified its own form to develop a highly specific creature, and once it was satisfied, it reproduced that creature by the thousands so that it would have servants enough to achieve its ultimate goal.

Then That-Called-the-Vlagh returned to its nest and began again, creating yet another form with yet another specific task.

And so it is that all of the varied creatures which emerge from the cocoon of the Vlagh are not the creatures of the Domains of the true gods of Dhrall, but rather are strange combinations, part insect, part reptile, part warm-blooded animal, and each of these variations has specific tasks in its service to the Vlagh.

The one and only characteristic the creatures of the Wasteland share is an obsessive need to expand the Domain of the Vlagh until the entirety of the Land of Dhrall lies in its grasp.

And the Vlagh sent forth many of its creatures to intrude themselves into the domains of the true gods of Dhrall, and carried those intruders back to the Vlagh everything which they had observed. And the Vlagh considered each tiny nibble of truth which its servants brought to it, and after eons uncounted, it perceived a flaw which it could exploit during the transfer of power and authority from one generation of gods unto the next.

For truly, the elder gods grew weary and forgetful as they longed for sleep; and the younger gods were yet only half awake.

And the spirit of the Vlagh was filled with anticipation at this revelation. And laid it then its plans and marshaled its servants in preparation for a war whereby it could surely destroy the true gods of Dhrall. And there in the Wasteland it dreamed of the day when its nest could expand into the more fertile regions of the Land of Dhrall, where there would be much to eat and where its need to spawn would no longer be restrained by the lack of food. And then the Vlagh dreamed further, yearning for the day when the entirety of the world englobed would be its nest, and its children would grow to numbers beyond counting, and all other living things would be their food.

Then and only then would the Vlagh be content.

Now, Mother Sea and Father Earth paid scant heed to the antics of any gods of any lands, and neither did they rest, for to them fell the task of maintaining the life of the creatures of earth and sea, and woe to him, human or divine, who threatens the perpetuation of life. For gentle though they may appear, Mother Sea and Father Earth have disasters beyond imagining at their disposal, should they appear necessary for the continuation of life.

Now, it came to pass long ago in the Domain of the North that a half-mad hermit had a vision of that which would one day become reality, and in that vision he saw sleeping children whose dreams could thwart the designs of That-Called-the-Vlagh, for the dreams could command, and Mother Sea and Father Earth could not disobey the commands of the Dreamers.

And most men of the Land of Dhrall scoffed at the vision of the hermit, for his madness was clearly evident. But the gods of East and West, North and South, scoffed not, for the hermit's vision resounded deep within their souls, and they knew it to be true. And troubled were the true gods of the Land of Dhrall, for they knew in their hearts that the arrival of the Dreamers would change all the world, and nothing thereafter would ever be the same again.

And the eons, as eons must, plodded on toward an uncertain future, and the younger gods grew older, and the cycle of their ascendancy neared its conclusion.

And it is here that our story begins.

THE ISLE OF THURN

1

Zelana of the West had grown weary of the brutish man-creatures of her Domain. She found them repulsive, and their endless complaints and demands irritated her beyond measure. They seemed to believe that she lived only to serve them, and that offended her.

And so it was that she turned her back on them and sojourned for several eons on the Isle of Thurn, which lies off the coast of her Domain. And there she communed with Mother Sea and entertained herself by composing music and creating poetry.

Now, the waters around the Isle of Thurn are the home of a rare breed of pink dolphins, and Zelana found them to be playful and intelligent, and in time she came to look upon them not as pets but rather as dear companions. She soon learned to understand—and to speak—their language, and they gave her much information about Mother Sea and the many creatures that lived in Mother's depths and along her shores. Then by way of recompense, she played music for them on her flute or sang for them. The dolphins came to enjoy Zelana's impromptu concerts, and they invited her to swim with them.

They were much perplexed by a few of Zelana's peculiarities after she joined them. So far as they could determine, she never slept, and she could remain under the surface of Mother Sea almost indefinitely. It also seemed odd to them that she showed no interest in the schools of fish which swam in the waters around the Isle. Zelana tried to explain to her friends that sleep and air and food were not necessary for her. Her periods of sleep and wakefulness were much longer than theirs, and she could extract the essential element of air from the water itself, and she fed on light rather than fish or grass, but the dolphins could not quite grasp her explanation.

Zelana decided that it might be best to just let it lie.

The man-creatures of the Land of Dhrall knew full well just who—and what—Zelana was. She held dominion over the West, but there were others in her family as well. Her elder brother Dahlaine held sway over the North, and he was grim and bleak. Her younger and sometimes frivolous brother Veltan controlled the South—when he was not exploring the moon or contemplating the color blue—and her prim and proper elder sister Aracia ruled the East as both queen and goddess.

The ages continued their stately march, but Zelana paid them no heed, for time meant nothing to her. Then on a clear day her dearest friend, a matronly pink dolphin named Meeleamee, surfaced near the place where Zelana sat cross-legged on the face of Mother Sea playing her newest musical composition on her flute. "I've found something you might want to see, Beloved," Meeleamee announced in her piping voice.

"Oh?" Zelana said, setting her flute aside in the emptiness just over her shoulder where she kept all her possessions.

"It's really very pretty, Beloved," Meeleamee piped, "and it's exactly the right color."

"Why don't we go have a look then, dear one?" Zelana replied.

And so together they swam toward the stark cliffs on the southern margin of the Isle, and as they neared the coast, Meeleamee sounded, swimming down and down into the depths of Mother Sea. Zelana arched over and followed, and soon they came to the narrow mouth of an underwater cavern, and Meeleamee swam on into that cavern with Zelana close behind.

Now, reason and experience told Zelana that this cave should grow darker as the two of them went deeper and deeper into its twisting passage, but it grew lighter instead, and the water ahead glowed pink and warm and friendly, and Meeleamee rose toward the light with Zelana close behind.

And when they surfaced in the shallow pool at the end of the passage, Zelana beheld a wonder, for Meeleamee had led her into a grotto unlike any other Zelana had ever seen. There was a rational explanation, of course, but mundane rationality could not tarnish the pure beauty of the hidden grotto. A broad vein of rose-colored quartz crossed the ceiling of the grotto, filling that hidden cave with a glowing pink light, and almost in spite of herself, Zelana feasted on that light and found it delicious beyond the taste of any other light she had savored in the past ten eons. And she shuddered and glowed with pure delight as she feasted.

Beyond that shallow pool at the entrance was a floor covered with fine white sand touched with the luminous pink of the prevailing light, and there was also a musically tinkling trickle of fresh water in a little niche at the rear, and all manner of interesting nooks and crannies along the curved walls.

"Well?" Meeleamee squeaked. "What do you think, Beloved?"

"It's lovely, lovely," Zelana replied. "It's the most beautiful place on all the Isle."

"I'm glad you like it," Meeleamee said modestly. "I thought you might like to visit here now and then."

"No, dear one," Zelana replied. "I won't need to visit. I'm going to live here. It's perfect, and I deserve a little perfection now and then."

"You won't stay here *all* the time, will you, Beloved?" Mee-leamee squeaked in consternation.

"Of course not, dear one," Zelana replied. "I'll still come out to play with you and my other friends, but this beautiful place will be my home."

"What is 'home'?" Meeleamee asked curiously.

It was on a day much like any other when Dahlaine of the North came up out of the passageway that led to Zelana's pink grotto to advise his sister that there was trouble in the wind in the Land of Dhrall.

"I don't really see how that's any concern of mine, dear brother," Zelana told him. "The mountains protect the lands of the West on one side, and Mother Sea protects them on the other. How can the creatures of the Wasteland ever reach me?"

"The Land of Dhrall is all one piece, dear sister," Dahlaine reminded her, "and no natural barrier is completely insurmountable. The creatures of your lands of the West stand in as great a danger as all the others. I think it's about time for you to come out of your little hideaway here and start paying attention to the world around you. How long has it been since you last surveyed your Domain?"

Zelana shrugged. "A few eons is all—certainly no more than a dozen. Have I missed anything significant?"

"The man-creatures have made a bit of progress. They're making tools now, and they've learned how to build fires. You really ought to look in on them once in a while."

"What in the world for? They're stupid and vicious, and they stink. My dolphins are cleaner and wiser, and their hearts are large and filled with love. If the creatures of the Wasteland are hungry, let them eat the man-creatures. I won't really miss them."

"The people of the West are *your* responsibility, Zelana," Dahlaine reminded her.

"So are the flies and ants and roaches, and *they* seem to be getting along well enough."

"You can't just ignore the world, Zelana," Dahlaine told her. "There are changes taking place all around you. The creatures of the Wasteland are growing restless, and it won't be too long before the Dreamers arrive. We need to be ready."

"It's not nearly the age of the Dreamers yet, is it, Dahlaine?" Zelana asked incredulously.

"The signs are all there, Zelana," Dahlaine said. "The servants of the Vlagh have begun to intrude into our Domains, which is a fair indication that the Vlagh is about to make its move, and we're not ready to face it yet. In a peculiar sort of way, this confrontation is the work of Mother Sea and Father Earth. Evidently, they know more than we do, and they're unleashing the Vlagh *now*—quite probably to force it to come against us before it's really ready. If we give it more time to modify its offspring, they'll swarm us under."

"We should have destroyed that hideous creature as soon as we realized just exactly where its instincts would send it."

"We can talk about all this some other time, dear sister," Dahlaine smoothly changed the subject. "What I *really* came here for was to give you something I thought you might like."

"A gift—for me?" Zelana's irritated humor seemed to vanish. "What is it?" she demanded eagerly.

Dahlaine smiled. Somehow the magic word "gift" always seemed to bring his brother and his sisters around to his way of thinking. Zelana in particular always responded in exactly the way he wanted her to. A gift wasn't really a form of coercion, but it served the same purpose, and it was a nicer approach. "Oh," he said in an offhand manner, "it's not really very much, sister dear. It's just a little something I thought you might enjoy. How would you like a new pet? It occurred to me that you might be getting a little tired of your dolphins after all these eons, since they can't really come out of the water to play with you here in your lovely grotto, so I brought you a pet that should be able to share your home."

"A puppy, maybe?" Zelana asked eagerly. "I've never owned a puppy, but I've heard that they're very affectionate."

"Not exactly a puppy, no."

"Oh . . ." Zelana sounded disappointed. "A kitten, then?" she said, her eyes brightening once more. "I've heard that the purring sound kittens make is very relaxing."

"Well, not quite a kitten either."

"What is it, Dahlaine?" Zelana demanded impatiently. "Show me."

"Of course," Dahlaine replied, concealing his sly smile. He reached both hands into the unseen emptiness he always carried along behind him and took a fur-wrapped bundle out of the air. "With my compliments, my beloved sister," he said extravagantly, handing her the bundle.

Zelana eagerly took the bundle and turned back the edge of the fur robe to see what her brother had given her. She gaped in obvious disbelief at the newborn pet drowsing in the warm fur robe. "What am I supposed to do with this thing?" she demanded in a shrill voice.

He shrugged. "Take care of it, Zelana. It shouldn't be much more difficult to care for than a young dolphin."

"But it's one of those man-creatures!" she protested.

"Why, so it is," Dahlaine replied in mock astonishment. "How strange that I didn't notice that myself. You're very perceptive, Zelana." He paused. "It's not an ordinary man-creature, dear sister," he added gravely. "It's very special. There are only a few of them, but they'll change the world. Care for it and protect it, Zelana. I think you'll have to feed it, because I don't think it can live on light alone as we do. You might have to experiment a bit to find something it can digest, but I'm sure that you're clever enough to solve that problem. You'll need to keep it clean as well. Infant man-creatures tend to be messy. Then, after a few years, you might want to teach it to talk.

There are things it's going to need to tell us, and if it can't talk, it won't be able to pass them on to us."

"What could one of these creatures tell us that we don't already know?"

"Dreams, Zelana, dreams. We don't sleep, so we don't dream. That baby in your arms is a Dreamer. That's why I brought her to you."

"It's a girl, then?" Zelana's voice softened.

"Naturally. I didn't think you'd get along very well with a boy. Care for her, Zelana, and I'll come by in a few years to see how she's coming along."

The baby in Zelana's arms made a cooing sound and reached out one tiny hand to touch Zelana's face.

"Oh," Zelana said in a trembling, almost stricken voice, clasping the infant more closely to her.

Dahlaine smiled. It had turned out rather well, he congratulated himself. All it had taken to totally enslave his brother and both of his sisters had been a few peeps and coos and one soft touch from an infant hand. He might have gloated a bit more, but his own baby Dreamer was home alone, and it was almost feeding time, so he really should get on back.

He swam out of Zelana's grotto and remounted his well-trained lightning bolt. Lightning bolts are noisy steeds—there's no question about that—but they can cover vast distances in the blink of an eye.

Zelana's first problem with her newfound charge was finding something to feed it. She rather hoped that Dahlaine had been mistaken. If the infant could live on light alone, as Zelana herself did, feeding it would be no problem. The vein of pink quartz in the ceiling of the grotto concentrated the sunlight into a glowing pink pool, which was presently centered on the bed of moss where Zelana occasionally rested. Hopefully she laid the fur-robed bundle on that moss bed and turned the robe back to allow the sunlight to touch the child.

The infant began to fuss a bit. Maybe the little creature didn't like the color. Zelana had discovered that a steady diet of pink light took a bit of getting used to. Pink, it appeared, was an acquired taste.

Zelana snapped her fingers, and the quartz obediently turned blue. The baby didn't stop fussing, though, and her discontent was growing louder.

Zelana tried green, but that didn't work either. Then she tried plain white. It was a little bland, but perhaps the baby wasn't ready for advanced colors yet.

The sounds the infant was making grew louder and more insistent.

Zelana quickly gathered the squalling infant in her arms and hurried down to the edge of the shallow pool at the mouth of the grotto. "Meeleamee!" she called in the piping language of the dolphins, "I need your help! Right now! Please!"

Now, Meeleamee had mothered many, many young, so she had great wisdom and much experience in such matters. "Milk," she advised.

"What is milk?" Zelana asked, "and where can I find some?"

Meeleamee explained in some detail, and for the very first time in her endless life, Zelana blushed. "What a strange sort of thing," she said, blushing even harder. She looked down at herself. "Do you think I might be able to . . ." She left it hanging.

"Probably not," Meeleamee replied. "There are some things involved that are just a little complicated. Can the young one swim?"

"I don't really know," Zelana admitted.

"Unwrap her and put her down in the shallow water here. I should be able to nurse her without too much trouble."

It was a bit awkward at first, but they found that if Meeleamee laid on her side and Zelana held the infant, things went quite well. Zelana felt a real sense of accomplishment—which lasted for nearly four hours.

Then they had to feed the child again. It seemed that there

was a great deal of inconvenience involved in caring for infants.

The seasons turned, as seasons always do, and summer drifted on into autumn, and winter followed shortly after. Zelana had never really paid much attention to the seasons. Heat or cold had little meaning for her, and she could create light whenever she grew hungry.

The female dolphins were taking turns feeding the infant, and Zelana noticed that the child seemed to be very affectionate. The dolphins were a bit startled by kisses at first, but after a while they even enjoyed being kissed by the grateful child, and sometimes there were even arguments about whose turn it was to nurse. The arguments broke off abruptly when the child sprouted teeth and began chewing on whatever was handy, though. Her diet changed at that point, and the dolphins offered her fish instead of milk. She still kissed them by way of thanks, so everything seemed all right again.

Since the child had always been fed in the shallow pool at the grotto's mouth, she was swimming even before she began to grow teeth, but she started walking—and running—not long after her diet changed, and she was soon toddling about the grotto, squeaking dolphin words as she went. She returned to the water whenever she grew hungry, however. The dolphins were careful to keep her more or less confined to the water at the mouth of the grotto, but they took to chasing fish in from the deeper waters of Mother Sea to give the child some experience in the business of catching her own food.

When the summer of the child's third year arrived, she ventured out of the grotto to join the younger dolphins in their forays along the coast of the Isle of Thurn. She spent her days now frolicking with the young dolphins and eating the bounty of Mother Sea.

Zelana approved of that. The child's independence freed her mistress at last so that she could return to poetry and music.

The young dolphins called the child "Beeweeabee," but Zelana didn't really think that was appropriate, since it approximately translated into "Short-Fin-With-No-Tail." Despite her habits and her companions, the little girl was still a land animal, so Zelana unleashed her poetic talents and ultimately arrived at "Eleria." It had a nice musical sound to it, and it rhymed with several very pleasant words.

The little girl didn't really seem to care for the name, but after a while she *would* answer to it when Zelana called her, so the name more or less did what it was supposed to.

The seasons continued to turn, but Zelana had long since realized that they could do that on their own, so she didn't have to prompt them.

Then, in the autumn of Eleria's fifth year, Dahlaine came by again. "How are things progressing with your child, dear sister?" he asked Zelana.

"It's a bit hard to say," Zelana replied. "I haven't had any contact with the man-creatures for more than ten eons, and I'm sure they've changed in that many years. I can't really be sure what's normal for them at Eleria's age. She spends most of her time in the water, though, so she doesn't stink the way most of her kind did when I turned my back on them."

"Where is she?" Dahlaine asked, looking around the grotto.

"Probably out playing with her friends," Zelana said, "most likely somewhere along the coast of the Isle."

"She has friends?" Dahlaine seemed a bit surprised. "I didn't know there were any people here on the Isle."

"There aren't, and even if there were, I wouldn't permit her to associate with them."

"You're going to have to get over that, sister. Eventually she *will* be required to have dealings with her own kind."

"What for?"

"She'll have to tell them what they're supposed to do, Zelana. If her playmates aren't people, what exactly are they?"

"Dolphins, of course. She and the young dolphins get along very well."

"I didn't know that dolphins can move around on dry land."

"They can't. Eleria swims with them."

"Are you mad?" Dahlaine almost screamed. "She's only five years old! You can't just turn her loose in Mother Sea like that!"

"Stop worrying so much, Dahlaine. She swims almost as well as her playmates do, and she finds most of her food out there in deep water. It saves me all sorts of time. She feeds herself, so I don't have to bother. She *does* seem to like berries—when they're in season—but most of the time she eats fish."

"How does she cook them if she's out there in the water?"

"What is 'cook'?" Zelana asked curiously.

"Just a custom, really," Dahlaine replied evasively. "You ought to try to keep her out of deep water, though."

"Why? She swims mostly along the surface, so what difference does it make how much water's down below her?"

Dahlaine gave up. There was just no talking with Zelana.

2

Though Zelana would not have admitted it even to herself, her life was much more pleasant now that she had Eleria to love and to care for. Since Eleria was able to find her own food and she had playmates enough to keep her occupied, her presence in the grotto in the evenings was hardly any inconvenience at all. Zelana was still able to create poetry and compose music, and Eleria served as a ready-made audience. She loved to have Zelana sing to her, and she seemed to enjoy listening to the recitation of Zelana's poems—even though she didn't understand a single word. She was now well into her sixth year, but she continued to speak exclusively in the squeaky, piping language of the dolphins.

Zelana considered that. It wasn't really all that much of a problem, since she herself was also fluent in that language. She decided, though, that perhaps one of these days she might teach the young one the rudiments of the language she spoke and shared with her sister and her brothers. It shouldn't be too difficult. Zelana had discovered that Eleria was very quick.

As it turned out, however, Eleria was about two jumps ahead of her. Zelana had been reciting poetry to the child since

Eleria's infancy, and one day in the early autumn of Eleria's sixth year Zelana happened to overhear the child reciting one of the poems to her playmates, translating each line into their own language as she went along. Zelana's poetry took on whole new dimensions when delivered in the squeaks and burbles of the dolphin language. Zelana was fairly sure that the young dolphins weren't really all that interested in poetry, but Eleria's habit of rewarding their attention with kisses and embraces kept them obediently in place. Zelana was very fond of dolphins herself, but the notion of kissing them had never occurred to her. Eleria, however, seemed to have discovered early in her life that dolphins would do almost *anything* for kisses.

Zelana decided at that point that it might not be a bad idea to start paying closer attention to the progress of the young child. Lately it seemed that every time she turned around, Eleria had a new surprise for her.

"Eleria," she said a bit later, when the two of them were alone in the grotto.

Eleria responded with a squeaky little dolphin sound.

"Speak in words, child," Zelana commanded.

Eleria stared at her in astonishment. "It is not proper that I should, Beloved," she replied quite formally. "*Thy* speech is not to be used for mundane purposes or ordinary times. It is reserved for stately utterances. I would not for all this world profane it by reducing its stature to the commonplace."

Zelana immediately realized where she had blundered. In a peculiar sort of way she'd treated Eleria in much the same way the child was now treating her dolphin playmates. Eleria had been something on the order of a captive audience—but not quite completely captive. The child had drawn her own conclusions. There was a certain logic behind Eleria's conviction that Zelana's language was reserved for poetry alone, since the only times when Zelana had spoken that language to her had been during those recitations. Ordinary conversations between them had been in the language of the dolphins.

"Come here, child," Zelana said. "I think it's time for us to get to know each other a bit better."

Eleria seemed apprehensive. "Have I done something wrong, Beloved?" she asked. "Are you angry with me because I told your poems to the finned ones? You didn't want me to do that, did you? Your poems were love, and they were for me alone. Now I have spoiled them." Eleria's eyes filled with tears. "Please don't make me go away, Beloved!" she wailed. "I promise that I won't do it again!"

A wave of emotion swept over Zelana, and she felt her own eyes clouding over. She held out her arms to the child. "Come to me," she said.

Eleria rushed to her, and they clung to each other. Both of them were weeping now, yet they were filled with a kind of joy.

Zelana and Eleria spent all of their time together in the grotto after that. The dolphins brought fish for Eleria to eat, and the trickling spring provided water, so there was no real need for the child to go out into Mother Sea. Her playmates were a bit sulky at first, but that soon passed.

Zelana spent many happy hours teaching Eleria how to create poetry and how to sing. Zelana's poetry was stately and formal, and her songs were complex. Eleria's poetry was still of a more ancient form, but much more passionate, and her songs were simple and pure. Zelana was painfully aware that the child's voice, clear and reaching upward without effort, was more beautiful than her own.

Eleria eventually came to realize that the language she had come to know as the language of poetry had a more colloquial form which they could use for everyday communication. She still insisted on calling Zelana "Beloved," however.

It was in the autumn of Eleria's seventh year when the child went out to play with her pink friends again. Zelana had suggested that Eleria had been neglecting them of late, and it was not really polite to do that.

Late that day Eleria returned to the grotto with a strange glowing object.

"What *is* that pretty thing, child?" Zelana asked.

"It's called a 'pearl,' Beloved," Eleria replied, "and a very old friend of the dolphins gave it to me—well, she didn't exactly give it to me. She showed me where it was, though."

"I didn't know that pearls could grow so large," Zelana marveled. "It must have been an enormous oyster."

"It was huge, Beloved."

"Who is this friend of the dolphins?"

"A whale," Eleria replied. "She's very old, and she lives near that islet off the south coast. She joined us this morning and told me that she wanted to show me something. Then she led me to the islet and took me down to where this enormous oyster was attached to a reef. The oyster's shell was almost as wide across as I am tall."

"How did you pry it open if it was that big?"

"I didn't have to, Beloved. The old whale touched the shell with her fin, and the oyster opened itself for us."

"How very peculiar," Zelana said.

"The old whale told me that the oyster wanted me to have the pearl, so I took it. I *did* thank the oyster, but I'm not sure it could understand me. It was a little hard to swim and hold my pearl at the same time, but the old whale offered to carry me back home."

"Carry?"

"Well, not exactly. I rode on her back. That is *so* much fun." Eleria held the pearl up. "See how it glows pink, Beloved? It's even prettier than the ceiling of our grotto." She nestled her pearl, which was about the size of an apple, against her cheek. "I *love* it!" she declared.

"Did you eat today?" Zelana asked.

"I had plenty earlier today, Beloved. My friends and I found a school of herring and ate our fill."

"Did the whale have a name, by any chance?"

"The dolphins just called her 'mother.' She isn't really their mother, of course. I think it's more like a way to let her know that they love her."

"She speaks the same language as the dolphins?"

"Sort of. Her voice isn't as squeaky, though." Eleria crossed to her bed of moss. "I'm very tired, Beloved," she said, sinking down onto her bed. "It was a long swim out to the islet, and mother whale swims faster than I do, so even though she slowed down, I had trouble keeping up with her."

"Why don't you go to sleep, then, Eleria? I'm sure you'll feel much better in the morning."

"That sounds like a terribly good idea, Beloved," Eleria said. "I'm really having trouble keeping my eyes open." She lay back on her bed of moss with the glowing pink pearl cradled to her heart.

Zelana was puzzled, and just a trifle concerned. It wasn't really natural for whales and dolphins to associate with each other in the way Eleria had just described, and Zelana was almost positive that they wouldn't be able to speak to each other and be understood. Something very peculiar had happened today.

Eleria appeared to be sound asleep now, and her limbs had relaxed. Then, to Zelana's astonishment, the glowing pink pearl rose up into the air above the sleeping child. Its pink glow grew steadily stronger, and the glow seemed to enclose Eleria.

"Don't interfere, Zelana," a very familiar voice echoed in Zelana's mind. "This is necessary, and I don't need any help from you."

Eleria awoke somewhat later than usual the following morning, and she had a somewhat puzzled look on her face as she sat cross-legged on her bed of moss with her pearl in her hand. "Why do we sleep, Beloved?" she asked.

"I don't," Zelana replied, "and I'm not sure exactly why other creatures seem to need to sleep every so often."

"I thought you and I were of the same kind," Eleria said. "We *look* very much alike—except that your hair is dark and glossy and mine is sort of yellow."

"I've wondered about that myself. Maybe I've just outgrown the need for sleep. I *am* quite a bit older than you are, after all." It was a simplified answer, but Zelana was quite certain that Eleria wasn't quite ready for the real one just yet.

"Since you don't sleep, you wouldn't know about the strange things I seem to see happening while I'm asleep, would you?"

"They're called 'dreams,' Eleria," Zelana told her, "and I don't think any other creature has the same kind of dreams you do. My brother Dahlaine told me that your dreams would be very special, and much more important than the dreams of the ordinaries. Did you have a dream last night that frightened you?"

"It didn't particularly frighten me, Beloved. It just seemed very strange, for some reason."

"Why don't you tell me about it?" Zelana suggested.

"Well, I seemed to be floating—except that I wasn't floating in Mother Sea the way I do sometimes when I want to rest and catch my breath. I was floating way up in the air instead, and all sorts of strange things were happening far below. Father Earth seemed to be all on fire, and his mountains were rising and falling, the way Mother Sea's waves do. Rocks were melting and running down the sides of some of Father Earth's mountains into Mother Sea, and some of his other mountains were spouting liquid fire way up into the sky. Could something like that really happen?"

"Yes, child," Zelana said in a troubled voice, "and it happened in exactly the way you just described it. I was there watching while it happened. It was at the very beginning of the world. What happened next?"

"Well, the fires kept burning for a long, long time, and then the land below me started to break apart, and the pieces floated off in different directions. Then trees began to sprout on the face of Father Earth, and Mother Sea started having children. It was along about then that I seemed to know that I wasn't alone. Others were having the same dream—only maybe for them it wasn't really a dream."

Zelana smiled. "No, dear, it wasn't. I was one of those others, and I certainly wasn't dreaming, and neither were my brothers or my sister."

"Then it was your family that was sort of hiding around the edges of my dream?" Eleria asked. "I thought you only had two brothers and one sister. There seemed to be two more brothers and a sister watching with me."

"They're another branch of the family, Eleria," Zelana told her. "We don't get together very often. We can talk about them some other time. Why don't you tell me what happened next in your dream? Dreams fade, I understand, and I'd like to hear your whole dream before you forget."

"Well, most of Mother Sea's children were fish, but some of them weren't. Those were the ones who crawled up onto the face of Father Earth. They sort of looked like snakes at first, but then they sprouted legs and they grew up to be very big. Some of them ate trees, but some of the others ate the ones who were eating trees. Then a great big rock that was on fire fell down out of the sky, and when it hit Father Earth it made an awful splash, except that it was rock that splashed instead of water, and everything got dark for a long time. It finally started to get light again, but the snakes with legs weren't there anymore."

"Did my relatives go away, too?"

"Some of them went to sleep, but they woke up after a while, and the ones who'd stayed awake went to sleep. There was one that never slept, though. That one's very ugly, isn't it?"

"Indeed it is, child," Zelana replied with a shudder. "It's an outcast, and we don't even like to think about it. What happened next?"

"There were a lot of things with fur wandering around, and there were birds and bugs too, but then some things who walked on their hind legs came along. They didn't look at all the way we do, though. Their skin was scaly, like the skin of large fish—or maybe snakes—and their eyes were huge and stuck way out in front of their faces. That went on for quite a long time, and then everything was all covered with white, and it got very cold. Mother Sea seemed to shrink, and she ran away from her shore. Then the white went away, and Mother Sea came back. That's when the man-things who look like me arrived. They didn't look exactly like me, though. They wrapped themselves up in animal skins for some reason, and you and I don't do that, do we?"

"It isn't necessary for us, Eleria. The skins help the man-things stay warm, and they're ashamed of their bodies."

"How peculiar," Eleria said, frowning slightly. "That was about all there was, Beloved, except that the awful-looking watcher was still way off at the edge of my dream, and I don't think it likes me very much. I get the feeling that it's afraid of me for some reason."

"If it has anything like good sense, it is," Zelana said. "Do you think you'll be able to manage here by yourself for a few days? There are some things I need to attend to. I won't really be gone for long."

"Can't I go with you?"

"I'm afraid not, Eleria. I have to go by myself this time. Maybe you can come along next time. We'll see."

Zelana swam out of her hidden grotto and onto a nearby gravel beach, where the waves rolled in and then receded with a mournful sound that seemed filled with regret. Then she raised her face to the sky to search for one of those winds that rushed far overhead in perpetuity, streaming eternally above the clouds and weather. She encountered several, but they were not moving in the proper direction, so she continued her search. Then at last she felt a wind that streamed northward toward the Domain of her elder brother, and she rose up and up through the buffeting of those winds which had not suited her until she reached that wind which rushed northward along the outer edge of the sky, and she bestrode that wind, and it obediently carried her toward the bleak Domain of her brother Dahlaine.

Now, Dahlaine dwelt in a cave deep in the bowels of the earth beneath the crags and eternal snow of Mount Shrak, which the people of the North believe is the tallest peak in all the world, and Zelana descended from the dark outer edge of the sky to the forbidding mountain that seemed almost to scowl down at her brother's Domain with a bleak expression of superiority. The mouth of Dahlaine's cave was a deep indentation in the north side of the mount, and Zelana entered there and followed the twisting passage that led down and down through glittering black rock to the vast chamber far beneath the mountain that was Dahlaine's home.

Zelana paused at the mouth of the passage. Her burly, grey-bearded brother, stripped to the waist, was standing over a ruddy fire, beating on something that glowed and made a sort of ringing sound. A small, glowing orb hovered just over him, bathing him with light.

"What in the world are you doing, Dahlaine?" Zelana asked.

Dahlaine turned sharply to look at his sister. "Why, Zelana!" he exclaimed. "You startled me. Is something wrong?"

"Perhaps—or perhaps not. Are you taking up music now? If you are, you're a little off-key."

"Just experimenting, dear sister," he replied. "Some of the people beyond Mother Sea have discovered something they call 'metal.' I wanted to see if I could duplicate it. Is something afoot?"

Zelana looked cautiously around Dahlaine's cave. "Where's your Dreamer?" she asked.

"Ashad? He's out playing with the bears."

"*Bears?* Surely you don't allow him to play with bears! They'll eat him, won't they?"

"Of course they won't, Zelana. They're his friends—in the same way the pink dolphins are Eleria's friends. Is something unusual happening?"

"Perhaps. Eleria had a dream last night, and I think it may have been significant. I thought you should know about it. There's something else that may be even more significant than the dream itself."

"Oh?"

"It appears that Mother Sea's taking a hand in this herself."

Dahlaine stared at her.

"Eleria was out playing with the young pink dolphins yesterday, and they introduced her to an old cow whale."

"I didn't know that whales and dolphins spoke the same language," Dahlaine said.

"They don't. That's what leads me to believe that it wasn't really a whale. Anyway, the old cow led Eleria to a small islet off the south coast of Thurn and showed her an oyster shell that was about fifty times bigger than any oyster *I've* ever seen. Then the whale touched the shell with one of her fins, and the oyster opened as if someone had just knocked on its door. There was a pearl inside—pink, and a bit larger than an apple."

"That's impossible!" Dahlaine exclaimed.

"You'll have to take that up with the oyster, Dahlaine. Then the whale told Eleria that the oyster wanted her to have the pearl, so Eleria took it, and the whale gave her a ride back to Thurn."

"Now, *that's* something I'd like to see," Dahlaine said, laughing. "It might be a bit difficult to saddle a whale."

"Did you want to hear the rest of this, or did you want to make funny remarks?" Zelana said tartly.

"Sorry, dear sister. Please go on."

"Eleria'd had a busy day, so she was very tired. She went to sleep almost immediately, and then some very strange things started to happen. That pink pearl rose up into the air above Eleria, and it started to glow—almost like a small pink moon—and its light shone down on Eleria. Then it spoke to me and told me to mind my own business. I recognized the voice immediately, since I've been listening to it since the beginning of time."

"You're not serious!" Dahlaine exclaimed.

"Very serious, brother dear. It *was* the voice of Mother Sea, and that seems to suggest that the whale might have been something other than an ordinary whale as well, wouldn't you say?"

"She's never done that before," Dahlaine said in a very troubled voice.

"You're being obvious again, Dahlaine," Zelana said. "I think we'd better step around her very carefully until we get a better idea of what she's doing and why. Mother Sea's the central force of the whole world, so let's stay on the good side of her."

"What happened next?" Dahlaine asked.

"Eleria had a dream, naturally. Evidently, that was the whole idea. In some peculiar way, that pearl's the essence of Mother Sea's awareness. Her tides still rise and fall, and her waves wash the shores of Father Earth, but she's awake now. I'm almost positive that the pearl, which is really Mother Sea incarnate, dictated Eleria's dream, image by image."

"Did Eleria tell you about her dream?"

"Of course she did. Why do you think I'm here?"

"What did the dream involve?"

"The world," Zelana replied. "Eleria saw it when it was still on fire, before the continents separated and before life began. Then she saw the continents move away from each other and watched living things crawl up out of Mother Sea. She saw the big lizards roam the world, and the falling star that killed them all. She was aware of us and of the others—the ones who are asleep now—and somehow she knew about the Vlagh. She saw the age of ice and then the more recent man-things. As closely as I can determine, she dreamt all the way from the beginning up until the day before yesterday."

"She managed to dream all of that in one night?" Dahlaine said incredulously.

"She had help, Dahlaine. I'm sure that the pearl was guiding her step by step. I think we'd better advise our alternates what's afoot here. Our cycle's very nearly reached its conclusion, and our alternates will be waking soon. We'd better warn them that the crisis we've been expecting since the beginning's very likely to boil to the top during their cycle."

"That's assuming that it doesn't come before our cycle's finished," Dahlaine said. "I think that we'd all better get together
and thrash this out. Why don't you go fetch Aracia, and I'll see
if I can run Veltan down. We need to make some decisions, and
we might not have much time."

"It shall be as thou hast commanded, my dear, dear
brother," Zelana replied with exaggerated formality.

"Do you have to do that, Zelana?" he said with a pained sort
of expression.

"When you're being obvious, yes. Go get Veltan, Dahlaine,
and I'll see if I can pry holy Aracia out of that silly temple of
hers. Do we want to meet here?"

"I think we'd better. It's more secluded than the other
places—except for yours, of course. We could meet there, I
suppose, but Veltan doesn't like to swim. And let's keep the
Dreamers away from our meeting. We don't want to contaminate their visions."

Zelana went up out of Dahlaine's cave and probed the northern sky until she found a wind that suited her purpose, and
then she rose up through the chill northern air to join with the
obliging wind, to ride it on down in a southeasterly direction
toward Aracia's Domain.

The arrival of the later variety of people had elevated Aracia's opinion of herself quite noticeably. Until their appearance,
Aracia had seemed sensible enough—a little vain, perhaps, but
not unbearably so. The later people, unlike the more brutish
early ones, had religious yearnings, and they longed for gods.

Aracia had thought that was very nice of them, and she'd
been more than happy to oblige. She'd suggested that a fancy
dwelling where she could stay while she was looking after
them might be appropriate, so her people built one for her—
several, actually. The first one had been a bit crude, since it had
been constructed primarily of logs. It had been all right for a

while, but the wind blew through the cracks, and the dirt floor grew muddy during the spring rains.

Aracia had then suggested stone blocks instead of logs, and the people who served her labored long and hard to build a dwelling for her that was *almost* as comfortable as Zelana's grotto or Dahlaine's cave. And now Aracia of the East dwelt in her splendid though drafty palace-temple with servants by the score to tell her how wonderful she was and how beautiful and how they could not possibly get along without her—and if it wasn't too much trouble, could she turn that fellow who'd been so insulting the other day into a toad and maybe make it rain because the oats really needed some water along about now, but not too much rain, since that made everything all muddy.

Zelana descended through the crisp autumn air to the marble dome of her sister's temple and adjusted her eyes to look through the polished marble at Aracia's regal throne room. It was sheathed in palest marble, of course, and there were tall columns around its outer edge, and red drapes behind Aracia's golden throne.

Aracia was garbed in a regal gown, and she wore a regal crown of gold and a regal sort of expression on her face.

A fat man garbed in black linen vestments and a tediously ornate miter was standing before Aracia's throne, delivering a tiresome oration of praise.

Aracia, Zelana noticed, seemed to hang on the fat man's every word.

Although she knew that it would be terribly impolite, Zelana simply couldn't resist a sudden impulse.

The fat orator broke off suddenly when Zelana, clad only in filmy gauze, abruptly appeared out of nowhere before the throne of her elder sister. Several plump, overfed servants fainted dead away, and a few of the more theologically inclined began to contemplate revisions of several articles of the faith.

Aracia gasped. "Cover yourself, Zelana!" she said sharply.

"What for, dear sister?" Zelana said. "I'm immune to the

weather, and I don't have any defects that I want to hide. If you want to wrap yourself in that silly-looking cocoon, that's your business, but I don't think it'll turn you into a butterfly."

"Have you no modesty?"

"Of course not. I'm perfect. Didn't you know that? Dahlaine needs to see us—now. Leave your Dreamer here, though. He'll explain why when we join him."

"If Dahlaine wants to explain something to me, he can come here and do it," Aracia said. "I will *not* bow down to him in that grubby hole in the ground where he lives."

"Splendid, dear sister of mine," Zelana said sweetly. "I'm sure all your fat servants will be delighted to see you bow down right here in your own temple—assuming, of course, that it's still standing after he arrives on that silly thunderbolt he always rides. It's a nice enough thunderbolt, I suppose, but the noise it makes when it passes shakes down buildings sometimes. Putting your temple back together should give your fat servants something to do while they're pondering the fact that the supreme goddess of the universe just bowed down to somebody who looks for all the world like some shaggy bear."

"*You* never bow down to him, Zelana," Aracia accused.

"Of course I don't," Zelana replied. "I don't have to, because I don't demand—or expect—anybody to bow down to me. That's the way it works, Aracia. Had you forgotten about that? It's time to shed your cocoon, my butterfly sister. The dreams have begun, and the Vlagh could be on our doorstep before the week's out. Let's go talk with Dahlaine while there's still time."

Zelana took her sister's hand, and they rode the wind toward the northwest. It was early autumn now, and the land far below was ablaze with color. The rivers sparkled in the autumn sun, and the mountains to the north of Aracia's Domain gleamed white beneath their eternal snow.

Just to be on the safe side, they skirted the northeastern

corner of the Wasteland. Many of the servants of the Vlagh had extremely sharp senses, and the sisters were certain that this wouldn't be a good time to alert their enemy. It might not have been really necessary, but there was no point in taking chances.

Actually, the sisters were rather looking forward to the meeting. There hadn't been a general family get-together for almost a dozen eons. There'd been occasional squabbles among them, of course. No family lives in absolute harmony forever, but in times of crisis the family was able to set their differences aside and work together to reach a solution.

"Isn't that Dahlaine's mountain?" Aracia asked, pointing at the land of the North lying far below.

Zelana glanced down. "No," she replied. "Mount Shrak's quite a bit taller."

"I've never looked at Father Earth from this high up before," Aracia said. "He looks different from up here, doesn't he?"

"Try looking at him from the edge of the sky some time, dear sister," Zelana suggested.

"Edge of the sky?" Aracia sounded puzzled.

"Up where it isn't blue anymore. After Eleria told me her dream, I needed to tell Dahlaine what she'd seen, but when I went looking for a wind that was blowing in his direction, the only one I could find was up at the outer edge of the air. You can even see the curve of the world from that high."

"Does it really curve?" Aracia asked. "Veltan told me that if you look at Father Earth from the moon, he looks like a round blue ball." She frowned. "I never *did* understand just why it was that Mother Sea exiled Veltan to the moon for all those eons. Did he do something to offend her?"

Zelana laughed. "Indeed he did, Aracia. He told her that she bored him."

"He *didn't!*"

"Oh, yes he did. You know how juvenile Veltan can be sometimes. He thought he was being terribly funny, but he just can't seem to get it through his mind that Mother Sea has absolutely no sense of humor. He kept clowning around with various absurdities—different shades of blue, and even the notion of 'stripes.' He was having all kinds of fun pestering her—probably hoping that he could make her laugh, but it didn't work out very well for him. She finally lost her temper and told him to go away. That's why our baby brother—who'll probably never really grow up—spent ten thousand years on the moon."

"And he passed the time cataloging shades of blue," Aracia added. "That seems to be his major preoccupation."

"How many shades of blue has he found so far?"

"Something in excess of thirteen million the last time I spoke with him. That was about an eon or so ago, though, so he's probably found more by now."

"There's Mount Shrak," Zelana told her sister, pointing toward the earth far below. "Let's go down and see if Dahlaine's managed to track Veltan down yet."

They descended through the lambent air toward the craggy peak of Mount Shrak, startling a flock of geese as they went. Zelana rather liked geese. They were silly birds most of the time, but their migrations marked the change of the seasons very precisely, and that added a certain stability to an unpredictable world.

The sisters came to earth near the mouth of Dahlaine's cave, and Zelana led Aracia down the long, winding passage toward their brother's underground home.

"Hideous," Aracia observed, looking around. "Did he put all those icicles on the ceiling himself?"

"They aren't ice, dear sister," Zelana replied. "They're stone. They sort of grow the same way, though, but they take quite a bit longer."

"He'll starve to death if he lives here in the dark for too long," Aracia observed.

"He has a little sun that follows him here in his cave," Zelana said. "It's a lot like a puppy, and it gives him all the light he needs."

"He's manufacturing suns now?" Aracia seemed a bit startled. "I tried that once, but the silly thing flew apart as soon as I started to make it spin."

"You probably didn't make it quite heavy enough. The balance of a sun has to be very precise—too light and it flies apart; too heavy and it collapses in on itself."

Aracia looked around cautiously. "Where's Dahlaine's Dreamer?" she whispered.

"Ashad? Dahlaine told me that he was out playing with the bears. We all seem to have our favorite animals, don't we? I love my pink dolphins, Dahlaine loves bears, Veltan's fond of sheep, and you're attached to the seals who nest along your coast."

Aracia shrugged. "They gave us something to play with while we were waiting for the man-creatures to grow up," she said. She peered back into the dim cave. "It seems that Dahlaine hasn't found Veltan yet," she noted. "I don't see them anywhere. How far back does this cave go?"

"Miles and miles, I think," Zelana replied. "Let's wait. I'm sure they'll be along soon. Has your Dreamer told you any interesting stories yet?"

"No," Aracia replied. "I don't think she's quite ready. From what you've told me, I'd say that your Dreamer might be the first. The story of the world sort of sets things up for the other Dreamers. Did she really see it right from the beginning in her dream?"

"It came very close to what really happened," Zelana replied. "Eleria has some problems with words once in a while. Her playmates were young dolphins when she was a baby, and she speaks dolphin much better than she speaks our language. It's probably my fault. I was too busy with poetry and music to train her." She shrugged. "We all make mistakes, I guess. Anyway, I'm fairly sure that Eleria still thinks in dolphin, and dolphin baby talk isn't too precise. She did her best, though. What's your child's name?"

"Lillabeth," Aracia replied fondly, "and she's the most beautiful creature in all the world."

"They seem to do that to us, don't they?" Zelana said.

"Do what?"

"Distort our perceptions, dear sister," Zelana replied. "I'd imagine that Dahlaine and Veltan feel the same way about *their* Dreamers. I know that *I* have exactly the same feelings about Eleria. It's probably very simple. We love them because they are *ours*."

"Could you be a bit more specific about this dream your Eleria had?" Aracia asked.

"Let's wait for Dahlaine and Veltan. There were some very complex things happening when Eleria began to dream, and I think Dahlaine's the best qualified to interpret them."

"That's assuming that he ever gets here," Aracia added.

It was probably late afternoon outside when a pair of shattering thunderclaps shook the air for miles around. "That is *so* childish," Aracia noted. "Do they *really* have to do that?"

"They're still little boys, dear," Zelana replied, "and showing off is part of their nature. Riding a lightning bolt is a sure way to get everybody's immediate attention."

"But they look so silly after they do that—glowing and with their hair standing on end the way it does."

"I think lightning does that," Zelana said. "It *is* a very fast way to travel, but I think I'll stick to riding the wind. It's almost as fast, and it doesn't make *nearly* so much noise."

A few moments later their brothers emerged from the twisting passageway that led down from the surface.

"What kept you?" Zelana asked mildly.

"I had a little trouble locating our baby brother," Dahlaine replied sourly.

"He can be such a grouch sometimes," the tall, fair-haired Veltan noted.

"I wouldn't be nearly so bad-tempered if you'd stop trying to hide from me," Dahlaine said. "Did you tell our sister about Eleria's dream, Zelana?"

"Not in any great detail, no," Zelana replied. "A number of her servants were there, and I didn't think they needed to know the full extent of what was happening just yet."

"Tell us all, then, my fishy sister," Veltan said, grinning at her outrageously.

"Of course, moon-boy," Zelana replied tartly. "A few days ago, Eleria was out playing with her dolphin friends, and they introduced her to a very old cow whale. The whale told Eleria that there was something nearby that she might want to see. Eleria went with her to a nearby island, and the whale showed her a huge oyster. The oyster obediently opened its shell, and Eleria saw a very large pink pearl. The whale told Eleria that she was supposed to take the pearl. Eleria did that and then brought the pearl home. She was very tired, and she fell asleep almost immediately. The pearl rose up into the air just above her, and it started to glow. Then it told me to keep my nose out of what was happening. It hung in the air over Eleria all night long, and when Eleria woke up, she told me about the dream she'd had. It was a nice little dream that more or less covered everything that's happened since the world was first formed right up to the present."

"You're just making this up, Zelana," Veltan scoffed.

"No, baby brother, I'm not. The pearl—and quite probably that whale as well—aren't what they seem to be."

"Our sister believes that Mother Sea's starting to tamper with things," Dahlaine said then, "and I think she might be right."

"Now we come to the interesting part, big brother," Zelana said brightly. "Just exactly who and what *are* these children you so generously gave us a few years ago?"

"The Dreamers, of course, Zelana," Dahlaine replied just a bit too quickly.

"And?" she pressed.

"And what?"

"What *else* are they, Dahlaine? You're so obvious most of the time that the rest of us can see right through you."

"You *didn't!*" Veltan exclaimed, his eyes almost popping out as he stared at Dahlaine.

"I don't quite . . ." Aracia began. Then her eyes bulged out as well. "Dahlaine!" she gasped.

"Well," he floundered, "it *was* kind of an emergency, wasn't it?" he asked plaintively.

"Are you *insane?*" Veltan demanded. "They *can't* be present during our cycle. As soon as they realize who they are, they'll usurp our Domains!"

"I was careful to blot out their previous memories before I woke them," Dahlaine replied. "And I modified them slightly to make them more closely resemble newborn man-creatures. They sleep and breathe and eat food instead of light. Their minds are still very infantile, and they have no idea of who— or what—they really are, so their presence during our cycle won't tear the Land of Dhrall apart. They're really nothing more than children, and our cycle will come to a close before they're fully mature and realize just who they really are."

"You've put the whole world at risk with this idiocy!" Aracia flared.

"Calm yourself, Aracia," Zelana said. "Now that I've had time to push my horror away, I think I'm beginning to see what Dahlaine had in mind. If the hideous thing in the Wasteland is on the verge of moving against us, we'll need all the help we can get, and the others have as much to lose as we do. Besides, we've never really gotten to know them, have we? They're really very sweet. I didn't really care for the idea of being supplanted before, but now that I've gotten to know Eleria, I love her. That was sort of what you had in mind when you came up with this scheme, wasn't it, Dahlaine? If we know them and love them, we can trust them. Isn't that the short and the long of this grand plan of yours?"

"Sometimes you're so clever you make me sick, Zelana," he said sourly.

"He's brighter than I thought he was," Veltan told his sisters. "If we awaken the others before the end of our cycle, we can raise them as if they were our children and prepare them for anything that might happen after we've gone to our rest."

"And then we can return the favor at the end of *their* cycle," Zelana added. "I get to mother Eleria this time, and then *she* mothers *me* next time."

"It sounds fair to me," Veltan said. Then he paused. "We've been strangers to the others for far too long, I think. We all have the same responsibilities, so a bit of cooperation might be in order. I'm still not too happy that you didn't tell the rest of us what you had in mind, Dahlaine, but we can set that aside for now. What's next?"

"First off," Zelana said, "I don't think we want to get too specific about what's happening when we're speaking with our Dreamers. They're still children, and children are impressionable, no matter what their species. We don't want to contaminate their dreams by explaining what these dreams really mean. As long as they believe that their dreams are just flights of fancy, they won't become too upset by any horrors that crop up. Then, too, if they realize what they can actually *do* with their dreams, they might try to tamper with them at the deepest level of their awareness, and *that* raises the possibility of total disasters. At that point, Mother Sea might decide to exile all eight of us to the moon—not just Veltan."

"You're probably right, Zelana," Dahlaine agreed. "Let's keep the dreams as pure as we possibly can." He scratched at his chin speculatively. "We've got a problem now," he said. "I'm almost positive that the Vlagh can sense these dreams—not the details, maybe, but the fact that the Dreamers are here and doing what they were sent here to do will certainly stir it to send the creatures of the Wasteland swarming across the mountains, and we don't have enough people to meet them. I seriously doubt that there are even a half-million man-things in the whole of the Land of Dhrall, and the Vlagh probably has at least ten times that many servants. The servants of the Vlagh aren't very bright, but the sheer numbers alone put us in an impossible situation. I think we'll have to bring in the outlanders from other parts of the world.

"Absolutely out of the question!" Aracia exclaimed. "Our people are pure and innocent. The outsiders are barbaric monsters. They're almost as bad as the creatures of the Wasteland."

"Not quite, Aracia," Dahlaine disagreed. "We can manipulate them if we need to. The only problem I can see is linguistic. The outsiders don't speak the same language our people speak."

"That's not really a problem, Dahlaine," Veltan told him. "I've looked in on several of the outsider cultures. Their babbling didn't make any sense at first, but I found a way to get around that."

"Oh?" Dahlaine said. "I'd like to hear about that."

"All you really have to do is step around language and go right straight to thought."

"He has a point, Dahlaine," Zelana said. "It didn't take me much more than a week to learn the language of my dolphins. If you listen with your mind instead of your ears, it comes very fast."

"Interesting notion," Dahlaine mused. "Unfortunately, I don't think people could do that."

Veltan shrugged. "I'll do it for them, then."

"Would you like to clarify that, Veltan?" Aracia asked.

"It's a little complicated, dear sister," he replied. "Are you really sure you want all the details?"

Aracia shuddered. "Spare me that, please. Just tell me what the results are likely to be."

"The outlanders will babble in their own language, and our people will babble in ours. Neither group will hear babbles, though. They'll *think* that they're listening to their own language, so they'll understand each other perfectly."

"Would it work that way between different groups of outsiders as well?" Dahlaine asked. "We'll probably be bringing in several different cultures."

"No problem," Veltan said. "We'll have to decide how far out we want to take it, is about all. We might want to limit it to the Land of Dhrall, though. The outlanders all speak different languages, and maybe we should keep it that way. If they can communicate with each other, they might start forging alliances, and that could cause trouble on down the line."

"You may have a point there," Dahlaine conceded. "Let's try it and see how it works."

"I'm against the whole silly notion!" Aracia said adamantly. "We can't bring those murdering barbarians here to the sacred land!"

"How sacred do you think it'll be after the unholy monsters of the Wasteland sweep over the mountains?" Dahlaine asked her pointedly. "The outsiders are a little crude, I'll admit that, but they *are* mostly warriors. Our people haven't even discovered iron yet, so they're still using stone tools. The people of the outside world have no idea of the significance of Dhrall, but they *do* know how to fight. They spend most of their time practicing on each other. I think maybe we'd all better visit those outlands and find those various warrior people. There are several tricks we can use to get them here to Dhrall, and once they're here, we can wave gold in their faces to get their interest."

"Gold isn't really very useful, Dahlaine," Veltan objected. "It's sort of pretty, but it's too soft for any practical uses. It's much like lead, when you get right down to it."

"The outlanders seem to like it, and if they hear about mountains of gold in the Wastelands of the interior, we won't be able to drive them away with whips. I don't think we've got much choice. Our people are too unskilled to face the armies of the Vlagh. We need large numbers of what Aracia calls howling barbarians, and we need them in a hurry. Let's go to the outer world and find warriors. It's the only way we have to save Dhrall from the forces of the Vlagh."

4

Zelana rode the wind westward from the coast of Dhrall for many, many leagues across Mother Sea. She knew that there was land far to the west—at least there had been before she'd gone to live in her grotto hideaway on the Isle of Thurn. Perhaps it had wandered off again.

Night was settling over Mother Sea when Zelana saw something rather peculiar far below. There seemed to be a small fire floating on the surface of the water. Fire and water do not mix well, and, overcome with curiosity, Zelana descended to investigate.

She drifted down through the twilight air, and as she came closer to the face of Mother Sea, she saw something very unusual. At first she thought it might be a floating house, but then she realized that it was probably an exceptionally large version of the canoes the people of her Domain used when they went out on the water to hunt fish. The fire she had seen appeared to be burning in a small glass box near the back of the oversized canoe.

She settled quietly onto the water and tiptoed closer. The floating object was obviously more advanced than anything the people of Dhrall could build, but it had probably been constructed for the same reason that the people of Dhrall made canoes. The outlanders were most likely fishermen.

The oversized canoe Zelana had found was very large—long and narrow—and the outlanders had even built low-roofed houses on it to shelter them when the weather went bad. For some reason, they'd seen fit to put a large tree trunk in the center. As Zelana approached it, she noticed that there was a distinctly unpleasant odor hanging over it.

Then a couple of man-creatures with hairy faces came out of a low, flat-roofed structure near the back of the alien canoe. They were both very tall and muscular, and their clothing was an odd mix of cloth and leather. They also had what appeared to be weapons of some sort belted to their waists, and that aroused Zelana's immediate attention. If these man-things were merely fishermen, they wouldn't really need to carry weapons all the time. That strongly suggested that these two weren't out here on the face of Mother Sea looking for fish. Zelana stepped back out of the light and opened her mind to what she was hearing in order to make the speech of the outlanders understandable.

"Looks to be a fair night, Cap'n," one of the creatures was saying.

"Aye," the other rumbled in a harsh voice, "and it's none too soon to suit me. I've had me a belly-full of foul weather here lately."

Zelana was satisfied that she could understand these outlanders, and a bit surprised to discover that Veltan's theory actually worked the way he'd said it would. Veltan's experiments seldom turned out exactly the way he wanted them to.

"You'd better get a lookout aloft, Ox," the one called Cap'n suggested. "Now that the weather's settled down, other ships might be under way hereabouts. We're not sailing the *Seagull* out here for entertainment, you know."

"Aye, Cap'n," the huge one called Ox replied. "The Trogite vessels usually hug the coast, but the storm might have swept a few of them out here to deeper water. If our luck's running good, we might be able to harvest a fair amount of Trogite gold while they're still floundering around out of sight of land."

"You're starting to think like a real Maag, Ox," Cap'n said with an evil grin. "The notion of picking Trogite vessels like apples off a tree lights a warm little fire in my belly. Come morning, put the crew to work patching the sails and clearing away the wreckage that storm made out of most of the rigging. It well-nigh drove us under a few times."

Zelana sat cross-legged on the surface of Mother Sea considering some interesting possibilities. The two outlanders, Ox and Cap'n, had referred to their canoe as a "ship," and there were obviously other ships in the vicinity as well. It was fairly clear that these man-creatures who called themselves "Maags" were not out on the face of Mother Sea in search of fish. Evidently they searched for the ships of other outlanders in order to take gold from them. Dahlaine's assessment of the outlanders had been correct. They *were* very interested in gold, though Zelana could not quite understand why. The *Seagull,* it seemed, might just be too good an opportunity to pass by. Now that Zelana could understand the speech of the outlanders, and if things went as the one called Cap'n seemed to hope they would, Zelana would be able to observe the outlanders who called themselves Maags in action. Should they prove to be suitable, their ship would make things very easy. A word or two with Mother Sea could produce a current which would sweep the *Seagull* to the west coast of the Land of Dhrall almost as fast as the wind could carry a mote of dust.

The more she thought about it, the more Zelana came to believe that these Maags might very well be exactly what she was seeking. She would need to watch and listen, though, and that suggested that she'd probably need to be somewhere inside the floating house called *Seagull*. That wouldn't be a problem of any magnitude. There were ways she could make herself inconspicuous while she watched and listened. Then, if these Maags proved to be suitable . . .

THE
SEAFARERS

1

Though he would deny it with his dying breath, if the truth were to be known, it was sheer coincidence that led to the discovery of the Land of Dhrall by Captain Sorgan Hook-Beak and the crew of his ship, the *Seagull*.

As all the world knows, Sorgan Hook-Beak of the Land of Maag is the greatest sea captain of all time. No man yet born can match him in the prediction of wind, weather, tides, or the probable value of the cargo of any ship unlucky enough to encounter the *Seagull* on the high seas.

The men of the Land of Maag are bigger than the men of lands farther to the south, and they took to the sea early in their history. The mountains of Maag march down to the sea, and their slopes seem almost to point seaward, mutely saying, "Go there." Mountains are fine for hunting, but not too good for farming, so the men of Maag farmed the sea instead, and her crops were bountiful. Fishhooks are much easier to hammer out of iron than plows are, and fishnets harvest bigger crops than scythes do. Then too, the men who harvest the sea aren't obliged to spend all those tedious months waiting for their crops to grow. The crops of the sea are always there, and they can be harvested in any season.

The people of the Land of Maag developed a quaint custom early in their history. They frequently used descriptions rather than names. Thus there could be several "Big-Foots" or "Buck-Teeth" in a Maag village, along with assorted "Slim-Wits," "Fats," and "Pigeon-Toes." More conventional names came along later, after the Maags had made contact with the more refined peoples to the south. Sorgan Hook-Beak was sort of proud of his name, since it suggested that others considered him to be an eagle, that noblest of all birds.

He went to sea early in his life, and his first captain was the legendary Dalto Big-Nose, a man whose very name struck terror into the heart of every Trogite sea captain who sailed the northern sea.

Now, the Trogites are an avaricious race, eager to snatch things that rightfully belong to others but which they haven't gotten around to discovering yet. At some time in the remote past a Trogite explorer in search of deposits of tin or copper which might prove profitable had discovered a peculiar region far back in the western reaches of the Land of Shaan, which stands to the west of the Land of Maag. The Maags grudgingly conceded that the Trogite explorer was a courageous fellow, since the natives of the Land of Shaan felt a moral compulsion to eat everything—or everybody—they killed. Being killed is one thing, but being eaten is quite another.

The Trogite explorer purchased the friendship of the savages of Shaan with a few worthless trinkets, and they had led him to that region where the rivers had sandy bottoms. Many rivers have sandy bottoms, but the sand in the rivers of interior Shaan is comprised mostly of flecks of pure gold. Word about the gold in the rivers of Shaan soon got out, and adventurers from all over the known world rushed there to claim their rightful share. After a few seasons, though, the word got out that adventurers who went to the Land of Shaan never came back.

The enthusiasm dropped off noticeably.

The source of the Trogite gold was well known, but the perils involved in seeking it were even better known. Gold, however, isn't really worth very much unless the owner can take it someplace where he can spend it. The Trogites came up with a quick solution to that problem. They started building ships to carry their wealth back to the Land of Trog. They were large ships, wide of beam and deep of hull, and they tended to wallow rather than sail. Maag vessels were narrow and swift. Moreover, the wealthy Trogites tended to be miserly, so they neglected to hire warriors to guard their treasure ships.

The Maags more or less abandoned fishing at that point. The Trogites winnowed gold from the rivers of Shaan, hauled it down to the coast, and put it aboard their wallowing treasure ships. Then the treasure ships sailed out to the northern sea, where the Maags waited for them.

Sorgan Hook-Beak had received an extensive education from Captain Big-Nose in the fine art of relieving Trogite treasure ships of all that excess weight. As a young man he'd squandered away his earnings in revelry, naturally. Young sailors are enthusiastic revelers, but after a few seasons, Sorgan realized that the captain's share of the ship's earnings was much, much larger than the share of an ordinary seaman, so he began to religiously set aside half of all his earnings, and he had soon saved enough to be able to buy his own ship, the *Seagull*.

The *Seagull* was not really in very good shape when Sorgan bought her from the crusty old pirate he'd happened to meet in a seaside tavern in the Maag port of Weros. Her sails were ragged, and she leaked quite noticeably. She was about the best Sorgan could afford at that time, though. Had the old man who owned her been completely sober during their negotiations, he'd probably have held out for more money, but his purse had just come up empty, and Sorgan had shrewdly delayed making his final offer until the poor old fellow's

tongue had been hanging out. He also shook his purse frequently while they were haggling, pretending that it was nothing more than an absentminded habit.

The musical jingle of money played no small part in the
tipsy old man's acceptance of Sorgan's final offer.

After he'd bought the *Seagull,* Sorgan had persuaded two
of his former shipmates, Ox and Kryda Ham-Hand, to join him
as first and second mates. Their rank hadn't really meant all that
much just then, though. What Sorgan had really needed at that
point in time had been their help in making the *Seagull* more
seaworthy.

It had taken the three of them more than a year to finish
the repairs, largely because they'd frequently run out of money.
Whenever that had happened, they'd had to suspend operations and take to the streets near the waterfront in search of
drunk sailors whose purses still had a few coins left in them.

Eventually, the *Seagull* had been marginally restored, and
then the three had been obliged to haunt the waterfront again
to find a crew.

The *Seagull* was a full-sized Maag longship, a hundred and
ten feet long and twenty-five feet wide at the beam, so she
needed a full-sized crew. Sorgan had done his best to keep the
size of his crew down to a minimum, but eighty men had been
about as low as he could go. He'd given a bit of thought to reducing the number of oarsmen, but Ox and Ham-Hand had
protested violently, pointing out that fewer oarsmen would
mean slower speed, and a faster ship would bring in more
money.

And so it was that now the *Seagull* roamed the waters of
the northern sea, looking for targets of opportunity.

It was about midsummer of an otherwise unimportant year
when the *Seagull* encountered one of those summer squalls
that seldom last very long—two days, perhaps, no more than
three. This one lingered longer, however, and the *Seagull*'s
crew endured bad weather for almost a week, helplessly

watching as the howling gale tore away the rigging and ripped the sail to shreds.

When the gale moved off, the *Seagull*'s crew labored long and hard to make her even marginally seaworthy again.

Captain Hook-Beak took it in stride. No ship ever sails on a perpetually sunny sea, so bad weather was simply something that had to be endured. Of course, the captain of a ship is seldom required to repair the rigging or patch the sail. Those chores are the duties of ordinary seamen, so Captain Hook-Beak retired to his cabin to catch up on his sleep.

It didn't quite turn out that way, though. Despite the fact that the *Seagull* was many leagues from land, a pesky fly had somehow found its way into Hook-Beak's cabin, and the buzzing sound of its wings was just enough to keep the captain awake. The times when it was not flying were even worse. He could actually feel its eyes on him, watching his every move, and that was much worse than the brainless buzzing. Try though he might, Sorgan Hook-Beak couldn't sleep.

Nothing at all seemed to be going right this season.

After her rigging and sail had been repaired, the *Seagull* got under way again, and she was running before the wind some distance out from the coast of Maag when Ox spotted a Trogite merchant vessel hull-down on the horizon. "Sail ho, Cap'n!" he roared in a voice that might well have shattered glass a league away.

"Where away?" Hook-Beak demanded.

"Two points off the starboard bow, Cap'n!" Ox shouted.

Hook-Beak relinquished the tiller to Kryda Ham-Hand and hurried forward to join Ox in the bow. "Show me," he told his burly first mate.

Ox pointed.

"Goodly distance," Hook-Beak said dubiously.

"The oarsmen are getting fat anyway, Cap'n," Ox replied.

"A good run might sweat some of the lard off 'em, even if we don't catch that ship."

"You've got a point there, Ox," Sorgan agreed. "All right, let's take a run at that ship and see if we can catch her. She looks to be Trogite, so it'll be worth the trouble."

"Aye, Cap'n," Ox agreed. Then he raised his voice. "Oarsmen to your places!" he bellowed.

There was a bit of grumbling, but the burly oarsmen hauled in their fishing lines, put away their dice, and went to their stations below the deck.

"More sail!" Ox shouted to the top-men aloft. Then he squinted forward. "I make it to be about a league and a half, Cap'n," he said, "and no Trogite vessel afloat can match the *Seagull* for speed when she's under full sail and the oarsmen are earning their keep. We should close on 'em afore the sun goes down."

"We'll see, Ox. We'll see." Sorgan always enjoyed a good run anyway, and the wallowing Trogite vessel gave him an excuse to stretch the *Seagull* out a bit. If nothing else, an invigorating run might clear away the memories of that cursed summer squall and the irritation of that pesky fly on the ceiling of his cabin. Hook-Beak was not particularly superstitious, but the prickly feeling of being watched had made him very edgy.

The Trogite vessel put on more sail, a clear indication that her crew had seen the *Seagull*'s approach, but the broad-beamed merchant ship was no match for her long and slender pursuer, so by late afternoon the *Seagull* was closing fast. Then the crewmen not otherwise occupied began to bring weapons up onto the main deck, and they stood at the rail, swinging their weapons and practicing their war cries.

As usual, the Trogites abandoned ship at that point. It was so much "as usual" that it was almost like a ritual. The *Seagull* paused briefly to give the Trogite seamen time enough to bail over the side and swim out from between the two ships. Then the Maags tied up alongside and stole everything of value.

Then they carried their loot back aboard the *Seagull* and pulled away so that the Trogites could climb back aboard their ship before anybody drowned. It was a civilized sort of arrangement. Nobody got hurt, no damage was done to either vessel, and they all parted almost friends. Hook-Beak smiled faintly. During the previous summer, he'd robbed one Trogite vessel so many times that he'd gotten to know her captain by his first name.

"Should we burn her, Cap'n?" Ox asked hopefully. Ox always wanted to burn the Trogite ships, for some reason.

"I don't think so," Hook-Beak replied. "Let them have their ship back. We've got what we wanted. Maybe if we don't burn her, they'll go back to Shaan and fill her back up. Then we can chase them down and rob them again."

After the Maags had left the Trogite vessel far behind, the *Seagull* was quartering the wind and moving off to the southeast, and that was when coincidence stepped in to alter the "as usual" part of the whole affair. Every seaman alive knows that there are rivers in the sea, but unlike land rivers, the rivers of the sea are largely invisible. Water is water, after all, and the surface of the sea looks much the same, whether it's just lying there or running fast just below the waves.

The *Seagull* was placidly moving southeast, and the crew was busily sorting through the loot, when there was a sudden surge, and the *Seagull* was abruptly swept sideways toward the northeast. First Mate Ox fought with the tiller, bending it almost to the breaking point. "We're in trouble, Cap'n!" he shouted. "A current just grabbed us!"

"Oarsmen to your posts!" Hook-Beak shouted even as Ham-Hand started bellowing, "Slack sail!"

There was a great deal of scrambling about, but nothing seemed to have any effect. "It's no good, Cap'n!" Ox cried. "It's got us, and it won't let go. The tiller's gone slack!"

"Maybe it'll slow down when the tide changes," Ham-Hand suggested hopefully.

"I wouldn't make no big wagers on it," Ox replied, working the tiller back and forth to get the feel of the current. "This one's moving faster than any current I've ever come up against. I don't think the tide's got much to do with it. The seasons might, but it's a long time till autumn, and we could end up a thousand leagues from home afore winter gets here."

"We're making purty good time, though," Ham-Hand noted.

"Are you trying to be funny?" Ox demanded angrily.

"I just thought I'd mention it," Ham-Hand replied. "You want I should tell the oarsmen to stand down, Cap'n?"

"No. Have them swing her so that she's going bow-first. If she keeps going sideways like this, a good ripple could swamp her. Then have the oarsmen ship their oars, but keep them in place. If we swirl in behind an island or a reef, I'll want them to dig in and pull us clear."

"Aye, Cap'n, if that's the way you want it," Ham-Hand replied, tugging his forelock in a salute of sorts.

It didn't happen that way, though. The *Seagull* continued to rush in a northeasterly direction for the next several days, moving farther and farther into unknown waters. The crew was growing more apprehensive as the days slid past. They'd been out of sight of land for more than two weeks now, and some tired old stories involving sea monsters, the edge of the world, demons, and vast whirlpools began to surface. Ox and Ham-Hand tried to stifle those stories, but they weren't very successful.

Then on one bright summer afternoon, the current slowed without any warning, and then it stopped, leaving the *Seagull* placidly sitting on a flat, empty sea.

"What's our plan, Cap'n?" Ham-Hand asked.

"I'm working on it," Sorgan replied. "Don't rush me." He looked at Ox. "How much water have we got left?" he demanded.

"Maybe a week's worth—if we ration it."

"How about food?"

"It's a little skimpy, Cap'n," Ox reported. "The Fat Man's been complaining about that for a couple of days now. The Fat Man's not the best cook in the world, but he does know how to pad up the beans and salt pork with seaweed if things get tight. I'd say that water's our main problem."

"Maybe it'll rain," Ham-Hand said hopefully.

" 'Maybe' don't drink too good," Ox said in a gloomy voice. "We'd better find some land, and we'd better find it fast; otherwise . . ." He left it up in the air, but the others got his drift.

2

The crew of the *Seagull* was on short rations for the next few days, but then, on a steel grey morning before the sun rose, Kaldo Tree-Top, the tallest man aboard, shouted, "Land ho!" from the topmast. A shorter man might have missed the low-lying smudge on the eastern horizon, but Tree-Top, well-nigh seven feet tall, saw it quite clearly.

"Are you sure?" Ham-Hand shouted up to the gangly look-out.

"Real sure," Tree-Top called back. "Two points off the port bow, and three, maybe four leagues away."

"Go wake Ox," Ham-Hand told Rabbit, the small, wiry crewman standing nearby.

"He don't like to get woke up this early," Rabbit replied. "It makes him real grouchy."

"Just kick his foot and then run," Ham-Hand suggested. "He'll never catch you. That's how you got your name, isn't it?"

"I can outrun my own shadow," Rabbit boasted, "but if I happen to trip and fall, old Ox'll tromp on me for the rest of the day."

"Shinny up the mast," Ham-Hand advised. "Ox don't climb

none too good. I need to let him know that we're about to make a landfall."

"I'd really druther not, Ham-Hand."

Ham-Hand clenched his huge fist and held it in front of Rabbit's nose. "I'd do a quick turnabout on my druthers if I was you, Rabbit," he said ominously. "Now, quit complaining and do as you're told."

"Don't get excited," Rabbit said, backing away. "I'm going."

Ox, however, surprised Rabbit with a sudden burst of enthusiasm. Of course, Ox required a great deal of food and drink because of his size, so an unexpected landfall brightened his entire day.

The *Seagull* was at least as fast as her namesake, and by the time the sun came up, the coast ahead was clearly visible. "Go tell the cap'n that we've made a landfall, Rabbit," Ox commanded.

"Why me?" Rabbit whined.

"Because I said so. Don't stand around and argue with me, Rabbit. Just go."

"Aye," Rabbit replied sullenly.

"He spends a lot of his time complaining, don't he?" Ham-Hand observed.

"He runs fast, though," Ox replied. "He's sort of timid, that's all. He's got a real wide streak of cautious that runs down his back, but if you lean on him some, he'll do like you tell him—sooner or later."

Captain Hook-Beak came forward immediately with a relieved look on his face. "Has anybody happened to see any towns on that coast?" he asked.

"None so far, Cap'n," Ox replied. "If we want anything to eat, we'll probably have to chase it down without no help."

"Better find a river or a creek first," Hook-Beak decided. "Let's get the water casks filled before we go hunting. Hungry's bad, but thirsty's worse."

"Not by very much," Ox said. "If my belly starts growling any louder, the people hereabouts will probably think there's a thunderstorm coming their way."

"Would you look at the size of them trees!" Ham-Hand exclaimed, staring at the thickly forested shoreline. "I ain't never *seen* trees that big afore!" Ham-Hand was perhaps a bit overly excitable, but this time Sorgan could see his second mate's point. The forest stretching up from the beach consisted of huge trees that were twenty to thirty feet through at the butt and rose like huge pillars to a height of at least a hundred feet before they sprouted a single limb.

"They do seem just a bit overgrown, don't they?" Ox agreed.

"A *bit?*" Ham-Hand said. "You could carve two *Seagulls* out of one of them trees and still have enough wood left over to cook breakfast."

"We can't eat trees," Sorgan told him. "Let's get the water casks filled and then go hunt up something to eat before Ox starts chewing up the sails or the anchor."

The *Seagull* sailed south along the forested coast for a league or so until Ox spotted a wide creek that emptied out into a small bay. Ham-Hand swung the tiller over hard and beached the ship on a sandy strip nearby. Then most of the crew went to work filling the water casks while Ham-Hand led a small party back into the forest in search of game animals.

The hunting party returned empty-handed along about sundown. "We seen some tracks, Cap'n," Ham-Hand reported, "and some pretty heavy-traveled game trails, but we didn't jump nothing worth wasting no arrows on."

"We can get by this evening, I expect," Sorgan told him. "The Fat-Man put out some setlines right after we beached the *Seagull,* and he brought in some pretty good-sized fish."

"I ain't all that fond of fish, Cap'n," Ham-Hand said.

"It beats eating leaves and twigs," Sorgan said, shrugging.

"Did you happen to run across any signs of people back there in the woods?"

"Nothing I could swear to, Cap'n. Nobody's been chopping down trees or building bridges or such. There *might* be folks hereabouts, but they ain't left no sign. I don't know as it'd be a good idea to leave the *Seagull* beached overnight. Might be better if we anchored a ways out, just to be safe. If there do happen to be folks living around here, maybe we should get to know a little about them afore we let down our guard. I sure don't want to be the main course at no dinner party."

"Good point there," Sorgan agreed. "See to it."

The *Seagull* moved carefully southward along the coast for the next few days. The crew found game animals—wild cows and a very large variety of deer—but they didn't encounter any people.

"There's *got* to be people here someplace, Cap'n," Ox said one afternoon about a week after they'd first made landfall.

"Why?" Hook-Beak said.

"There's always people, Cap'n—even along the coast of Shaan."

"Let's hope they ain't like the Shaans—if there are people here," Ham-Hand put in. "I could go for a long time without meeting folks who eats other folks."

"It might just be that we made landfall too far to the north," Sorgan said. "It's still summer here, so we don't really know what winters here are like. It might just be that any people hereabouts live farther south."

The *Seagull* continued south along the empty coast, but an hour or so later Tree-Top called down from the topmast. "Ho, Cap'n!" he shouted. "There's a village on up ahead. I don't see no people about, but there's smoke coming from some of the houses."

"You see, Ox," Sorgan said. "You worry too much." He

looked up at the topmast. "How far off is that place, Tree-Top?" he shouted.

"Just on t'other side of that sand spit on ahead," Tree-Top called back. "I kin see some skiffs hauled up on the beach, but nobody's anyplace near them."

"We must have scared them off," Hook-Beak said. "I think we might want to go in sort of slow and easy. We don't want to stir anybody up." He turned. "Ho, Rabbit!" he called.

"Aye, Cap'n?" the little man replied.

"Go get that horn of yours and blow it a few times. There's a village just ahead, and I'd like for the people there to know that we're coming and that we're peaceable."

"Aye, Cap'n," Rabbit said. He went below for a moment and emerged with a large, curled cow horn. He put it to his lips and blew a long, mournful-sounding bleat that echoed back into the dark forest.

Hook-Beak and the others listened intently, but there was no immediate reply.

"Try again, Rabbit," Sorgan said. "See if you can make it sound a little more cheerful this time."

Rabbit blew a high-pitched note that ended with an off-key squeak.

"I think maybe Rabbit should practice some," Ox said critically. "That one sounded a lot like a cat who just got her tail stepped on."

Then from somewhere back in the forest there came an answering note that was quite a bit mellower than Rabbit's squeak.

"Now we're getting somewhere," Hook-Beak said. "Keep blowing, Rabbit," he instructed. "Try to make it sound a little friendly, if you can."

"I'm doing my best, Cap'n," Rabbit whined. "Nobody on board likes it when I practice tooting, so I'm sort of rusty."

The *Seagull* rounded the tip of the sand spit, and the crew gathered near the bow to look at the village crouched at the head of a shallow inlet.

"Not too fancy," Ox observed. "Mostly sticks chinked with grass."

"You weren't expecting palaces, were you, Ox?" Sorgan asked. "I'm just as happy not to see stone walls and such. We're only one ship, so we don't really *want* to find folks with all kinds of civilization to back them up. It looks to me like we might have found this place before the Trogites did. Tell the crew not to start waving swords and spears. We don't want to make these folks nervous. Those woods are pretty close to the edge of that village, and I'd rather not sprout a dozen or so arrows while I'm trying to talk to the head man. Take the *Seagull* on into the bay, Ox, but we'll drop anchor a little ways out from the beach. I'll take the skiff on in a little bit closer and then stop. I expect the villagers'll get my point. I want to talk, not pick a fight."

Ox grunted and eased the *Seagull* on into the inlet. When she was about a hundred yards from the beach, he ordered the crew to drop anchor, and several crewmen lowered Hook-Beak's skiff.

"I'll stay within bowshot," the captain said to Ox, "but tell the crew to keep their weapons out of sight—unless things start getting sticky." Then he climbed over the side and lowered himself into his skiff. He set his oars in place and rowed on in a ways. Then he stopped and waited.

Several people from the village came down to the beach, and they seemed to be holding some kind of discussion. Then a tall, lean man with long blond braids and wearing leather clothing got into a kind of canoe, and the other villagers pushed the canoe into deeper water. Then the blond man paddled out to where Hook-Beak waited. He seemed to be very skilled at it. As he came closer and the men on the *Seagull* could see him more clearly, Sorgan felt a brief chill. This was quite obviously a man to be taken very seriously. He was quite lean, and his face was hard. It was his eyes, however, that had so chilled the captain of the *Seagull*. There was a sort of determination there that Sorgan had seldom seen before. When this particular native wanted something, he would almost certainly go to any lengths to obtain it. Sorgan was fairly certain that it was time to walk very carefully.

"What do you want?" the stranger asked. He didn't sound particularly belligerent, and Hook-Beak took that to be a good sign. He was just a bit surprised that the other man spoke the language of the Maags. That should make things a lot easier. "We aren't here to cause any trouble, friend," he said. "We're strangers in these parts, and we don't know exactly where we are."

"This is the Land of Dhrall," the other man replied, "and this is the Domain of Zelana of the West. Does that answer your question?"

"I don't believe I've ever heard of Dhrall before," Sorgan said. "Of course, we're a long way from home, and that might explain why. Is this Zelana your king, or something along those lines?"

"Not exactly. You'll be meeting her before long, I expect. You're Sorgan Hook-Beak, aren't you?"

"How did you know that?" Sorgan was startled.

"Zelana of the West told us that you were coming. She said you wouldn't really know much about Dhrall, so I'm supposed to answer any questions you might have."

"How could she have possibly known that we were coming?" Sorgan demanded. "We certainly didn't *intend* to wander off this far from the Land of Maag."

"But a sea current caught you and brought you here. Wasn't that what happened?"

"You seem to know a great deal about us, stranger, and I don't even know your name yet."

"I was just getting to that, Sorgan Hook-Beak," the tall man said. "I am Longbow of the tribe of Old-Bear, and Zelana of the West instructed me to direct you to White-Braid, chief of the village and the tribe of Lattash. There are three tribes between here and Lattash, and they'll build fires on the beach to guide you. You *can* count as far as three, can't you?"

"Of course I can." Sorgan was more than a little offended. "How is it that you came by the name 'Longbow'?"

"I'm somewhat taller than the other men of Old-Bear's tribe, so my bow's longer." He held up his bow to let Sorgan see it. He didn't move it very fast; there was no arrow anywhere in sight, and he was not holding it as if he intended to use it. Both Longbow and Sorgan were being careful not to make any quick moves, since there were probably several dozen arrows pointed at them right now.

"Nicely crafted," Sorgan said.

"It does what I want it to do," Longbow said modestly. "It hasn't yet missed at any range."

Sorgan assumed that the blond man was boasting, but he sounded so sincere that Sorgan wasn't entirely certain. "Just how far south is this Lattash place?" he asked.

"As far as a man can walk in ten days," Longbow replied. "After you pass the fires on the beach, you'll come to a narrow inlet that leads on into a fairly large bay. Lattash stands at the head of that bay, and Zelana awaits you at Lattash."

Sorgan squinted at the water, making some calculations in his head. "I'm just guessing, but I'd say that the *Seagull*—that's my ship over there— should make it in three days."

"I wouldn't take much longer, if I were you," Longbow advised. "Zelana's impatient, and you don't want to irritate her. I'm supposed to ask you if the word *gold* has any meaning for you."

"Oh, yes!" Sorgan replied fervently.

"I wouldn't know myself, but Zelana told me to say 'gold' to you. Have you enough food and water for three days? I don't think Zelana will let you stop again on your way south."

"How's she going to stop me?"

"I don't think you really want to know, Sorgan Hook-Beak. We'll probably meet again, but for right now you'd better move along as quickly as you can. Things will go better if you do."

3

"Did he have any weapons aside from that bow, Cap'n?" Ox asked when Sorgan returned to the *Seagull*.

"He had a bundle of arrows and a spear in the bottom of the canoe," Sorgan replied. "He didn't touch it, but it was right out in the open where I could see it. I'm pretty sure he wanted me to know it was there. The funny thing about it was that the spear point wasn't iron. It'd been made from stone instead."

"The people who eat other people in the Land of Shaan make their tools and weapons out of stone, too," Ox said. "That don't make me feel none too comfortable, Cap'n. Just the idea of getting et makes me go cold all over."

"I don't think these people are that kind, Ox," Sorgan said. "The fellow in the canoe seemed to be almost friendly. He knew my name, and he wanted to be sure we had enough food and water on board. There's a place called Lattash about three days south of here, and there's a woman named Zelana there who wants to talk with us. Longbow told me that there might be gold involved in the discussion. That sort of suggests that the Zelana woman wants to hire people who know how to fight, and she'll pay good gold to get them."

"I ain't about to start taking no orders from no woman, Cap'n," Ham-Hand protested.

"Don't worry about it, Ham-Hand," Sorgan told him. "You'll take your orders from me, just like always. *I'll* be the one who deals with this Zelana woman. Hoist up the sail, and let's go south. There's a lady down there who wants to talk to me about gold, so let's not dawdle."

Once the *Seagull* was clear of the inlet, a good following breeze came up, and Sorgan's ship was soon skimming lightly over the waves a league or so out from the coast of Dhrall. By evening the *Seagull* was a goodly distance south of Longbow's village, and Sorgan prudently hauled in on the leeward side of a small islet and dropped anchor. Nobody in his right mind sails through strange waters after dark.

Sorgan rose at first light and went up on deck to have a look at the weather. He found Ham-Hand and Rabbit leaning over the rail on the starboard side. "What's afoot?" he asked them.

"There's some real strange critters in these here waters, Cap'n," Rabbit replied. "I've seen dolphins and porpoises afore, but I ain't never seen any of them as was pink."

"You're not serious!" Sorgan said.

"Strike me dead iff'n I ain't," Rabbit said. "I heared them splashin' an' gigglin' out there afore it got light, an' I couldn't believe my eyes once it got light enough for me to take a good look."

"He's right, Cap'n," Ham-Hand said. "The little rascals is as pink as a new sunrise, and they're skipping around out there on the water like little children having a good time."

"There's one right now, Cap'n," Rabbit said, pointing off to starboard.

Sorgan stared. The creature was definitely a dolphin, and it really was pink.

Then there were others swarming around the *Seagull,* leaping and splashing and giggling as they frolicked about. "This is the strangest place," Sorgan muttered, half to himself. "The next thing we know, we might come across purple sharks or bright green whales. Rouse the crew, Ham-Hand. The weather looks good, so let's get under way."

"Aye, Cap'n," Ham-Hand replied.

The *Seagull* continued south, but she was no longer alone. The pink dolphins accompanied her, racing along ahead of her bow and chattering to the crew on both the starboard and port sides. "It's almost like we got an escort, ain't it, Cap'n?" Ox suggested. Then he squinted speculatively at the creatures playfully leaping out of the water on all sides. "I wonder what dolphin meat tastes like," he said.

"No!" Sorgan said sharply. "Our luck's running good, Ox. Don't tamper with anything. You might bring down a squall or even a waterspout, and it's a long swim back to Maag."

"Those things splashing around out there don't have anything to do with the weather, Cap'n," Ox scoffed.

"Maybe not, but I'm not about to take any chances. Don't fool around with things, Ox. Just leave them exactly the way they are."

And so the *Seagull* proceeded south at a goodly rate with dolphins leaping along in front of her bow as rosy dawn tinted the eastern sky.

"There's a fire on the beach, Cap'n," Tree-Top called down from the topmast.

"Keep your eyes peeled," Hook-Beak called up to him. "There'll be two more farther on south. After we pass the third one, we'll need to keep a sharp eye out. There'll be an inlet that leads into a fair-sized bay. That's the place we're looking for."

"Aye, Cap'n," Tree-Top called back.

*   *   *

The *Seagull* passed the third bonfire in the early afternoon of the third day after Sorgan's meeting with Longbow, and Hook-Beak ordered the crew to keep a sharp eye off to port.

They rounded a headland, and just beyond there was what appeared to be a narrow channel stretching back between two rocky promontories.

"I'll take her, Ox," Sorgan said, laying one hand on the tiller. "Get the oarsmen in place, and drop the sail. Let's not run her aground this close to the rich lady's home village."

"Aye, Cap'n," Ox agreed.

Hook-Beak considered his options as he steered the *Seagull* through the channel and on into the sizeable bay lying beyond. He was fairly sure that Longbow hadn't been trying to deceive him, but it might be better to take things a little slow and steady here. He didn't know these people, and they didn't know him. He glanced at the sky. It was midafternoon now, and it'd probably take some time to locate the village and row up the bay to wherever it was. That could possibly bring them to this Lattash place at sundown or even later. It might be safer to drop anchor a ways out from shore and wait until morning. That way they'd arrive in broad daylight, and everybody could see what everybody else was doing.

"Shinny up the mast, Ham-Hand," he told his second mate. "See if you can spot that village, and then find us a place to anchor for the night. We'll sit tight until morning, and *then* we'll go talk with the rich lady."

"Aye, Cap'n," Ham-Hand agreed. "Let's not rile up the natives if we don't have to."

They anchored the *Seagull* off a rocky shore where there was no discernable beach. Hook-Beak didn't want anybody to come creeping up to his ship in the dark. He stationed lookouts aloft and others in the bow and on the stern, just to be on the safe side.

The night passed quietly, and everything seemed to be all

right the next morning. The lookouts had seen several fires near the broad, sandy beach at the head of the bay during the night, and Sorgan called the crew of the *Seagull* to the aft deck for a little conference. "I want you men to mind your manners when we go into that village," he told them. "Don't start getting any ideas about their womenfolk or try to grab any trinkets from the men. We're probably going to be outnumbered by about ten to one, so let's all be real polite. These people seem to need some help from us, and there's been some talk of gold as payment for that help, so behave yourselves. Don't start waving your swords and spears around, and don't snarl or shake your fists at anybody. We could be talking about a lot of gold here, and I'll be *very* unhappy with anybody who does anything to upset the applecart. Have I made myself clear?" He looked around at his crew with bleak eyes and an even grimmer expression.

They all seemed to get his point almost immediately.

They raised anchor as the sun was just coming up, and the oarsmen slowly rowed the *Seagull* up to the head of the bay where the nighttime lookouts had seen the fires.

"Take her on in until we're about a hundred yards from shore, Ox," Sorgan instructed. "We'll drop anchor there and wait to see how the natives behave. If they seem peaceful, fine. If they act belligerent, we'll turn the *Seagull* around and go someplace else."

"I get your drift, Cap'n," Ox agreed.

Sorgan noted that the village of Lattash was quite a bit larger than the one where he'd met Longbow, and there were many canoes on the sandy beach, and fishnets drying on poles near the canoes. It appeared that the natives of Lattash were primarily fishermen. The houses, if they could be called that, were made, for the most part, of tree branches tightly woven about dome-shaped frames, and, though they appeared to be a bit crude, Hook-Beak was fairly sure that they kept the weather at bay. There was nothing in the village that could really be called a street, since the individual huts appeared to have been randomly placed.

There was also a well-packed ridge or berm between the village and the river, which came down out of the mountains just there, and that strongly hinted at the possibility that the river sometimes overflowed its banks.

It wasn't long before a dozen or so canoes were paddled out from the beach by leather-clad natives. Sorgan noted that they were all fairly well armed. Their arrows and spears had stone points, but a well-sharpened stone point could probably find a man's vitals almost as well as an iron one could.

The canoes drew up in a sort of half-circle between the *Seagull* and the beach, but a single one was paddled up to within a few yards of Sorgan's ship. There were only two natives in the canoe. The one who was doing the paddling appeared almost as burly as Ox, and he had a flaming red beard that reached halfway to his waist. The other native was much older, and he had snowy hair, which he wore in braids.

The red-bearded native skillfully brought the canoe to a stop, and his older companion rose to his feet. "Welcome to Lattash, Sorgan Hook-Beak," he said in a deep, rolling voice. "Long have we awaited your coming."

"I am honored by your greeting," Sorgan replied. A certain formality seemed to be in order here. He didn't know these people, so he didn't want to take any chances.

"I am White-Braid of Lattash," the man in the canoe introduced himself, "and the younger men of this village even heed my advice—every so often." The old man smiled faintly.

Sorgan had noticed that Longbow had also seemed to have a similarly dry sense of humor. He straightened. "I have been told that the Lady Zelana would have words with me, Chief White-Braid," he said.

"I have heard so myself," White-Braid replied. "This is my nephew, Red-Beard," he said, gesturing toward the native who'd paddled the canoe. "He will escort you to the cave where she dwells. I shall remain here so that your men will need have no concern about your continued well-being. In time, these precautions may no longer be necessary, but we are strangers still, so let there be no possibility of deception."

"You are very wise, Chief White-Braid," Sorgan said, "and I shall be guided by you in this matter." If White-Braid wanted formality, Sorgan was ready to pile formality on him until he was hip-deep in it.

The two of them rather carefully changed places. White-Braid came on board the *Seagull,* and Hook-Beak climbed down into the canoe. "Treat our friend well, Ox," Sorgan called up to his first mate.

"Aye, Cap'n," Ox replied respectfully.

"Why does the lady called Zelana live in a cave instead of in the village with the rest of the tribe?" Sorgan asked the red-bearded native, who was paddling the canoe smoothly toward the beach.

"She doesn't really belong here, Sorgan Hook-Beak," Red-Beard replied, "and she isn't very fond of us."

"I thought that she was the queen of this part of Dhrall," Sorgan said.

"Not exactly," Red-Beard replied. "Our legends say that she's lived forever, but that she doesn't care for people very much. She went away a long, long time ago. She came back just recently, and now she's staying in that cave at the edge of the village. My uncle tells us that she's very powerful, and that if she wants something to happen, it *will* happen. Uncle White-Braid gets a little strange when he talks about her. I think he's afraid of her, and that's most peculiar, because he's not really afraid of anything. She never comes out of that cave, and the only servant she has is a little girl. The child comes out of the cave to tell us what Zelana wants us to do."

"What does she look like?" Sorgan asked.

Red-Beard shrugged. "I've only seen her twice, and she keeps her face covered. I overheard my uncle once when he was talking with some of the other old men of the village, and he was telling them that she changes every so often."

"Changes?"

"She doesn't always look the same." Red-Beard stopped paddling. "When we get to the beach, I'm supposed to lead you right along at the edge of the water. Uncle White-Braid told me to be very careful to keep you right out in plain sight all the way to the cave of Zelana so that your men won't have any cause for concern."

"Your people seem to be very cautious, Red-Beard," Sorgan observed.

"Uncle White-Braid seems to prefer it that way. Old men are like that sometimes."

"That might explain how they lived long enough to get old."

"You're probably right," Red-Beard conceded, taking up his paddle again. "We'll have to go ashore just ahead. There's some sharp rocks just below the surface of the water farther on down the beach, and I'd rather not rip the bottom out of my canoe."

"How far is it to this cave?" Sorgan asked.

Red-Beard pointed with his paddle. "It's in the side of that hill near the end of the beach."

"It's quite a ways from the village," Sorgan observed, noting that the hill was oddly dome-shaped and its sides were mostly bare rock with scant vegetation.

"The one called Zelana doesn't seem to like the way we smell."

"Am I supposed to bow down to her or anything like that?" Sorgan asked.

"I don't think so. Uncle White-Braid would have mentioned it. Just tell her who you are. She'll probably know already, since she's been describing you ever since she first got here." Red-Beard drove the prow of his canoe up onto the beach, and then he and Sorgan pulled it on up until it was clear of the water.

Then they walked on down the beach, being careful to stay in plain sight of the *Seagull*.

"Have you heard anything about some kind of trouble that might be coming this way?" Sorgan asked.

"There's always trouble in this part of the world, Sorgan Hook-Beak," Red-Beard replied. "The tribes can go to war about almost anything. Here lately, though, we've heard some stories about the creatures of the Wasteland."

"Where's that?"

"Off beyond the mountains," Red-Beard replied vaguely. "I don't really know very much about it, because the old men don't like to talk about the Wasteland. The creatures who live there are supposed to look sort of like people, but I don't think they *are* people. Zelana can probably tell you more about them. I think that's why she wants to talk to you. There's the mouth of her cave right over there." He pointed at an irregular opening in the rocky hillside. "My uncle told me to make some noise before we go on inside. He said that we don't want to startle Zelana."

They approached the cave mouth with a certain caution. "Zelana of the West," Red-Beard called into the echoing cave, "I am Red-Beard of the line of White-Braid the chief, and I have brought an outlander named Sorgan Hook-Beak to speak with you."

They waited for a few moments, and then a beautiful little girl with fair hair came out of the dark cave. "What kept you so long, Hook-Beak?" she asked Sorgan. "The Beloved was start-ing to worry about you. Come along, but wipe your feet before you come inside. She gets very peevish when somebody tracks mud into her cave."

Sorgan and Red-Beard followed the little girl through the irreg-ularly shaped opening and on through a twisting, narrow pas-sageway into a large chamber where a small fire burned some distance back from the cave mouth. A woman with dark hair and wearing a filmy gauze garment was seated near the fire with her back to them. "It's about time you got here, Hook-Beak," the woman said. "Has the *Seagull* gone lame?"

"It *is* a fair distance from Longbow's village," Sorgan replied, feeling more than a little offended.

"That didn't bother her very much when she was chasing down that Trogite treasure ship a little while back."

"How did you know about that?" he demanded.

"The Beloved knows everything, Hook-Beak," the little girl told him. "Everybody knows that."

"That'll do, Eleria," the woman in gauze said. Then she turned to look at Sorgan.

Sorgan's knees went weak at that point. She was by far the most beautiful woman he'd ever seen.

"Don't stare, Sorgan," she said primly. "It isn't polite."

"Forgive me," he said, flushing slightly. "Your appearance startled me. You must be used to that by now, though."

"It does happen every so often," she admitted. "At least you're strong enough not to swoon at the sight of me. That can be *so* irritating. I see you've brought Red-Beard with you."

"Actually, he's the one who brought *me*," Sorgan replied, his voice still trembling a bit. "He showed me the way."

"Then you know each other. Good. He'll be going with us when we return to Maag. We'll have to stop and pick up Longbow as well, but we can go into the details later. Let's get down to business here. I need warriors, and I pay in gold. Are you interested?"

"The word 'gold' is *very* interesting," he replied. "Who do you want me to kill, and how much gold will you give me after he's dead?"

"You're a blunt man, Sorgan," she said.

"It saves time," he said with a shrug. "Are we talking about some kind of war here?"

"Well, sort of. How much do you know about the Land of Dhrall?"

"I'd never even heard of it until I met Longbow about three

days ago. Red-Beard here was telling me something about some people that live over beyond the mountains. I gather that they're the ones you'd like to have me kill. Is this some sort of tribal squabble? That sort of thing happens in Maag all the time."

"It goes a long way past 'squabble,' Hook-Beak," she said. "The people of Dhrall dwell mostly along the coastline, where the fishing's good, but there are other creatures here as well who dwell in the Wastelands of the interior. They're starting to grow restless, and we want you and your warriors to persuade them to go back home where they belong. That's why I sent for you. I want you to enlist your fellow Maags to come here and help us drive the creatures of the Wasteland back across the mountains. We'll tell the Maags that I'll give them gold if they come here and help us."

"It's easy to *say* gold, Lady Zelana," Sorgan said, "but I think I'll need to *see* gold before I'll be very convincing when I talk with the other Maags."

"That sounds reasonable." Zelana turned to the little girl. "Take him back to where the gold is, Eleria," she said. "Let him see how much there really is."

"Of course, Beloved," the little girl replied. "It's back in the cave a ways, Hook-Big," she told Sorgan.

"That's *Hook-Beak*," he corrected her.

"Ah," she said. "That does make a little more sense, doesn't it? I must have misunderstood the Beloved when she told me your name. It seemed to me that it was backwards, but 'Big-Hook' wouldn't make sense either, would it? How much of this gold did you want to look at?"

"As much as possible," Sorgan replied eagerly.

"I don't think we have that much time, really," Eleria said. "The Beloved's in sort of a hurry."

Then the gauze-draped Zelana made a kind of squeaking sound, and Eleria responded in the same fashion. Sorgan assumed that it was some sort of foreign language.

Then Zelana reached out and took a glowing lump of fire out of the empty air and handed it to Eleria. "It's dark back in the cave," Eleria told Sorgan. "This little sun should light our way. You should feel honored, Hook-Beak. The Beloved was going to have this for lunch." She held out the glowing lump of fire. "Here," she said. "You can carry it, if you like."

Sorgan put his hands behind his back. "No, that's all right," he said, perhaps a bit too quickly. "You can carry it." So far as Sorgan was able to determine, the lump was not enclosed in glass—or anything else, for that matter. It appeared to be raw fire, but the little girl seemed very casual about the whole thing.

"All right. Come along, then." She led him back into the cave, holding up the fire to light the way.

"Doesn't that burn your hand?" Sorgan asked Eleria as they went on back into the rocky passageway.

"No, not really," she replied. "The Beloved asked it not to."

"Why do you keep calling her 'the Beloved'?" he asked.

"That's what the pink dolphins always call her," Eleria replied. "I used to play with the pink dolphins when I was younger."

"We saw some of those when we were coming here from Longbow's village," he said.

"I know. The Beloved asked them to show you the way to get here. She didn't want you to get lost. The gold you want to look at is right around this corner."

Sorgan followed her, but then he stopped suddenly, his eyes almost starting out of their sockets. The rocky passageway he and Eleria had been following was blocked by a solid wall of what appeared to be gold bricks.

"Will this much do for now?" Eleria asked him. "The Beloved can send for more, but it might take Red-Beard and the rest of the villagers a while to carry it here."

"How far back does this passage go?" Sorgan asked in a trembling voice.

"I'm not really sure," Eleria replied. "Quite a long way, I think. Hold me up in the air and I'll take a look."

Sorgan picked her up and sat her on his shoulder. She held out her ball of fire and peered back into the cave. "The light doesn't reach all the way back," she reported, "but there's gold back as far as I can see. It's nice enough, I suppose, but it'd be prettier if it was pink instead of yellow. Yellow's sort of tiresome, don't you think?"

"It doesn't tire *me* out much," Sorgan disagreed.

"Let's go on back," Eleria suggested. "The Beloved's sort of impatient."

"Would it be all right if I took a couple of these bricks to show my men?" Hook-Beak asked her.

"I'm sure it would," she said with a sunny smile. "There are lots of them here, aren't there?"

"Oh, yes," Sorgan said fervently.

They went on back to the front of the cave.

"Was there enough gold there to suit you, Hook-Beak?" Zelana asked.

"It looks about right to me," he replied. "I could probably buy the whole Land of Maag with that much. I'll have to take some of it with me to show to the other Maags, though. They probably won't believe me when I tell them about it."

"Not *too* much, Sorgan," Zelana told him. "The *Seagull* isn't built to carry a lot of weight, and we don't want her to sink out from under us when we sail back to Maag, do we?"

"We?" Sorgan asked sharply.

"Eleria and I'll be going with you, and so will Red-Beard and Longbow."

"You don't really have to come along, Lady Zelana," Sorgan protested.

"I think I do, Hook-Beak," she disagreed. "We need to hurry, and I can persuade the *Seagull* to go faster—*and* make sure that you don't forget about your obligation to return."

"But . . ." he started weakly.

"No buts, Sorgan," she cut him off. "We sail on the afternoon tide. Go back to the *Seagull* and get her ready. I'll have Red-Beard make the arrangements to put some gold on board before we leave. Take Eleria with you. I'll have to talk with my brother before we leave."

"I haven't agreed to any of this yet," Sorgan protested.

"Were you going to say no?"

"Well . . ." His objection sort of dribbled off as he remembered that solid wall of gold bricks.

"I didn't really think so," Zelana said smugly. "Now go."

He looked longingly toward the back of the cave.

"Quickly, quickly, Sorgan," she said, snapping her fingers at him. "The day runs on, and we want to be well on our way before the sun goes to bed."

THE
LAND
OF
MAAG

1

Now, Old-Bear was the chief of the tribe, and though he seldom spoke, Longbow's parents had told their son when he had been but a child that Old-Bear was very wise. Longbow had been busy being a child at that time, so he had accepted what his parents had told him without question and had continued his childhood with great enthusiasm.

The village of Old-Bear's tribe at that time had been located atop a high bluff where the deep forest lay at its back and the shining face of Mother Sea stretched from the foot of the bluff to the far western horizon. Longbow had been certain that there could be no better place in the entire world to be a child.

It had been in the late summer of Longbow's fifth year when many members of Old-Bear's tribe had been overcome by a strange illness that had first burned them with fever and then had wracked them with chill. Their skin had been marked with purple splotches, and they had seen things which had not really been there—things so horrible that they had screamed for many days—and then they had died.

Now, One-Who-Heals was the shaman of Old-Bear's tribe, and he was very skilled in the healing arts, but the pestilence which had crept out of the night resisted his every attempt to conquer it, and fully half the tribe of Old-Bear had been carried off. And among those who had been lost had been the parents of Longbow and the mate of Chief Old-Bear. And One-Who-Heals, realizing that the pestilence had defeated him, had gone to the lodge of Old-Bear and had urged his chief to gather up those members of the tribe who still lived and to flee.

In sorrow, Old-Bear had agreed and had commanded the survivors to burn their lodges, and then he had led them to a new location near the shore of Mother Sea, where they could build lodges on uncontaminated ground, and he had taken the orphaned Longbow into his new lodge and had reared him as if he were his own son.

Now, Old-Bear had a daughter named Misty-Water, but the children had not, as children often do, contended with each other for Old-Bear's attention but rather had joined together in their grief. Though they had grown up together in the same lodge, Misty-Water and Longbow had never thought of each other as brother and sister—perhaps because Old-Bear had always referred to Longbow as their "guest."

Even as a child, Longbow had been very perceptive, and it had seemed to him that Old-Bear's use of the word "guest" had been his way to carefully manipulate the thinking of the two children in his lodge. The ultimate goal of the clever chief had been fairly obvious, but as Misty-Water had matured, Longbow had seen no real reason to complain. Misty-Water had grown up to be the sort of girl who made men stop breathing as she walked by. Her long hair was as black as a raven's wings, and her skin was pale as the moon. Her eyes were large, and her lips were full. She was quite tall and slender, and as she began to mature, other interesting aspects emerged as well. Longbow had found that it was very difficult to take his eyes from her.

The fathers of attractive girls are frequently very edgy as young men begin to gather in large numbers about their daughters, but Old-Bear remained tranquil because Longbow was attending to the matter. Even as a young man scarcely past his boyhood, Longbow was quite tall and well muscled, and he could be very persuasive. After only a few incidents, the other young men of Old-Bear's tribe came to understand that the pursuit of Misty-Water could be most hazardous.

Misty-Water appreciated Longbow's actions, since she had concerns of her own that required her undivided attention. She had observed that several of the other young women of the tribe viewed Longbow with a great deal of interest, and it seemed to her that it might be prudent to encourage *dis*interest. It didn't really take Misty-Water very long to persuade those other young women that Longbow wasn't really available. In most cases, she had accomplished this with a few hints, but a couple of the young women of the tribe had required a more direct approach. There had been a few bruises involved, but very few really serious injuries.

Old-Bear had watched their little games. He hadn't said anything, but he had frequently smiled.

The other young men of the tribe viewed Longbow with a kind of awe. He had taken up his bow very early, and he had never been able to explain exactly how it was that every arrow he loosed from his long, curved bow went precisely where he wanted it to go, even at incredible distances. He had tried to explain the sense of oneness he felt with every target his arrows unerringly found. The unity of hand and eye and thought lies at the center of every archer's skill, of course, but Longbow had realized very early that the target must be included in that unification. It was that sense of joining that lay at the core of Longbow's unerring accuracy. He believed that his target seemed almost to draw his arrow, and that is a very difficult concept to explain.

Misty-Water, however, had not had any difficulty understanding Longbow's point. She had been unified with *her* target since early childhood.

Everyone in Old-Bear's tribe knew by now that it wouldn't be too long before a certain ceremony would take place, but exactly *when* was entirely up to Chief Old-Bear, and the chief didn't seem to be in any great hurry.

Longbow and Misty-Water were fairly certain that the chief's delay was no more than his way of teasing them, but they didn't really think it was very funny at all.

It was in the early summer of Longbow's fourteenth year that Old-Bear finally conceded that the children of his lodge were probably mature enough, so with some show of reluctance he agreed that Misty-Water and Longbow could go through the ceremony which would join them for life.

The celebration began immediately. Misty-Water's father was the chief, and the young couple was very popular in the tribe, so their joining promised to be the happiest event of the summer. The young women of the tribe gave Misty-Water small gifts, and their gatherings around her were often punctuated with giggles.

The young men gave Longbow well-made arrowheads, spear points, and knives, all chipped from the finest stone, and they helped him build the lodge where he and Misty-Water were to dwell.

Finally the day of their joining arrived, and in keeping with tradition, Misty-Water arose at dawn to go alone to a quiet pool in the nearby forest to bathe and then to garb herself in the soft white deerskin garment she was to wear during the ceremony.

Longbow was not supposed to look upon her that day until the time of the ceremony, and so he kept his eyes tightly closed as he lay on his pallet while Misty-Water gathered up her ceremonial garment and quietly left her father's lodge. "Hurry back," he said softly as she went out into the morning light, and she laughed a pearly little laugh that touched his very heart.

The sun rose above the deep forest to the east, and the blue shadows of morning gradually faded as that most special of days plodded slowly along. Longbow garbed himself with some care, and then he waited.

But Misty-Water did not return.

By midmorning Longbow was frantic. Misty-Water was as impatient as he was to go through the ceremony of their joining, and *nobody* could take this long to bathe. Finally Longbow cast custom and tradition aside and ran out of the village along the path that led to the quiet pool in the forest. And when he reached it, his heart stopped.

His mate-to-be, garbed all in white deerskin, was floating facedown in the still water of the pool

Desperately Longbow rushed into the water, gathered her in his arms, and struggled back to the moss-covered edge of the pool. He laid her facedown on the moss and pressed her back as One-Who-Heals had instructed the young men of the tribe to do to revive a drowning victim, but despite everything Longbow tried to revive her, Misty-Water showed not the faintest sign of life.

In agony Longbow raised his face and howled as all meaning faded from his life.

When Longbow, insensible with grief, carried the still body of Misty-Water back to the village, Chief Old-Bear wept, but in time he sent for the shaman of the tribe, One-Who-Heals. "She could not have drowned, could she?" the sorrowing chief demanded. "She swam very well, and that pool in the forest is not deep."

"She was not drowned, Old-Bear," One-Who-Heals replied grimly. "The marks on her throat are the marks of fangs. It was venom that took her life."

"There are no venomous snakes in this region," Old-Bear protested.

One-Who-Heals pointed at the marks on Misty-Water's throat. "No snake of any size has fangs this large. It is my thought that these are the fang-marks of one of the servants of

That-Called-the-Vlagh. There are many stories about the servants of the Vlagh. Old stories seldom have much truth to them, but it seems that the stories about the creatures of the Wasteland might well be true. It was That-Called-the-Vlagh that made them, and we are told that the Vlagh gave them venom so that they would need no weapons."

"Why would a servant of the Vlagh kill our beloved Misty-Water?" Old-Bear demanded in a voice filled with grief.

"There are rumors in the air which tell us that That-Called-the-Vlagh grows restless and that it sends its servants out of the Wasteland into the coastal domains to watch us so that the Vlagh might come to know of our weaknesses. Those servants do not wish to be seen, I think, so they will most probably kill any of us who happen to see them, so that they may continue to watch us and to carry what they have seen back to the Vlagh."

"It might be well, then, if none of the servants of the Vlagh return to the Wasteland with this knowledge," Old-Bear said grimly. "I will speak with my son Longbow of this. His grief may be a wellspring for eternal hatred, and I think That-Called-the-Vlagh may come to regret what its servants have done this day."

"Send him to me before he goes to the hunt, my chief," One-Who-Heals suggested. "Let him grieve first, though. He'll think more clearly after his grief has run its course, and while he grieves, I will use the time to gather more information about the servants of the Vlagh so that I can advise him of their peculiarities."

It was late in the winter of the following year when Old-Bear decided that it might well be time to take the still-grieving Longbow to the lodge of One-Who-Heals, for Longbow's grief showed no signs of fading, and so he bleakly commanded his despairing son to accompany him.

And so they trudged through the melting snow to the

shaman's lodge, and when they entered, One-Who-Heals opened a bundle of dried bones and spread them out upon a blanket for them to see. "Since little is known of the creatures of the Wasteland who serve That-Called-the-Vlagh, I thought it might be well if we had a dead one to examine, so that we might better understand its peculiarities," he told them.

"Where did you find this dead one?" Longbow asked in a flat, unemotional voice.

"I didn't really find it, Longbow. After the death of Misty-Water, I went out to trap one of them. They know very little about the forest, so it's easy to conceal a trap from them. I found many tracks of their small feet, which told me where I might have some luck with a trap, and then I dug a pit and concealed it under fallen leaves and twigs. It was a fairly deep pit, and I lined the bottom with sharpened stakes, and then, when it was well-concealed, I waited. It took a while, but finally one of the Vlagh's servants fell into my trap, and the stakes at the bottom greeted it. Everything worked out quite well, except that it took the creature two days to finish dying. Then I pulled it up out of the pit and boiled all the meat off its bones so that we might better see its peculiarities." One-Who-Heals shrugged. "After we've learned what we need to know, you might want to take the skull to Misty-Water's grave as a gift to her spirit."

Longbow's eyes, which had seemed almost dead, suddenly brightened. "It might please her spirit at that," he conceded, "and more of these heads might even please her spirit more."

"It's quite possible, my son," Old-Bear agreed.

"Now, then," the shaman said, picking up the skull, "notice that this creature's fangs are folded back to keep them concealed—much in the same way that the fangs of a venomous snake are hidden. The fangs spring forward when the creature strikes. This is how it hides its weapons until it attacks." He set the skull aside and picked up the bones of one of the creature's arms. "As you can see, the creature has sharp spines along the outer sides of its arm from the wrist to the elbow. The spines are much like the stings of wasps or hornets. The spines, like the fangs, are venomous, and they also remain out of sight until the creature wishes to attack. Then they spring forward. Be wary when you approach one of these creatures, Longbow, for they can move very fast. That-Called-the-Vlagh has made a very effective killer, but it has to be close to kill. It cannot kill from any great distance."

"That's a useful thing to know," Longbow said, his voice coming to life now. "Does this venom cause pain?"

One-Who-Heals nodded. "Unbearable pain, I think."

"And is it even able to kill creatures of its own kind?" Longbow pressed.

"I'm certain that it can."

"Then if I were to smear the venom of one of them on the point of my arrow, it would carry pain and death to any other one I happened to meet, wouldn't it?"

One-Who-Heals blinked. "Why would you need to do that? You never miss your target when you shoot one of your arrows."

"The creatures of the Wasteland have caused me much pain, and I think I owe them a great deal of pain in return. An honest man always pays what he owes."

"Be very careful, Longbow," the shaman cautioned. "These creatures hunt by concealing themselves, and they strike only when their intended prey is very close."

"I'm a hunter, One-Who-Heals," Longbow reminded the shaman. "Nothing in the forest can hide itself from me. The servants of That-Called-the-Vlagh have been sent into our lands because the Vlagh hungers for information. I think it will be my lifelong task to make certain that the Vlagh's hunger remains unsatisfied, for I will kill all servants it sends here and deliver their heads to Misty-Water's grave as gifts to her spirit, as a sign that I love her still."

"And will you now go to the hunt, my son?" Chief Old-Bear asked.

"If it pleases you, my father."

"It pleases me very much, Longbow."

And so it was that Longbow of the tribe of Old-Bear vanished into the forest to seek out the venomous servants of That-Called-the-Vlagh. It was rumored over the next decades that the Vlagh sent many of its servants into the lands of the tribe, but few if any of its servants returned, for Longbow had become one with the forest, and the creatures of the Wasteland could neither see nor hear him, nor could they even catch his scent as death sprang upon them from his bow.

The return of the legendary Zelana of the West stirred great excitement in all the tribes of her Domain, and the people of Old-Bear's tribe felt greatly honored when word reached them that she would soon come to visit. Longbow, however, had felt no great need to meet with her, and so it was that when word of her approach reached the village of Old-Bear, Longbow simply faded back into the forest to continue his hunt.

She had sought him out, however, and he had found that to be disturbing. He had been certain that no one could find him in the forest if he did not wish to be found, but Zelana had unerringly come to the place where he was to ask him for his aid.

"I'm not really interested, Zelana," he had told her bluntly. "I have a responsibility of my own right now. I think you'd better choose someone else."

"This is *very* important," she had pressed.

"Not to me, it isn't. There's only one thing that's important to me, and it's what I'm doing right now."

"You don't like us very much, do you, Longbow?" the little girl who'd accompanied Zelana had asked shrewdly. "You don't really like anybody, do you? You don't have any room inside you for 'like,' because you're all filled up with 'don't like,' aren't you?"

"It goes quite a bit further than 'don't like,' little one," Longbow had told her, his voice softening slightly. "The servants of That-Called-the-Vlagh killed she who was to become my mate, so now I kill them."

"That sounds fair to me," the little girl had said. "How many of them have you killed so far?"

He had shrugged. "Hundreds, I suppose. I don't really keep count anymore. I've been doing this for twenty years now."

"If that's all that really matters to you, we know how you can kill thousands, don't we, Beloved?"

"Perhaps even more than that, Eleria," Zelana had replied. Then she looked Longbow straight in the face. "We hate the creatures of the Wasteland almost as much as you do, Long-bow, and if this turns out the way I want it to, we'll kill them all, and then we'll go into the Wasteland and kill That-Called-the-Vlagh. How does that sound to you?"

"It's interesting enough to make me want to hear more," he had conceded.

He was just a bit puzzled by these two. Zelana had been very arbitrary, demanding that he obey her commands. Eleria, how-ever, appeared to have seen right to the core of his abrupt re-fusal to accept Zelana's command, and had cleverly waved "kill them by the thousands" in front of him almost like waving bait before a fish.

Longbow ruefully admitted to himself that he'd taken Ele-ria's bait almost without thinking. "Maybe I'd better keep a very close eye on that little one," he murmured to himself. "There's much more going on here than seemed right at first."

Longbow had been a bit dubious when Zelana had assured him that the ship of the Maag called Hook-Beak would come across the face of Mother Sea to the Land of Dhrall, and even more skeptical when she'd told him that the Maags would do *any-thing* for gold, but when the long, narrow ship of Hook-Beak arrived at the village of Old-Bear almost exactly when she'd told him that it would, Longbow's skepticism began to fade. Moreover, Sorgan Hook-Beak had responded to the word *gold* even as Zelana had suggested that he would.

Zelana had been right twice so far, and if the Maags would be as useful as she seemed to believe, the long voyage to their homeland could be worth the time and trouble.

Longbow had not killed a servant of the Vlagh for many days now, and that made him a bit ashamed. Misty-Water had always been patient, though, so he was fairly sure that her spirit would be willing to wait while he gave Zelana of the West the assistance she needed to bring the men of Maag to the Land of Dhrall to help Longbow kill all the servants of the Vlagh—and ultimately, of course, the Vlagh itself.

Longbow was quite certain that the spirit of Misty-Water would be quite pleased when he brought the head of the Vlagh to her grave and laid it there as a present for her.

2

The *Seagull* returned to Old-Bear's village late one blustery afternoon, announced somewhat in advance by the booming sound of her sail. Longbow immediately saw the advantage of the sail, but when the wind was just right, a sail could be very noisy.

"Will you leave now, Longbow, my son?" Chief Old-Bear asked when the Maag ship hove to a short way out from the pebbled beach.

"It may be that it will be in the best interest of the tribe, my father," Longbow replied. "Zelana of the West has told me that the Maags can show us ways to kill more of the creatures of the Wasteland, and that may please the spirit of your daughter Misty-Water."

"Then it is proper for you to go, my son," Old-Bear agreed. "Do not be concerned about your absence. I myself will attend to the grave of Misty-Water while you are gone."

"I would appreciate that, my father," Longbow said. "It may be that in time you and I will be able to bring the head of the Vlagh itself to the grave of your daughter, and that should please her spirit."

"I know that it will please mine," Old-Bear said approvingly. "Go, then, my son, and may the spirit of Misty-Water watch over you."

"It shall be as you have said, my father," Longbow said quite formally. He went on down through the village to the pebbled beach, pushed his canoe out from the shore, and took up his paddle to cross the choppy water to the *Seagull*. The village and his forest were fading behind him, but he didn't look back.

"Nice little skiff you got there, friend," a fellow with enormous hands observed, leaning over the rail of the *Seagull*.

"Skiff?" Longbow was puzzled by the word.

"That skinny little boat you got there. It goes real fast, don't it?"

"It takes me where I want it to go."

"You want we should bring it on board?"

"It might be best. I don't know the tribe of the *Seagull* as yet, and if it happens that I don't get along very well with them, I might need the canoe to take me back to where I belong."

The man with the big hands laughed. "There's been a few times when maybe I could have used a skiff of my own for the same reason. I've been at sea for most of my life now, and every so often I've had trouble my very own self getting along with my shipmates. You're Longbow, aren't you?"

"That's what they call me."

"They call me Ham-Hand," the man at the rail said. "It's not much of a name, but I guess I'm stuck with it now. Come on board, Longbow. The cap'n wants to see you. I'll take care of your canoe for you."

"I should tell Zelana of the West that I'm here," Longbow said.

"She's with the cap'n in the cabin back at the stern," Ham-Hand advised. "She took his cabin away from him back at the place called Lattash. He wasn't none to happy about that, but she's the one who's paying us, so he didn't argue with her. He still uses the cabin for business during the daytime, but he bunks with me and Ox after the sun goes down."

Longbow handed the braided thong attached to the front of his canoe to Ham-Hand and climbed smoothly aboard the Maag ship. "Just exactly where's the stern?" he asked.

"The back end of the ship," Ham-Hand explained.

"Who's this one you call 'Cap'n'?" Longbow asked. "I'm not familiar with that word."

"You talked with him the last time we passed through here," Ham-Hand replied. "His name's Sorgan Hook-Beak, and he owns the *Seagull* here."

"That clears things up a bit. We Dhralls would probably call him 'the chief.' I'll talk with him and let Zelana know that I'm here."

"I'm not sure you should take that there bow with you," Ham-Hand said dubiously. "It might just make the cap'n a little nervous."

"It goes any place where I go," Longbow said curtly. "If that bothers the people here on the *Seagull,* I'll go back to the forest where I belong."

"Don't get excited," Ham-Hand told him. "We're all on the same side here."

Longbow grunted and walked on back toward the stern of the ship.

There was a burly Dhrall with a flaming red beard leaning against the low structure at the rear of the boat. "I am Red-Beard of the tribe of White-Braid," he introduced himself rather formally.

"And I am Longbow of the tribe of Old-Bear. I was told that Sorgan Hook-Beak wished to speak with me and that Zelana of the West is with him."

"They are in there, Longbow of Old-Bear's tribe," Red-Beard said, pointing at a rectangular opening in the front of the low-roofed structure.

"We will speak again, Red-Beard of White-Braid's tribe,"

Longbow said. The formalities might fade as he and Red-Beard became better acquainted, but for right now formality was probably the more proper way to go.

The child Eleria leaned through the opening Red-Beard had indicated. "He's here, Beloved," she called back over her shoulder. "It's that one who spends all his time killing those he doesn't like."

"It's not right for you to say that, child," Longbow chided her.

"It's the truth, isn't it?"

"Perhaps, but it isn't polite to come right out and say so."

"Oh, poo," she said. Then she held her arms out to him. "Carry me," she said.

"Did you forget how to walk?"

"No, but I like to be carried, that's all."

Longbow smiled faintly, picked her up, and carried her into the place that smelled of tar and had a low roof.

"Welcome, Longbow," Zelana said. "Why are you carrying Eleria?"

"She wanted me to," Longbow replied, "and it didn't particularly bother me."

"He's very nice, Beloved," Eleria said. "He didn't object in the least little bit to carrying me." Then she kissed Longbow's cheek. "You can put me down now," she said.

"He's not a dolphin, Eleria," Zelana chided.

"I know," Eleria agreed, "but he'll do until we go back home. I need to kiss things every now and then. You know that."

Zelana sighed, rolling her eyes upward. "Oh, yes," she said. "This is Sorgan Hook-Beak of the Land of Maag, Longbow. I believe you've met him before."

"Yes," Longbow replied. He looked at Sorgan. "The man called Ham-Hand told me that you wanted to speak with me," he said.

"It's not really all that important, Longbow," Sorgan said. "I just wanted to let you know that we'll make you as comfortable as we can during our voyage. Is there anything you'll need?"

Longbow shrugged. "A little time every day to fish, is about all. I get hungry now and then."

"You can eat with the crew, Longbow. We can talk more later. Right now I'd better go get us under way." Sorgan rose to his feet and went out.

"He isn't speaking in our language, is he, Zelana?" Longbow asked.

She blinked. "How could you possibly know that?"

"His lips are not shaping the words which are coming from his mouth. Something seems to be changing the language he speaks into ours even while he talks."

Zelana laughed with obvious delight. "This will embarrass my brother to no end," she chuckled. "I probably should have noticed that myself. You're very observant, Longbow."

"Isn't that why we have eyes?"

"You're going to take a bit of getting used to. Do you always jump right to the point like this when you speak?"

He shrugged. "It saves time. Now, will you tell me exactly why you sought me out to come with you? What is it that I'm supposed to do to help you persuade the Maags to come to the Land of Dhrall to kill the servants of the Vlagh for us?"

"I want you to shoot arrows, Longbow."

"Who or what do you want me to kill?"

"I don't really need to have you kill anything just yet, Longbow," she replied. "We're going to the Land of Maag to fetch warriors to help us fight the creatures of the Wasteland. I want you to shoot arrows at things which are a long way away from where you're standing, and to hit as many of them as you can. The Maags need to know that the warriors of Dhrall can be as dangerous as the warriors of Maag are. We need their help, but we also need their respect."

Longbow considered it. "Geese, I think," he suggested.

"I beg your pardon?"

"People always seem to be startled when they see geese falling down out of the sky with arrows sticking out of them," Longbow explained. "They don't seem to realize that arrows can hit things up in the air as well as down on the ground."

"Can you actually do that, Longbow?" Eleria exclaimed. "I mean, can you really bring geese down from way up in the sky with your bow?"

"It's not really very difficult, little one," Longbow said. "Geese fly in straight lines, so it's easy to know where they'll be when your arrow reaches them. They're good to eat, too, so I won't be killing them for no reason. It's not right to do that."

"I think we should keep this one, Beloved," Eleria said. "And if you don't want him, can I have him?"

That startled Longbow just a bit.

3

Red-Beard sleeps with the Maags Sorgan calls 'the crew,'"
Zelana told Longbow later that afternoon. "He's a jovial sort of
fellow, but he's very observant. We need to know more about
the Maags, so Red-Beard's taking care of that for us. I think you
should sleep in here with Eleria and me, though. We'll tell the
Maags that you're here to guard me so that nobody gets any
improper ideas. The *real* reason is that I'd like to keep you just
a bit separate from the Maags, if possible. In a little while, you'll
be doing some fairly spectacular things with your bow, and it
might be useful if the Maags of the *Seagull* have a certain
amount of awe in their voices when they tell other Maags about
you."

Longbow shrugged. "Whatever seems best to you," he
replied. "How long is this task likely to take?"

"Not too long," she replied. "Sorgan's bringing quite a bit of
gold back to Maag with him. When he starts showing it to the
other Maags, they'll probably flock to him like vultures." She
frowned. "That didn't come out exactly right, did it?" she said.

"It's a possibility we should keep in mind, though," Longbow suggested. "I'll watch them. If they seem to be getting *too*

hungry, there are ways to persuade them to go eat somebody else."

Longbow arose at first light the following morning, and he was a bit surprised to find that Zelana was awake. "You don't sleep very much, do you?" he asked her.

"It isn't really necessary for me, Longbow," she replied. "Why are you up so early?"

"I thought it might be useful for me to get to know these Maags a bit better. The more a hunter knows about the creatures he hunts, the more successful he is."

"You aren't here to kill them, Longbow," she chided.

"No," he agreed, "but *capture* is sometimes more difficult than *kill,* isn't it?" He took up his bow and went out into the grey light of morning.

There was only the faintest hint of a breeze, but there was enough to tell Longbow that it was coming from the east, and that was very unusual for this time of year. Evidently, Zelana was tampering with things.

There was a faint ringing sound coming from the front of the *Seagull,* and Longbow went forward to see if he could determine the source of that sound.

A small Maag was standing near the front of the *Seagull,* and he was pounding on something that glowed almost as if it had fire deep inside of it.

"What is that," Longbow asked curiously, "and why are you pounding on it?"

"It's called iron," the little Maag replied, "and I'm shaping it with my hammer. Ham-Hand broke his knife the other day, and he wants me to make him a new one. He's sort of clumsy, so he breaks things all the time."

"Where is it that you find this iron?"

"I haven't got no idea at all where it comes from, but all I have to do is work with it. I don't have to go out and find it. You're the one called Longbow, aren't you?"

"That's what they tell me. Does this iron glow like that all the time?"

"No. I have to heat it up in my fire first. That makes it soft and easier to work with. They call me Rabbit, by the way—probably because I forgot to grow up some time way back when. Anyway, we make all our tools and weapons out of iron. One of my chores here on the *Seagull* is hammering fishhooks out of iron. I'm glad you came along, though. The cap'n told me that maybe I ought to hammer out some arrowheads for you."

"Stone arrowheads are customary in the Land of Dhrall," Longbow told him. "They've worked well for us in the past. I don't see any reason to change."

"Could I see one of your arrows?"

"Of course." Longbow took an arrow from his quiver and handed it to the small man.

Rabbit carefully examined the arrow. "Do you make these your very own self?" he asked.

"Naturally. If I'm going to be the one who shoots them, I want to be sure that they've been made correctly."

"It must take quite a while to chip one out," Rabbit observed, "and they wouldn't all have the same weight, would they?"

"They're close enough."

"Why don't I hammer a few out of iron, and you can look them over. I think they might surprise you. That lady who orders everybody around told me that someday soon you're likely to need a whole lot of arrows, but she didn't come right out and tell me how come."

"I'm going to shoot some geese for the entertainment of your people," Longbow told him.

"That sort of explains why you'll need so many," Rabbit said. "You must lose a lot of arrows when you start whanging them up in the air."

"They're easy to find again, Rabbit. The dead geese float."

"What about the ones that don't hit no geese?"

"That doesn't happen."

"Are you trying to tell me that you don't never miss?"

"It wouldn't be useful to miss. How do you go about making arrowheads from this iron?"

"Like I said, I heat it up in a fire until it starts to glow. That means that it's soft enough to pound into the shape I want."

"A soft arrowhead wouldn't be very useful, Rabbit."

"It don't stay soft. After I hammer it into the right shape, I dunk it in cold water, and it gets hard again."

Longbow looked at the beach sliding slowly past as the *Seagull* moved west. "If we're going to make arrows, we'll need arrow shafts. I don't think it'll be much longer before the *Seagull* leaves the Land of Dhrall behind, so you and I should probably go to the beach and cut saplings before we begin making arrowheads. I'll speak with Sorgan and tell him what we need to do."

"That makes sense," Rabbit agreed. "We'll have plenty of time to hammer out arrowheads once we get out on the open sea. It's a long ways between Dhrall and Maag—a whole lot farther than the cap'n seems to realize."

"But *you* realize how far it is, don't you?" Longbow said shrewdly.

Rabbit looked around quickly to make sure there wasn't anybody close. "I think I'd rather you didn't say anything about that to the cap'n, Longbow," he said quietly. "He doesn't pay too much attention to the sky after the sun goes down, and if you know what you're looking for, you can tell by the location of certain stars just where you are. When that sea current took hold of the *Seagull*, it took her a whole lot farther east than the cap'n— or anybody else—seems to have realized."

"You're a very clever man, Rabbit," Longbow observed. "Why do you go to so much trouble to conceal it?"

Rabbit shrugged. "It makes my life easier," he said with a sly little grin. "If the cap'n and Ox and Ham-Hand don't realize that I've got something besides air in my head, they won't expect too much from me. If they happen to find out that I can tell my right hand from my left, they might start ordering me to do things that aren't quite as easy as the things I have to do now. I've always believed that 'easy' is a lot nicer than 'hard,' don't you?"

"Your secret's safe with me, Rabbit. Someday, though—and I don't think it's very far off—you and I might have to explore the land of 'hard,' and our lives may depend on how well we do it."

"You just had to go and say that, didn't you, Longbow?" Rabbit said sourly.

"I just thought I'd warn you, that's all."

The *Seagull* turned westward a few days later, and the Land of Dhrall receded behind her, soon dropping below the eastern horizon. The open sea made Longbow a bit edgy. He had always been a creature of the forest, and the vast emptiness of Mother Sea disturbed him.

He also felt twinges of guilt, since he had abandoned his lifelong purpose. He was supposed to be in the forest killing the servants of the Vlagh, or at the burial ground tending to Misty-Water's grave.

His memory reached back to his meeting with Zelana of the West and child Eleria. Zelana held dominion over the West, and her command to him should have been the law, but it hadn't been the word of Zelana which had made him agree to go with her to the Land of Maag; it had been the clever word of child Eleria. Her suggestion that the Maags could provide a way to kill more servants of the Vlagh in a short time than he'd be able to kill by himself during a lifetime of hunting had moved him to come on board the *Seagull*.

The more he thought about that, the more peculiar it seemed. Zelana had absolute authority in her Domain, but he'd refused her peremptory command quite easily. Eleria, however, had lured him into acceptance with numbers. In a peculiar sort of way Eleria had just imitated Zelana's approach to Sorgan. Zelana had bought Sorgan with a large number of gold blocks, and then Eleria had bought Longbow with a large number of dead enemies. Their tactics had been almost identical, and that raised a very interesting possibility. Just exactly who *was* Eleria? Her evidently simpleminded need for affection could conceal a hard but devious drive to get what she wanted, which made Zelana look soft by comparison.

Eleria's little game had *almost* succeeded, but she'd taken it a step or two further than had been necessary, and that had alerted Longbow's instincts. If Eleria wanted to play games, Longbow was more than ready to show her that he could play much better than she could.

It might just turn out that this tiresome journey would be much more interesting than he'd thought.

"Hook-Big just doesn't believe her, Longbow," Eleria said a few days later, when they were alone in the tar-smeared cabin at the stern of the *Seagull*. "When the Beloved told him that your arrows *always* go where you want them to go, he said that nobody could do that."

"Hook-Big?" Longbow asked.

"He seems to be terribly full of himself," Eleria replied with a naughty little grin. "That's why I call him 'Hook-Big.' "

"That's unkind, little one."

"I know," she admitted. "Fun, though."

Longbow laughed. Eleria was an absolute delight, and it was that, perhaps, that made her even more dangerous than Zelana herself.

"Fun isn't a bad thing, Longbow," she said, nuzzling at his cheek like a small kitten.

"Why don't you speak with Zelana?" Longbow suggested. "This might be a good time for a flock of geese to fly over the

Seagull. Let's brush away Hook-Big's doubts so that they won't concern him anymore."

"That would be nice," Eleria said. And then she giggled.

It was not a very large flock, Longbow observed as the geese came out of the north, just before the sun sank into a red-flushed bank of clouds low on the western horizon—six or seven birds at most. It should be enough, however, to make a believer out of Hook-Beak. Longbow took up a handful of his new iron-tipped arrows and his bow and went to the stern of the *Seagull,* where Sorgan, Ox, and Ham-Hand spent most of their time. "I'm growing a bit tired of eating fish, Sorgan-Captain," he said politely. "Would you find it offensive if I bring us something different to eat?"

"What did you have in mind?" Sorgan asked.

"Those," Longbow replied, pointing at the incoming geese. "I haven't made any contribution to what we eat here on the *Seagull,* and that isn't proper. I think that geese might be a welcome change for you and your men."

"Them geese are pretty high up in the air," Ham-Hand suggested dubiously.

"Not quite high enough," Longbow assured him.

Ox squinted off to the west, the fiery sunset painting his face red. "The sun's going down, Longbow," he said. "You might be lucky enough to hit one or two of them geese, but finding them floating in the water after it gets dark won't be very easy, will it?"

"I'll do what I can to make it easy," Longbow promised.

It took a bit of careful calculation, but Longbow had chosen the time of day quite deliberately. Killing the geese with his arrows would be simplicity in itself. Hitting them in the dim twilight and making them all fall on the deck of the *Seagull* instead of into the water would be a bit more difficult—but hardly impossible. Zelana wanted him to impress Sorgan and his men with his skill, and this would probably be the easiest way to do that.

It rained geese onto the deck of the *Seagull* not long after Longbow had spoken with Hook-Beak, and Sorgan and his crew began to treat Longbow with a great deal of respect—tinged with a certain degree of awe. Longbow was accustomed to that. The men of Old-Bear's tribe had been looking at him with a similar expression since he'd been very young.

4

"She's a lot older than she looks, Longbow," Rabbit was saying the next morning. "From what I've heard, she was a pretty battered-up old tub when the cap'n bought her from the old Maag who owned her before. It took the cap'n, Ox, and Ham-Hand better than a year to fix her up. About the first thing they did was to add this." Rabbit stamped one of his feet on the deck. "Up till then she was a lot like an open rowboat. They decked her over and built in those long, narrow ports for the oars. I guess part of the idea was to protect the oarsmen from foul weather, but the main reason for adding the deck was to give them as was going to do the fighting some running room. If you're going to jump from one ship to another when the water's choppy, you need to be moving pretty fast. If you're not, you'll probably get wet."

"It does make some sense, I suppose," Longbow conceded. "Back in Dhrall we don't fight out on the face of Mother Sea. It's not a good idea to irritate her."

"We get along with her pretty good," Rabbit said. "Anyway, the notion of decking over a longship's fairly recent. It was, oh, maybe twenty years ago when a shipbuilder down in Gaiso came up with the notion—probably because some ship cap'n wanted to have his own cabin so that he wouldn't have to sleep with his crew. Some ship cap'ns get kind of uppity sometimes."

"Isn't it a bit difficult for the oarsmen to steer when they can't see where they're going?" Longbow asked.

"That's where the tiller comes in. If you look back toward the stern, you'll see Ox standing there holding on to a long handle that's attached to a post. The post runs all the way down into the water, and there's a big flat board built out from the bottom of the post. It's called the rudder, and it makes the ship turn this way or that way when Ox pulls on the handle to one side or the other. The oarsmen do the rowing, but Ox does the steering." Rabbit grinned. "I don't get stuck with that chore too often. It takes a pretty beefy man to steer a ship as big as the *Seagull*. Ox is pretty good at it, though. He's got muscles on top of muscles from his neck down to his toenails. He could probably pick up something that only had one end if he really wanted to."

"I haven't seen many things with only one end," Longbow noted.

"They are just a bit rare," Rabbit agreed.

"We like to think that it's the prettiest place in the world," Rabbit was telling Longbow and Eleria a few days later, when the three of them were sitting near the bow of the *Seagull*. "Of course, I grew up there, and everybody I've ever met seems to think that no place in the whole world is half as nice as the place where he grew up."

"It's proper for you to be loyal to the home of your childhood, Rabbit," Longbow told him. "Loyalty to place and people is the beginning of honor."

"I'm not all that big on honor, Longbow," Rabbit confessed. "No matter where I go or who I hook up with, I'm always the runt of the litter. Every Maag I've ever known seems to think that bigger is better, so they always think that I'm not really worth much because I'm short and scrawny."

"But you like it that way, don't you, Bunny?" Eleria said shrewdly. "You *want* them to think that your mind is just as teenie-weenie as your body is. That's why you always talk so sloppy around them, isn't it?"

"Bunny?" Rabbit protested.

"It's a friendlier sort of name," Eleria told him from her usual place on Longbow's lap, "and I feel very friendly about you, since you're almost as teenie-weenie as I am. Longbow here is one of the biggies, so he doesn't really understand us teenie-weenies. I do love him, but he has a few flaws. But then, nobody's perfect—except the Beloved, of course."

"Eleria's very quick, Rabbit," Longbow told the small Maag, "and you should probably know that sometimes she can make you do things that you'd prefer not to do. I'd still be back in the forest if Zelana hadn't brought Eleria with her when she sought me out. I had 'no' halfway out until Zelana turned Eleria loose on me. I swallowed 'no' not long after that."

Eleria stuck her tongue out at Longbow, but then she laughed. "You have to be careful around this one, Bunny," she cautioned. "He watches all the time, and he sees things that others are trying to hide. I guess everybody has things they want to hide, but they don't have much luck when they try to hide them from Longbow."

"I've noticed," Rabbit said dryly. "I've been pretending to be stupid since I was just a boy, and it's always worked before, but he saw through me before I'd turned around twice." He paused, and one of his eyebrows went up slightly. "As long as it's come up anyway, maybe *you* ought to know that Longbow and I aren't fooled a bit by your little game of silly. You grin and giggle a lot, but Longbow and I both know that you're as hard as iron underneath. You *always* get what you want."

"Why, Bunny," Eleria said in mock chagrin, "what a thing to say. I'm shocked at you. Shocked."

"We're not going to spread this around, though, are we?" Rabbit said to both of them. "All three of us have peculiarities that other people here on the *Seagull* don't really need to know about, do they?"

"If they can't see this for themselves, they probably wouldn't believe us if we told them," Longbow agreed.

"There's somebody coming," Eleria warned in a soft whisper.

"What's the name of this place where you grew up, Rabbit?" Longbow asked, speaking a bit louder.

"The folks over there in Maag all calls it Weros," Rabbit replied, lapsing back into his usual slovenly speech pattern, "and they're all just jumping up and down to go there and have theirselves a real bang-up good time. A real Maag'll go a long ways to have hisself a good time." He glanced casually over his shoulder at a seaman who was busy tying off a rope. Then the sailor turned and went back toward the mainmast. Rabbit lowered his voice. "If I'm reading the position of the stars right, we should sail into the harbor of Weros on the day after tomorrow—which doesn't seem possible, since we were a *lot* farther from home than Sorgan and the rest of the crew seemed to realize."

"I wouldn't spread that around, Bunny," Eleria told him. "It isn't really necessary for them to know how far it is from Maag to Dhrall, and the Beloved doesn't really want them to find out. She needs an army, and the people she wants might not want to go that far away from home."

"How *did* we get there so fast?" Rabbit demanded.

"The Beloved can make things happen when she *wants* them to happen, Bunny," Eleria replied. "Do you *really* want to know exactly how she does that?"

That seemed to jerk Rabbit up short. He swallowed hard. "Ah . . ." he faltered, "no, I don't think so."

"Isn't he nice?" Eleria said to Longbow. Then she squirmed

down from the big Dhrall's lap and approached the small Maag. "Kiss-kiss, Bunny," she said.

"What?" Rabbit sounded very confused.

"It's one of her habits," Longbow told him. "It's not too painful, and it makes her happy, so we all put up with it."

"Shush, Longbow," Eleria said. Then she wrapped her arms about Rabbit's neck and kissed him soundly. "You really ought to take a bath, Bunny," she told him, wrinkling her nose.

"I washed off no more than a month ago," he protested.

"It's time to do it again, Bunny. Soon. Please."

The weather turned sour, and it was blustery and rainy for the next two days as the *Seagull* doggedly pushed her way west. Longbow was accustomed to rain, since the northwest coast of the Land of Dhrall was the native home of rain. The Maag sailors seemed dispirited by the weather, though, and the mood on board the *Seagull* was gloomy until the coast of Maag, hazy and indistinct in the steady drizzle, appeared on the western horizon.

The Maag town of Weros stood at the head of a narrow inlet, and the *Seagull*'s oarsmen took their places without the usual grumbling, despite the weather. Coming home after a long time seemed to brighten things for sailors.

Weros was a sizeable town, though the houses all seemed jammed tightly together, almost as if the inhabitants were afraid to be alone. The muddy streets wandered about aimlessly, strongly suggesting that the people who lived there had made it up as they'd gone along. Most of the buildings were constructed of squared-off logs, and they appeared to be more substantial than the lodges of Old-Bear's tribe back in Dhrall. Iron tools, it seemed, made better houses. A pall of smoke drifted out from the town, obscuring the nearby fields. Long piers extended from the water's edge, and there were many Maag longships tied to the piers or anchored some distance out in the harbor.

As the *Seagull* approached the town, an eddy in the wind carried a rancid smell out across the water. Longbow's nostrils were very acute because he was a hunter, and he hoped that they wouldn't have to stay in Weros for very long.

The sailors dropped heavy iron anchors off both ends of the *Seagull,* and Eleria came looking for Longbow. "The Beloved asked me to find you," she told him. "Hook-Big wants to tell us how he intends to use gold to persuade other Maag ship captains that it might be nice to visit the land of Dhrall. The Maags all seem to find square lumps of gold very pretty, and they'll do almost anything to get their hands on as many of them as their ships can carry."

"Owning things seems very important to the Maags, doesn't it?" Longbow observed.

"That makes things easy for us, though, doesn't it? They'll do what we want them to do so that they can own gold, but we end up owning them instead. Let's go see what Hook-Big has to say." Eleria held out her arms to him. "You can carry me, if you'd like."

"Of course," Longbow said, taking her up in his arms, although he knew that it was part of her game and that it played an important part in persuading people to do what she wanted them to do. Zelana commanded, but Eleria charmed. The intent and results were usually the same, but Eleria's approach was more pleasant, and usually more effective.

Longbow carried Eleria to Sorgan's cabin at the stern of the *Seagull.* Ox and Ham-Hand were already there, as was Red-Beard. "The best way I know of to get people's attention in a hurry is to show them gold," Sorgan was saying, "and this is the way we're going to do that. Ox, I want you and Ham-Hand to spread the word that the *Seagull*'s got stacks and stacks of gold blocks down in her hold. They probably won't believe you— which is right down at the core of our little scheme. As soon as some ship captain says that he thinks you're lying, tell him that you'll be happy to show him, if he'd like. Don't bring any ordinary seamen or tavern loafers out here, and don't waste my time on the ones who call themselves captains but only have an oversized rowboat and fifteen or twenty men. We only want the captains of full-sized longships with full crews. If somebody doesn't have eighty men at his command, I don't want to see him. Now then, just to keep things from getting rowdy, don't bring more than two or three to the *Seagull* at any one time, and let it get spread around that those of us here on board won't look kindly on uninvited guests. We only want two or three at a time."

"I get your drift, Cap'n," Ox said. "Me and Ham-Hand'll take care to keep our visitors from turning into a crowd that the crew can't handle."

"Do your people really have little boats, Hook-Big?" Eleria asked.

Sorgan made an indelicate sound. "They're leeches for the most part," he replied. "They call themselves real Maag sea captains, but their boats are really nothing more than old fishing sloops, and the men who make up the crew don't know the first thing about fighting. A *real* Maag longship's better than a hundred feet long, and she's got at least eighty men on board—fifty oarsmen, twenty-five to deal with the sail, three officers, a cook, a smith, and a carpenter." He looked at Zelana. "How soon do you want the fleet we'll put together to reach your country?" he asked.

"We have a bit of time, Sorgan," she replied. "The creatures of the Wasteland aren't in position to attack us as yet."

"That gives us until next spring, doesn't it? Nobody in his right mind tries to march an army across a range of mountains in the dead of winter."

"The Vlagh has a different kind of mind, Sorgan. It doesn't care how many of its servants die along the way when it wants something. I want the Maag fleet standing off the coast of Dhrall before the snow starts to pile up."

"That's only two months or so, Lady Zelana," Sorgan

protested. "I won't be able to gather that many ships in so short a time. The ships aren't all in one place, so I'm going to have to chase them down. I *might* be able to have a fair-sized advance fleet there by then, but it'll probably take a while longer to bring the main body across. I'm just scraping a number off the wall here, but I think six hundred ships should be about right. With eighty or so men on board each one, you'll have a good-sized army—fifty thousand or so anyway. The main problem's going to be getting the word out to all those sea captains. A lot of them are cruising around out there in deep water looking for Trogite treasure ships."

"Doesn't that mean that they're between us and the Land of Dhrall?" Red-Beard asked.

"I suppose so. Why?"

"We'll encounter them along the way then, won't we?"

"That's open water out there, Red-Beard. If those ships aren't right in our path, we won't even see them."

"Are there paths in Mother Sea now?" Red-Beard asked mildly. "I hadn't heard about that. Is there some reason that I don't know about that all the ships of the fleet absolutely *must* trail along behind the *Seagull*? Wouldn't it be better if they spread out as they sailed to the land of Dhrall? I've fished the waters of Mother Sea many times, and over the years I've found that my luck's much better if I fish in waters that haven't been recently worked by other fishermen."

"Well . . ." Sorgan began, but whatever he'd intended to say dribbled off.

"It will still be your fleet, Sorgan Hook-Beak," Zelana assured him. "All the Maags on all the ships will know that you command. Do you really have to have them clinging to your tail feathers all the way to Dhrall?"

Sorgan looked a bit sheepish. "I've never had a whole fleet to follow me," he admitted. "I really wanted to see all those ships massed up in one place and to know that it was *my* fleet. I was being sort of childish, wasn't I?"

"It's all right to be a child, Hook-Big," Eleria told him. "Look at all the fun I've been having lately."

Sorgan sighed. "I guess it'll be all right if the fleet spreads out to bring in those other ships," he said regretfully.

"That's a good boy," Eleria said affectionately.

"Just what's this all about, Sorgan?" a lean Maag sea captain, among the first group Sorgan had invited to visit the *Seagull* in the harbor of Weros, asked as he climbed up the rope ladder to the deck of the *Seagull*.

"Come on back to my cabin, and I'll explain it," Sorgan replied, glancing at the two other Maags in the skiff Ox had just rowed out to the *Seagull*.

Longbow drifted along behind them as they went aft.

Zelana and Eleria were up near the bow of the *Seagull*, looking at the town of Weros, so the cabin was empty at the moment.

"Who's he?" the other Maag asked, pointing at Longbow.

"This is Longbow, and he works for the lady that's paying me to gather up a fleet."

"Is it safe to talk in front of him?"

"He knows what this is all about, cousin Torl," Sorgan replied. "Didn't Ox tell you about all the gold we've got piled up down in the hold?"

The lean Maag snorted. "You didn't really think I'd believe him, did you?"

"We'll go look in just a minute. There's a war in the works over in a place called Dhrall, and the lady who sort of runs things over there needs men who know how to fight to join up with her people, and she pays in gold. I brought about a hundred bars here with me to prove to the ship captains I come across that it'll be worth their while to join up."

"I think you might have lost your mind, Sorgan. Nobody with his head on straight starts waving gold in front of Maag ship captains."

"That's why we're having this little talk, Torl," Sorgan replied. "I think I'd feel a lot more comfortable if I had a fair number of my kinsmen close by when I start showing the gold I've got stacked up down in the hold to other Maags."

"That makes a certain amount of sense, I guess. Just where is this place, Sorgan?"

"It's a fair distance off to the east."

"I take it that this lady who's got all the gold hasn't got any kind of real army to work with?" Torl asked.

"I think it might surprise you, Torl. This is Longbow, and I've never seen anybody who could even come close to him when it comes to shooting arrows, but I guess Lady Zelana doesn't have enough people to fight off her enemy. That's where we come in. Right now, though, I want to get the word out to as many kinsmen as I can locate. Do you happen to know where Malar and Skell are right now?"

Torl scratched the side of his face. "The last I heard, Malar was whooping it up with his crew down in Gaiso. They had a stroke of luck here recently, so they're celebrating. You know how our cousin is. Once he starts to party, it goes on until he runs out of money."

"Do you think you could get word to him that I want to talk over a business opportunity with him?"

"I'll see what I can do. We'll have to wait until he's sober, though."

"Where's Skell?"

"Up the coast in Kormo. His ship needed repairs after he came up against a Trogite ship that rammed her off the north-east coast. That's something you should know about, Sorgan. The Trogites have taken to reinforcing the bows of their ships, and they've added what they call a ram. It's a real thick pole with the front end cased in iron. It sticks out in front of the Trogite ship, and it's right at the waterline. The Trogites don't just give up so easy when they see one of us coming anymore. They row their ships right into us now, and that ram puts a hole a man could walk through right in the side of any ship it smashes into. From what I hear, the Trogites have already sunk a half-dozen or so Maag longships with those cursed rams."

"That's terrible!" Sorgan exclaimed.

"Trogites have always been terrible, Sorgan. I thought you knew that. . . . You promised to let me and the other captains look at all this gold you've managed to pick up."

"All right, but then we'll need to start getting word out to the rest of our family. I'll sleep a lot better if I've got a dozen or so ships that belong to people I can trust anchored around the *Seagull*. After you see what I've got stacked up in the hold, you'll understand why."

Longbow considered what he had just heard. The Maags, it appeared, had a very primitive culture. Their technology was more advanced, certainly, but their social structure had a long way to go.

At first light a few days later, Longbow came out of the cabin at the stern of the *Seagull* to take a look at the weather, and he saw Red-Beard leaning against the railing at the bow. "You're up early, Red-Beard," he said as he joined the man of White-Braid's tribe.

Red-Beard shrugged. "Habit, I guess. I like to look at the sky before the sun comes up. Do you fish very much, Long-bow?"

"Once in a while. I really prefer hunting." Longbow hesitated. "I noticed something the other day when Hook-Beak was talking with one of his relatives. You've spent quite a bit of time with the ordinary Maag sailors. Does it seem to you that family's more important to them than tribe?"

"I don't think they even *have* tribes, Longbow, and as far as I've been able to discover, there's no such thing as tribe—or customs, or rules, or chiefs. Their weapons are better than ours, but aside from that, they're absolute savages."

"I sort of saw things much the same way. Customs might be a bit tedious, but they do seem to hold a tribe together."

"I don't know if you're aware of this, Longbow," Red-Beard said then, "but you're quite famous all over the Domain of our Zelana."

"I don't really stray very far, Red-Beard, so I wasn't aware of that."

"You can tell me that it's none of my business, if you want to, but why do you spend all of your time killing the creatures of the Wasteland?"

Longbow hesitated, but Red-Beard was about the closest thing to a friend he had here. "It was something that happened a long time ago," he explained. "There was a young woman in our tribe named Misty-Water, and she and I had decided that we should mate. On the day of the ceremony, she went into the forest to bathe and dress herself in her new deerskin. While she was alone in the forest, one of the poison-fanged creatures of the Wasteland killed her. Since that day, I live only for vengeance."

"I'm sorry, Longbow," Red-Beard apologized. "I didn't really mean to pry like that. I understand now, though. You want to kill them all, don't you?"

"If I possibly can," Longbow admitted. "No day is really complete for me if I haven't killed at least one of those beasts. That's what finally persuaded me to join Zelana and come here to the Land of the Maags. Little Eleria suggested that if I had Maags to help me, I could kill thousands of the servants of the Vlagh—or maybe even kill them all."

"That might take some doing, from what I've heard about those beasts," Red-Beard suggested. "Would it offend you if I kill a few dozen of them? Just as a sign of friendship, of course. It's courteous to kill the enemies of one's friends, isn't it?"

Longbow smiled briefly. "It wouldn't bother me in the least, Red-Beard. Enjoy yourself. One thing, though. When we reach the Wasteland, remember that That-Called-the-Vlagh is *mine.*

It's my thought that the spirit of Misty-Water might be pleased if I placed the head of the Vlagh at the foot of her grave as a sign of my continued love for her."

"I wouldn't dream of interfering, friend Longbow," Red-Beard declared. "Would it be all right if I held your cloak for you while you chop That-Called-the-Vlagh into small pieces?"

"I think I could stand that, friend Red-Beard," Longbow replied with mock solemnity.

Then they both laughed.

5

Sorgan managed to gather several of his relatives about the *Seagull* as he continued to recruit unrelated Maag ship captains in the harbor of Weros. Longbow had been called upon several times to demonstrate his proficiency with his bow, and the Maags all treated him with a great deal of respect by the time the growing fleet left Weros to move south along the coast of Maag. The *Seagull* hove to each time she came to a coastal village where there were more than two or three ships anchored in the harbor.

"I've got some of my kinsmen scouring the towns to the north of Weros for more ships and men," Sorgan advised Zelana one evening a few days later during the customary meeting after supper in his former quarters. "The word's getting out that I'm hiring and that the pay's good, and that's making things go a lot faster than I'd thought they might. We'll probably have our fleet put together before too much longer."

"I certainly hope so," Zelana replied.

"I'll be sending the advance fleet to Dhrall in just a little bit," Sorgan assured her. "I've been holding off until my cousin

Skell joins us. He's more reliable than some of my other relatives."

"How's Skell going to find Lattash, Cap'n?" Ox asked. "That coast stretches on for a long way, as I recall."

"I could go with them and show them the way," Longbow offered.

Sorgan shook his head. "I need you here, Longbow," he said. "You're the only man I know who can shoot arrows through knotholes from a hundred paces away, and that's one of the things that I use to persuade others to join us."

"*I* could go with them, though," Red-Beard suggested. "I'm not doing anything here but growing longer whiskers, and I don't imagine that my beard—splendid though it is—has persuaded many to join us."

"It makes sense, Sorgan," Zelana said, "and if your cousin follows Red-Beard's advice and spreads his fleet out, they'll encounter other Maag ships out on the face of Mother Sea. Then they can say the magic word 'gold' to the captains of those other ships, and we could very well have twice as many ships approaching the coast of Dhrall than we sent from the coast of Maag."

"That's the way we'll do it, then. You're paying, so we'll dance to your tune—but not until Skell joins us. He's a lot more responsible than some of the other ship captains, so he'll be able to prevent any enthusiasts from raiding the coastal villages instead of preparing to meet the army of the Wasteland. That would irritate your people, and I could lose half of my army before I even get there if the other Dhralls are even half as good with their bows as Longbow here is."

It was foggy the next morning, and Longbow stood near the bow of the *Seagull,* listening to the voices coming out of the fog from nearby ships. Sounds, he noted, always seemed to carry farther in the night or in dense fog. Perhaps there was some sort of agreement between the eyes and the ears involved.

Red-Beard came along the deck from the stern and joined Longbow. "Murky," he observed quietly.

"I noticed that myself," Longbow agreed. "I don't think this would be a good day for hunting."

"The fishing might be good, though." Red-Beard looked around and leaned closer. "Zelana wants to have a word with you," he said very quietly. "Something happened during the night that's bothering her."

"I'll go right away," Longbow replied in a similarly quiet voice. Then he spoke a bit louder. "Do you suppose you can watch the fog without any help, Red-Beard?" he asked. "I should probably go find out if Zelana has anything she wants me to do today."

"I think I'll be able to manage here by myself," Red-Beard replied. "I'll have somebody fetch you if it gets to be more than I can handle."

"Very funny," Longbow muttered.

"I'm glad you liked it," Red-Beard said with a broad grin.

Longbow went aft toward the stern of the *Seagull*. Red-Beard was from a different tribe, but Longbow liked him anyway. The present crisis was altering many of Longbow's preconceptions in ways that would probably have been impossible no more than a year ago.

He tapped lightly on the door to the aft cabin.

"Come in, Longbow," Zelana's voice responded.

He went on into the low-beamed cabin that smelled of tar and quietly closed the door behind him. Zelana was sitting in a chair behind the nailed-down table, and she had a slightly worried look on her face. Eleria was standing just behind her, and *this* time she didn't come running to Longbow with her arms held out.

Red-Beard said that you wanted to speak with me," Longbow said. "Is there trouble of some kind?"

"I think there may very well be," she replied. Then she looked him full in the face. "I believe that the time's come for us to clear something away. Have you ever heard of the Dreamers?"

Longbow shrugged. "It's a very old story. It tells us that the coming of the Dreamers will be a sign that the elder gods will soon go to sleep."

"It goes quite a bit further than that, Longbow. Time tends to distort things, and old stories don't always come out the same as they did originally. The story of the Dreamers deals with the current situation, and it's ultimately the Dreamers who'll confront the Vlagh."

"And defeat it?" Longbow asked.

"Well, we can hope, I guess." She looked at him in a peculiar kind of way. "You already see where I'm going with this, don't you, Longbow? Yes, as a matter of fact, Eleria *is* one of the Dreamers, and she's already stolen you away from me."

"I did *not!*" Eleria protested.

"Don't try to deceive me, Eleria," Zelana accused the child. "You've been just a little obvious."

"I like him, Beloved, that's all. I wouldn't steal anything from you."

"That's a lie, and you know it," Zelana said angrily. "You stole my dolphins, and now you're trying to steal my most trusted servant."

"Maybe if you were nicer to them, they wouldn't be so eager to come to me," Eleria declared. "You've turned mean and hateful lately, Beloved. What's the matter with you?"

Longbow gave them a cold look. "I'll come back some other time," he told them in a flat, unemotional voice. "Let me know when you've settled your differences." He started toward the door.

"You come back here!" Zelana screeched.

"I don't think so. If you two want to scream at each other,

I'll just be in your way." Then he left the cabin, softly closing the door behind him.

The silence coming from the cabin was louder than thunder.

Longbow went over to the rail and stood looking out at the fog while he waited.

Eleria came out of the cabin even sooner than he'd expected. "Everything's all right again, Longbow," she said. "The screaming's all over now."

"That was quick," he observed.

"You frightened us. The Beloved isn't used to people who walk away from her the way you just did. We stopped arguing right after you left. We cried for a while and hugged each other, and everything's all right now. It's safe for you to come back."

"Good. Did you want me to carry you?"

"Maybe we'd better not," she said regretfully. "Let's not get her started again."

They went back inside the cabin, and Zelana appeared to have regained her composure. "We were talking about the Dreamers, Longbow," she said as if nothing had happened. "They have some unusual abilities when they dream. They can look back into the past, and occasionally they dream about the future. That's what happened last night. Eleria had a dream about the future, and we'll need to take steps to make sure that it doesn't come true."

"Can we do that?" Longbow asked her. "I've heard all the old stories about the Dreamers, and they all say that those dreams lock the future in stone."

"The old stories are wrong. Eleria's dream last night told us what *might* happen, not what will *definitely* happen. It was more in the nature of a warning. Tell him about your dream, Eleria, and about your pearl."

"If you want me to, Beloved," Eleria replied obediently. The little storm of screaming seemed to have passed. Eleria looked at Longbow. "Have you ever heard of the Isle of Thurn?" she asked.

"It lies off the west coast of Dhrall, I've been told," Longbow replied, "and we're forbidden to go there."

"That's probably the Beloved's idea. She lives there, and she doesn't really care much for the idea of having neighbors. Anyway, there are pink dolphins in the water around the Isle, and the Beloved talks with them, and she's very fond of them. When I was a very small child, the younger dolphins were my playmates."

"And you also speak their language, then, don't you?"

"It's the language I spoke first. It was only a little while ago when the Beloved taught me how to speak *her* language."

"That's odd. Most mothers teach their children to speak their own language."

Eleria laughed a sparkling little laugh. "What in the world ever gave you the absurd idea that the Beloved is my mother?" she asked. "I think we're related in some way, but she's not my mother, certainly."

"We can talk about that some other time," Zelana said quite firmly. "Tell him about the pearl, Eleria."

"I was just getting to that, Beloved. It was last year when I was out playing with the younger dolphins off the coast, Longbow, and an old cow whale came to where we were playing, and she told me that she wanted to show me something. I followed her and we went down to the bottom of Mother Sea. There was a huge oyster down there, and the cow whale touched the oyster with one of her fins, and the oyster opened its shell." Eleria went to the narrow bed where she slept, and rummaged around under the blankets. Then she drew out something that was about the size of an apple. "This is what the oyster was hiding inside its shell," she said, holding it up for Longbow to see. "It's called a pearl, and the cow whale told me that I was supposed to have it."

Longbow was startled by the size of the pink pearl. He had seen pearls before, but never one so large.

"The pearl controls Eleria's dreams, Longbow," Zelana said, "and I think the dream she had last night was a warning. Tell him about it, Eleria."

"Of course, Beloved," Eleria agreed. "I guess that other people have dreams too, Longbow," she said, "and most of the time my dreams are probably like theirs, but the one I had last night wasn't at all like the dreams I usually have. I seemed to be floating up in the air above the *Seagull*. She was anchored in the harbor of some little Maag town, and it was nighttime. There were five other ships sitting around her to protect her, but some of the little boats the Maags call skiffs came paddling up to them, and then all the ships around the *Seagull* caught on fire. The Maags got very excited, and they were running around trying to put the fires out, and that's when five *other* ships came out of the dark and tied themselves to the *Seagull*. There was a big fight, and everybody on the *Seagull* was killed. Then the strangers went down into the place where Hook-Big keeps those gold blocks he likes so much. After they'd taken them all, they set fire to the *Seagull* and rowed away. It was then that I saw someone with a hood up over his head watching from the beach, and he was laughing. Then I woke up and told the Beloved what I'd just dreamed, and that's when she sent Red-Beard to find you and ask you to come here."

"How big was the one on the beach who was laughing?" Longbow demanded intently.

"Not nearly as big as the other Maags," Eleria replied. "It was only about as big as Bunny."

"Could you see what color its hood was?"

"Sort of grey, I think. Is it important?"

"I think it might be. The servants of the Vlagh aren't very large, and they all wear grey hoods. There seems to have been more in your dream than you might have realized. It would seem that a few of the creatures of the Wasteland have found some way to follow us here, and now they're trying to find ways to keep us from bringing an army of Maags to the Land of Dhrall." He looked at Zelana. "Is there some way we can prevent this from happening?" he asked her.

"I think we've already begun to change things, Longbow," she replied. "Just knowing about it is the first step."

Longbow had grown tired of the endless procession of Maag sea captains coming to the *Seagull* to look at Sorgan's gold blocks. It seemed that they couldn't accept the word of others, so they just *had* to see for themselves. Eleria's dream, however, changed Longbow's attitude immediately. If the dream meant what it *seemed* to mean, five of the ship captains had—or would have—little interest in the Land of Dhrall.

Longbow was a hunter, and hunters learn early to watch and to listen—and to be as unobtrusive as possible when they do so. Most of the visitors to the *Seagull* were genuinely enthusiastic about the opportunity Sorgan was offering. Others made some show of a similar enthusiasm, but there was something about what they did that didn't ring quite true.

Longbow continued to watch and listen, but he said nothing.

It was in the harbor of a coastal village called Kweta that Sorgan's lean and sour cousin Skell joined them, and after some discussion, Sorgan and Skell agreed that it was time to send a portion of what they called "the fleet" eastward to the land of Dhrall, with Red-Beard to guide them.

"My cousin Skell's a dependable man, Lady Zelana," Sorgan declared as the advance fleet prepared to depart. "He'll have about a hundred and twenty ships and almost ten thousand men to deal with any surprise attacks by your enemy, and if there's a major invasion of the coastal region of your Domain, he'll be able to hold the enemy off until we get there."

"How much longer do you think it's going to be until the rest of us sail to Dhrall?" Zelana asked him.

"Not too much longer, really. The word's out now, and just about every ship captain in Maag's eager to join us. The only real problem is that they all want to *see* the gold in the *Seagull*'s hold for themselves before they make any final decisions." Sorgan made a rueful face. "I hate to admit it, but maybe we brought *too much* gold back to Maag. When you get right down to it, a dozen blocks would probably have been enough. Most people here in Maag would take my word if I'd said 'a dozen.' When I tell them that I've got a hundred in the hold, they want to see them to make sure I'm not lying to them. I think I might have overbaited my fishhook."

"Nobody's perfect, Hook-Big," Eleria said.

"Hook-*Beak*," Sorgan absently corrected her.

"Whatever," she said with mock indifference.

6

I've already shown you the gold, Kajak," Sorgan said to a bone-thin Maag the next morning when a group of visitors came on board the *Seagull*. "Didn't you believe what you saw?"

"I'm helping you, Sorgan," the lean Kajak replied. "I sent out word to a whole lot of my kinfolks and promised to introduce them to you when you hauled into the harbors of their home ports. If things work out the way I think they will, I should be able to bring a couple dozen more ships to join your fleet."

"Splendid, Kajak," Sorgan said. "It looks like you can see past the end of your own nose. I keep coming across men who can't quite see why we need more ships and men once they've joined us. They seem to be afraid that more ships means smaller shares for everybody who's already joined the fleet. They can't quite understand how much gold we're talking about."

"There's some out there that have trouble with big numbers, Sorgan. Would it be all right if I take my cousins here down into the *Seagull*'s hold and show them your gold?"

"Be my guest, Kajak," Sorgan replied.

Longbow had been sitting off to one side in Sorgan's cabin while Sorgan and Kajak had been talking, and he noticed that Kajak's four cousins had seemed just a bit edgy as they stood behind Kajak in the aft cabin. Eleria, as always, was sitting in Longbow's lap. "Those might be the ones I saw in my dream," she whispered in his ear.

"The number's right," Longbow agreed, "but number alone isn't quite enough to be certain that these are the ones we have to watch out for. Climb down, child. I think I'll drift along behind when they go down to look at Sorgan's gold."

Longbow followed Kajak and his four kinsmen at some distance. They seemed to be a bit nervous, but there were several of Sorgan's heavily armed crewmen close by, and that would explain their apparent apprehension.

When they came back up out of the hold, they all had that look of awe that had become quite common. They hadn't done anything out of the ordinary yet, but Longbow wasn't ready to dismiss the possibility that these were the five ship captains in Eleria's dream.

"It's a family that hasn't got the best reputation here in Maag, Longbow," Rabbit said later that day when Longbow privately asked him about Kajak and his cousins. "There've been times when other Maag ships sailed along with a few of them to go hunting Trogite treasure ships, and those other Maags never came back. If they've got any ideas along those lines this time, though, they aren't likely to try anything just yet. Skell and the other captains in the advance fleet are still provisioning their ships for the voyage to Dhrall, so there are a lot of Maag ships nearby."

"But Skell's fleet won't be here for much longer, Rabbit," Longbow reminded him. "They'll be sailing off to Dhrall within the next few days, and then there won't be very many ships here to guard the *Seagull*."

"*That's* when we might need to start worrying just a bit,"

Rabbit conceded. "Sorgan's going to be sending ships away, and Kajak's going to be calling ships in. I think maybe I'll go visit a few taverns this evening. Maag sailors do a lot of drinking when they're in port, and drunk sailors talk an awful lot. Sometimes they say things they wouldn't say if they were stone-cold sober. If I set my mind to it, I can look a whole lot drunker than I really am, so people don't pay too much attention to me. I'll let you know what I find out."

"That might be useful, Rabbit," Longbow agreed. "I'll tell Zelana about our suspicions, but I don't think we need to tell Sorgan about them just yet. We'll need to know more before we get him all worked up." He turned and went aft to Zelana's cabin.

"What have you been doing, Longbow?" Zelana asked him when he came in.

"Looking for sign," he replied.

"What a peculiar term."

"It has to do with hunting. The animals of the forest leave marks on the forest floor and on the trees and bushes that a hunter can follow if he knows how to recognize them. Rabbit's helping me."

"You really like him, don't you?" Eleria asked.

"He's very clever, but he hides his cleverness well. He's going to the beach this evening to look for sign in the taverns where the Maag seamen drink the juice that makes them foolish. It's possible that some seamen of Kajak's tribe will become foolish enough to say things that Kajak would rather they didn't. If Kajak is really the one you saw in your dream, the ordinary seamen of his ship and those of his cousins will know about it. Rabbit's going to be off in some corner pretending that he's far gone in drink. Kajak's people will think that he's asleep, and they'll talk to each other as if he wasn't there."

"You've changed, Longbow," Zelana observed. "You wouldn't have done this sort of thing back in Dhrall."

"It's not all that much different from what I did back in the forest, Zelana," he disagreed. "I still hunt, but the hunting ground has changed, that's all. My eventual target is still a creature of the Wasteland, but I may have to kill several shiploads of the kinsmen of the one called Kajak before I can get a clear bowshot at the servant of the Vlagh. In good time, however, I *will* find it, and then I'll kill it. That's what hunting is all about, isn't it?"

"It turns out that you were right, Longbow," Rabbit said very quietly when the two of them met in the bow of the *Seagull* at dawn the following morning. "A fair number of Kajak's crewmen were falling-down drunk last evening, and their mouths were running a mile a minute. I was lucky enough to catch a few bits here and some pieces there, and it's starting to come together."

"You're a good hunter, Rabbit," Longbow congratulated his little friend. "Where does the trail you found go?"

"That's a woodsy way to put it," Rabbit noted, "but down at the bottom it comes fairly close. Kajak's sailors were all agreed that the idea of letting *any* gold get away from him makes Kajak want to break down and cry. Cap'n Sorgan told him about all that gold over in Dhrall, but that was only words. Kajak saw *real* gold here on board the *Seagull,* and he wants it. He'll worry about the gold in Dhrall *after* he steals the gold here in Maag. You were also right when you said that Kajak and his cousins won't do a thing until after Skell leads most of the fleet off toward the east. They said that so many times that I got a little sick of hearing about it. They don't know exactly when Skell's planning to sail away, but they're hoping that he won't do it for several more days. They've got five ships here in the harbor of Kweta, but there's more on the way. They aren't *too* thrilled about taking on the ships that guard the *Seagull* when there's an even match. They'd be a lot happier if they could make their move when they outnumber us by about three to one. The way they seem to see it is that they'll have to make their move during the night after Skell moves out. The word's out all over Maag about what the cap'n's doing and how much he'll pay, so more ships are coming here every day. If they hold off too long, they'll be outnumbered again. If Skell sails before their friends get here, they'll have to move whether they like it or not. They *have* come up with an idea that might give them an edge, though."

"And it involves fire, doesn't it?" Longbow suggested.

"You knew that all along, didn't you?"

"It was just a guess. It needed some confirmation before I could base any plan on it."

"We'd better warn the cap'n," Rabbit said gravely.

"That won't be necessary. The captain and the rest of the crew would only get in our way."

"Are you trying to tell me that just the two of us are going to fight off five Maag longships all by ourselves?" Rabbit demanded incredulously.

"Of course not, Rabbit," Longbow replied with a faint smile. "Zelana and Eleria will help us. That's all the help we're going to need."

"Have you been drinking?" Rabbit asked suspiciously.

"Rabbit's visit to the local taverns confirmed our suspicions, Zelana," Longbow reported a little later. "It *will* be Kajak who'll come bearing fire. That's going to be our first enemy. Can you make it rain?"

"I'll speak with Mother Sea about it. I'm sure she'll be happy to oblige. What did you have in mind?"

"When Kajak's men row their skiffs up to the ships of Sorgan's kinsmen and throw their torches, rain would put out the fires before they could spread. Then Kajak's going to have to fight five ships when he only wants to fight one. He might just give up at that point and try to sail away from here." Longbow paused and thought for a moment. "I don't think we should let him get away. There are a lot of Maag ships nearby, and Kajak's not the only greedy one. Other Maag ship captains might find his plan very interesting. If he's dead, he won't be able to tell his plan to others here in the world of the living. I don't think we'll need to be very worried about what he says in the world of the dead, but I don't know very much about the world of the dead. If you think it might cause us some problems, you might want to look into it."

"You're teasing me, aren't you, Longbow?"

"I wouldn't even consider doing something like that, holy Zelana," he replied with an absolutely straight face. "I've given this a great deal of thought, and I don't think we'll want to bring this to Sorgan's attention. Rabbit and I can deal with it by ourselves, and Sorgan would just be in the way."

"You've been in the Land of Maag too long. You seem to have picked up their habit of boasting. You don't *really* believe that you and Rabbit can attend to Kajak all by yourselves, do you?"

"Kajak's *only* got five ships, Zelana. That shouldn't be much of a problem."

"He said that as if he really believes it, Beloved," Eleria noted.

"I know. And that's starting to worry me."

Sorgan's cousin Skell was finishing his preparations to set sail for the Land of Dhrall with the Maag ships that had been gathered so far, and Longbow spoke privately with Red-Beard. "It's not a matter of any great concern," he told his friend. "I'll see to it that Kajak doesn't live to see the sun come up on the morning after he comes to visit the *Seagull*. One or two of his kinsmen may see that things aren't going very well, and they might decide to leave here in a hurry. If they should happen to try to join Skell's fleet, you might want to let Skell know what they tried to do here in the harbor of Kweta. I don't think Skell's going to want people like that in his fleet."

"I'll do that," Red-Beard promised. "Should I warn Skell that the servants of the Vlagh are venomous?"

Longbow considered it. "Probably not until his fleet reaches Lattash," he decided. "Let's get him there before we tell him the whole truth. The Maags are much bigger than the creatures of the Wasteland, so they have a much longer reach. Their swords and spears should give them an advantage when the fighting starts."

"We'll do it that way, then," Red-Beard agreed. "Do you want me to carry some message to your chief, Old-Bear?"

"If you happen to be near him at any time after you return to Dhrall, you might tell him that I'm well, that I'll rejoin the tribe before the snow grows too deep, and that we're now almost ready to fight a war."

"I'll do that, friend Longbow."

"You're a very dependable man, friend Red-Beard, and much, much wiser than your humorous behavior makes you appear."

"It's paid off many times, friend Longbow," Red-Beard replied with a broad smile. "When people are laughing, they'll usually do what you want them to do."

"You're even more clever than I'd thought, friend Red-Beard." Longbow smiled faintly. "These are very unusual times, aren't they? I've never called a man of another tribe my friend before."

"It's a very rare thing," Red-Beard agreed. Then he flashed a quick grin at Longbow. "Fun, though," he added in an imitation of one of Eleria's favorite expressions.

Longbow burst out laughing, and the two of them clasped hands in an age-old gesture of friendship.

7

How can you be so certain that it's going to rain, Long-bow?" Rabbit asked as the two of them crouched well out of sight near the bow of the *Seagull* watching as the five skiffs approached the ships of Sorgan's kinsmen.

"You wouldn't believe me if I told you, Rabbit," Longbow replied. "It'll rain when it's necessary, and the ships guarding the *Seagull* won't burn. Now, then, this is the way we're going to do this. I want you to stay low and hand me arrows just as fast as you can. My right hand's going to stay in one place— very close to the bowstring—and you're going to put the arrows right between my fingers. If we do it like that, we'll be able to put out twice as many arrows as I could shoot without your help."

"There's going to be five shiploads of unfriendly people out there, Longbow. No matter how fast you can shoot, that's still an awful lot of people to kill off."

"We don't *have* to kill them all, Rabbit," Longbow patiently explained. "A ship won't go where its captain wants it to go unless there's somebody at the tiller to point it in the right direction. You and I'll only have five targets to shoot at, and between us, we can have five arrows in the air all at the same time."

"So *that's* why you're so convinced that you and I can do this all by ourselves, isn't it? A ship without a steersman at the tiller's likely to wander around all over the harbor for the rest of the night." Rabbit squinted across the dark water. "That's going to take some pretty fancy shooting, Longbow," he observed.

"No more difficult than shooting geese out of the sky, my little friend," Longbow said. It occurred to him that he'd been calling a goodly number of people "friend" here lately. It seemed appropriate, but it was very odd. Longbow hadn't called anyone "friend" for at least a half-dozen years.

Can you hear me, Longbow? he heard what seemed to be a whisper in his left ear.

Very clearly, he soundlessly replied.

I'll need to know exactly when those people throw the torches at the ships around us. I don't want to worry you, so you should know that this rainstorm won't be very big. It'll rain on those ships, but it won't rain anyplace else, and *it's only going to rain long enough to put out the fire coming from the torches. We don't want the crews of those five ships hiding from the rain in the cabin or down in the hold. They need to be where they can protect their own ships.*

Right, Longbow silently agreed.

"If you're going to do a rain dance or something, you'd better start now," Rabbit said urgently. "The men in those skiffs just fired up their torches."

"The rain's going to start *after* they throw the torches, Rabbit," Longbow told him. "We'll want to be sure that they've thrown every torch they have before we bring down the rain."

"You're cutting it a little fine, Longbow," Rabbit said in a worried tone.

"Trust me."

"I *hate* it when somebody says that to me," Rabbit complained. "Do you want me to blow out that lantern at the bow?"

"Why?"

"So that your arrows will be coming out of the dark. I've seen how fast you can shoot arrows, and if between the two of us we can put out twice as many arrows as that, those people out there won't have any idea of how many people are shooting at them. That'll probably scare them silly, and maybe they'll just give up and run away."

"Not a bad idea, Rabbit," Longbow conceded. "If they run, we won't have to waste arrows killing so many. Go blow out that lantern."

Rabbit scampered forward and extinguished the lantern at the *Seagull*'s bow. "There go the torches, Longbow!" he called in a hoarse whisper, running back to his place.

Rain, Zelana! Rain! Longbow's thought crackled.

I thought you'd never ask, she replied mildly.

There was a sudden flash of lightning and a sharp crack of thunder, immediately followed by a roaring downpour of rain.

The rain stopped as quickly as it had begun, but Longbow was certain that *nothing* would be able to set fire to the five ships now, since water was pouring down their sides in rushing sheets.

"Now, Rabbit!" Longbow said sharply, and he began loosing arrows as fast as he could, dropping the Maags in the skiffs first and then concentrating on the steersmen of each of Kajak's vessels.

There was much dimly heard shouting coming from the five floundering ships. The oarsmen were in place, of course, but with no one at the tillers, the five ships wandered about the harbor like lost puppies, and every time someone was brave enough—or foolish enough—to rush to the tiller, an arrow came out of the darkness to welcome him. Longbow felt a certain grim amusement when the seamen aboard those ships chose to leap over the sides rather than rush to take the tillers when the captains commanded them to.

It was most probably the terror inspired by silent arrows coming out of the darkness with deadly accuracy that ultimately sent the seamen aboard five ships over the sides to swim through the chill, choppy waters of the harbor to the safety of the beach, and Longbow added to that terror by placing his arrows where they would be very visible. An arrow in the heart will kill a man, certainly, but in most cases few men will see the fatal arrow protruding from the dead man's body. Longbow, therefore, carefully took aim at foreheads rather than chests, and of course he never missed. Three or four dead men with arrows protruding from their foreheads convey a message too clear to be misunderstood.

Rabbit, crouched low in the darkness, fed arrow after arrow into his friend's right hand, and Longbow fed arrow after arrow to the men of Kajak's ships.

Finally, all hope aboard the five ships fluttered and died when Kajak, screaming orders and curses, broke off quite suddenly when *his* forehead sprouted a single quivering arrow. *Everybody* went over the sides of the ships at that point.

"We won!" Rabbit exclaimed. "We actually won!"

"Not quite yet," Longbow said, carefully taking up one of his old stone-tipped arrows. He rose to his feet, his eyes searching the beach. "There," he said, drawing his bow and loosing his arrow all in a single move.

The arrow arched high over the dark water of the bay, and it unerringly found the grey-hooded figure which had been howling in frustration since the rain had extinguished the fires on the five ships surrounding the *Seagull*.

The hooded figure shrieked in agony as the venom-tainted arrow buried itself in its chest. Then it fell writhing on the sand, stiffened, and went limp.

"What was that all about?" Rabbit demanded.

"That one was the true enemy, my little friend," Longbow

replied. "It's gone now, though, so we don't need to worry about it anymore."

"There were enough enemies out here to suit *me*, Longbow," Rabbit said. "I can't believe that we actually came out on top. There were only two of us, so I wasn't about to place any large bets on this. Why did you shoot everybody in the forehead like that?"

"I wanted the ones who were still alive to realize just exactly what to expect. An arrow in the chest might not be visible if the dead man falls forward. An arrow in the head's almost always right out in plain sight."

"I still can't hardly believe that only two people could win a fight with the crews of five ships."

"The fight wasn't really all that serious, Rabbit. Our arrows were coming out of the dark, so no one on Kajak's ships could be certain just exactly where we were, and as long as nobody was steering the ships of the man who used to be called Kajak, the *Seagull* was in no real danger."

"You've got a very peculiar way of looking at the world, Longbow. If they used to call him Kajak, what do they call him now?"

Longbow shrugged. " 'Dead,' probably," he replied.

"The one on the beach isn't laughing anymore," Longbow briefly advised Zelana and Eleria a short while later.

"Good," Zelana replied. "I told you that those iron arrowheads would be better than the stone ones."

"Perhaps," Longbow admitted, "but I saved a few of the old ones for special occasions."

"Whatever for?" Eleria asked.

"My stone arrows had all been dipped in venom," Longbow explained. "It seemed proper to me that the creature of the Wasteland who was behind what happened here tonight receive something special."

"I'm sure it appreciated that," Zelana said dryly.

"The shouts it was making after my arrow reached it were not exactly shouts of joy, Zelana," Longbow said with a faint smile.

Then Sorgan, Ox, and Ham-Hand came bursting into Zelana's cabin. They all seemed to be agitated. "Why didn't you tell us what Kajak was up to, Longbow?" Sorgan demanded. His voice was just a bit shrill.

"It wasn't necessary," Longbow replied. "Rabbit and I were able to deal with it. It's always best in such situations to use as few warriors as possible. The more that we involve, the more confusion's likely to turn up."

"But *Rabbit?*" Ox exclaimed. "Rabbit's never been any good in a fight. He's too small."

"He did what was necessary," Longbow pointed out. "He's as quick with his hands as he is with his feet. He passed arrows to me faster than any other man on the *Seagull* could have, and that's what I needed. I didn't need to kill *all* the men on those ships, only the ones manning the tillers. Rabbit and I were able to do that without any help. Everything came out the way we wanted it to, so why are you all so excited now that it's over?"

"You're a cold one, Longbow," Sorgan observed. "Nothing rattles you at all, does it?"

"I'm a hunter, Sorgan. A hunter who gets excited at the wrong time doesn't eat regularly."

"About all that saved us was that freak rainstorm," Ham-Hand declared accusingly. "If that hadn't come along, we'd have been in a lot of trouble. How did you know it was coming?"

Longbow touched his nose. "I smelled it," he lied glibly. "Have you been at sea for all these years without learning how to recognize the smell of approaching rain?"

Sorgan looked directly at Zelana. "If you've got an army of men like Longbow working for you, why do you need us?" he demanded.

"Because I *don't* have that many Longbows, Sorgan," she replied. "He's unique. There's nobody else like him in the whole world. He shoots arrows very fast, but he thinks even faster. The time will come—before very long, I believe—when he'll make certain suggestions. If you want to go on living, pay very close attention to what he says, and do exactly what he tells you to do."

Eleria came to where Longbow was sitting and held out her arms to him. He picked her up and seated her on his lap. "I'd do as the Beloved tells you to do, Hook-Big," she said.

"That's Hook-Beak," he absently corrected her again.

She shrugged. "Whatever. Longbow's the best in the world, and the Beloved says that he's *mine*, so you'd better be awfully nice to me, don't you think?"

"Every time I turn around, somebody *else* is trying to give me orders," Sorgan complained.

"It does seem to be working out that way, doesn't it?" Eleria said, yawning. "If we've said everything that needs to be said, I think I'll take a little nap. I didn't get much sleep last night because of all the shouting and running back and forth. Do me a favor and try to fight quieter battles, Hook-Big. I really need my rest." Then she kissed Longbow, snuggled down in his arms, and immediately went to sleep.

THE JOURNEY OF VELTAN

1

Charity?" the ragged beggar said in a tentative sort of voice as Veltan of the South passed him on a quiet street near the forum of the Trogite city of Kaldacin on a blustery winter morning.

"Of course," Veltan replied, fumbling around for his purse. Veltan was still having some problems with the concept of money. He had to admit that it was much more convenient than barter, but he kept losing track of the relative value of coins made from different metals. He gave the beggar a few brass coins and continued down the street toward the forum.

It was winter now, and Veltan didn't care much for winter, since his Domain in the Land of Dhrall was largely given over to farming, and farmers much prefer spring and summer. The winter sky was perpetually overcast, the bare trees all seemed dead, and there were no flowers. The Trogites of Kaldacin, however, appeared to be immune to the innate melancholy of the season. Trogites in general had very high opinions of themselves, no matter what part of the Empire they called home, but the Trogites of Kaldacin seemed to believe that their city was the very center of the universe, and that simply living inside its walls automatically elevated them far above not only the people of other lands, but also above those Trogites unfortunate enough to live in some other city or village.

The city itself was magnificent, of course. Quite obviously, an unimaginable amount of labor had gone into its construction, but Veltan could not quite grasp the "why" of the entire thing. Nobody really *needed* houses that big. The towering walls around the city might possibly have been necessary—assuming that there were enemies in the vicinity—but Veltan had a strong suspicion that the walls were merely for show.

The Trogites favored stone for their houses and other buildings, and that certainly made sense to Veltan. Wood burns, but stone usually doesn't. The marble sheathing was decorative, certainly, but hadn't the Trogites of Kaldacin had anything better to do with their time?

The "public buildings" made no sense whatsoever at first, but as Veltan had come to know the Trogites a bit better, he had begun to realize that they all seemed to desperately need grand displays to prove to others (and probably to themselves even more) that they were very important. Any hint of a lack of importance seemed to gnaw at the very soul of the average Trogite.

Thus it was that there were enormous marble-sheathed palaces, meeting halls, temples, and mercantile establishments, usually perched atop the hills within the city walls.

Grandest of all, of course, was the imperial palace, the home of the glorious Emperor Gacian. The palace teemed with assorted servants, counselors, and other miscellaneous hangers-on, all vying for the exalted emperor's attention. After a few hints, Veltan managed to buy his way into an audience with His Imperial Majesty, but the exalted Gacian turned out to be a brainless incompetent with little or no understanding of the meaning of the word *army*.

"You're wasting your time here, you know," an elderly, mantle-clad counselor in the palace of Gacian had advised Veltan after the two of them had become acquainted. "The real authority here in Kaldacin lies in the hands of the Palvanum. They make the laws and decide what course the Empire will take."

"And where will I find them?" Veltan asked.

"In the forum at the center of the city. If you tell the Palvani what you want and what you're willing to pay, I'm sure you'll be able to strike an accord with them."

It hadn't turned out that way, however. The individual Palvani were all quite willing to accept Veltan's money in return for vague promises to "bring the matter to the attention of my colleagues," but the matter never seemed to come up in the august chamber where most of the Palvani slept through the endless orations of their fellow members.

Veltan of the South wasted yet another afternoon in the forum trying to find somebody—*anybody*—with enough authority to have control over the Trogite army.

As the cloudy sky to the west flamed with the incipient sunset, Veltan gave up and went back toward the south gate of Kaldacin. There were lodgings available within the city, of course, but Veltan was immune to the weather and he didn't need sleep. He much preferred to spend his nights out in the fields. The air was sweeter, and he could see the moon more clearly. Veltan was very fond of the moon, and he missed her.

He hadn't felt that way when Mother Sea had first banished him. He still felt a certain resentment about Mother Sea's peremptory response to his joking suggestion that she might be prettier if she wore stripes. Mother Sea seemed to have no sense of humor at all. She took everything so seriously. Veltan obviously hadn't been serious when he'd gone on at great length about the beauty of contrasting shades of blue and how lovely Mother Sea would look if she adorned her surface with carefully blended stripes ranging from pale, pale blue all the way across the spectrum to royal purple. He'd intended simply to amuse her, but she hadn't laughed. Instead, she had pointed at the moon and said, "Go there, Veltan! Go now!"

"But . . ." Veltan had protested.

"Go!"

And so it had been that Veltan had spent the next ten eons camped out on the pocked face of the world's baby sister, staring longingly down—or up—at the round blue ball he'd once called home. He'd ventured out among the stars a few times, but that was even worse. There was a dreadful emptiness between the stars that filled Veltan with an overwhelming loneliness. At least he could look at the earth from the surface of the moon. It had made him homesick, of course, but it was better than the vast blackness of the universe.

In time he'd grown fonder of the moon, and she'd evidently sensed his growing affection for her, and she had finally spoken to him. "That was a silly thing to say, you know," had been her first words to him. "Stripes, Veltan? You're lucky that she didn't feed you to her fish."

"I was only joking," he'd protested.

"I know that," the moon had replied, "but the Sea doesn't know how to laugh. Everybody knows that. I'll speak with her and see if I can persuade her to relent."

"She never listens," he'd replied in a gloomy voice.

"You're wrong, Veltan. She *always* listens to me. I can disrupt her tides any time I choose, and she absolutely *hates* that." Then, to Veltan's astonishment, the moon had giggled. They'd gotten along very well after that. Unlike Mother Sea or Father Earth, the moon definitely had a sense of humor, and Veltan had passed the endless centuries telling her outrageous jokes.

Even after Mother Sea had relented and allowed him to come home again, Veltan had continued to maintain contact with the moon, and he frequently visited her.

"Charity?" It was that same ragged beggar Veltan had seen the previous morning.

"Is this your customary place of business?" Veltan asked him.

The beggar shrugged. "It's fairly well protected from the wind, and if it starts to rain, I can take shelter under that archway. You seem troubled, stranger. What's bothering you?"

Veltan sat down on the curbstone beside the beggar. "I thought this city was the center of power here in the Trogite Empire, but I can't seem to find anybody here who has any kind of authority. I've been trying to find somebody here who'll rent me an army, but I can't find anybody who's willing to even discuss it."

"Did you speak with the soldiers themselves?"

"I didn't think that was permitted. Don't I have to go through someone in authority? I thought that the army of the Empire takes orders from the government."

The beggar laughed. "That hasn't been true for centuries, stranger. The imperial government found it inconvenient to give the soldiers full pay in peacetime, and before long, beggars such as me were better off than the average soldier. It was at that point that the soldiers went into business for themselves. There are little wars breaking out all the time—usually between the various noblemen who rule the provinces—so the assorted armies can find steady work. Why do you need an army?"

"There's trouble in the wind at home," Veltan replied evasively. "It's a little complicated, but it looks as if we're going to need professional soldiers to help us deal with it."

A young Trogite in tight black leather clothing came into the narrow street. He was wearing a metal helmet, and he had a long spear in one hand. "I need to talk with you, Commander Narasan," he said apologetically to the beggar.

"What is it now, Keselo?" the beggar demanded, "and don't call me 'Commander.' I threw that away on the day when I broke my sword."

"Things are really falling apart on us, sir," the young man reported. "Won't you please reconsider your decision? Nobody knows what to do anymore."

"Give them some time, Keselo. They'll learn."

"We don't *have* time, sir," the youthful Keselo said. "The seventh cohort's completely out of control. They've gone outside the city and they've been raiding manor houses and robbing travelers out on the high road. We sent orders to them to come back where they belong, but they ignored us."

"Go kill them," the beggar said bluntly.

"Kill?" Keselo gasped. "We can't do that! They're our comrades. It's not right to kill one's comrades."

"They're operating outside the rules, Keselo, so they're not your comrades anymore. They've broken off from the army, and that's a violation of the oath they swore when they joined us. If you don't punish them, other cohorts will do the same thing, and the army'll disintegrate. You know what has to be done, Keselo. Go do it, and stop bringing these silly problems to me. Was there anything else?"

"No, sir." The young man's face grew desperate. "Won't you please reconsider and come back to our headquarters?"

"No. You *do* grasp the meaning of 'no,' don't you, Keselo? And you should know me well enough by now to know that I mean what I say. Now, go away."

Keselo sighed. "Yes, sir," he said. Then he turned and left.

"He's a good boy," the beggar told Veltan, "and if he lives, he might go far."

"It appears that you're not what you seem to be, my friend," Veltan noted.

"Appearances can be deceiving. I'm exactly what I seem to be. That won't change just because I used to be something else. Narasan the army commander is now Narasan the beggar."

"Why did you decide to change careers?"

Narasan sighed. "I made a stupid decision and got several thousand of my men killed. That's very hard to live with, so I don't want to do what I used to do anymore. Time's running out anyway, so in a little while it won't make any difference *what* I do."

"You aren't *that* old, my friend."

"I wasn't talking about me," Narasan said in a gloomy voice. "I was talking about the world. It's just about to come to an end, you know. It won't be long before it's gone."

"I doubt that," Veltan disagreed. "What led you to this gloomy conclusion? Is it perhaps one of the tenets of the Trogite religion?"

Narasan made an indelicate sound. "Religion's nothing but a bad joke filled with lies and superstition," he declared scornfully. "The priests in the temple use it as an excuse to rob the gullible so that they can live in luxury in those fancy temples. I came to understand what's happening on my own. Time's running out. It'll stop any day now." There was a hopelessness in the ragged man's voice.

"I think you've seen what very few others have," Veltan said, "but you didn't go quite far enough. The world's approaching the end of a cycle, not the end of time itself. One cycle nears its end, but another will begin, and time, as she always does, will continue. Don't despair, Narasan. Time has no end—or beginning either, if the truth were known."

"And just how is it you know that?" the beggar demanded.

"I've seen the cycles change before," Veltan told him, "many, many times. The seasons turn and the years pass. The young grow old and long for sleep, and the sleeping ones awaken to resume their tasks. This is the natural order of things."

"You're not from around here, are you?"

"I think I already mentioned that. I'm looking for an army, and I'm ready to pay, but I haven't been able to find anybody yet who was willing to talk about it." Veltan's face took on a rueful cast. "I think my mind must be shutting down. I've walked past the man I need to talk with dozens of times and scarcely even saw him."

"Oh? Who's that?"

"You, my friend. It's time to set aside your sorrow and your gloomy speculation about the end of time and of the world.

Time will continue her stately march, and the world will abide, no matter what we do to destroy her."

"You're not at all like other men," the beggar observed in an awed tone. "I don't think you're really a man at all. You're something entirely different from man, aren't you?"

"The differences aren't really all that great, my friend. I've been to places where you couldn't go, and I can see things that you can't, but I still love and serve my homeland, and that's all that's really relevant, Commander Narasan. I need your army, and I'll pay gold for its services. The war will be difficult, I'm sure, but if we arrive in good time, we'll probably win, and winning's all that really matters, whether it's war or dice."

"That's a practical sort of approach," Narasan said. He stood up. "It looks like my holiday's over. It was sort of nice to sit around doing nothing, but it'll be good to get back into harness again. The army compound's over by the west wall. Shall we go?"

"We might as well," Veltan agreed, also rising to his feet.

The winter evening was settling over the city of Kaldacin as Veltan and Narasan walked through the shadowy streets. Workmen in shabby smocks carrying the tools of their assorted occupations hurried past in the chill air.

"The only honest men in the whole corrupt city," Narasan noted. "It's the same everywhere, though, isn't it?"

"I don't think I quite follow you," Veltan admitted.

"I suppose you wouldn't at that," Narasan conceded. "You've got money, so you don't really have to get your hands dirty, do you?"

Veltan laughed. "Have you ever tried farming, Narasan? Farmers get to know dirt very well. The people of my region are mostly farmers, and I've worked alongside them many more times than I can remember."

"You're a very unusual sort of fellow, then. Most landowners here in the Empire would sooner die than go out into the fields. That's the main reason we have money. A man with money can pay people to do the hard, dirty work."

"We don't use money, Narasan. We have a barter economy. It works out quite well."

"How did you plan to hire an army, then?"

"Does the word 'gold' have any significance here?"

"Indeed it does. Gold *means* money to most Trogites."

"So I've noticed. When I first arrived here, I had several gold bricks, and I found a fellow who almost broke down and cried when he saw them. He gave me bags and bags of coins for them. I still haven't quite determined the relative value of those coins. They're made of various metals, and some of the metals must be more valuable than the others."

Narasan laughed. "I think you might have been swindled, Veltan. If somebody gave you copper and bronze and silver for your gold bricks, he was only giving you about a tenth of the real value of your gold."

Veltan shrugged. "It doesn't really mean anything, Narasan. There are mountains of gold not far from where I live. I can get as much of it as I need."

"I wouldn't mention that here in the Empire, Veltan," Narasan cautioned. "The word 'gold' tends to make Trogites come unraveled in the head."

"I'll bear that in mind. How much farther is it to where your army lives?"

"Not too far. We're on the other side of the forum. It's an old imperial barracks that our forebears commandeered after they decided to go into business for themselves."

"Didn't the government object?"

"Of course. It didn't do them any good, though. They didn't have any army to put our forebears out, remember?"

"Why didn't those independent armies just seize power and take over the whole Empire?"

"And take on all the tedious chores involved in governing? Why bother? We're making more money this way, and the high-ranking idiots in exalted positions get to do all the worrying. That suits us right down to the ground."

The compound of Commander Narasan's army was a no-nonsense sort of place where everything was laid out in straight lines. Straight lines, it appeared, were very dear to the military mind. Veltan much preferred curves himself. They were softer and less rigid. Of course, no military man had viewed Father Earth from the moon, so soldiers weren't aware of the fact that straight lines were an unnatural imposition of a human concept upon a far more complex entity. Veltan smiled faintly. The assertion by rigid humans that the world was obliged to do what they told it to was an absolute absurdity, but Veltan had always seen a certain whimsical charm in absurdity.

Though Commander Narasan was still unshaven and dressed in his beggar's rags, his soldiers recognized him immediately, and the very air in the compound seemed to heave a vast sigh of relief. Order had been restored, and all was right with the world again.

"I take it that this compound's reserved for *your* army, Commander," Veltan observed as the two of them entered a large stone building in the center of the enclosure.

"It works out better that way, Veltan," the commander replied. "When you put two armies in the same compound, fighting usually breaks out after a few days. If we want to look the truth right in the eye, we'll have to admit that wars between the various armies aren't that uncommon. We work for pay, not for idealism, so every now and then one army's working for one side, and another army's working for the other. Blood gets shed, and old grudges lurk in the shadows. That's one of the reasons our compounds are walled in. We can defend them if we need to."

They entered a large room where a goodly number of Trogites in tight-fitting black leather clothing lounged in comfortable chairs, talking and drinking from metal tankards. There were heavy drapes at the tall windows, assorted weapons hanging on the walls, and animal skins with thick fur on the polished floor. Veltan felt a sense of ease and camaraderie in the room. Evidently, this was the place where the higher-ranking Trogite soldiers came to relax when they had nothing better to do. Everyone in the room stood up as Narasan came through the door.

"Oh, stop that," Narasan told them irritably. "You know it's not necessary here. That's just for public show."

"Did the weather finally drive you in off the streets, Narasan?" a balding man of middle years asked, grinning.

"I've been rained on before, Gunda," Narasan replied. "It was opportunity that brought me home. This is Veltan of the Land of Dhrall, and he needs an army. Since we're not doing anything else at the moment, I thought we might accommodate him. Put your tankards aside, gentlemen, and let's go to the war room." Then he went on through the large room where the soldiers had been lounging, and the others fell in behind him.

They trooped on down a wide corridor to the other end of the building and entered a cluttered room with iron-tipped spears and other weapons stacked in the corners, what appeared to be models of various war engines on a large central table, and white walls with extensive drawings on them— drawings that reached as high as the ceiling. Veltan examined the drawings. They had no color, and there didn't seem to be any central point to draw the beholder's eyes. "What are these pictures supposed to represent, Narasan?" he asked.

"Land," Narasan replied. "We call them maps, and they're supposed to look more or less like the ground of various regions." He pointed at one of the larger drawings. "That's the Trogite Empire."

Veltan went closer to the drawing. "It's not very accurate, you know." He pointed at the upper part of the drawing. "If that's supposed to be the north coast, it doesn't even come close to the real thing."

"It looks close enough to me," the balding Gunda objected. "My family lives in that district, and I don't see very many mistakes."

"That might explain some of the errors," Veltan said. "We all tend to overemphasize our ancestral home." He pointed at a jutting peninsula on the representation of the north coast. "Your family lives *here,* doesn't it, Gunda?"

"How did you know that?"

"The picture shows it to be at least twice as big as it really is."

"That's our Gunda," another soldier laughed. "He seems to think that everything about him is twice as big as it really is."

"Is this big enough to suit you, Padan?" Gunda asked, holding up his clenched fist.

"All right," Narasan said wearily, "that's enough of that. Just exactly where *is* this Land of Dhrall you were telling me about, Veltan?"

Veltan looked around the room at the various maps. "It's not on any of these," he replied. "It's about five hundred leagues to the north of Gunda's home territory."

"There's nothing up there but ice," a bone-thin officer called Jalkan scoffed.

"It's beyond the ice," Veltan told him. "There's a sea current that comes down from the far north, and it carries those large ice floes down from the eternal ice. The ice floes form a barrier of sorts. The fishermen of the south coast of Dhrall know all about them, and they know how to avoid them."

"Could you draw us a map?" Narasan asked.

"Of course."

"I think it'll be too risky, Narasan," Jalkan warned. "No Trogite vessel I've ever heard of has made it through those floating ice mountains in one piece."

"The Maags don't seem to have much trouble, Jalkan," the soldier named Padan said. "They've been raiding our north coast for years now."

"Their ships aren't as big as ours, and they're faster," Jalkan pointed out. "They can get out of the way if an ice mountain's bearing down on them. Our ships are bigger and slower. We'll lose at least half of our army if we try to go through that zone of floating ice."

"We're going to have to work out a few details, I think," Narasan told Veltan, "and it's likely to take us a while. For right now, why don't we talk about payment? How much are you prepared to give us for our help?"

"How much do you want?"

"Why don't you make me an offer?"

"Why don't you tell me how much you expect?"

"How does one gold crown per man strike you?" Narasan asked tentatively.

"It fills me with confusion," Veltan replied. "We don't have what you Trogites call money in the land of Dhrall. I picked up a few brass and copper coins when I first came here, but that's about the extent of my familiarity with your money. Just what exactly is a gold crown?"

"It's one ounce of pure gold," the young soldier Keselo supplied.

"And what exactly is an ounce?"

"Somebody show him a crown," Narasan said.

The soldiers all sorted through the leather purses each of them carried at his belt, and eventually the one called Jalkan managed to find a gold coin. "I'll want this back," he told Veltan as he handed the coin over.

"Of course," Veltan replied. He bounced the coin thoughtfully on the palm of his hand. "All right," he said, handing the coin back to Jalkan. "We have gold in Dhrall, but we usually store it in the form of bricks. As closely as I can determine, each brick would weigh as much as five hundred or so of those coins. How many men do you have in your army, Narasan?"

"I can field a hundred thousand."

Veltan made a quick computation. "That would be two hundred bricks," he said. "That seems to be a reasonable number."

"You're taking a lot of the fun out of this, Veltan," Narasan complained. "Don't you want to argue with me just a little?"

"What's there to argue about?"

"Nobody *ever* pays the first price we ask. You're supposed to tell me that I'm asking too much. Then we bicker back and forth until we come to the *real* price."

"What a waste of time," Veltan murmured. "I need to speak with my elder brother anyway, so I'll bring some of the bricks with me when I come back." Veltan squinted at the map. "Which one of those coastal towns will you sail from?"

"What do you think, Gunda?" Narasan asked.

"Castano," Gunda replied immediately. "It's the biggest town on the coast, and it's got the most protected harbor."

"Very well," Veltan said. "I'll meet you gentlemen in Castano in three, maybe four weeks. I think we'd better move your army to Dhrall by spring—sooner if we can manage it. We've all got work to do, so I'll get out from underfoot so that you can do yours. My work might take a bit longer, but please be ready to sail from Castano when I come back. Hopefully, I'll have a better idea of when the war's likely to start when I return." Then he turned and walked briskly from the war room.

2

The night sky was clear and the stars were very bright when Veltan left the city of Kaldacin. The pale moon had not yet risen, but Veltan knew her very well, so he was certain that she'd soon put in an appearance. He walked on out across the brown-stubbled, sleeping winter farmland beyond the walls of Kaldacin before he summoned his pet thunderbolt. She always seemed a little bad-tempered when he was obliged to awaken her after the sun went down, and she made more noise at night than she did in the daytime. It was highly unlikely that the Vlagh had agents here in the Trogite Empire, but Veltan didn't really think that announcing his presence with a shattering crash of thunder just outside the walls of Kaldacin would be very prudent.

He was several miles from the city when he stopped and looked up at the night sky. "I'm sorry to have to wake you, dear," he apologized, "but I really need to go home."

The thunder grumbled off in the distance.

"Oh, don't do that," he chided her. "It's not really all that far, and you can go back to sleep as soon as we get home."

She grumbled some more, but he could hear her stirring, and there were flickers of light along the eastern horizon.

Then there was a sudden crash, and she was at his side.

"Good girl," he said, patting her fondly. Then he mounted. "Let's go home, baby," he said.

She obediently arched up toward the north, leaving the Trogite Empire behind in the blink of an eye and flashing across the northern sea in a few heartbeats. They flew over the wide strip of ice floes that separated the Trogite Empire from the southern coast of the Land of Dhrall, and Veltan considered that barrier as his thunderbolt carried him over it. The ice belt had been his sister Aracia's idea, and she'd put it in place while Veltan had been living in exile on the moon. The notion had come to Aracia when she'd realized that the various outlanders had begun to build ships that were much more advanced than the simple rafts that had been prevalent at the beginning of the current cycle. Aracia had reasoned that it might be well to put some sort of barrier in place to keep the outlanders' ships away from the coast of Dhrall. The barrier had made good sense in the past, but it was likely to cause problems in the current situation. "I think I'll have to work on that a bit," he muttered.

His thunderbolt crackled inquiringly.

"Nothing, dear," he replied. "I was just thinking out loud."

She muttered something as they reached the coast of Dhrall.

"I didn't quite catch that, dear," Veltan said as the thunderbolt put him down on the doorstep of his own house, somewhat farther up the coast.

She repeated what she'd just said, shaking the very ground under his feet.

"That wasn't nice at all," he scolded. "Where in the world did you pick up that kind of language?"

She said a few things that were even more colorful, and then she streaked off into the darkness to sulk.

Veltan smiled faintly. It was a little game he and his pet had been playing since the beginning of time. She would shower him with assorted profanities, and he'd pretend to be shocked. They both enjoyed the game, so they played it all the time.

He opened the massive front door of his house and went on inside. Unlike his sister Aracia, Veltan had made his own house, and he suddenly realized that he probably shouldn't bring Narasan's Trogites here. The various buildings in Kaldacin had been constructed of squared-off stone blocks, much as Aracia's temple had been. When Veltan had made his house, he'd made it with a single thought, willing a huge rock into existence in the shape he wanted. It definitely kept the weather out, but it might be just a bit difficult to explain to Narasan's people. The conversion of thought into reality in a single act of will was obviously something the Trogites wouldn't be able to comprehend, and that might cause some problems.

All in all, though, it was good to be home again. Traveling about the world was nice enough, but home was much more comfortable. Veltan reached the end of the central corridor and then started up the stairs to the tower where he and Yaltar spent most of their time. "I'm back," he called up the stairs.

The door to the tower room opened, and Yaltar stood waiting for him. Yaltar was a slender little boy dressed in an ordinary peasant smock. He had dark, dark hair and huge eyes. "Did you have any luck, uncle?" he asked.

"Things turned out rather well," Veltan replied. "It took me quite a while to find the man I really needed to talk with, but once I found him, we came to an agreement in almost no time at all. Has anything been happening here?"

"Nothing that I've heard about. Omago's wife, Ara, was nice enough to feed me while you were gone."

"She's a treasure," Veltan agreed. Then he noticed something. "What's that you have around your neck, Yaltar?" he asked.

"Omago tells me that it's an opal, uncle. I found it just lying on the ground outside our front door a few days after you left."

The boy untied the leather thong that held the opal as a pendant about his neck, and raised the milky stone up for Veltan to see. "Isn't it beautiful?" he said proudly.

"It is indeed, Yaltar," Veltan agreed, trying his best to sound casual. He could feel the enormous power of the fiery jewel from halfway down the stairs. It was obviously time to step very, very carefully. Veltan knew for a fact that there weren't any deposits of opals in his Domain, and if Yaltar had found it just outside the front door, it had obviously been put there specifically for the boy to find. The jewel was quite large, somewhat bigger than a plum. It was oval-shaped, with multi-colored fire flickering deep within it. Worse yet, Veltan could feel its awareness even as he looked at it. It was a peculiar sort of awareness, but still very familiar.

"Oh, before I forget," Yaltar said, tying his pendant back around his neck, "Omago asked me to tell you that he'd like to talk with you when you come home."

"I'll go see him tomorrow," Veltan said as he reached the top of the stairs.

They went on into the tower room. Although Veltan's house was very large, he and his young charge had spent most of their time in this room since Yaltar had been an infant. It was large enough to serve their purposes, and it had the feel of home to them. There was a fire on the hearth, as usual, and the clay pots nearby suggested that Yaltar had been trying his hand at cooking. The room was none too tidy, but Yaltar had been alone for several weeks, and "cleaning up" was an alien concept for the little boy.

"I've missed you, uncle," Yaltar said gravely. "I get lonesome when you aren't here, and I've been having a bad dream. It's always the same, and it seems to come back every night." Yaltar was a very serious little boy who seldom smiled.

"Oh? What does it involve?"

"People are killing each other," Yaltar replied with a shudder. "I don't really want to watch, but the dream forces me to see everything."

"Did the surroundings look at all familiar?"

"It's not anywhere around here, uncle. There are mountains that're very close to Mother Sea. The sun comes up from behind the mountains, and it goes down somewhere beyond Mother Sea herself."

"That would put it somewhere in Zelana's Domain," Veltan mused.

"Isn't that where Balacenia lives?"

Veltan almost choked at that point. "Where did you hear the name Balacenia, Yaltar?" he asked.

Yaltar frowned. "I'm not really sure, uncle. It just seems to me that I know someone named Balacenia, and she lives in the western Domain. Maybe it's just part of that dream that keeps coming back over and over again."

"That's altogether possible, I suppose." Veltan glossed over Yaltar's use of a name he could not possibly have heard about. "Did anybody in your dream put a name to any mountains or rivers that might possibly have given you some landmarks?"

"I heard some people talking about 'Maags' once, and others said some nasty things about somebody called 'the Vlagh,' but I don't think those words had anything to do with rivers or mountains." Yaltar frowned. "Now that I think about it, though, sometimes the people in my dream said things about 'Lattash.' I think that one might be a place because of the way they talked about it. If somebody says, 'I just came here from Lattash,' he almost has to be talking about a place, doesn't he?"

"It sounds reasonable to me, Yaltar. Did your dream give you any kind of idea about what time of year it was?"

"Well, sort of, maybe. There wasn't any snow on the ground, so that sort of rules out winter, doesn't it? It wouldn't mean too much around here, because we don't get much snow in the winter, but the snow really builds up in the mountains during that time of year, I've heard."

"That it does, Yaltar. Were you ever able to get any idea of why the people in your dream were killing each other?"

"Nothing very clear, uncle. Some of them were coming west across the mountains, and others seemed to be trying to stop them. Does that make any sense at all?"

Veltan forced a gentle smile. "Dreams aren't supposed to make sense, dear boy. If they made sense, they wouldn't be fun, would they?"

"I'm not really having very much fun with this one that keeps coming back, uncle. It's *awful!*"

"Try not to think about it, Yaltar. If you ignore it, maybe it'll go away. I need to go talk with my big brother. I hate to have to keep leaving you alone like this, but there's a sort of family emergency right now. Hopefully, we'll be able to put it behind us before long, and things should return to normal."

"Could you see Omago before you leave, uncle? He seems to think it's fairly important, and he even said that he wouldn't mind if you woke him up to hear what he has to say."

"Now that's *very* unusual. Once Omago goes to sleep, not even a thunderstorm can wake him. Is there anything else you think I should know before I leave?"

Yaltar snapped his fingers. "I almost forgot something, uncle. After the last time I had that awful dream I was telling you about, I drew a picture of the ravine where it seemed to be happening. If you're at all interested, I could show it to you."

"That would be nice," Veltan replied blandly, resisting a sudden impulse to jump up and dance on the table.

Omago was a sturdy farmer with fertile fields and an extensive orchard. The other farmers of Veltan's Domain frequently sought his advice, and during their discussions with him they almost always passed on gossip, observations, and other tidbits of information. It was widely believed in Veltan's Domain that if a stray dog trotted down a village street anywhere in the region, Omago would know about it before the sun went down. Omago was a very good listener, and many times people would tell him of things they might have been wiser to keep to themselves.

Veltan liked him, and he'd come to rely on him for information.

The sun had not yet risen when Veltan went through Omago's now bare-limbed orchard, where last summer's leaves lay thick along the low stone wall to the south. Omago's whitewashed cottage seemed almost to nestle drowsily under its overhanging thatched roof. Veltan smiled faintly. It seemed sometimes that almost everything in his Domain viewed winter as a good time to catch up on its sleep. Veltan went along the neatly made stone walk to the door of Omago's cottage and rapped on the door. Ara, Omago's slender and beautiful wife, opened the door. Ara had long, dark auburn hair, and she was by far the loveliest woman in the village. As was her custom, she wore no shoes, and she had very pretty feet.

Her kitchen was quite large and warm, and it was filled with the lovely fragrance of her cooking. Veltan had no need for food, of course, but he always enjoyed the smell of cooking.

"Good morning, Ara," he greeted the lady of the house. "Is Omago awake yet? Yaltar tells me that he wants to have some words with me."

"He's stirring a bit, dear Veltan," she replied. "You know Omago. He can sleep through almost anything—except the smell of breakfast. Come in. I'd offer you something to eat if I thought you'd accept."

"The smell of your cooking is tempting, dear Ara, but no, thanks all the same." He followed her into the warm golden light of her kitchen. "I'd like to thank you for looking after Yaltar while I was away, Ara," he said, seating himself at the table. "Sometimes I forget that he needs food quite regularly—probably because I don't."

"You're missing one of the better parts of life, dear Veltan."

She looked at him. "I've always wondered if light has any sort of flavor," she said curiously.

"I don't think 'flavor' is exactly the right term, Ara," Veltan replied. "Different colored lights have a different sort of feel to them. I taste things with my eyes, not with my tongue. Could you see if Omago's awake yet? I'm a little pressed for time right now."

"I'll fetch him for you, dear Veltan." She took a generous slice of warm, fresh bread and went back to the place where her husband slept, her long blue dress swirling about her ankles as she moved.

A few moments later she returned, leading her nightshirt-garbed husband by the simple expedient of holding the fragrant piece of bread just out of his reach.

"Good morning, Omago," Veltan greeted him. "I see that Ara's managed to get your attention."

"She does that every morning, Veltan. I swear that she could wake the dead with that wonderful smell." Omago took the piece of bread from his wife and wolfed it down.

"Don't eat so fast," Ara cautioned. "You'll choke."

"Yaltar said that you wanted to tell me something," Veltan said. "He seemed to think it might be important."

"It could be, Veltan," Omago replied. "I've been hearing about a fair number of strangers drifting around in your Domain here lately. They're pretending to be traders from the Domain of your sister Aracia of the East, but they can barely speak our language, and all other traders from that part of Dhrall speak the same language we do. They don't seem to have anything of value to trade, and all they're really doing is asking questions."

"What sort of questions?"

"They seem to be curious about how many people live up near the Falls of Vash. Why in the world would anyone want to live *there?* It's all rock, and so steep that a man'd have to tie himself to a tree to harvest anything that might sprout. The thing they seem to be most curious about is how much contact there is between the people here and the tribes of your sister Zelana's Domain and just how close you and Zelana are to each other. I've been catching some hints that they'd be much happier if you hated her."

"That's absurd!"

"I'm just passing on what I've heard, Veltan. I thought you should know about it."

"I'll look into it when I come back from my brother's Domain, Omago. I need to talk with him about a little family matter. Eat your breakfast before it gets cold."

"I'll see to it that Yaltar gets enough to eat," Ara promised. "We wouldn't want him to start wasting away, now, would we?"

"Isn't she a treasure?" Omago said fondly.

"Indeed she is," Veltan agreed.

"Come back soon, dear Veltan," Ara said.

"That I will, treasured one," Veltan promised with a broad smile.

"Does this look at all familiar to you?" Veltan asked his older brother later that morning in the cave under Mount Shrak. He handed the picture Yaltar had drawn on a sheet of parchment to Dahlaine. "I get the feeling that it's somewhere in Zelana's Domain."

"Your boy's quite gifted, Veltan," Dahlaine observed. "He's got a good eye for perspective."

"Notice that he hasn't included any sign of snow. I didn't want to make too big an issue of it, so I didn't press him too hard, but he told me that there wasn't any snow on the ground in his dream—of course, that might not be all that significant. The war had already begun at the beginning of his dream, I think. He *did* mention the name Lattash. Isn't that a village somewhere in Zelana's Domain?"

"Yes, it is," Dahlaine agreed, studying the drawing. "There," he said, pointing at a twisted tree in the middle distance on Yaltar's drawing. "My thunderbolt did that quite a long time ago, and Zelana scolded me about it for years. Notice the way it's all twisted and bent over that ravine. I recognize that tree, and I know exactly where it is. This is that ravine that comes down out of the mountains above Lattash."

"Of course!" Veltan said, snapping his fingers. "All right then, Yaltar's dream put the battle in that ravine, and he overheard people talking about the Maags. Hasn't Zelana been trying to persuade the Maags to help her fight off the creatures of the Wasteland?"

Dahlaine nodded. "They're pirates, so I don't know how dependable they are, but maybe your boy's dream means that Zelana's winning them over. This might just be very useful, Veltan."

"Maybe," Veltan replied, "but can we be sure that this will be the first attack? Dreams aren't too specific, Dahlaine. Isn't it possible that the attack on Zelana's Domain will come some time *after* attacks on the other Domains? Yours? Mine? Aracia's? For all we know, Yaltar's dream could be taking place long after the war's begun."

"That wouldn't make too much sense, Veltan. The Dreamers are here to help us, not to add to the confusion." Dahlaine frowned. "There *could* be a problem there, though. We don't really know all that much about the Dreamers, or if there's any kind of logic or sequence to their dreams. If the dreams are just popping up at random with no connection to sequence, they could give us more trouble than help."

"Oh, before I forget, when I told Yaltar that his dream was quite probably taking place in Zelana's Domain, he asked me if that was the region where Balacenia lives."

"He said *what?*"

"He called Eleria by her true name, brother."

"That's not possible!"

"He called her by name. Vash and Balacenia have always been very close, so evidently he's aware of her presence, and he doesn't think of her as Eleria. The young ones are at least as perceptive as we are, Dahlaine, and Yaltar—or Vash—has somehow managed to slip around the barrier you set up when you arranged their premature rebirth. I think we'd better start being very careful. Our cycle hasn't run its full course yet, and if we break the pattern, everything could start falling apart."

"Now I've got something *else* to worry about. Thanks a lot, Veltan."

"Don't mention it." Veltan frowned. "Do you have any idea at all about what sort of creatures we'll be facing when this all starts?"

"A few—and they're not very pretty. The Vlagh tampers and experiments, and it has very little understanding of what we look upon as natural development. We've always permitted the creatures—and plants, for that matter—to develop and grow as their innate nature and their surroundings dictate. There's a certain harmony in our Domains, but there's no harmony in the Wasteland. The Vlagh seizes on certain characteristics and it crossbreeds to bring those to the fore. From what I've seen, it seems that it's attracted to venomous reptiles and stinging insects for some reason."

"There *is* a certain practicality there, Dahlaine," Veltan pointed out. "Poisonous creatures wouldn't need any weapons, would they? Their weapons are built right into them."

"That's true, I suppose," Dahlaine conceded.

"The only problem I can see with that is that insects and reptiles are dormant during the winter, aren't they?"

"It seems that That-Called-the-Vlagh steps over that problem," Dahlaine responded. "Its crossbreeds also involve warm-blooded creatures. Insects are enormously strong, snakes have deadly venom, and most warm-blooded creatures remain active in the winter. As closely as I've been able to determine, the dominant traits derive from certain insects—bees and ants, for the most part. Have you ever examined the colonizing activities of those kinds of bugs?"

Veltan shuddered. "Not so that you'd notice it, big brother. Bugs are hideous—or were you aware of that?"

"They're very well designed, though. Their skeletons are on the outsides of their bodies to maintain their shape and also to serve as armor."

"Perhaps, but they're stupid beyond belief."

"As individuals, perhaps, but there seems to be a sort of group awareness involved in the behavior of some varieties. The group is wiser by far than the single individual."

Veltan squinted at his older brother. "What on earth ever persuaded you to take up the study of bugs, Dahlaine?" he asked.

Dahlaine shrugged. "I was bored, Veltan. Cycle after cycle sort of ambled along before any creature with anything remotely resembling intelligence came along. Bugs were all that there was, so I studied bugs."

Veltan frowned. "I think there might be a hole in your theory, though. I've heard that there have been men—who look like men—who've been roaming around in my Domain, nosing around and asking questions. If they can communicate with my people, they almost have to be smarter than bugs, don't they?"

"What sort of questions are they asking?"

"They're curious about how many of my people live near the Falls of Vash, and if there's very much contact between Zelana's people and mine. From what I gather, they'd really be a lot happier if Zelana and I hated each other."

Dahlaine frowned. "I hadn't anticipated that," he admitted. "The Vlagh may just be more clever than we'd thought. Evidently it's not going to rely on sheer brute force if it's sending spies into our Domains. This might just turn out to be a more interesting war than we'd expected. Have you managed to locate any warriors yet?"

"It took me a bit longer than I'd expected, Dahlaine. I went on down into the Trogite Empire thinking that all I'd have to do would be to wave gold in front of some high official, but it doesn't quite work that way. Once I'd located the right man, though, it went more smoothly." Veltan snapped his fingers. "I nearly forgot something. Are you likely to be in contact with Aracia any time in the near future?"

"Probably. Why?"

"Could you tell her that I'm going to cut a channel through her ice zone? I'm hiring a Trogite army, but it won't do us any good unless I can get it here to the Land of Dhrall. Aracia created that ice zone to keep the Trogites away, but the circumstances have changed. We *want* the Trogites here now."

"Why don't *you* tell her?"

"She won't listen to me, Dahlaine. You should know that by now. She's older than I am in this cycle, and she seems to think that she outranks me. *You're* the only one she'll listen to this time, because you're the only one who's older than she is. I'm not really looking forward to the next cycle, when *she'll* be the eldest. Maybe I'll just go back to the moon and wait her out."

"You can't do that, Veltan. You know you can't."

"It was just a thought. Have you managed to find *your* army of outlanders yet?"

"I'm still working on them. Have you ever heard of Malavi?"

"Aren't they the ones who ride cattle?"

"Malavi call them horses, and they don't exactly think of them as cattle. There aren't any horses here in Dhrall, so the creatures of the Wasteland are going to be in for a nasty surprise if they decide to come north."

"Is Aracia working on anybody in particular?"

"She's negotiating with some people off to the east. She wasn't very specific about just who they are."

"I'd better go see if I can find Zelana," Veltan said. "Things seem to be coming to a head, and since there's a strong possibility that the first confrontation's likely to take place in her Domain, I think it's time for her to come home. Do you think you might have time to go warn her people about the possibility that the creatures of the Wasteland might be coming to call before very long?"

"I'll see to it, Veltan," Dahlaine promised. "Go warn Zelana, and I'll let her people know what's afoot."

3

I need you again, baby," Veltan silently summoned his pet thunderbolt as he left Dahlaine's cave under Mount Shrak.

As always, she grumbled a bit, and the flickers of light and distant rumbles of her discontent came to him from far to the south. "Oh, quit," Veltan chided her. "We've hit a busy season, that's all. Things should go back to normal in a while, so don't be so bad-tempered."

There was a sudden flash of light and a crash that shook the very earth, and she was there.

"Good girl," Veltan said fondly. "We need to find Zelana. Dahlaine says that she's somewhere off to the west. We may have to jump about a bit to find her, but it's very important. If you're extra, extra good, maybe we can have a bit of fun a little later. There's a band of ice mountains floating off the south coast of Dhrall, and I'm going to need an open channel through them before too much longer. I think we'll be able to smash our way through, don't you?"

The lightning bolt skittered around enthusiastically.

"I thought you might like the idea. For right now, though, let's go find Zelana. Don't make *too* much noise when we cross Mother Sea, though. We don't want to irritate her, now, do we?"

The thunderbolt rattled her agreement, Veltan mounted, and they were off.

It was the dead of winter, and the face of Mother Sea was clouded and stormy. Veltan shuddered. Mother Sea's face was as dreary as it had been on that awful day when she'd banished him to the moon. He'd probably be there still if the friendly moon hadn't interceded for him.

His thunderbolt reached the coast of a land far to the west of the Land of Dhrall much earlier in the day than it had been back in Dhrall. That was one of the advantages of going westward. If a traveler moved right along, he could pick up hours of extra time.

"Set me down here, baby," Veltan told his pet when they were a mile or so out from the coast. "I'll walk on in from this point. Let's not disturb the aliens if we don't have to."

She muttered something.

"I won't be long, dear. Stop all your grumbling." He smiled then. "As soon as we find Zelana and tell her what's going on, you and I can go home and amuse ourselves by smashing that floating ice. Won't that be fun?"

She crackled enthusiastically. Lightning was a simple natural force, and it wasn't too hard to entertain her.

She set Veltan down on the stormy face of Mother Sea, and he walked the rest of the way to shore. He was just a little surprised when Mother Sea calmed her surface to make the going easier for him. Either she'd recovered from her bout of bad temper, or she realized just how serious the present situation really was. He stepped right along and reached rocky shore in short order. "Thank you, Mother," he said politely to the source of all life.

"Don't mention it," she replied silently within his mind. "Zelana and Eleria are farther south," she added helpfully.

"Ah. Could you give me some sort of landmark?"

"The coast along here's fairly level, Veltan, so there isn't anything that really stands out. Just go on south until you come to a place where there are quite a few floating trees gathered near the shore. The man-things call them 'ships,' and they ride on them when they visit me."

"I've seen a few of those, yes." Veltan squinted at the alien land he'd just reached. "I think I'll nose around a bit, Mother. The people here won't know that Zelana's my sister, so they might tell me things they wouldn't mention to her. If we can come here, it's possible that the creatures of the Wasteland can as well, and if they do happen to be here, I think we should know about it." He hesitated. "There's something you should probably be aware of, Mother," he added. "Before very long, I'm going to have to open a channel through Aracia's ice zone that lies off the south coast of Dhrall. I'm sure that Aracia received your approval before she put it there, but now I'll need to push it aside so I'll be able to move the army I just hired to our homeland. Is that going to offend you?"

"Not particularly, no. Aracia didn't bother to ask me before she put it in place, so it only seems fair for you to brush it aside without her permission as well. Actually I could do it for you, you know. All you had to do was ask."

"I didn't want to bother you, Mother. I learned quite some time ago that it's not a good idea to offend you."

"I'd forgotten all that silly 'stripes' business a long time ago, Veltan. I thought you'd realized that by now." She paused. "Why did you remain on the moon for so long?" she asked.

"The moon told me that you were still angry with me."

"And you actually *believed* her? Oh, Veltan, you should know me better than that by now. You could have come home after a month or so. You didn't really have to remain on the moon for ten thousand years."

A dark suspicion intruded on Veltan's awareness. "Evidently the moon was feeling just a bit lonely," he muttered. "She kept telling me that you hated me."

"She lied. Everybody knows that you can't trust the moon."

"*I* didn't. She seemed so sincere."

"Oh, Veltan, what am I going to have to do with you to make you grow up? You're so gullible sometimes. The moon enjoyed your company, so she lied to you to keep you there. Your responsibilities are *here,* not out there."

"When all this business with the Vlagh and the creatures of the Wasteland is over, I think I'll go have a nice long chat with the moon," he said darkly.

"Whatever entertains you, Veltan. She won't listen, of course, but if scolding her will make you feel better, I suppose it's all right. Don't hurt her, though, and don't offend her *too* much. My tides depend on her, so step around her rather carefully. If you think that silly business about stripes made me angry, you'll come face to face with *real* anger if something disrupts my tides."

"I'll be careful, Mother," Veltan promised.

Veltan modified his clothing and quickly pushed out his scanty facial hair to make himself look much like an ordinary Maag, and then he went on into a coastal town the Maags called Weros. He drifted unobtrusively around the narrow, muddy streets near the waterfront, listening but saying very little. Since he was listening to thought rather than speech, he could hear whispered conversations from a long way away.

He soon discovered that the Maags were a noisy, rowdy kind of people who spent much of their time in taverns, soaking up beer and grog by the gallons. Fights seemed to break out very often in the area near the waterfront, and it was not uncommon to see a Maag peacefully sleeping in the gutter in that part of Weros.

Veltan strolled along, occasionally looking into taverns as

if he might just be looking for some friend or acquaintance. Such conversations as he happened to overhear were usually garbled, since most of the Maags in this part of town were far gone in drink.

He wasn't really accomplishing very much, but then he heard someone off to his left speaking in a voice that seemed uncontaminated by strong drink.

"It was a good enough plan, I guess," the speaker was saying to someone else, "but it went all to pieces when Kajak and his men tried to set fire to the ships Hook-Beak had anchored around the *Seagull*."

"Exactly what went wrong?" The voice that asked the question chilled Veltan all the way to his core. It was a rasping sort of voice that could not have come from a human mouth.

"I wasn't there to see it personally," the first speaker replied. "My hive-mate had been controlling Kajak from the very beginning, but I guess just the thought of all that killing excited it more than it should have, so it was down on the beach—far too close, as it turned out. One of the man-creatures killed it from a great distance away. By the time I got there, most of the survivors had scattered to the winds. I nosed around in Kweta and managed to pick up the gist of the story from various Maags who'd spoken with the survivors before they fled back into the surrounding countryside. It's fairly obvious that Sorgan—or someone in his crew—knew about Kajak's entire scheme. As soon as the men in those little rowboats threw torches onto the decks of the ships that were guarding the *Seagull,* a rainstorm came out of nowhere and doused the fires before they could spread. Then long arrows began to come out of the dark with unbelievable accuracy. I managed to get my hands on the arrow that killed my hive-mate, and the arrowhead was made of stone—like the ones we've encountered back in the Land of Dhrall—*and* it'd been dipped in venom in the same way. That sort of says that the

Dhrall who's been killing my hive-mates for all these years is here, and he's still killing us. The arrows he used to kill the Maags had iron arrowheads, though. As we've come to expect, he's extremely clever. He disabled Kajak's ships by killing the steersmen, and he terrorized everybody on the ships by driving his arrows through the head of anyone who went near the tiller. Kajak's men panicked and went over the sides of their ships. Kajak was screaming at them to come back when *he* took an arrow right between the eyes, and the whole thing ended right then and there."

The one with the chilling voice began to swear.

"I feel the same way," the first speaker agreed. "I think you'd better go advise the Vlagh that your scheme didn't work. The Maag fleet's on the way to Dhrall, and there's nothing we can do now to stop it. Our war in the west won't be as easy as we thought, I'm afraid."

"I am not foolish enough to be the one who takes that message to the Vlagh," the one with the rasping voice replied. "Bad news angers the Vlagh, and those who tell it things it does not wish to hear seldom live long enough to watch the sun go down."

"I've noticed that. I'd say that you've got a bit of a problem. Your scheme was clever enough, but Kajak was a poor choice to carry it off."

Veltan sauntered past the muddy little alleyway where the two had been speaking, and they both tried to shrink back into the shadows to stay out of sight, but Veltan had already seen enough. The one who'd brought the news looked much like any other Maag on the streets of Weros—fur-clad, hooded, bearded, and dirty—but he was much smaller than an ordinary Maag. The other one was also wrapped in a hooded cloak, and Veltan caught a single glimpse of a face with huge, bulging eyes, a mouth surrounded by mandibles, and two long antennae sprouting from the top of an oval head.

Veltan strolled on past the alley as if he hadn't seen or heard anything out of the ordinary, but he was quickly revising a few preconceptions. Given the general tone of what he'd just heard, it was fairly obvious that the insect outranked the human in the social structure of the Wasteland. They were both far more intelligent than Veltan had expected, however. The term "hive-mate" hinted at an insectlike mentality, and that raised the possibility that That-Called-the-Vlagh might just be "the queen bee of the Wasteland."

The intelligence of the two in the alley sort of confirmed a notion that Veltan had reached during his sojourn on the moon. It had seemed to him that intelligence might just be a characteristic driven by necessity. If your enemy was large, size would be very important, so each generation would be larger than the preceding one. That had suggested to Veltan that a clever enemy would virtually demand the expansion of one's mind in response. The alternative would be extinction.

"Enough," he muttered, walking purposefully through the rest of Weros to the edge of the town. He crossed the stump-dotted field to the west of Weros, and once he was in the woods, he called out to his thunderbolt. "Let's get out of here, dear one. I've heard and seen enough. It's time for me to have a talk with my sister."

It didn't take Veltan very long to find Sorgan's fleet. There were a few ships in the harbor of each village he and his pet passed as they flew south along the coast of Maag, but Mother Sea had implied that there would be many ships at the place where Zelana was. The difference between "few" and "many" wasn't too precise, but Veltan was fairly certain that two or three didn't exactly qualify as many, so he kept going south.

Then his pet carried him to a shabby village far to the south of Weros, where dozens of Maag ships were anchored. "I think this is the place, dear," he told his pet. "Put me down a little ways out, and I'll walk on in. You're lovely beyond words, but we don't want to attract attention. You'll be able to crash and boom to your heart's content when we go back to Dhrall and start smashing ice."

She flickered affectionately at his cheek and then set him down at the edge of a large grove of trees a little way to the west of the village.

Since Zelana had come to Maag to recruit an army, Veltan was fairly certain that the one the aliens had called Sorgan was the one he should try to find, and that his sister would probably be on board the ship called the *Seagull*.

The weather was unpleasant as Veltan walked down across the open field toward the shabby village. A gusty wind swept in from the east, and a steady drizzle of rain swirled in from the harbor, wreathing like fog and half obscuring the shabby buildings.

When he reached the village, he found it teeming with sailors despite the chill drizzle. It didn't take him long to locate a small group of men who served on board the *Seagull*, since every seagoing man he spoke with pointed them out to him. They were down near the waterfront, loading barrels and big, bulky sacks into several small boats. A large fellow with a neck like a bull seemed to be in charge.

"Excuse me," Veltan said politely to the big man, "I'm looking for a lady named Zelana. Do you happen to know where I might find her?"

"She's on board the *Seagull*," the sailor replied. "Is it important?"

"I believe it is. She's my sister, and I've got some information for her that's probably quite significant. Things are heating up in the Land of Dhrall, so it's time for her to come home."

"Rabbit!" the big man barked. "This is Lady Zelana's brother, and he needs to talk with her. Row him out to the *Seagull*."

"But it's raining," the small sailor whined.

"What's that got to do with anything?"

"Couldn't we wait a bit? It could clear up before long."

"Almost any day now, but you're not going to wait, Rabbit. You're going right now." The big man's voice was hard, and the look he gave the smaller man was threatening.

"All right, all right. Don't get excited. I'm going." The little man grumbled as he led Veltan out onto a rickety dock, and he continued to mutter as the two of them climbed down into one of the small boats.

"How's my sister been lately?" Veltan asked as the little man rowed them out into the rain-swept harbor.

"She was sort of worried up until a few days ago," the little fellow replied. "Things brightened up for her after me and Longbow killed a whole bunch of people who were planning to cause trouble."

"The one you call Longbow's the archer, isn't he?"

"That he is, and he's the best there is in the whole wide world. Me and him are real close friends." The little man stopped rowing and wiped the accumulated water off his nose with his sleeve.

"Is Eleria with my sister?"

"They don't never get too far apart. That's one sweet little girl, ain't she?"

"Indeed she is," Veltan agreed. "It was Longbow, then, who shot arrows into the foreheads of the enemy sailors, wasn't it?"

"Word about that seems to have gotten out. Where did you hear about it?"

"It was in a town up the coast a ways. I happened to overhear a conversation between a pair who'd really wanted Kajak to succeed. They were both terribly disappointed, and more than a little afraid. The one they work for doesn't take bad news very well."

"What a shame," Rabbit said with a sly grin. Then he turned and looked over his shoulder. "That's the *Seagull* just ahead. Once we get on board, you'll be able to tell your sister what's afoot back home."

"She lied to me, Zelana. Can you *believe* that?" Veltan said to his sister in the snug cabin at the aft end of the ship while Rabbit went back to his skiff to return to the little village on the beach. "Mother Sea told me that I could have come back home after just a couple months, but the moon deceived me, and I stayed there for ten eons."

"Oh, Veltan!" Zelana exclaimed. "Everybody knows that the moon isn't to be trusted."

"*I* didn't. Actually, though, it wasn't really all that bad. The moon can be a delightful companion when she wants to be. Let's get down to business here. Where's this Sorgan that everybody keeps talking about?"

"He's off somewhere in the harbor talking with the other ship captains. He should be back before too much longer."

"Let's hope so. I've arranged to bring a Trogite army to Dhrall. If all goes well, they'll be landing in my Domain in late winter or early spring."

"How big an army are we talking about here?"

"About a hundred thousand men, dear sister."

"That should carry quite a bit of weight."

"We can hope, I guess. Now things start to get a little interesting. When I returned home, Yaltar was wearing a beautiful fire opal as a pendant, and he told me that he'd found it lying on our doorstep one morning. Then he told me that he'd been having a recurrent nightmare. It's fairly obvious that his opal is having the same effect as Eleria's pearl, wouldn't you say?"

"It's entirely possible, I suppose, and if the pearl *is* the voice of Mother Sea, wouldn't that suggest that the opal might very well be the voice of Father Earth?"

Veltan blinked. "I hadn't thought of that," he admitted. "It would seem that we have some powerful friends, wouldn't it?

Anyway, Yaltar's nightmare involved a war, and Dahlaine and I were able to pinpoint its location. It's going to take place in your Domain, dear sister, and most of the fighting's going to be in a river gorge that leads down to a place called Lattash."

"How very fortunate. As it happens, I've already got an advance force of Maags in the harbor of Lattash."

"You knew this was coming, didn't you?"

"Of course I did, Veltan. I just didn't know exactly where or when. Now that we've pinpointed where, all we need to know is when."

"Spring, maybe. I questioned Yaltar, without being too obvious about it, and there wasn't any snow in the ravine that leads down to Lattash during the battle he kept dreaming about. I wouldn't lock 'spring' in stone, though. Yaltar's dream started in the middle of the war, so we can't be sure just *when* it started. The Vlagh's keeping an eye on us, and it might just try an early strike to catch us off guard. There have been strangers wandering around in my Domain asking questions. They're curious about how many people live in the vicinity of the Falls of Vash, and whether you and I are on speaking terms."

"It should know that we're close, Veltan. We *are* brother and sister, after all."

"The Vlagh wouldn't understand that, Zelana. It doesn't have a family, so it knows nothing about love. You had a bit of excitement here recently, didn't you?"

"Oh, yes—very exciting. There was a Maag named Kajak who was *very* interested in the gold Sorgan was using for bait to attract other Maags to go to Dhrall and fight our war for us."

"It went just a bit further than that, dear sister. The Vlagh has people—and things—here in Maag as well as in Dhrall, and they encouraged this Kajak to attack your Maag, Sorgan. I happened to overhear a couple of the Vlagh's agents talking in an alley up in Weros, and they weren't very happy about the way things turned out. The Vlagh's agents were a very odd pair, let me tell you. One of them appeared to be an ordinary Maag, except that he was only about half as big, but the other one was a very large insect."

"You're not serious!"

"I'm afraid so. Dahlaine told me that the Vlagh's been experimenting, and it's tampering with the natural order of things by crossbreeding assorted species. The insect I saw in that alley in Weros was as tall as a man, and it could talk—and think. As I understand it, their scheme fell apart because of a Dhrall you brought with you."

Zelana smiled. "Indeed it did, Veltan. His name is Longbow, and he never misses when he shoots an arrow at something."

"I thought that little Maag who rowed me out to this ship was exaggerating, but he might have been actually telling me the truth."

"That was probably Rabbit. He and Longbow are good friends. You've been very busy, haven't you, Veltan?"

"I haven't *quite* met myself coming around a corner yet, but that may happen in a week or so. How big an army have you managed to gather so far?"

"We're approaching fifty thousand men. I wish I could get more, but the Maags spend most of their time at sea robbing Trogite treasure ships."

"I'd heard about that. The Trogites dislike the Maags intensely. That could cause a few problems, but I think we'll be able to work our way around them. When I go back to pick up my army, I think I'll send you some help. Trogites are very good soldiers, so they might be useful."

"What a nice person you are, Veltan," Zelana said, smiling fondly at him.

"Family obligation, sister." Veltan looked around. "Is Eleria anywhere nearby?" he asked quietly.

"No, she's out on the deck playing in the rain."

"She's *what?*"

"She loves water. Longbow's keeping an eye on her."

"There's something else you should know about, sister of mine," Veltan said very quietly. "When Yaltar was telling me about his dream, I made a quick guess and suggested that the battle he'd dreamt about would take place in your Domain. Then he said, 'That's where Balacenia lives, isn't it?' I can't for the life of me understand how, but it seems that he knows her real name."

"That's impossible!"

"Dahlaine said the same thing, but Yaltar definitely said 'Balacenia' when he spoke of her. Our big brother may *think* he's put a wall between our Dreamers and their past, but I think that wall may have just a few holes in it."

Eleria and the archer Longbow came in out of the rain a little while later. Eleria was dripping wet, but Longbow had evidently been watching her from a sheltered place on the deck. "Did you have a nice time, dear?" Zelana asked.

"It was sort of nice," Eleria replied. "Not as nice as swimming, but Hook-Big's people get all excited when I jump off the rail, and the water here's awfully dirty."

"Go dry yourself off and change clothes, dear," Zelana told her. "You're dripping all over the floor."

"Yes, Beloved," the little girl replied, going to the place where she slept and taking up a thick cloth.

Veltan was more than a little startled by Zelana's Dreamer. She was by far the most beautiful child he'd ever seen, and he sensed a towering though not fully developed intelligence in her.

"Longbow," Zelana said to the tall, silent Dhrall, "this is my brother, Veltan of the South, and he's brought us some news about what's been happening at home."

"It's an honor to meet you, Veltan," Longbow said. "Has Zelana's Domain been attacked as yet?"

"Not as far as I know," Veltan replied, "but I'm afraid it won't be too much longer."

"We'd better go home, then, Zelana," Longbow suggested.

"I think you're right," she agreed. "Sorgan's cousin should be in the harbor of Lattash by now, but if the creatures of the Wasteland come now, Skell could be badly outnumbered. We might have more time than I originally thought we would, but I'd rather not take any chances. As soon as Hook-Beak returns, I'll talk with him."

"It could just be that the advance fleet of Trogites I'll be sending will reach Lattash before Sorgan's fleet does," Veltan suggested. "That could be very useful in the event of a sudden emergency."

"That's assuming that the Maags and Trogites don't kill each other before the war even starts. They aren't really very fond of each other."

"We're the ones in charge, Zelana, and we're the ones who'll pay them. I don't think you fully understand the power of money, dear sister. They won't have to *like* what we tell them to do; they just have to do it. If they decide that they'd rather not, we just tie the purse shut. That river that comes down the ravine to Lattash has two sides, though. If we deploy the Maags on one side and the Trogites on the other, we should be able to keep the bloodshed to a minimum."

Eleria came back from changing clothes and climbed up into Longbow's lap. Veltan gave his sister a questioning look.

"It'd take much too long to explain, Veltan," she said with a sigh.

Captain Sorgan returned to the *Seagull* as the rainy afternoon was moving on toward evening, and the crewmen who'd been loading supplies for the long voyage to Dhrall made their final trip of the day at about the same time. Zelana sent word to the Maag ship captain that she needed to talk with him and with two other sailors as well: one she called Ox, and another known as Ham-Hand. Maags, Veltan noted, had peculiar and usually unflattering names. Veltan immediately saw that Sorgan, like most of the other Maags he'd encountered, was about half again the size of an ordinary man, and he and his friends seemed to be very grubby and dirty. Maags evidently didn't bathe very often. If Zelana was anywhere close to being right, though, the Maags were very clever. Veltan smiled faintly. Zelana's Maags and his Trogites probably weren't going to get along very well.

"This is my brother Veltan," Zelana introduced him to the oversized Maags, "and he's brought us some interesting news about certain events in the Land of Dhrall."

"It's always good to know what's going on," Sorgan said. He looked at Veltan. "What's afoot over there?" he asked.

"We had a stroke of luck here recently," Veltan told him. "We managed to discover exactly where our enemy's planning to make its initial attack, and as luck has it, it's going to take place in the vicinity of a spot you're familiar with, and better yet, a part of your fleet's already bound for that region."

"The enemy's going to attack Lattash?" Sorgan demanded shrewdly. "So *that's* what this has been about right from the start, hasn't it?"

"I don't think I quite follow you," Veltan confessed.

"Lattash is the place where Lady Zelana keeps all her gold. Didn't you know that? Now this war's starting to make sense."

"I think we'd better haul anchor and put on full sail, Cap'n," the burly Ox said. "If we don't get to that Lattash place afore the enemy does, we'll come up empty when pay time rolls around."

"He's got a point, Cap'n," the Maag named Ham-Hand chipped in. "Skell *might* get there in time to hold the enemy off, but *might* is pretty shaky ground to stand on right now. You've been hiring just about every Maag ship along this coast with promises about the gold in that cave, and if the cave's empty when we get there, you ain't going to be none too popular."

"The enemy knows that you're coming, Captain Sorgan," Veltan told him, "and they're doing everything they can to delay you. I was coming through the town of Weros a few days ago, and I happened to overhear a conversation between a couple who don't care much for you. They were very unhappy about what had happened to a fellow named Kajak. They wanted you dead with all their hearts, but as I understand it, Longbow sank their scheme without so much as a ripple. Kajak wanted your gold, but those strangers wanted your life. Without you, Lattash lies helpless before the enemy."

"Let's haul anchor, Cap'n," Ox repeated his suggestion.

"I'd really like to gather up more ships and men," Sorgan said, "but I think you might be right, Ox."

"Isn't your kinsman Torl still here, Sorgan?" the archer Longbow asked. "Couldn't he stay behind and gather more ships and men?"

"I suppose he could," Sorgan conceded, "but he might have trouble persuading other ship captains to join us if he doesn't have any gold to show them."

Longbow shrugged. "Leave the gold with him, then."

Sorgan blinked. "Well, I'll have to think about that just a bit," he said dubiously.

"Don't you trust your cousin, Hook-Big?" Eleria, still nestled on Longbow's lap, asked. "It's not like the gold really *means* anything, does it? You saw how much of it there is in the Beloved's cave, didn't you?"

"It's something to think about, Cap'n," Ham-Hand said. "Torl's going to need that gold a lot more than we are. He's going to have to have *something* to show any new ship cap'n who might be interested. When you get right down to it, all that gold really is, is bait, and Torl's the one who'll be fishing after we leave."

"It just seems *unnatural*," Sorgan said. "Giving gold away really goes against my grain."

"We'll give you more, Hook-Big," Eleria told him. "You worry too much." Then she yawned. "I'm a little sleepy," she said. "If it's all right with everybody, I think I'll take a little nap. And even if it's not all right, I'll do it anyway." Then she snuggled down in Longbow's arms and promptly fell asleep.

4

Veltan's thunderbolt enjoyed herself enormously as she enthusiastically blasted a channel through the mountainous mile-long ice floes lying to the south of the Land of Dhrall. She seemed to take particular delight in the steam that came boiling out and the huge fragments that went flying each time she shattered an ice mountain. Veltan felt that she was probably overdoing things, but she was having so much fun that he didn't have the heart to rein her in, so he leaned back and let her play.

Her first pass at Aracia's arbitrary zone of ice left a path of slush a half mile wide. Her next pass doubled the width of the path, and the steam she generated was very much like a fog bank.

"Enough, Veltan!" Mother Sea said sharply.

"She's not really hurting anything, Mother."

"Oh, yes she is. The water's starting to boil, and it's killing all the fish. Make her stop."

"Yes, Mother," he replied obediently. "Could you perhaps push the slush aside, though? Ice seems to bother the Trogites, for some reason. Their ships are slow enough to begin with, and if they start being overly cautious, it could be midsummer before they reach the coast of Dhrall."

"I'll take care of it, Veltan, and I'll add a little current behind them to hurry them along."

"That would be very nice, Mother," Veltan thanked her. He hesitated. "Would it be all right if I let my pet smash a few more of these ice mountains? I won't let her boil the water, but she's having so much fun that I hate to make her stop just now. She'll get tired in a little while, and then I'll put her to bed. I've been running her a little hard here lately, so she needs a bit of play-time."

"Oh, all right, I suppose, but be sure you don't let her boil the water anymore."

"I promise," he replied.

Castano was a large seaport on the north coast of the Trogite Empire, and the harbor was filled with broad-beamed vessels that were obviously designed to carry a great deal of cargo. The city itself was surrounded by thick, high walls, and what Veltan could see of it raised some memories of the town of Weros, over in the Land of Dhrall. For some reason, the more civilized people of the world seemed to be afraid of open space, since their houses were all tightly crowded together. Unlike the houses in Weros, however, most of the houses of Castano were made of stone. That made them sturdy, of course, but they were probably cold and damp in the winter. Like the Maags, the Trogites appeared to believe that the streets of their towns were the most convenient place to dispose of their trash.

Veltan saw a large encampment just to the south of the city. He assumed that Narasan's army was there, but he didn't stop. He was fairly sure that Narasan wouldn't move until he received at least a token payment, so he passed on over Castano and went on to a small fishing village of perhaps a dozen houses a few leagues off to the west and rather carefully examined several fishing sloops to get a general idea of how they were constructed. Then he moved on to a deserted beach and built one of his own with a single thought. It was faster to do it that way than it would have been to duplicate Trogite coins and then spend the rest of the afternoon haggling with some smelly old fisherman.

The sloop he'd just built appeared to be a fair duplicate of the ones he'd seen in the harbor of the village, so he pushed her off the beach. It took him a little while to determine which of the ropes raised, lowered, or turned the single sail, but it wasn't really all that complicated, so his sloop was soon running before a good following breeze back along the coast in the general direction of Castano. He found it to be quite exhilarating, and he wondered why he'd never tried sailing before. Of course, the weather wasn't bad, and the breeze was going in the right direction, so things weren't too difficult.

When he reached Castano he sent out a searching thought and located the soldier named Gunda, whom he'd met in Narasan's compound back in Kaldacin. He eased his little sloop up to the pier where Gunda was conferring with several other Trogites. "Ho, Gunda!" he called.

"Is that you, Veltan?" Gunda sounded startled.

"It was the last time I looked. Is Commander Narasan anywhere nearby?"

"He's over in the encampment just south of town. What in the world are you doing in that rickety little sloop?"

"I thought it might be easier to come here from Dhrall by boat than it'd be to walk."

"Very funny, Veltan. Did you actually sail all the way from Dhrall in that rickety thing?"

"It wasn't too bad. We've had a stroke of luck, and I think we should take advantage of it while we can. Some freakish ocean current just opened a channel through the ice floes, and if we hurry, we should be able to get through before it closes up again. Could you send for Narasan, please? You might mention the word *pay* in your message. That should bring him running."

"You've got *that* much gold in that broken-down sloop?" Gunda demanded incredulously.

"Do I really look that stupid, Gunda? Let's just say that I've got enough with me to get Narasan's attention. I'll give him the rest when we reach Dhrall. You'd better start things moving. I think we'll want to leave here first thing tomorrow morning. That channel through the ice won't last forever, so we'd better get cracking."

Veltan made some show of tidying up his little sloop after Gunda had left, squaring away the sail, coiling ropes, and generally making her presentable. He stayed at it long enough to bore any curious onlookers, and then he went up to the bow and ducked down out of sight. He reached back over his shoulder and took a gold brick out of nowhere. He set it at the very bow. Then he took another brick and put it behind the first one. When there were ten of them, he stood up and covered them with a bit of canvas. If his calculations were correct, he had roughly the equivalent of five thousand Trogite gold crowns to get Narasan's attention, and if Narasan wanted to see more, the channel through the ice was open now, so taking him to the Land of Dhrall should be fairly easy.

Narasan had discarded his beggar's rags, and he looked quite imposing in his tight-fitting black leather uniform and heavy metal helmet and breastplate. He was also wearing a sheathed sword belted at his waist, and the heavy-looking handle suggested that the sword was for business, not for show. "Where in the world did you get that tub, Veltan?" he demanded from the pier, looking at Veltan's sloop with a certain disdain.

Veltan shrugged. "I bought her from a fisherman. I needed a boat. She doesn't look like much, but she sails well."

"Is that a Dhrallish boat?"

Veltan shook his head. "It's a Trogite fishing sloop. Dhralls don't build sloops, and I didn't feel up to paddling a Dhrall canoe all the way here. I have something I'd like to show you, and then we'll need to talk."

"All right," Narasan agreed. "See if you can hold your sloop steady. I don't swim very well—particularly not in full uniform." He gingerly climbed down the ladder that was attached to the pier, while Veltan snugged his sloop up against the ladder with a long-handled hook. Narasan awkwardly dropped the last few feet into the sloop. "What was it you wanted me to see?" he asked Veltan.

"It's up in the bow. Drag that canvas out of the way."

Narasan went forward and turned the canvas back. "Well, well, well," he said, staring at the gold bricks, "aren't they pretty."

"I thought you might like them."

"That's hardly two hundred, though."

"I know. I didn't really want to sink my sloop with all that weight. Let's just call it a demonstration of good faith. The rest of the gold's back in Dhrall. These should give you some idea of the size and weight of the standard block."

Narasan hefted one of the bricks. "Heavy," he noted. "How can you buy anything with something this bulky?"

"We don't use them for money, Commander." Veltan reminded him. "They're mostly just for decoration—ceilings, bracelets, door handles, and the like. . . . Now, then, we'll need to move at least part of your army to Dhrall immediately. We've discovered that the enemy forces will attack very soon. We have other soldiers that are already in place, but you'll probably have to reinforce them. My sister's been hiring an army off to the west, and she's sent a part of that army to her Domain. She has more on the way, but they might not reach Dhrall in time."

Narasan's eyes narrowed. "The only people I've ever heard of that live beyond the western sea are the Maags."

"So?"

"We don't get along very well with the Maags."

"I've heard about that. This war doesn't really have anything to do with friendship. You don't have to like the Maags, Commander Narasan; you just have to fight alongside them. The only thing you and the Maags need to concern yourselves about is the gold we're paying you—and whether you'll live long enough to spend it."

"That's blunt enough, but it gets your point across."

"I don't really have time for diplomacy, Commander. I *must* help my sister ward off an invasion. You'll be meeting a Maag sea captain who goes by the name of Sorgan Hook-Beak before long. My sister believes that he's competent, but I'll let you make your own judgement about that when the fighting begins."

Narasan grunted. "You're the one who's paying the bills," he conceded. "Did you happen to remember that map you promised to draw for us?"

"Of course," Veltan lied. "I'll go get it for you." He went off toward the stern of his sloop, conjuring up a picture of Dhrall in his mind as he went. It occurred to him, however, that the map didn't need to be *too* accurate. There might very well be times in the not too distant future when he'd need to move soldiers from one place to another in the Land of Dhrall in a hurry, and if the real distances between here and there were represented accurately on the map, the Trogites might begin to realize that more was happening than he'd told them. *Some* people in this world have no difficulty with the notion of miracles, but Veltan was fairly certain that Trogite soldiers weren't very likely to fit into that category. The map he created sort of resembled the Land of Dhrall, but it was a much smaller version.

He rolled the vellum map up and took it to the bow of the sloop, where Narasan was fondling the gold bricks. "This is about as close as I can come, Commander," he apologized, handing the map to the soldier. "Some of the distances aren't really very accurate."

"That's all right, Veltan," Narasan said. "All I really need is a general layout of the territory." He studied the map for a few moments. "Do your people have any kind of army that might be of any use at all?" he asked.

Veltan smiled faintly. "My people don't even know what the word 'army' means, Commander," he confessed. "Zelana's people have occasional squabbles with each other, but they have a tribal society, and that means that all the men pick up their weapons and go out in a disorganized mass to meet the enemy tribe. After a dozen or so men are killed, they usually suspend hostilities and enter into extended negotiations. Most of their weapons are fairly crude and ineffective. The only exception to that is the archers. There's a Dhrall in my sister Zelana's Domain named Longbow who doesn't seem to know how to miss, and he can have four arrows in the air all at the same time."

"Now, *that* I'd like to see."

"I'm sure you'll meet him before too long. The people of the Northern Domain of my brother Dahlaine are pretty much the same as the people of the West. The Domains of my sister Aracia and mine are mostly farmland, and our people are primarily farmers. They don't fight people; they fight the soil and the weather instead." He paused. "How many men can you put to sea right now?"

Narasan squinted at the sky. "Probably about twenty thousand. The bulk of my army's still marching here from Kaldacin. You arrived here about a week early, so we aren't quite ready."

"Twenty thousand might be a little light, but I guess it'll have to do." Veltan looked at the Trogite ships. "I don't think your ships will move very fast, so you and I should go on ahead."

"In *this* thing?" Narasan demanded.

"She may not look like much, Commander, but she's very fast. Your second in command's Gunda, right?"

Narasan nodded.

"I think we'd better go have a talk with him. There's an

open channel through the ice zone right now. It's one of those seasonal things. Gunda shouldn't have any trouble reaching the coast of Dhrall, but he needs to know exactly where to put your advance force ashore. We'll be several days ahead of him, and that should give you and Sorgan Hook-Beak time to work out some details. There's snow up in the mountains now, but the weather could break at any time, and as soon as it does, the enemy army will invade my sister's Domain, and we'll have to be ready to meet them."

Narasan shrugged. "You're the one who's financing all this, Veltan," he said, "so we'll do it your way."

LATTASH

1

Rabbit had no memories of his mother. He'd been raised from early childhood by Ashar Beer-Belly, a relative of some sort, Rabbit assumed, though Beer-Belly could never quite remember exactly what that relationship was. In general, Beer-Belly was a kindly blacksmith in the port city of Weros on the west coast of the Land of Maag, and when he was sober—which didn't happen too often—he gave his small nephew instructions in the fine art of working with iron. Despite his bad habits, Rabbit's uncle Beer-Belly was a truly masterful smithy, and his teachings took Rabbit far beyond the capabilities of ordinary apprentices.

And so it was that by the time that Rabbit was about twelve years old, his skills went far beyond those of most adult blacksmiths. He concealed that out of necessity. More and more frequently, Uncle Beer-Belly's fondness for strong drink incapacitated him, and Rabbit was obliged to deceive prospective customers with assorted excuses, which had almost no element of truth in them. Of course, "He's not here right now," was very true, given Beer-Belly's condition at the time.

The smithy's regular customers noticed a distinct improvement in the products of Beer-Belly's smithy at about that time.

There were a few drawbacks, however. Rabbit could do most of the work during the daylight hours, but the finer details required a certain amount of caution on his part, so he was obliged to close all the doors and windows and work at night, as quietly as possible.

Several neighbors complained about "all that whangin' and bangin' in the middle of the night," but Rabbit had come up with a long line of excuses, so he was able to fend them off— most of the time.

By then, Uncle Beer-Belly had begun to see things that weren't really there, and every so often he'd been seized by convulsions. Rabbit hoped against hope that the seizures would go away, and he found that he could control them to some degree by keeping Uncle Beer-Belly's large tankard filled to the rim with strong grog.

It was on a chill winter morning some months later when Rabbit's world came crashing down around his ears. He'd risen early and fired up the forge in the smithy, and then he went back into the living quarters to check on Uncle Beer-Belly's condition.

Uncle's eyes were open, and he didn't seem to have the shakes as he had for the past several months. His face seemed to be rather relaxed.

"Are you feeling a little better, uncle?" Rabbit asked. "Would you like something to eat?"

Beer-Belly didn't answer, and he kept staring at the ceiling.

"I'll fry us up some bacon," Rabbit said. "You really ought to eat something." He put some wood in the stove and then went back into the smithy, dug some glowing coals out of the forge with a small scoop and fired up the cooking stove. "Are you going to be all right, uncle?" he asked as he sliced strips of bacon. "I have to finish up that frying pan for Old Man Gimpy today, so I'm going to be busy this morning."

Beer-Belly didn't answer, and he kept staring at the ceiling.

"Would you like a touch of grog to go with your bacon?" Rabbit asked.

Beer-Belly continued to stare at the ceiling.

A sudden chill came over Rabbit. He laid down the cutting knife and went to uncle's bed. "Uncle?" he said. "Are you all right?" He reached out and put his hand on uncle's shoulder. Then he snatched it back. Uncle's skin was very cold, and he seemed quite stiff.

"No!" the boy gasped. He looked more closely. Uncle Beer-Belly wasn't breathing, and his eyes were still fixed on the same spot on the ceiling.

"Oh, no!" Rabbit moaned, shrinking back. "What am I going to do now?"

Several possibilities flashed through his mind. He immediately threw announcing uncle's condition out the window. If the word that Uncle Beer-Belly had just died got out, the neighbors would come in and ransack the smithy, and the tools and just about everything else would be gone by noon. He was obviously going to have to hide uncle, but where?

He shrank back from the obvious answer, but there wasn't really an alternative. He was going to have to hide uncle somewhere—permanently—and he'd have to do it before very long. Dead people were probably like dead animals, so uncle would almost certainly start to smell in a few days.

Their living quarters had a solid wood floor; the dirt floor of the smithy was hard-packed, and customers frequently came in without much warning. The storeroom on one side of the smithy also had a dirt floor, though, and it had a door that was usually closed. There was all sorts of rubbish in the storeroom, but Rabbit was sure that he could drag most of it out—enough, anyway, to give him room for digging.

"At least he'll still be here," Rabbit murmured sadly.

*　　*　　*

At first, Rabbit had no serious problems at the smithy. Just about everybody in Weros knew that Uncle Beer-Belly had "bad days," and Rabbit had been doing most of the work for over a year now. As time went on, though, more and more of their regular customers came to realize that their old friend wasn't visiting his favorite taverns anymore, and they drifted away. Rabbit was sure that they just didn't believe that he was skilled enough to complete anything beyond the simplest of tasks, quite probably because his small size had convinced them that he was much younger than he claimed to be.

It soon reached the point where not a single customer would come to the smithy for weeks on end, and things began to get very tight.

There was plenty of money in Weros, but Rabbit wasn't getting what he felt to be his fair share. "Well, uncle," he murmured to the storeroom door, "it looks like I'm going to have to do something else. I think maybe I'll try the waterfront for a while."

The waterfront of Weros was famous in the Land of Maag as one of the favorite places for sailors (or pirates) to celebrate recent successes. A sailor's favorite form of celebration involved large amounts of strong drink, and it was not at all uncommon to see sailors sleeping under the tables in taverns or even in alleys or gutters. A sailor that far gone in drink seldom had much money left in his purse, but Rabbit didn't really need all that much. He needed money to buy food, but that was about all.

As he spent more and more time on the waterfront, Rabbit became fascinated by the longships. A sailor on a longship would be as free as the wind, and he'd have money to burn any time he reached a port.

There was one ship in particular that seemed to Rabbit to be the most beautiful one in the harbor. She was called the *Seagull,* and Rabbit frequently dreamed of sailing out to sea as a member of her crew. It was a dream that had almost no chance of coming true, of course. Maag sailors were very large men, tall and bulky. Rabbit was positive that Sorgan Hook-Beak, the captain of the *Seagull,* would howl with laughter should he be foolish enough to apply for a berth on board his ship.

But then he discovered that among the members of the crew of every longship afloat there was a smith. That bit of information raised some interesting possibilities. Rabbit had recently turned sixteen, and his whiskers were thick enough to convince people that he wasn't really a child, despite his short stature. If he could somehow persuade Sorgan to give him a chance to display his skills as a smith, he might very well become a member of the *Seagull*'s crew.

A few careful questions gave him the name of the *Seagull*'s current smith, a bulky fellow named Borkad, and Rabbit's quick mind came up with a somewhat devious plan.

First he was going to need a bit more money, so he roamed about the muddy streets on the waterfront for most of the night, looking for targets of opportunity.

By the time the sun came up, Rabbit's purse had started to get fairly heavy. There had been a few occasions when the sailor whose purse Rabbit had just filched wasn't quite as far gone in drink as he'd appeared, but, as his name suggested, Rabbit could run very fast.

He asked around the waterfront and found the name of Borkad's favorite tavern, and then he went back to the smithy to catch a few winks. He'd definitely have to be on his toes this coming evening, and he was almost falling asleep on his feet right now.

His plan wasn't really all that elaborate. He'd locate Borkad and slip in the fact that they practiced the same occupation. Then, while they were talking shop, he'd buy the *Seagull*'s current smith enough strong grog to put an entire ship's crew to sleep. He wanted to be absolutely certain that when the *Seagull* sailed from Weros, Borkad would not be on board.

He woke up just before sunset and went on back to the waterfront. He glanced into The Sailor's Home and saw Borkad sitting by himself at a table at the rear of the tavern. It appeared that he was not completely sober, and it seemed to Rabbit that he was spacing his drinks out. That suggested that he was getting close to the bottom of his purse, so it was time to move in on him.

Rabbit went on into the tavern and approached Borkad's table. "I've heard tell that you're the smith on one of those ships out in the harbor," he said.

"What's it to you?" Borkad demanded.

"I'm a smith myself, and I've always been curious about how a man can practice our trade out at sea."

"It ain't really all that much different from the way you landbound smiths do your job," Borkad said.

"The one thing that sort of puzzles me is how you manage to avoid having the sparks from your anvil set fire to the ship," Rabbit said, sitting down across the table from Borkad.

"Easiest thing in the world," Borkad declared. "All you've really got t'do is pour buckets of water on the deck afore you start t'hammer."

"I *knew* there had to be an answer. Let me buy you another tankard of grog."

"I'd appreciate that," Borkad conceded. "My purse is about to come up empty."

"More grog!" Rabbit called to the tavernkeeper. "There's another thing that's been pestering me," he went on. "Is there really all that much for a smith to do on a ship?"

"We always spend a lot of time bangin' the anvil with our hammer."

"What for?" Rabbit asked. "Why do that?"

Borkad gave him a bleary-eyed grin. "Just pretendin' t'be busy," he admitted. "If'n the smith on board a ship ain't poundin' on 'is anvil, the fellers as tells the crew what to do will find other things t'keep him busy."

The tavernkeeper brought them two brimming tankards, and Rabbit paid him.

"Thankee, little friend," Borkad said.

"My pleasure," Rabbit replied.

After three more tankards, Borkad was barely coherent, and Rabbit suggested that they might want to visit a different tavern. He was quite sure that the other sailors on board the *Seagull* knew that Borkad spent most of his time in Weros at The Sailor's Home, so it was very important to make sure that the tipsy smith wasn't there when they came looking for him.

It was about midnight, and they were in a small, seedy-looking tavern some distance from the waterfront when Borkad slid off the bench where they were sitting to lie snoring under the table.

Rabbit quietly stood up and went outside. "So far, so good," he murmured, walking back toward the waterfront.

The *Seagull* was tied to a wharf not far from The Sailor's Home tavern, and Rabbit crouched in the shadows at the foot of the wharf to look things over. There were a couple of sailors on deck who were probably supposed to be keeping watch, but they didn't seem to be taking the job very seriously. They were both back near the stern, and they were paying much closer attention to a brown jug than they were to anything else.

Rabbit's frequent conversations with seagoing men in the taverns of Weros had given him a fair idea of the general layout of the standard Maag longship, and it seemed to him that the best place to hide on the *Seagull* would probably be in what sailors called the "rope locker." On most longships this was a small compartment below the deck and at the very bow, where it was too narrow for anything else. If the sailors had been telling Rabbit anything at all close to the truth, the rope locker was *never* opened during the first month or so after the ship left port, since all the rigging was carefully checked before the ship set sail.

The *Seagull*'s mooring line gave Rabbit easy access, and he was below the deck at the bow of the *Seagull* in a few moments. Then he waited, listening intently, but he heard nothing. In all probability, most of the crew were still ashore, enjoying their fifth, or maybe sixth, "last drink."

He crept forward in the darkness with one hand outstretched. After he had gone no more than a few feet, his hand touched a wooden panel. He located two metal hinges on one side and the handle on the other. "This *has* to be it," he exulted. He carefully opened the door, wincing as the hinges squealed. Then he reached inside, and his hand encountered well-coiled rope.

He carefully checked his water flask and the half loaf of bread he'd brought with him, and then he crawled inside his temporary home and quietly pulled the door shut behind him.

He remained in the rope locker for two days to make sure that the *Seagull* was a long way out to sea. Then he braced himself and went up onto the deck. "Where would I find the cap'n?" he asked a sailor who was leaning on the rail.

"Back near the stern," the sailor replied. He looked more closely at Rabbit. "You're a new man, ain't you? I don't think I've ever seen you afore."

"Fairly new," Rabbit replied evasively. Then he braced himself and walked on back to the stern. He'd never actually met Sorgan Hook-Beak, but the captain wasn't too hard to recognize. His broken nose was a clear indication of how he'd come by his name. "Ho, Cap'n," he called.

Sorgan broke off the conversation he'd been holding with two other men. "Who are you?" he demanded.

"My name's Rabbit, and I'm the new smith here on the *Seagull*."

"How did you come up with that peculiar notion, little man?" a sailor with enormous hands demanded.

"I came across a man named Borkad back in Weros, and he sold me his position here on the *Seagull*. Since I'm probably the best smith in the whole Land of Maag, the *Seagull*'s lucky that I chose her, rather than some other ship."

"It don't look t'me like you're even big enough to pick a hammer up, much less swing one," a huge sailor standing at Hook-Beak's side scoffed.

"I manage," Rabbit said tersely.

"I don't see that we've got much choice, Ox," Hook-Beak said. "Nobody could find Borkad before we sailed out from Weros, so now we're out here without a smith. Let's not make up our minds until we see what this little man can do."

And that, of course, had been the one thing that Rabbit had really wanted.

"That's a mighty fine looking weapon," the man called Ox said admiringly when Rabbit presented him a well-made war axe.

"That *is* a pretty good-looking axe there," the one called Ham-Hand agreed. "It looks to me like we might just have come up lucky. The little fellow ain't none too big, but he seems t'know what he's doing. It's up t'you, cap'n, but I'd say that we might want t'keep him. Old Borkad couldn't'a made an axe like that one in a hunnerd years."

"Let me see that," Sorgan said, taking the axe from Ox. He looked closely at it, absently scraping his thumb across the edge.

"Careful, Cap'n," Ox warned him. "She's sharp enough t'shave with."

Sorgan gave the axe a couple of experimental swings. "Not bad at all," he admitted. "What's your name, little man?"

"They call me Rabbit, Cap'n, probably because I can run about twice as fast as anybody else."

"Don't run off right now. We'll give it a try and see how you're going to work out, but I'm getting a hunch that you're going to be with us for quite a long time."

"Whatever suits you, Cap'n," Rabbit agreed, resisting a strong urge to dance for joy.

*   *   *

Rabbit discovered that there were a few drawbacks to life at sea. The weather wasn't always calm and sunny, and sometimes the wind was ferocious. There was also the tiresome business of standing watch. It was sort of necessary, of course, but standing in the bow of the *Seagull* looking at empty water could get very boring after a few hours.

Night watch, of course, was even worse. The hours seemed to drag by so slowly that each night on watch seemed to last for a week or more.

Rabbit could never really recall just exactly when it was that he became aware of the fact that the stars were not always in the same place in the night sky. At first he was quite certain that like the sun and the moon, they rose and set as they circled the world; but as he watched them more closely, he came to realize that it wasn't that way at all. He didn't mention his speculation to the other sailors on the *Seagull,* but his curiosity even led him to volunteer for night watch.

After a few months of close observation, it came to him that it was not the stars that were moving. It was the *Seagull.* If she was sailing east, certain stars—or groups of stars—rose higher in the night sky. If she was sailing westward, back toward the Land of Maag, they sank back down toward the eastern horizon.

Then one night it dawned on him that the friendly stars had been giving him the exact location of the *Seagull* every time he looked up at them.

He thought that was terribly nice of them.

Rabbit had always been painfully aware of the fact that the men of the Land of Maag who were of "normal" size viewed small men as defective—not only in their stature but also in their mental capabilities. The notion that small size meant small brains was locked in stone in the general Maag consciousness, and Rabbit carefully and very gradually began to take advantage of that prevailing prejudice. If he pretended to be simple-minded, he could quite easily avoid the more unpleasant chores on board the *Seagull*. The crew recognized his skill as a smith, but over the years they all seemed to reach the conclusion that his mind shut down when the fire in his forge went out. That suited Rabbit right down to the ground. To his way of looking at things, "easy" outranked "hard" more than just a little bit.

Things were going along very well for Rabbit, but then on a summer day, just after the men of the *Seagull* had looted yet another slow-moving Trogite ship, a sudden sea current grabbed the *Seagull* and swept her off in an easterly direction, and no amount of rowing by the oarsmen could pull her free.

Rabbit was more than a little worried as the *Seagull* rushed eastward. The stars were telling him that she was moving faster and farther than he'd ever thought possible. It was obvious—to Rabbit, at least—that something very unnatural was going on here.

Eventually, they made landfall on the coast of a very unfamiliar land covered with enormous trees. It seemed at first that the strange land was devoid of humans, but then they came across a village of crudely built huts, and a tall, bleak-faced man called Longbow told Captain Hook-Beak about an opportunity that seemed to Rabbit just too good to be true.

Rabbit observed that the Land of Dhrall was a peculiar sort of place with peculiar people and peculiar animals. When the *Seagull* reached the village of Lattash, he added the rulers of that land to his list of peculiarities. Lady Zelana was beautiful, there was no question about that, but she had Sorgan Hook-Beak bent over backward in almost no time at all. Rabbit had his suspicions about Sorgan's awed report of the amount of gold she had piled up in her cave. If she was that rich, why was she living in a hole in the ground?

Rabbit decided to avoid her, just to be on the safe side, but he did enjoy the company of the sweet, pretty little girl, Eleria.

When the *Seagull* returned to the first village she'd visited, the tall, grim-faced native called Longbow joined them, and he almost immediately saw right through the clever game Rabbit had spent years perfecting. They got along quite well, though, and Rabbit offered to replace Longbow's stone arrowheads with much superior ones made of iron. As the two of them worked together during the long voyage back to the Land of Dhrall, they became much better acquainted. Unlike the Maags, Longbow made no issue of Rabbit's size, and he encouraged his new friend to assert himself a bit more.

Captain Hook-Beak had devised a clever plan involving gold bricks to recruit other Maag ship captains to assist him in the upcoming war in Zelana's part of the Land of Dhrall, but Rabbit fully agreed with his friend Longbow that *some* of the captains might very well have slightly different plans.

The situation almost compelled Rabbit to drop his clever pose as a little dimwit and to take an active part in Longbow's ridiculous plan to counter the scheme of an unscrupulous ship captain who went by the name of Kajak. He didn't like it too much, but Longbow was the only friend that Rabbit had ever had since the death of Uncle Beer-Belly, so Rabbit wasn't about to let him down.

2

Rabbit still had mixed feelings about the Kajak affair as Sorgan's fleet set sail from the harbor at Kweta. His sudden celebrity as "the little fellow who helped Longbow that night" had given his ego quite a boost, there was no question about that, but celebrity was the last thing Rabbit really wanted. Inconspicuousness had been his goal since the day he first joined the crew of the *Seagull*. The standard Maag conviction that "bigger is better" had made the pose fairly easy, and his mock simplemindedness had convinced Sorgan and the others that a few easy tasks were about all he was good for. It had made his life less exhausting, and that was all that really mattered.

The only significant task that had ever been laid on his shoulders had involved the *Seagull*'s smithy, and that had worked out rather well. If he happened to be standing at his anvil tapping on a piece of iron with his hammer, Ox and Ham-Hand would find other sailors to attend to the more tedious chores.

He was required to stand watch, of course. No sailor can escape that task, and Rabbit much preferred night watch, when

217

the captain was asleep. When things were going well, Rabbit could go for weeks on end without once seeing Sorgan.

That didn't particularly bother him.

Rabbit had based his previous computations of the *Seagull*'s speed and location on the location of a specific cluster of stars in the night sky relative to the eastern horizon, and in the past he'd found that if the *Seagull* was moving at her normal rate of speed, those stars would be a hand's breadth higher in the sky than they had been the previous night. It all fit together quite well, and Rabbit had been certain that his numbers were very accurate. When the current had seized the *Seagull* and swept her off to the Land of Dhrall however, Rabbit had almost discarded his entire set of computations, but now that he knew that Zelana could alter things to suit her purposes, he dropped the term "impossible." When Zelana was involved, nothing was really impossible.

Sorgan's fleet left the harbor at Kweta at first light on a blustery winter morning, and once they were at sea, the wind seemed almost to die. Then it came up again, but now it came out of the west. Most of the crew of the *Seagull* viewed the change of the wind as a stroke of good luck. Rabbit, however, was fairly certain that luck had very little to do with it.

Despite the fact that it was winter now, Sorgan's fleet made good time, and they rounded the northern end of the Isle of Thurn after little more than two weeks at sea. Had the sky been clear, Rabbit might have been able to keep better track of their progress, but the clouds hid the stars from him.

He didn't think that was very nice at all.

"Does she really need to blot the stars out like that?" he complained to Longbow one evening as the fleet made its way down the forested west coast of Dhrall.

"Go ask her," Longbow suggested.

"Ah—no, I don't think I'll do that. I wouldn't really want to irritate her."

"Good thinking," Longbow said without so much as a smile.

It was about midday on a chill day when the fleet turned into the narrow inlet that opened out into the bay of Lattash, where the fleet of Sorgan's cousin Skell lay at anchor. The sky was cloudy, so there were no shadows, and it seemed to Rabbit that the village huddled in the chill air with the snowy mountains looming ominously above it.

Rabbit noticed that the village had more than doubled in size since he'd last been there, but most of the additions appeared to be temporary. The new huts were along the edges of the old village, for the most part, and there were even several of them standing atop the berm that separated the original village from the river. The smoke from the huts seemed to hang in the chill air, and what few natives were out in the open wore thickly furred capes, and they stepped right along. Rabbit knew that winter was an unpleasant time almost anywhere, but it seemed even worse here in the Land of Dhrall.

A narrow canoe came skimming out across the bay from the village. Red-Beard was in the rear of the canoe, and Sorgan's cousin Skell, a lean, sour-faced man in a heavy fur cloak, was seated in the bow. Rabbit laid his hammer down on the anvil to watch and listen.

"You must have picked up a good following wind, Sorgan," Skell called when the canoe came to within shouting distance.

Sorgan shrugged. "Lucky, maybe," he called back. "How have things been going here?"

"Not all that great," Skell replied as Red-Beard paddled his canoe up beside the *Seagull*. "You and I can keep our men pretty much under control, but some of these ship captains you saddled me with seem to have no idea of the meaning of the word 'discipline,' and they've got barrels and barrels of grog on board their ships. As soon as we got here, a fair number of the men in the fleet went on a rampage. I guess they thought that every hut here in Lattash had walls of solid gold, and they all seemed to get *those* kinds of ideas about the womenfolk here. That caused a lot of trouble. The Dhralls killed a few dozen of the rowdier ones, and things were real nervous for a while. I had a few sailors—and a couple of ship captains—flogged, and things quieted down after that."

Sorgan winced. "Wasn't that a little extreme?"

"We were right on the edge of open war, Sorgan," Skell replied. "I had to do *something* to get back on the good side of the Dhralls."

"Have you seen any sign of the enemy yet?"

"I haven't personally," Skell said as Red-Beard pulled his canoe alongside the *Seagull,* "but the Dhralls were scouting up on the rim of the ravine that river comes down through, and they told us that the invaders were coming downriver and that they had us outnumbered by more than just a little. The weather turned foul on them, though, and I don't think they'll be moving very much for a while. They're bogged down in about fourteen feet of snow right now."

"It sounds like luck's on our side for a change," Sorgan observed.

"I wouldn't reach for my dice just yet," Skell said, standing up and reaching for the rope ladder hanging down the side of the *Seagull.* "The weather around here can change in the blink of an eye." He climbed up the ladder to the *Seagull*'s forward deck, and he and Sorgan gravely shook hands off to one side of Rabbit's anvil.

Sorgan looked across the harbor to the village. "There seems to be quite a few more huts than there were when I came here last summer." He said.

"Old-Bear's tribe came here right after the local Dhralls saw the enemy coming down the ravine," Skell reported. "The two biggest tribes here in western Dhrall are here, and there are more on the way."

"Were you able to get any of your men up into the ravine before the weather turned bad?" Sorgan asked.

"Quite a few. We had to scout up on the north side of the ravine because a snowslide had blocked off the side closer to the village, but I picked the narrowest spot I could find and put a couple dozen ship crews to work building a fort across it. I doubt that they got much of it done before that snowstorm came out of nowhere. I haven't been able to get anybody up there to find out, though. The snow's too deep." Skell looked out at Sorgan's fleet. "It looks a little skimpy to me, Sorgan. Was that the best you could manage?"

"Things got a little wild back in Kweta right after you left, Skell. Do you remember Kajak?"

Skell made an indelicate sound.

"That comes close to what he really was," Sorgan agreed. "He came up with a scheme to get his hands on all that gold I had on board the *Seagull,* but he came up against Longbow and Rabbit here. You wouldn't *believe* how many people the two of them killed in short order. Anyway, after that I went back to hiring more ship captains, but then Lady Zelana's brother came by and told her that things were starting to heat up over here, and that her people were going to need us before too much longer. I left your brother Torl back there to recruit more ships and men. He should be along in a couple of weeks."

"We'll probably need him," Skell said, "but the way things stand right now, I don't think anybody's going to be able to move around very much until the snow melts."

"We'd better start making plans for what we'll need to do after that happens," Sorgan said. "The snow might hold the invaders off for a while, but it won't last forever. When it melts, we'd better be ready to deal with them."

"That's what we're getting paid for, I guess," Skell agreed.

"Where's Longbow?" Red-Beard quietly asked Rabbit as Sorgan and Skell continued their discussion.

"He's back in Lady Zelana's cabin," Rabbit replied. "Do you need to talk with him?"

"There are a few things he should probably know about. You might as well come along too, Rabbit. That way, I won't have to tell the story twice."

They went on back to the stern of the *Seagull,* and Rabbit tapped lightly on the door of Sorgan's old cabin.

"You can come in if you want, Bunny," Eleria called, "but don't forget to wipe your feet."

Rabbit sighed, rolling his eyes upward.

"Does she say that very often?" Red-Beard asked.

"Every single time," Rabbit said, opening the door.

As usual, Eleria was sitting on Longbow's lap, but the tall man firmly put her down on the floor and stood up. "Has there been any trouble between the tribes?" he asked Red-Beard.

"Right at first I guess there was," Red-Beard replied with a faint smile. "The younger men didn't get along with each other too well—you know how that goes."

"Oh, yes," Longbow agreed with a note of resignation.

"Things had quieted down by the time I came back here with Skell's fleet, though. My chief, White-Braid, and your chief, Old-Bear, spoke *very* firmly with the young ones of the two tribes, and everyone's behaving now."

"Does that sort of thing happen very often here in Dhrall?" Rabbit asked.

"All the time," Red-Beard said with a shrug. "Young men seem to need the attention of others, and as soon as one of them says, 'My tribe's better than your tribe,' the fights begin."

"That has a familiar ring to it," Rabbit said with a faint smile. "Tavern brawls over in Maag break out for almost exactly the same reason. I guess that the only good thing about being young is that you'll get over it—eventually."

"Where did Chief Old-Bear set up his lodge?" Longbow asked Red-Beard. "I should probably speak with him before too long."

"His lodge is near the berm," Red-Beard replied. "He spends quite a bit of his time with your tribe's shaman, doesn't he?"

Longbow nodded. "They get along with each other quite well. One-Who-Heals is very wise—and very practical. He explained many things to me before I went to the hunt." He paused. Rabbit got the distinct impression that they were approaching a subject they weren't supposed to mention in his presence. "There seems to be more snow on the ground than there was when we left," Longbow continued quite smoothly. "How long did the storm last?"

"Ten days or so, actually," Red-Beard said. "It was a very unusual kind of snowstorm, though. I can't remember the last time I saw snow falling out of a clear blue sky."

"That *would* be a bit peculiar, wouldn't it?" Longbow agreed.

"Storms that come out of nowhere seem to be turning up fairly often here lately," Rabbit observed.

The three of them looked inquiringly at Zelana.

"All right," she said. "I cheat a little bit now and then. Don't make a big issue of it. I just wanted to be sure that nothing serious got under way until Sorgan's fleet reached Dhrall. Snow isn't quite as cold as ice, but if there's enough snow, it pretty much freezes everything in place."

"Couldn't we just leave all that snow up there in the mountains, Beloved?" Eleria suggested. "The bad things won't be able to move until it melts, and if it never melts, they'll have to stay right where they are."

Zelana shook her head. "Father Earth wouldn't permit that, Eleria. A year without a summer would kill too many plants and animals, and plants and animals are as dear to him as people are. We can keep that snow up there for a few weeks longer, but then we'll have to let it melt off. If Veltan can get here before the snow melts, everything should be all right. If he's delayed, things might start to get interesting."

"Your brother's bringing help?" Red-Beard asked.

Zelana nodded. "Trogite soldiers."

"Trogites!" Rabbit exclaimed. "You expect Trogites to help Maags? That's not very likely, you know. Trogites hate us like we were some kind of disease."

"Veltan's paying them *not* to hate you," she told him. "You can go back to hating each other after the war's over and you've all gone home."

Rabbit shrugged. "It's your war, Lady Zelana, so we'll do things any way you want us to, but I think there might be trouble before the war's over."

"There's all the trouble we're likely to need camped up at the head of the ravine right now, Rabbit," Red-Beard said.

"Did any of those rampaging sailors happen to find Lady Zelana's cave?" Rabbit asked him.

"No," Red-Beard answered. "Chief White-Braid told the young men to cover the cave mouth with bushes and tree limbs and then put a couple of huts in front of it. There were guards, but they weren't too obvious."

"I think it's time for Eleria and me to go back to the cave," Zelana decided.

"I'll take you there," Red-Beard offered.

"That would be nice," Zelana said. "Rabbit, go tell Hook-Beak that he can have his cabin back now."

"I'll need to get my canoe out of the forward hold," Long-bow said to Zelana. "Do you want me to bring Rabbit to the cave?"

"I think so, yes. See what Sorgan has to say about it first, though. Let's not ruffle Hook-Beak's feathers if we don't really have to."

Rabbit was a bit surprised by Zelana's decision to include him in the rather select society of the cave. Despite what had happened in Kweta, Rabbit still didn't think of himself as one of any kind of inner circle. He gave it some thought as he went forward to the bow of the *Seagull*. "Lady Zelana's going ashore now, Cap'n," he reported. "She says you can have your cabin back now."

"Well *finally*," Sorgan said. "Things might go back to being normal now. Has she left yet?"

"She's on the way, Cap'n. Red-Beard's taking her and Eleria ashore in his canoe. Longbow's hauling his canoe up out of the forward hold as well, so we'll have the *Seagull* to ourselves for a change."

"I think maybe you should go stay in that cave with Lady Zelana, Rabbit," Sorgan said with a thoughtful squint. "She likes you, so keep her happy. Let's not lose sight of the fact that a lot of the gold in that cave's going to be ours when this is over. Make sure that it's well guarded."

"I'll do the best I can, Cap'n," Rabbit promised. Then he went back out on deck and helped Longbow lower his canoe into the water.

"Did he argue with you about it?" Longbow asked as they both settled into the canoe.

Rabbit grinned at his friend. "I didn't even have to ask. He really, *really* wants somebody he knows near all that gold stacked up in the cave."

Longbow nodded and then pushed his canoe away from the *Seagull* with his foot, picked up his paddle, and started them toward shore. "Lattash seems much larger than our village," he observed as they approached the beach.

"Some of that's probably because the people of your tribe moved here while we were off in Maag trying to pick up a lot of ships," Rabbit suggested. Then something occurred to him. "You've never been down here, have you, Longbow?" he asked.

"We usually avoid the villages of other tribes, Rabbit," Longbow explained. "The chieftains of the various tribes occasionally meet, but usually in open meadows, where there's not much chance of surprises."

"You folks here in Dhrall are kind of nervous, aren't you?"

"Cautious, Rabbit, cautious. It's very rare for the people of one tribe to completely trust the people of other tribes. Wars between the tribes are very common." Longbow beached his canoe, the two of them pulled it up farther onto the sand, and then they trudged up toward the cave mouth.

Eleria was waiting near the front of one of the huts Red-Beard's people had erected to conceal the cave mouth. "What kept you?" she asked. "We've got company. The Beloved's big brother came here a little while ago, and they're talking right now back in the cave."

"Veltan again?" Rabbit asked her.

"No, Bunny, it's Dahlaine. He's the oldest one in the family, and he thinks he's the most important creature in the whole world. He tries to order the Beloved to do things, but she doesn't pay too much attention to him." Eleria giggled. "That drives him absolutely wild."

"You live with a very strange group of people, baby sister," Rabbit said.

"I know, and it's loads of fun."

Rabbit and Longbow followed her through the empty hut and back into the cave, where Rabbit saw Zelana speaking with a large, burly fellow dressed in bearskins. He had piercing eyes and an iron grey beard.

"Veltan told me that he might be able to lend me some of his Trogite soldiers," she was saying, "but I suppose that might depend on how soon he can get them here to Dhrall."

"I'll talk with him," the grey-bearded man promised. "Veltan's just a bit reticent sometimes. Are the Dhralls of your Domain gathering to meet the invaders?"

"Chief White-Braid was dealing with that while Eleria and I were busy over in Maag. I hate to admit this, Dahlaine, but I really should have paid more attention to what's been going on here in the West. There are some very serious animosities between several tribes that I might have been able to smooth over if I hadn't spent all those years swimming with my dolphins.

Fortunately, when White-Braid and Old-Bear joined together, they were fairly intimidating. Some of the tribes here didn't really want to join with the others, but they were prudent enough not to say so."

"Have you told your Maags about the true nature of the servants of the Vlagh yet?" the bearded Dahlaine asked his sister.

"Do we really want to go into the details before Veltan's Trogites arrive, Dahlaine?" she said a bit dubiously. "Once our outlander armies are here, we can keep them here, but if the word gets out too soon . . ." She left it hanging.

"You could be right, dear sister," Dahlaine conceded. He looked sternly at Rabbit. "Can we trust this one?" he asked.

"I think so. He's more clever than he appears to be, and he and Longbow are fairly close. There are still a few things he doesn't need to know quite yet. Why don't we let Longbow decide when to tell the outlanders what they'll be coming up against?"

"I think we should let One-Who-Heals describe our enemies to the Maags and the Trogites," Longbow suggested. "He knows much more about our enemies than anyone else. He trapped one of them when I was just a boy, and after it died, he boiled all the meat off so that only the bones were left. Then he showed me all of the creature's peculiarities. They aren't really very hard to kill, but one needs to be a bit cautious. I'll be speaking with Chief Old-Bear soon, and I'll ask him to speak with One-Who-Heals about this."

"That might be the best way to handle this, Dahlaine," Zelana said.

Rabbit looked at them suspiciously. There was something ominous about all this, and it was making him more than just a little uneasy.

Just then Red-Beard entered the cave. "You wanted to speak with me, Zelana?" he asked.

"Yes," she replied. "I think you and Longbow should show the members of the other tribes your new arrowheads and give them a few demonstrations. Sometimes people object to new things. Show them how well the new arrowheads work. Rabbit, I want you to go tell Hook-Beak that I want every loose bit of iron on every ship in his fleet, and I'll need the use of everybody who knows the least bit about working with iron. We're going to need as many iron-tipped arrows as possible."

Rabbit sighed. "Somehow I knew that something like this was going to turn up. Pounding out arrowheads day after day's likely to get tedious after a while."

"But you're the expert, Bunny," Eleria reminded him. "After you show the other iron-pounders how it's done, you'll spend all your time watching and telling them if they're doing it wrong."

"That's true, I suppose. When you get right down to it, I'll be the captain of the smiths, won't I?" The notion of being able to *give* orders instead of taking them lit a warm little fire in his heart.

"Don't let it go to your head," Zelana advised.

3

Rabbit set up his arrow shop on the beach near Zelana's cave, and there was trouble right from the start. The smiths from the other Maag ships objected violently when Rabbit told them that they'd be required to contribute every scrap of iron on board their ships, and they really didn't care much for the notion of working from dawn to dusk for weeks on end. A sea-going smith normally has life fairly easy. He might occasionally have to repair a pot for the ship's cook, repair a broken pulley, or sharpen a few swords and axes, but that was usually the extent of his labor.

"I don't see the point of this," Hammer, the bull-shouldered smith from the *Shark*, the ship of Sorgan's cousin Skell, declared. "We're the ones who'll do all the fighting, aren't we? If these natives are too timid to fight their own wars, they won't be of much use when the fighting starts."

"I'm not so sure about that, Hammer," one of the ironsmiths who'd been in the harbor of Kweta during Kajak's failed attempt on the *Seagull* said. "I've seen what that tall one they call Longbow can do with arrows when he sets his mind to it, and every enemy the Dhralls kill from a long way off is one less that *we'll* have to kill up close."

"I still think it's a waste of time and good iron," Hammer declared stubbornly.

Longbow came out of the cave just then, and Rabbit saw a quick way to put an end to all the complaining. "Are you busy right now?" he asked his friend.

"Not really, Rabbit. Why?"

"Hammer here doesn't quite see the point of what we're doing. I think this might go smoother if you show him and some of the others what you can do with your bow. Why don't you prove it to them?"

"No trouble at all," Longbow agreed. He looked around the beach and then went down to the water's edge and picked up a clamshell. Then he came back and handed it to Hammer. "Why don't you take this on down the beach?" he said. "I'll show you what a well-aimed arrow can do."

"That's a pretty small target," Hammer said dubiously.

"I've got good eyes. Hold it up over your head as you go so that I can see it."

Hammer grumbled a bit, but he started on down the beach holding the clamshell up over his head. "About here?" he called back after he'd gone a hundred paces.

"Farther," Longbow replied.

Hammer kept walking "Here?" he called at two hundred paces.

"Farther," Longbow called back.

"This is silly!" Hammer shouted as he walked on down the beach.

"Do you think that might be far enough to persuade them?" Longbow asked Rabbit.

"If you can hit it from here, I don't think we'll get any more arguments about this."

"Let's find out," Longbow agreed, drawing his bow.

"Aren't you going to tell him to lean it up against a log or something?"

"I can see it well enough where it is," Longbow replied, loosing his iron-tipped arrow.

The long, slender bow sang, and the arrow arched up and over the sandy beach. Then it began its descent.

The clamshell shattered into a thousand pieces when Longbow's arrow smashed it out of Hammer's hand.

Hammer danced around, swearing and shaking his hand. "You almost tore my fingers off!" he shouted.

"You were holding it too tight," Longbow called. "Should we break up more shells, or would you rather make arrowheads?"

Things went more smoothly after that. The ironsmiths of Sorgan's fleet hammered out arrowheads by the score, and the Dhralls of Lattash brought bundles of slender shafts. Soon there were dozens of arrows stacked in neat piles near the front of Zelana's cave. Rabbit felt a real sense of accomplishment as the sun settled slowly in the west.

The work proceeded rapidly for the next several days, and then the weather turned sour again, with rain along the coast and more snow up in the mountains. Rabbit had to suspend operations while the Dhralls of Lattash erected well-roofed sheds over the anvils and forges to keep the rain from putting out the fires.

It had been raining for three days, and the sheds were still under construction when Eleria came out of the cave and walked down to where Rabbit was sourly looking up at the murky sky. "How much longer are we going to have to put up with all this rain, baby sister?" he asked her.

"As long as the Beloved thinks we need it, Bunny," she replied. "I need a hug," she said then, holding her arms out to him. "Everybody's so busy that they don't have time for me anymore."

Rabbit embraced her, and she kissed him soundly. "That's

better," she said with a sunny smile. "Don't say bad things about the rain, Bunny. It's rain here, but it's snow up there in the mountains. The bad people can't move when it's snowing. Are you busy right now? The Beloved wants you to go fetch Hook-Big. There's somebody coming that she wants him to meet."

"I'll go get him," Rabbit agreed, and he turned and went on down the rain-swept beach to find somebody who could paddle a canoe without tipping it over.

Red-Beard wasn't doing much except watching the rain, so he agreed to paddle Rabbit out to the *Seagull*.

Sorgan was in his cabin, sourly looking out at the dismal rain. "This is the soggiest place in the whole world," he growled as Rabbit joined him.

"It's that time of year, Cap'n," Rabbit reminded him. "Lady Zelana wants you to meet somebody in her cave."

"Can't she bring him out here?"

"I suppose I could go ask her, Cap'n, but I don't think you'd like her answer very much."

Sorgan sighed and pulled on his heavy fur cape. Rabbit smiled, being careful not to let it show. His position on board the *Seagull* had noticeably changed over the past few weeks. Captain Hook-Beak, Ox, and Ham-Hand no longer ignored him or treated him like some feebleminded errand boy. His position as Longbow's assistant that night back in Kweta had rather quickly changed everybody's opinion of him.

Rabbit was of two minds about that. His new status definitely boosted his ego, but he was certain that he'd no longer be able to slip back into his previous anonymity. Whether he liked it or not, he did have a certain prominence now.

Captain Hook-Beak led the way out of his cabin to join Red-Beard on the rain-swept deck. "Does it rain like this every year?" Sorgan asked the leather-clad Red-Beard as they climbed down into the canoe.

"It's not unusual," Red-Beard replied. "It isn't cold enough to snow here on the coast, but the snow's really piling up in the mountains above us. That's not really a bad thing, you know. The enemy can't attack through deep snow."

"There's that, I suppose," Sorgan conceded grudgingly. "Just who is it Lady Zelana wants me to meet, Rabbit?"

"Eleria didn't say, Cap'n. Maybe Lady Zelana wants to surprise you."

"I can live without too many surprises," Sorgan grumbled.

Red-Beard smoothly beached his canoe not far from the mouth of Zelana's cave. There was an odd-looking boat anchored near the beach some distance on to the south. Rabbit was almost positive that it hadn't been there when Eleria had come out of the cave to tell him what Zelana wanted. "What kind of tub's that, Cap'n?" Rabbit asked.

"I think it's what they call a fishing sloop, Rabbit," Sorgan replied. "People on to the south of Maag have lots of them out on the water at certain times of the year when the fish are running. I'm not all that fond of dried fish myself, but Southerners seem to like them."

The three of them pulled Red-Beard's canoe above the high-water mark and then went on up the hill to the rickety-looking hut that concealed the mouth of Zelana's cave. Longbow, Chief White-Braid, and Chief Old-Bear were waiting for them, and they led the way on into the cave.

"Ah, there you are, Sorgan," Zelana said. "Now we can get started. You've already met my brother Veltan. The antique over there is our older brother, Dahlaine, and the overdressed lady is my big sister, Aracia. They've come to watch you destroy the invading force."

"I'll try not to disappoint them, Lady Zelana," Hook-Beak said. Then he looked inquiringly at the stranger standing beside Zelana's brother Veltan. The man had dark hair touched with silver at the temples, and he wore tight-fitting, glossy black leather clothing. His upper body was encased in a sort of iron vest, and he had a rounded iron helmet under one arm. There was a sheathed sword belted to his waist, and it reached almost down to his ankles. The hilt of the sword was quite heavy and long, suggesting that it was commonly wielded with both hands.

"This is Commander Narasan of the Trogite Empire, Captain Hook-Beak," Veltan introduced the soldier. "He's bringing a sizeable force here to aid you during the current unpleasantness."

"Captain," the Trogite said with a brief nod.

"Commander," Sorgan responded, also nodding. Then he straightened. "I guess we'd better get this right out in the open," he said. "Up until a little while ago I made my living robbing Trogite treasure ships, and I was very good at it. Lady Zelana persuaded me that I could earn much more gold if I gathered up a fleet and came here to fight this war for her. I know that it seems unnatural, but that puts you and me on the same side, and Maags and Trogites have never gotten along very well. Is this going to give you any kind of problems?"

"I'm a soldier, Captain Hook-Beak," the Trogite replied, "but I fight wars for gold, not for patriotism. I've fought wars against men I've called friends beside people I didn't like in the past. Then too, I don't really have much use for the greedy Trogites who swindle the natives of Shaan. Those poor savages don't even realize what gold's worth, so they're willing to trade it for worthless trinkets. Rob as many of those swindlers as you want to, Hook-Beak. It doesn't hurt my feelings in the slightest. There's plenty of gold here in the Land of Dhrall, and we'll earn every ounce we get by fighting this war. We won't cheat each other, and we won't cheat the people who pay us."

"We'll get along fine, then," Sorgan said with a faint smile. "I haven't seen the enemy myself, but the Dhralls tell me that I'm probably going to be seriously outnumbered when the snow melts and the enemy comes down through that river valley. How many men can you bring here, and how long do you think it'll take them to get here?"

"I have twenty thousand or so men on the way, Sorgan. They should be here in a week or so."

"I can probably hold out at least that long," Sorgan assured him. "I sent my cousin here with an advance fleet, and he had his people building fortifications a ways on up the ravine that'll probably be the enemy's invasion route. Everything stopped a few weeks ago, though. My cousin tells me that a snowstorm buried everything up there in the ravine, so nobody's moving at all." Sorgan scratched his cheek. "I really wanted to gather more ships and men back in Dhrall, but Lady Zelana was a little worried about what was happening here, so she ordered me to get here as soon as I could. I've got another cousin back home who's gathering up more ships and men, but I can't be certain sure when he'll get here. If things start to get tight, you and your army might just save the day for us. The way things stand right now, though, the enemy's buried up to his ears in snow up at the head of the ravine, and it looks like there's more snow on the way. We may not have to do any serious fighting until midsummer."

"This promises to be a very interesting war, doesn't it?" the Trogite Narasan observed mildly. "That's assuming that we don't kill each other before the *real* war starts."

"We'd really rather that you didn't, Narasan," Veltan said with a faint smile.

The Trogite's expression grew thoughtful. "It occurs to me, Captain, that even though we've both fought wars in the past, we probably don't fight in exactly the same way. As long as we're both here anyway, and since there's nothing of any urgency in the wind, wouldn't it be useful to pool our experience and get to know each other better? Is there anything in particular that you need right now?"

Sorgan squinted and scratched his cheek. "Not that I can think of right offhand."

"Uh . . . Cap'n," Rabbit said a bit hesitantly, "I really need more iron."

"Have you used up all we gave you when we first got here, Rabbit?" Sorgan asked, sounding a bit surprised.

"We're getting down to the bottom of the barrel, Cap'n. I've got a lot of smiths working on this, and if the rain ever lets up, we'll go through what little iron is left in a hurry."

"What are you building that needs so much iron, Sorgan?" Narasan asked.

"Arrowheads for the Dhralls. This tall one here is Longbow, and he's the only man I know of who can thread needles with his arrows from a half mile away. When we were gathering the fleet back in Maag, I was using gold for bait, and there was a greedy ship captain named Kajak who really wanted my gold. Five ships came at me one night in the harbor of a town called Kweta. Longbow stopped them with only Rabbit here to help him. People start to get real jumpy when everybody nearby suddenly starts sprouting arrows out of their foreheads. The Dhralls aren't really as helpless as they look, but they chip their arrowheads out of stone. Iron's better, so we started making iron arrowheads for them when we got here. Every Maag ship has a smith on board, and they've used up just about every scrap of iron in the whole fleet hammering out arrowheads. I've talked it over with Longbow, and we pretty much agree that when the time comes, I'll lead my men up along the bottom of the ravine while the Dhralls move along the rim on both sides. If there's a steady downpour of arrows out in front of my men, it'll cut down on the number of enemies we'll have to fight."

"Shrewd," Narasan said. "Who's your smith?"

"Rabbit here," Sorgan replied. "He's not very big, but he really knows how to work with iron."

"Are you familiar with other metals as well, Rabbit?" Narasan asked.

"I can work with copper if I have to," Rabbit told him, "but it's really too soft to make anything very useful."

Narasan reached into a leather pouch at his belt and took

out a handful of large round coins. "Could you make arrow-heads out of this?" He handed one of the coins to Rabbit.

Rabbit bounced the coin on the palm of his hand. It wasn't as heavy as iron, but it seemed harder and denser than copper. "It's possible, I suppose. What kind of metal is this?"

"It's called bronze. Trogites use bronze coins to buy things that aren't very expensive. I've got a fair-sized fleet coming along the coast, and there'll be thousands of those coins on those ships, as well as assorted tools and ornaments. The fleet should be here before long, and once it arrives, you'll proba-bly have all the bronze you'll need."

Rabbit thoughtfully snapped his fingernail against the bronze coin. "How hot a fire does it take to melt this?" he asked.

Narasan smiled. "I haven't the faintest idea. Why?"

"We've got forges as well as hammers and anvils," Rabbit explained. "If we can stoke up the fires in the forges and get them hot enough to melt this bronze, we could make molds out of clay while we're waiting for your fleet to get here. We'll bake the molds to make them hard, and pour melted bronze into those molds. That'd be a lot faster than hammering them into shape on our anvils. We'll turn out arrowheads by the thou-sands instead of hundreds."

"Ah . . . Commander?" Zelana's brother Veltan said then. "Correct me if I'm wrong, but aren't the anchors on your ships made of bronze?"

Narasan blinked, and then he started to laugh. "I guess I overlooked that," he admitted. "I wasn't alone, though. If I re-member correctly, the anchor on your little sloop's also made of bronze. That should give our little friend here enough for some experimentation, wouldn't you say?"

4

The steady drizzle continued for the next few days, and Rabbit brought his forge into Zelana's cave so that he could continue his work with Veltan's bronze anchor. Things went much faster, he discovered, if he chopped the anchor into chunks instead of trying to melt it down all at once.

The first few bronze arrowheads he produced were not quite heavy enough to satisfy Longbow, so he made his mold larger and then larger again. Once he'd produced one Longbow found satisfactory, he used it to produce clay molds with the help of the village potters. There was quite a bit of trial and error involved, but he finally got the procedure smoothed out, and then he concentrated on making more and more of the hard-baked clay molds. He was certain now that when Narasan's fleet arrived with all that bronze, he'd be ready. Once he'd produced several arrowheads that Longbow found to be satisfactory, his friend went off to the lodge of his chief. It seemed that Longbow and Old-Bear were very close, and the two of them conferred very often with the scrawny old fellow they called "the shaman." Rabbit wasn't exactly sure what the title meant. It seemed to be an odd mixture of religion, healing various illnesses, and tending to wounds and injuries.

Narasan was staying in Zelana's cave, awaiting the arrival of his fleet, and Sorgan Hook-Beak came by every day so that they could confer. They spent many hours poring over Veltan's roughly sketched map of the ravine above the village of Lattash while Rabbit was dressing off the bronze arrowheads.

"I wish this had more details," Narasan complained one morning, pushing the map aside.

Sorgan shrugged. "It's all we've got, so it'll have to do, won't it?"

Red-Beard and Longbow escorted their chiefs into the cave about then.

"Ah, Red-Beard," Narasan said. "You're just the man we wanted to see." He reached for the map. "This is a sort of picture of that ravine where we'll probably meet the enemy. Take a look at it and tell us what you think. Is it anywhere at all close to the real ravine?"

Red-Beard briefly examined the map. "This won't really help you very much," he said, handing the map back. "I've been involved in a few tribal wars in the past, and war's very much like hunting—except that the one I'm hunting is also hunting me. You can't hunt well if you base your decisions on a flat drawing. You need to look at the real ground."

"It's buried in snow right now," Sorgan reminded him.

"Your picture doesn't show you where the hills and gullies are, how much is covered with trees, or where the steep places are. If you're going to fight this war up in that ravine, your life could depend on those details."

"I would listen closely, Sorgan Hook-Beak," old Chief White-Braid advised in the stiffly formal manner that Longbow had told Rabbit was common among tribal chieftains. "Red-Beard has hunted that ravine since he was but a child, and he knows every tree and rock personally. We *must* win this war, since the creatures of the Wasteland will show us no mercy if we should lose."

"That's blunt enough," Sorgan replied. "But how can anybody draw a picture that isn't flat?"

Rabbit set his whetstone aside and carefully ran his thumb across the edge of the arrowhead he'd been sharpening. It was probably sharp enough to shave with, he concluded. The molds he'd made to cast the bronze arrowheads seemed to be working out very well.

Two things seemed to come together in his mind just then. "I think there might be a way to make a picture that isn't flat, Cap'n," he said.

"Lumpy ink, maybe?" Sorgan replied in a sarcastic tone of voice.

"Not exactly, Cap'n. Why not use wet clay instead? Red-Beard knows that ravine like the back of his hand, and the potters who helped me make the arrowhead molds told me that there's a huge clay-bank down by the river that they've been using for generations. If they bring basket-loads of that clay here to Lady Zelana's cave, maybe Red-Beard could make a lumpy picture out of clay somewhere in here out of the rain."

"What do you think, Red-Beard?" Sorgan asked.

"I don't know very much about making pots," Red-Beard said dubiously, "and my fingers are a little thick for fine details, I think."

"The potters have tools for that," Rabbit told him. All you'd have to do would be to tell them what shape you want. They can add clay or shave it off until they get it right."

"Almost like sculpture," Narasan mused. "It's got possibilities, Sorgan. Even if it's not absolutely accurate, it'll be much better than the rough sketch we've been using."

"It's worth a try, I guess." Sorgan agreed. Then he looked at Chief White-Braid. "How much longer is it likely to be until all that snow up in the mountains melts off?" he asked. "My people need to finish the forts they're building up in the ravine, but they can't get much work done when they're hip-deep in snow."

The silvery-haired old chief looked a bit startled. "How much snow falls in the Land of Maag?" he asked.

"Oh, we get snow, right enough, but nothing like these three-week storms you get here, and our snow usually melts off before the next snowstorm arrives."

"Ah," White-Braid said. "That might explain your lack of understanding of certain dangers here in the Land of Dhrall. Winter is old, and he patiently builds his snowbanks in the mountains over many long nights; but spring is young, and she's sometimes enthusiastic. Her breath is very warm, and the snow which patient old winter laid upon the mountains inch by inch will disappear overnight when she breathes upon it. Melted snow is water, and water yearns to rejoin Mother Sea. It is most unwise to be in one of the ravines when this happens. The river will overflow its banks, and like some huge wave, it will rush on down to the sea, tearing all that stands in its path from the place where it was."

"I would listen very closely here, Sorgan Hook-Beak," Longbow's Chief, Old-Bear, said firmly. "There is much snow in the mountains this year, and when winter's grip loosens, the water rushing home to the sea will rip rocks away from where they now rest, and it will uproot trees as if they were no more than twigs. No one with any sense lingers in a ravine at this time of year."

"So *that's* the purpose of that berm along this side of the river," Narasan observed. "It didn't seem to make any sense when I first saw it, but it does now. Does it keep the water back?"

White-Braid nodded. "We put it there to make it easier for the water to go on down to the sea rather than to wander around in our village. Do not, as Chief Old-Bear warned, remain in the ravine when the warm wind begins to blow, for if you do, you'll be washed away."

"That gets right to the point, doesn't it?" Sorgan said. "I think my cousin had better get word to his men up there. It's time for them to leave their forts and find some place where their feet won't get wet."

"Does this same sort of thing happen all along the coast, Chief White-Braid?" Narasan asked. "I've got about twenty thousand soldiers on board ships that are coming up from the south, and we need those soldiers *here*, not fifty leagues out to sea."

Longbow had been standing off to one side, listening but not saying anything. "I think we might be overlooking something," he said finally. "Our enemies live in the barren Wasteland, where there are few streams, so they probably know little or nothing about these spring floods. I've spent many years hunting the creatures of the Wasteland, and I've seen very few of them in the winter. It's very difficult to move through the mountains when they're covered with snow, and even if That-Called-the-Vlagh *does* send its servants here during the winter, it's my guess that most of them will freeze to death up in the mountains or drown during the spring flood. That suggests that the Vlagh has no knowledge of these yearly floods, doesn't it?"

"Well, maybe," Sorgan agreed. "Where are you going with this, Longbow?"

"Red-Beard's scouts tell us that the invaders are camped among the snowdrifts right on the banks of the river that runs down through the ravine, and that's not really a safe place in the springtime. But if the Vlagh doesn't know about these spring floods, those who serve it wouldn't know either, would they? Isn't it quite possible that the spring flood will come as a complete surprise to them? Their march down the ravine might go quite a bit faster than they'd planned, but I don't think they'll stop when they reach Lattash. They'll invade Mother Sea instead, and very few people who live in deserts know how to swim. It might just turn out that we'll win this war without even raising a hand. The seasons and Mother Sea might just win it for us."

"We'll still get paid, though, won't we?" Hook-Beak demanded in a slightly worried tone of voice.

"I think you'd better take a look at this sculpted model of the ravine Red-Beard and the village potters are putting together, Skell," Sorgan was telling his cousin as the two of them trudged up the beach to Rabbit's arrow shop in the drizzling rain. "The time's going to come before much longer when you'll have to get your men up out of the ravine in a hurry. If old Chief White-Braid's anywhere close to being right about these spring floods, you're going to have something a lot like a tidal wave coming down the ravine without much warning."

"I think I should have held out for more gold, Sorgan," Skell said sourly. "This isn't turning out to be anything at all like I expected. This yearly flood could wipe out half my men."

Rabbit trailed along behind them as they entered the cave.

"The Beloved's busy right now," Eleria told them.

"We won't need to bother her," Sorgan replied. "I just want to show my cousin here Red-Beard's model of the ravine. How's he doing, by the way?"

"He was talking with Longbow this morning," Eleria replied. "He said that things are going a lot faster now, and that the potters should finish up by tomorrow. They don't need so much clay now."

"Oh?" Sorgan said. "Why not? I thought they'd need even more the farther uphill they go."

"Red-Beard was complaining about that, too," she said. "I made a little suggestion, and now they don't need nearly so much clay."

"What suggestion was that, baby sister?" Rabbit asked.

"They didn't really have to pile clay up in those great big heaps. We've got all those yellow blocks in that long passage, so I told them to stack the blocks up on the cave floor where they're building that model of the ravine and then slather clay on top of the blocks to make only the surface. It seems to be working quite well."

"You're slopping wet clay all over those gold bricks?" Sorgan almost screamed.

"It'll wash off after the war's over, Hook-Big," Eleria assured him. "It was just sitting there not doing anything, so I thought we might as well put it to work."

Sorgan spluttered a bit, but then he threw his hands in the air. "I give up," he said.

"Isn't he nice, Bunny?" Eleria said with a fond little smile.

Red-Beard was standing near the foot of his sculpted map, carefully inserting spruce twigs into the damp clay that represented the south side of the ravine.

"Is the forest there really *that* dense, Red-Beard?" Commander Narasan, who was standing nearby, asked.

"Denser," Red-Beard replied. "It thins out farther on up, but the forest near the bottom of the ravine is so thick that the only way to get through is to follow the game trails."

"That might give my soldiers a bit of trouble," Narasan mused. "We aren't used to fighting wars in thick brush. We like open fields where we can see the enemy."

Red-Beard shrugged. "If we can't see them, they can't see us. If Longbow's right about how stupid the servants of the Vlagh really are, we probably won't encounter very many of them near the bottom of the ravine. The spring flood should thin them out for us. We might start seeing a few of them farther on up the ravine, but the trees up there are much farther apart."

"How are things going, Narasan?" Sorgan asked.

"Better than any of us had anticipated, Sorgan. I think mapmaking just grew up. Red-Beard's sculpture here makes every map I've ever seen look like the scribblings of a child."

"Can you point out the place where your men were building their fort before the snow came, Skell?" Sorgan asked his cousin.

Skell peered down into the imitation ravine. "It's right about here, I think," he replied, pointing at a spot some distance upstream. "The riverbanks are narrow, and that makes things a lot easier. That wasn't the main reason I picked that spot, though. The walls of the ravine are straight up and down there, and if I butt walls right up against those flat faces, I'll be able to block off the whole ravine. Nobody's going to get past me, Sorgan."

"How far along had your men gone before the snow came?"

"We had the north bank fairly well blocked off by then. The south bank should be simpler. Four or five big boulders are about all it's going to take. Then we'll start on the walls that'll block off the benches."

"Do you think your fort down by the river's going to stay put when that spring flood comes down the ravine?"

"It should, cousin. We didn't build it out of pebbles. We levered large boulders off that shelf that runs along both sides of the river. Things went faster that way, and if a boulder's so big that it takes a hundred men to budge it, it'll probably stay put no matter how much water comes down the ravine. I wasn't really thinking about floods when we picked the spot, though. I was just looking for a place that'd be easier to defend."

"How did you learn so much about land warfare, Skell?" Narasan asked curiously. "I thought you Maags did your fighting at sea."

Skell smiled. "When Sorgan and I were only boys, we joined the crew of a Maag ship captain called Dalto Big-Nose, and Big-Nose was famous for going after gold, no matter where it was—at sea or on land. His crew learned about fighting on land the hard way. We know which kinds of barricades are the most difficult to get across because we used to have to climb over all kinds of them to get at the gold Big-Nose wanted. A man can learn a lot about barricades when he's standing behind one, but he learns a lot more when he's trying to get over them."

"Ah," Narasan said. "That *would* be educational, I suppose."

Zelana quietly came into the torch-lit chamber and glanced at Red-Beard's handiwork. "Very nice," she observed.

"Good morning, Lady Zelana," Sorgan greeted her. "I was sort of hoping that you'd stop by. Is it possible that the river used to be a lot wider than it is now? Those rocky benches about halfway up the sides of the ravine look to me like they might have been gouged out a long time ago."

"They were," she replied. "There was once a vast inland sea where the Wasteland is now, but Father Earth shuddered and shifted, and that sea broke loose and ate its way down out of those mountains."

"I'd say that we might want to use those benches when we go upriver, Narasan," Sorgan suggested. "It looks to me like it'd be faster that way than it'd be down along the riverbanks. The benches seem to be wider and not so cluttered up with boulders and thick brush, but that'll come later—*after* that spring flood's over. Right now, I think our main problem's going to be getting Skell's men up out of the ravine without alerting the enemy. I'm sure they've got scouts watching everything we do. If Skell's men pack up and move out, won't that let the enemy know that it's dangerous down at the bottom of the ravine? We're sort of hoping that the spring flood's going to take them by surprise, but if Skell's men run away, won't they get a little suspicious?"

"I'm afraid you might be right, Sorgan," Narasan said, frowning, "and I can't see any way around the problem."

Rabbit was carefully examining the model of the ravine. "What are all these little cuts that run down from the rim?" he asked Red-Beard.

"Small streams," Red-Beard replied. "They're dry for most of the year, but they fill up during the spring runoff, and over the years they've eaten their way down to the main river."

"Could a man get up to the rim if he followed one of them?"

"I've hunted deer in many of them. They're steep and narrow, but a man can make his way to the top through them if he really thinks it's necessary."

"Then if Skell's men got some sort of warning that the flood was about to start, they could get out of the ravine in a hurry if they went up through those cuts, couldn't they?"

"It's possible," Red-Beard conceded, "but who's going to warn them in time for them to escape the flood?"

"Which direction does that warm wind usually come from?"

"From across the sea to the west, and there's no 'usually' involved. The spring wind *always* comes from the west."

"Then it'll blow through Lattash quite a bit sooner than it'll go on up the ravine, won't it?"

"What are you getting at, Rabbit?" Sorgan asked.

"If it's that hot wind that sets off the flood, then Skell's men can stay right where they are until the wind starts to blow, but it might cut things a bit tight if they wait until it gets that far up the ravine. They won't really have to wait, though. There are a lot of Maag ships anchored out in the bay, and if you anchored a few way out at the inlet that leads into the bay, that hot wind would hit them hours before it made its way up to Skell's fort."

"So?" Sorgan asked.

"There's at least one sailor on every Maag ship with a horn, Cap'n, and if I remember right, the Dhralls have horns, too. If Red-Beard and Longbow were to space out their horn-blowers up there on the rim of the ravine, they can blow *their* horns as soon as they hear ours blowing out in the bay. We could send Skell all the warning he's likely to need by passing toots from the bay all the way up to the fort, and the toots will get there quite a while before the hot wind does. That'll let Skell know that it's time to pack up and get out of the ravine."

Skell gave Rabbit a hard, unfriendly look.

"It sounds like a good idea to me," Sorgan said.

"Would *you* like to wade through hip-deep snow to get up

there and tell the men at the fort to start listening for toots, Sorgan?" Skell demanded.

"I couldn't really do that, Skell," Sorgan replied with mock seriousness. "They're *your* men, after all, and it just wouldn't be right if I ran up there and started ordering them around, would it?"

The weather cleared off a couple of days later, and there was definitely a faint smell of spring in the air. Rabbit and the other Maag smiths were still hammering arrowheads from the last few scraps of iron they'd scavenged from Sorgan's fleet, but Rabbit periodically set his hammer aside and walked away from the loud banging noise of the arrow shop to listen carefully for the sound of the horns which were to announce the approach of the warm wind. Just about everybody in Lattash was listening for the horns. They all wanted that wind to arrive, but there were still many things that needed to be done first, so they were of two minds about it.

There was no sound of horns that day, but a fleet of lumbering Trogite ships sailed into the bay of Lattash about midafternoon. That definitely brightened Rabbit's day. His supply of bronze had finally arrived.

The Trogite Commander Narasan went down to the beach to greet his army, and after a bit of discussion he came back up the beach accompanied by four other armored Trogites. They were quite a bit shorter than the Maags Rabbit was more familiar with, and like Commander Narasan, they all wore tight-fitting black leather clothing, iron vests, and helmets. Their heavy swords were belted to their waists, and their boots were sturdy and well made.

Narasan paused as the Trogite delegation passed the arrow shop. "Would you like to join us, Rabbit?" he asked. "We're going to discuss our strategy with Sorgan and the others, and you may have some contributions to make."

"I'll sit in if you want," Rabbit agreed, "but I don't know too much about strategy and the like."

"That's what I'm hoping, Rabbit," Narasan replied. "Professionals tend to have their concepts locked in stone, so we overlook possibilities that might occur to a clever but inexperienced fellow like you."

Rabbit was a little dubious, but he joined the Trogite soldiers walking toward Zelana's cave.

"I don't want to be offensive," a very young and sincere-sounding Trogite soldier said to Rabbit, "but aren't you just a bit small for a Maag? I've never encountered Maags before, but I've heard that most of them are about seven feet tall."

"You wouldn't believe how many other people have noticed the same thing," Rabbit replied sourly.

"My name's Keselo, by the way," the young fellow introduced himself. "Is your name *really* Rabbit?"

"That's what they call me. I don't like it all that much, but up until a little while ago, the name served its purpose. My main goal in life was to sort of stay out of sight. Then Longbow came along and spoiled everything."

"Longbow?"

"He's a Dhrall archer who's so good with his bow that if we gave him enough arrows, he could probably win this war all by himself."

"You're joking, of course."

"I wouldn't be too sure," Rabbit replied.

Rabbit and Keselo followed Narasan and the three other Trogites into the cave, where Hook-Beak, Ox, and Ham-Hand were waiting.

"My men have finally arrived, Sorgan," Narasan said. "This bulky one who's going bald is Gunda. His lanky friend is Padan, the thin one is Jalkan, and the boy is Keselo. Gunda, Jalkan, and Padan have been with my army quite a while, and Keselo's sort of an apprentice."

"Gentlemen," Sorgan said with a brief nod, "this is my first mate, Ox, and the other one's my second mate, Kryda Ham-Hand."

"Colorful names," Padan observed.

"It's a Maag peculiarity, Padan," Narasan said. "Their names tend to be descriptive."

"Ah," Padan said. "My friends, Hairless Gunda, Scrawny Jalkan, and I are pleased to make your acquaintance, gentlemen."

"Watch your mouth, Padan," Gunda growled.

"I'm glad your people made it, Narasan," Sorgan said. "The weather could turn just about any time now, and once the snow melts off, things are likely to get exciting up in that ravine. I wouldn't want them to miss any of the fun."

"Did your cousin manage to get back up to where his people are building that fort?" Narasan asked.

"He hasn't sent word back yet, but he's probably there. Once Skell sets his mind to something, he usually manages to pull it off. He's stubborn and bad-tempered, but I can always count on him to do what he's supposed to do. Something came to me last night that we might want to think about. You and I are professionals, Narasan, and when we're working for money, we don't let old dislikes get in the way. Some of our people get excited when they come across traditional enemies, though—the younger fellows for the most part. I think it's one of those things a man has to outgrow. If we're going to move up the ravine along those benches on either side of the river, I think maybe I'd better take one side, and you should take the other. That'll put the river between us. The young fellows can shout curses at each other, but that's about all."

"I get your point, Sorgan," Narasan agreed. "Which bench do you want? North or south?"

"I'm going to move my ships away from yours anyway," Sorgan replied. "We don't want them to be anchored side by side for the same reason that we don't want our armies on the same side of the river. That'll put me closer to the north bench, so I'll take that one, if it's all right with you."

"Quite appropriate, Sorgan. Maags are Northmen, and we Trogites are Southerners."

"You know, I've noticed the same thing myself," Sorgan said.

5

The day was cloudy and calm, and the smiths were busy melting down Trogite bronze to cast more arrowheads in the clay molds. It was about midafternoon when Longbow came out of Zelana's cave. "I think you'd better come inside, Rabbit," he said. "There's something you should probably know about."

"Is it important? I'm sort of busy right now."

"Your friends here know what they're doing. You don't have to stand over them. This is a matter of some seriousness."

"Hammer," Rabbit called out to the smith of Skell's ship, the *Shark,* "take over here. Lady Zelana needs to talk with me."

"If you say so, Rabbit," Hammer agreed.

Hammer's obedient attitude gave Rabbit a warm little glow. He knew that it was sort of childish, but his recent elevation among the ranks of the Maags was very satisfying for some reason. "What's afoot?" he asked Longbow as the two of them went toward the mouth of Zelana's cave.

Longbow smiled faintly. "I wouldn't want to spoil the surprise for you, my little friend."

"Why do you always have to be that way?"

"For the fun of it, I suppose."

"You've been spending way too much time with baby sister, Longbow," Rabbit said sourly.

There seemed to be quite a crowd of people in Zelana's cave. Most of them were fairly important, and that suggested to Rabbit that there might be some sort of crisis in the wind. The two chiefs, White-Braid and Old-Bear, were standing off to one side, along with the thin old man who seemed to have quite a bit of authority in Old-Bear's tribe. Sorgan and Narasan, along with several other Maags and Trogites, were also there, and Zelana, her two brothers, and her older sister were at the back of the large chamber where Zelana spent most of her time. Eleria was there as well, along with three other children.

"I guess we'd better get started," Zelana said. "Perhaps I should apologize, but I'm not really very good at that, so I don't think I'll bother. The spring flood that's going to come down the ravine almost any day now will probably take the servants of That-Called-the-Vlagh completely by surprise, and most of them in the ravine right now aren't very likely to survive. That-Called-the-Vlagh has many, many servants, though, so after the flood subsides, the Vlagh will just send more. Sooner or later, our friends from the Land of Maag and the Trogite Empire will begin to encounter the creatures of the Wasteland, and those creatures have certain peculiarities that our friends need to be aware of, and that's why we're here today."

"Get to the point, Zelana," her bearded older brother told her.

"Do *you* want to do this, Dahlaine?" she asked tartly.

"It's your Domain, Zelana," he gave up. "Do it any way you want to."

"Thank you." Her tone was flat, even unfriendly. There seemed to be quite a few tensions in Zelana's family. "Now, then," she continued, "when Veltan and I first spoke with our outlander friends, we may have glossed over a few things they should probably know about now that they're here."

"Oh?" Sorgan said. "We know that the enemies are fairly

primitive, but it won't hurt if we know a little bit more about them. Do they happen to have some sort of exotic weapons or something?"

"Well . . . sort of," Zelana replied. She looked at Longbow. "Perhaps you should introduce them to One-Who-Heals," she suggested.

He shrugged. "If you wish," he replied. He gestured at the thin old Dhrall standing near Chief Old-Bear. "That is our shaman, One-Who-Heals," he told them. "As some of you know, I've been hunting and killing the servants of the Vlagh for twenty years now, but before I began, One-Who-Heals told me many things about those I wanted to kill." There was a flat, unemotional quality to Longbow's voice that sent chills through Rabbit. "I have spoken with our shaman, and he has agreed to tell you things you should know *before* you meet our enemies."

"I will do the best I can, Longbow," the old man replied. He squinted at the Maags and Trogites a bit dubiously. "What I am about to tell you may seem quite strange and unlikely," he told them, "but it would be wise of you to take what I say very seriously. That-Called-the-Vlagh holds dominion over the Wasteland, and it tampers with its servants in many peculiar ways so that they may better serve it. They who rightfully hold dominion over the Land of Dhrall—East and West, North and South—do not tamper with living creatures as does That-Called-the-Vlagh, so we have become what we are in response to the world around us. Life has many forms, and each form remains true to its origins. That-Called-the-Vlagh, however, crosses the boundaries between the various forms of life, min-gling characteristics to build creatures which often have most unnatural capabilities. When you see one, it will look very much like a small man wearing a hooded garment made of cloth. That is not what it is, however. It is only partially a man, and its garment is spun out from its own body, even as the web of a spider is."

"Are you saying that they're part *bug?*" Gunda exclaimed.

One-Who-Heals nodded. "But they are also part man and part reptile. That-Called-the-Vlagh, it would seem, ignores the boundaries which separate the various creatures in the Wasteland, and it joins them in ways which are most unnatural, to make them more suitable for their tasks. Those which we have seen here in the Domain of Zelana have snakelike fangs in their mouths and insectlike stingers above their wrists. They have no weapons of the kinds we carry, because they have no need for them. *Their* weapons are a part of their own bodies, because their fangs and stingers are venomous, and their venom kills almost instantly."

"You seem to have neglected to tell us about this, Veltan," the Trogite commander observed in a cool, unfriendly voice.

"If you take some care, it's not really a serious problem," Longbow said calmly. "I've been killing them by the hundreds for twenty years now."

"Naturally," Sorgan said, "but not too many of us are good enough with a bow to stick arrows into somebody who's a half mile away."

Longbow shrugged. "It's not that big a problem, Sorgan. The venom in their fangs and stings will kill anything—even others of their own kind. I've had quite a bit of success by simply sticking my arrowheads into the venom sacks of those I've already killed. The enemy has to be close enough to bite or sting you. A long spear with its point dipped in venom should keep you fairly safe."

"That's very interesting, Longbow," Sorgan said, "but just where are we going to be able to get our hands on that much poison?"

"In just a few days a flood should be coming down the ravine, Sorgan," Longbow reminded Rabbit's captain. "It'll carry all sorts of things down the river: trees, branches, old logs, dead enemies, bushes, and twigs. If we fish the dead enemies out of the river and drain their venom sacks, we should have more than enough poison to treat every spear, sword, and arrowhead we'll be using to kill the servants of the Vlagh."

"Well, maybe," Sorgan said dubiously.

Rabbit suddenly remembered something. "That strange-looking little fellow you killed with one of your old stone arrows back in Kweta was one of the things we're going to have to fight, wasn't it?"

"Of course," Longbow replied. "That's why I used one of my old arrows. They'd already been dipped in poison."

"I think we'll have to fort up, Commander," Gunda suggested. "We don't want to get too close to those things, do we? If they have to climb a wall to get to us, we should be able to poke them off that wall with poisoned spears, and after a while they'll get the point and go play someplace else."

"They will not do that," One-Who-Heals disagreed. "Once they have been told to attack, they will keep coming at you until they swarm over you or until the last one has been killed—and they will come at you in numbers beyond counting. They are not intelligent enough to be afraid."

Narasan was frowning. "I think this changes quite a few things, Sorgan. We'd better take a long, hard look at our plans. *If* this spring flood clears the ravine of all the enemies, we should probably hurry right along and get to the head of the ravine just as quickly as we can and build a strong fort up there to hold the rest back."

"What if they don't all get drowned?" Sorgan asked.

"We might have to just go up as far as your cousin's fort and stop there. If we start getting involved in little hand-to-hand skirmishes, we could lose half of our men, and neither of us would like that very much, would we?"

"Not even a little bit," Sorgan agreed. He scratched at his cheek. "Now that I've had a bit of time to digest this business of the snake-men, I don't know that it really changes all that much. All we really have to do is stay a little ways away from them. If we do most of our fighting with long spears, the snake-people won't get close enough to bite us, and since they don't have any weapons except their teeth and those stingers along the sides of their arms, they should be fairly easy to defeat, wouldn't you say?"

"You've got a point there, Sorgan," Narasan conceded. "And if we can gather up enough of the venom to poison all of our spear tips, all that our people really need to do is scratch a charging enemy or give him a little poke with the spear to kill him right there in his tracks. He'll be too busy dying to come any closer. This might just turn out to be an easy war after all."

"And the nice part of it is that the enemy supplies us with the poison we'll use to defeat him," Sorgan added.

"I know," Narasan said with a broad grin. "I think that's terribly generous of him, don't you?"

"Wake up, Bunny. It's time to toot."

Rabbit struggled up out of sleep to stare at the strange chubby little girl who'd just roused him. "You're Lillabeth, aren't you?" he asked. "The little girl who came here with Zelana's sister, Aracia?"

"That's me," the dark-haired little girl replied. "Zelana asked me to wake you. You're supposed to go outside and blow your horn."

"I don't understand." Rabbit was still only about half awake, and his mind seemed a little foggy.

"It's very simple, Bunny. Take up your horn, go outside, pucker up, and blow." She pointed at the cave mouth. "Go! Now!"

Rabbit didn't care much for her attitude, but he struggled to his feet, took up his horn, and went out into the night. He was getting a little tired of having everybody tell him what to do.

The wind blowing in from the bay was quite warm, and it seemed that every Maag with a horn in the fleet out there in the bay was responding to a signal from farther out. This was obviously the day they'd all been waiting for. Rabbit climbed up to the shoulder of the hill above the cave's mouth to make sure that the sound of his horn would carry up to the rim of the ravine. Then he raised his horn and blew a long, mellow-sounding note. He stood listening intently for a response. After a few moments, a mournful-sounding reply came down from out of the mountains above Lattash. The reply was coming from some distance off, and the echoes resounded from the nearby hills and crags. A few moments later, Rabbit heard yet another reply, which was much fainter but nonetheless stirred its own echoes. Fainter and fainter responses, each trailing echoes, faded back up into the mountains. "That should do it," Rabbit muttered to himself. "I hope somebody's awake in Skell's fort." He turned and went on back down the hill.

When he reentered the cave, he found that Zelana's relatives and the children were all there. The young Trogite, Keselo, was standing somewhat behind Veltan with a look of absolute bafflement on his face.

Everybody in the cave was watching Eleria intently as she lay sleeping on a fur robe near the fire with what appeared to be a pink ball in her hand.

"Did the warning reach Sorgan's cousin?" Zelana's elder brother, Dahlaine, asked.

"They were passing it along," Rabbit replied. "I listened for a while, and the sounds of the horns were getting fainter and fainter as they moved up the ravine. I'd say that the word's reached Skell by now."

"How warm is the wind?" Zelana's sister asked him.

"Warm enough, I'd say. If it's still that warm when it reaches the head of the ravine, the snow up there—and in the surrounding mountains—won't last very long. Why are we all watching Eleria like this? Is she sick or something?"

"She's dreaming, Bunny," the stout little girl who'd awakened him replied.

"Everybody has dreams. What's so unusual about hers?"

"How much does this one know, Zelana?" Dahlaine asked in a quiet voice.

"Probably quite a bit more than he's supposed to," Zelana replied. "He's a member of the crew of Sorgan's ship, and Longbow found him to be very useful. He's caught me tampering with things on several occasions already. I don't think we'll be able to hide very much from him. Eleria's very fond of him, and Longbow's his friend."

"Does he know enough not to tell everybody he encounters just who and what we are?"

"I think so, yes."

"What about this other one?" Dahlaine asked, pointing at the young Trogite Keselo.

"He's young and inexperienced," Veltan replied, "but Commander Narasan believes that he has a great deal of potential—assuming that we don't get him killed."

A sharp sense of apprehension came over Rabbit. He was almost positive that Dahlaine was about to tell him and the young Trogite some things that they didn't really want to know.

"All right, then," Dahlaine said, turning a stern eye on the pair of them. "We'd take it as a kindness if the two of you keep what I'm about to tell you strictly to yourselves. Of course, nobody from the outlands would believe you anyway, but let's not start circulating rumors and exaggerations if we can avoid it. As you heard last night, there's trouble in the wind here in my sister Zelana's Domain, and Eleria's currently dealing with it."

"Baby sister?" Rabbit exclaimed. "Why don't you or Lady Zelana take care of it?"

"That's not permitted," Dahlaine told him.

"Lady Zelana tampers with things all the time," Rabbit protested. "She can do *anything*."

"Not anything that kills people," Dahlaine disagreed. "That's *one* of the things that we aren't permitted to do."

"But Eleria *is?* That doesn't make any sense at all."

"*She* isn't doing it. It's her dream that kills. The dream

brings natural forces into play. In this case, it's going to be a very warm wind, I think—probably quite a bit warmer than is usually the case. Mother Sea controls the weather, but Eleria's dream can override Mother Sea's preferences. It gets just a bit complicated. To put it in the simplest of terms, Mother Sea wants to preserve all life—even the lives of the monstrous slaves of That-Called-the-Vlagh. Eleria's dream will unleash a very hot wind that will cause a flood that's going to be much more savage than the usual spring flood, and that flood will do most of your job here. It will kill most of the enemy creatures who are currently in the ravine above Lattash, so That-Called-the-Vlagh will be obliged to gather up more of its servants and command them to invade Zelana's Domain again. That will take time, and we hope that extra time will give you outlanders the chance to occupy the ravine and hold back that second incursion."

"I really think you should take this up with Commander Narasan, sir," Keselo protested. "I'm not really experienced enough to put this information to good use."

"I'm sorry, young man," Dahlaine said firmly. "Somebody in each of our hired armies needs to know what's really happening. That person should be close enough to the army commander to persuade him to do what needs to be done. Narasan listens to you, and Hook-Beak listens to Rabbit."

"Why do I always get saddled with these chores?" Rabbit complained.

"Because you're quick, clever, and very inventive," Zelana told him, "and because Longbow and Eleria both like you. That might become important later on. Quit sniveling, Bunny. Just smile and do as you're told."

"I wish all you people would get off the 'Bunny' business."

"Eleria calls you Bunny all the time," Lillabeth said. "It's a sign of her affection."

"If you people are going to keep on babbling like this, take it on outside," Zelana's older sister Aracia told them pointedly.

"If you happen to interrupt Eleria's dream, all our plans are going to fly out the window."

"We're almost done, Aracia," Dahlaine told her. He turned back to Rabbit and Keselo. "This is only the first war," he told them. "There'll be three more, and your people will be involved in all of them. I've observed Sorgan and Narasan, and I'm quite certain that they'll stay here and fight if we offer them more gold. We'll also be bringing in the Malavi horsemen and the woman-warriors from the Isle of Akalla to join us in our struggle. Eventually, we'll probably have to march our armies into the Wasteland and deal with That-Called-the-Vlagh permanently. Now the two of you know what's really happening here. You're both clever enough to lead your chieftains, or whatever you want to call them, down the proper path. We'll be close enough to keep you advised if the Dreamers are about to unleash any other natural disasters, so you'll be able to warn your leaders."

"Sorgan and Narasan are coming along the beach," Zelana warned them. "Rabbit, you and Keselo had better stay here. The rest of you go on back in the cave. Let's not alert them to what's really happening."

Her brothers and sister took the children back toward the passageway where Zelana kept her gold, and a moment or two later, Sorgan and Narasan entered, along with Ox, Ham-Hand, Gunda, Jalkan, and Padan. Longbow, the two chiefs, and Red-Beard weren't far behind them, and they all had serious, businesslike looks on their faces.

"That wind out there is really gusting," Sorgan reported, "and it's as warm as midsummer. Chief White-Braid here tells us that the river's going to start to rise before morning, and it'll run out of its banks by noon. He's fairly sure that dike his people built will protect the village. We've talked it over, and we all agree that it might be best if all of us outlanders went back on board our ships out in the bay and sat out the flood there. That way we won't get scattered, and we'll be able to see when the flood begins to subside. Then we'll come back ashore and move on up the ravine."

"The plan seems sound, Hook-Beak," Zelana approved. "I'll keep Rabbit and Keselo here, just in case I need to send messages out to you. The Dhralls will be up on the rim, so they'll be able to keep an eye on the river. When it returns to its banks, they'll sound their horns again, and Rabbit and Keselo can pass the word on to you gentlemen out there in the bay."

"This is turning out even better than I'd hoped," Narasan said. "This annual spring flood's likely to do about half of our job for us."

"We'll see," Sorgan replied cautiously. "It's all going to hinge on whether or not the invaders stay down at the bottom of the ravine. If they recognize the danger and make a run for higher ground, we'll have to face their whole poison-fanged army, and we might be just a bit shorthanded for that."

6

The warm wind was still coming in from the sea when the sun rose the next morning, and Rabbit and Keselo climbed the hill above the cave mouth to keep an eye on the river.

"I don't really see all that much difference, do you?" the young Trogite said.

"It'll need to do a lot better than that if it's going to do our job for us," Rabbit agreed. Then he looked curiously at Keselo. "It's probably none of my business, but what made you decide to take up soldiering? Is the pay really all that good?"

Keselo shrugged. "Not really, but we eat regularly, and we don't have to sleep in the street. I wasn't really interested in politics or buying and selling, so my father bought me a commission in Commander Narasan's army."

"What's a commission?" Rabbit asked.

"I'm an officer instead of an ordinary soldier. I'm supposed to tell the ordinary soldiers what to do—'dig a ditch'; 'build a wall'; 'kill those people over there'—things like that."

"Ah," Rabbit said. "You'd be sort of like Ox and Ham-Hand, then. They're the first and second mates on board the *Seagull*. The cap'n tells them what he wants done, and then they tell us ordinary seamen to do it and hurry. It sounds to me like being a soldier isn't all that much different from being a sailor. We all take orders, don't we?"

"I suppose I hadn't really thought of it that way," Keselo admitted. "How did you Maags get involved in this war?"

"Lady Zelana took the cap'n into the back of her cave and showed him about ten tons of gold bricks. Then the cap'n took a hundred or so of the bricks back to Maag and showed them to just about everybody who owned a ship over there. Every Maag sea cap'n *loves* the sight of gold, so we didn't have too much trouble gathering up a fleet to come across and fight this war."

Keselo smiled. "Veltan did much the same thing when he hired us. Of course, he had to find Commander Narasan first."

"Oh? Was he lost?"

"Not really. We all knew where he was, but he didn't want to be a soldier anymore. We'd been involved in a war that hadn't worked out very well, and Commander Narasan blamed himself. He threw his uniform away and set up shop as a beggar. The army was right on the verge of falling apart after he left. We tried everything we could think of to persuade him to come back, but he wouldn't listen to us. Then Veltan came along, talked to him for a little while, and Commander Narasan came back home. It could have been the promise of gold that persuaded him, but I think it might have been something a little more than that. For some reason, it's awfully hard to say no to someone in Veltan's family."

"You've got *that* right," Rabbit agreed. "And if one of *them* can't bring us around, they turn the children loose on us. It's impossible to say no to one of the children. Longbow's made out of solid iron, and he didn't want any part of this war. Zelana turned Eleria loose on him, and that little girl wrapped him around her finger in no time at all."

"Is Longbow *really* as good an archer as everybody claims he is?" Keselo asked.

Rabbit shrugged. "He doesn't know how to miss, that's all."
Then Rabbit laughed. "When we first got here, the cap'n told
me to set up an arrow shop on the beach. The Dhralls had always chipped their arrowheads out of stone, but when we
were sailing across to the Land of Maag, I hammered out some
iron ones for Longbow, and they seemed to work a lot better.
Anyway, Hammer—he's the smith on the *Shark*—wanted to
argue with me about it. Longbow handed him a clamshell and
told him to walk on down the beach a ways and hold the clamshell up over his head. Hammer was about two hundred and
fifty yards on down the beach when Longbow's arrow smashed
that clamshell right out of his hand. Everybody stopped arguing with me about arrowheads along about then."

"Are the other Dhralls that good as well?"

"Close, maybe, but nobody in the world's as good as Longbow."

Zelana's brother Veltan came up the slope to join them on
the hilltop. "Anything unusual yet?" he asked.

"Not as far as we've seen so far," Keselo replied.

"It's coming. You can be sure of that."

"I wish it'd get on with it" Rabbit said. "We've got a lot
hanging on this flood business. Is baby sister still sleeping?"

Veltan nodded. "Why do you call her that?" he asked.

Rabbit shrugged. "It's sort of silly," he admitted. "It just
popped into my head when she came up with that 'Bunny'
business. She says 'Bunny' and I say 'baby sister.' It's sort of
childish, I know, but she *is* a child, after all, and she seems to
like it. Wait until she starts climbing up and sitting in *your* lap."

"You love her, don't you?"

"Everybody loves Eleria. You just can't help yourself."

"Zelana's very much the same," Veltan said. "I'm sure that
she taught Eleria all the little tricks."

Keselo was staring at the mouth of the ravine. "I think the
river's starting to rise now," he observed.

Rabbit looked quickly. The river was higher now, and its

surface was littered with broken tree branches and other debris from the mountains. "I was expecting something a bit more spectacular, Veltan. If it just rises slow and steady like it's doing now, the snake-people are going to have lots of time to get out of the way."

"This is only the beginning, Rabbit," Veltan told him. "Eleria's still sleeping and dreaming. She isn't finished yet."

The sun was well above the horizon by now, and the wind from the west was still brisk and warm, but the river at the mouth of the ravine remained well within its banks. Then Rabbit heard a faint roaring sound echoing down from the ravine. "What's that noise?" he asked Veltan.

"It's what we've been waiting for, my little friend," Veltan replied with a broad grin. "There's a winter's worth of snow coming down that ravine all at once."

The roaring sound grew louder and louder until it was much like thunder, and then a solid wall of water burst out of the mouth of the ravine. As closely as Rabbit was able to determine, it was at least fifty feet high, and it was tearing trees up by the roots as it blasted out into the open. The crest of the huge wave curled forward, and the thunderous sound shook the very earth.

"What was holding it back before?" Keselo asked.

Veltan shrugged. "It probably hadn't built up enough pressure to break through. The hot wind turned the snow on the mountainsides to slush, and the slush slid down into the river to form a sort of dam. The water backed up behind the dam and then broke through all at once. Nice little flood, isn't it?"

"It looks good to me," Rabbit agreed. "I sure hope our toots gave Skell enough warning. How long do you think it'll take for the river to go back where it belongs?"

"Four or five days at least. A week might come closer."

Large logs were tumbling over the crest now, and mixed with the debris were a goodly number of limp, dead creatures: deer, wild cows, and smaller animals as well. There were also quite a few tiny, oddly dressed men among the animals. "The flood seems to be doing its job," Keselo observed. "I'd say that there probably aren't too many invaders left up there in the ravine."

"What a shame," Veltan said.

The water continued to rush out of the mouth of the ravine for the rest of the day, flooding the low-lying ground on the north side of the river. The coastal village of Lattash had been built on the slightly higher ground on the south side of the river, but it was still the earth berm the Dhralls of White-Braid's tribe had built between the river and the village that held the flood at bay.

Rabbit and Keselo came down the hill above the village and joined Longbow and Red-Beard on the berm.

"Has the spring flood ever come over the top of the berm?" Keselo asked Red-Beard.

Red-Beard shrugged. "A few times," he admitted, "but no more than a few feet. It's a little inconvenient, but it doesn't do any serious damage. I've heard that once, a long time ago, the flood broke through the berm and destroyed most of the village. When the people here rebuilt the berm, they used rocks instead of dirt as a base, and that kept the river away much better."

"I think we should speak with our chieftains, Red-Beard," Longbow suggested. "We need quite a few people up here on the berm to drag in those drowned enemies. They have something that we're going to need before too much longer."

"I think you're right, my friend," Red-Beard agreed. "I've been trying to forget about that venom business. It makes me go cold all over."

"We'll bring in as many of the dead ones as we can and pile them up here on the berm. Then we can use our canoes to gather up the ones that get past us and we'll pile those on the beach."

"How do you go about getting the venom out of the dead ones?" Red-Beard asked.

"I'm not entirely sure," Longbow confessed. "All I've done in the past has involved stabbing my arrows into the venom sacks on a dead one and then leaving the body in the forest for the vultures."

"I don't think that'll work too well here, Longbow," Red-Beard said. "We'll have thousands of them stacked up on the beach, and things here in Lattash might start to get fragrant along about midsummer."

"Burn them," Rabbit suggested. "Eleria's wind should carry the smoke on up the ravine, and that might make life unpleasant for any enemy snake-men left up there."

"Wouldn't it be better if we had some way to store the venom in jugs or something like that?" Keselo asked. "If we need to repoison our spear points later on, we should have a supply of venom handy."

"It's not a bad idea, Longbow," Red-Beard agreed. "The potters here in Lattash could make jugs for us, but fooling around with something that'll kill me if I happen to get a drop of it into any scratch I happen to have on one of my fingers doesn't light any warm little fires in my heart."

"I think maybe I should have a little talk with One-Who-Heals," Longbow said. "If anybody can come up with a safe way to do this, it'll be him."

"Wise move there, Longbow," Red-Beard agreed.

The river continued to rise for the rest of that day, but it crested late the following afternoon, and then the flood slowly began to subside.

Skell's brother Torl arrived with about seventy more Maag ships about noon on the following day. Rabbit was fairly sure that Captain Hook-Beak had expected more ships, but Torl was at least as sour as his brother, so he seemed to put people off. Torl's ships anchored near Sorgan's fleet, and the harbor of Lattash was now choked with ships. All that was left to do was to wait for the river to go down.

Longbow conferred with the old healer of his tribe at some length, and the old man gathered a sizeable number of young men of both tribes and began to train them in the process of draining the venom from the bodies of the dead enemies that were beginning to pile up along the berm and the beach at the river mouth. The procedure was moderately revolting, but it produced dozens of jugs of the deadly venom. One-Who-Heals firmly instructed his pupils to smear lard on their hands before they went to work, and that seemed to provide enough protection.

The bonfires on the beach sent a thick cloud of black smoke up the ravine, and Rabbit was profoundly thankful that he wasn't upriver at Skell's fort.

Rabbit and Keselo stayed in Zelana's cave for the next several days, periodically going down through the village to have a look at the water level. A wary sort of friendship began to grow between them as time inched its way along, and Rabbit came to understand the Trogites a bit better. They weren't as rowdy as Maags, but then, who really was?

Longbow had gone up to the rim above the ravine to keep an eye on the flood, and time seemed almost to stand still as everyone waited for the flood to subside. That, of course, would be the signal to start.

"I need to talk with the cap'n," Rabbit called up to Ham-Hand as he eased Red-Beard's canoe up alongside the *Seagull* in the steel grey light of dawn several days later.

"He's still asleep, Rabbit."

"That's too bad. I just got the word that it's time to go to work. You want to toss that rope ladder over the side? I'd better wake him up myself. Longbow told me a few things that the cap'n needs to know about."

Ham-Hand pushed the rolled-up rope ladder over the rail.

"I hope Longbow knows what he's talking about," he said dubiously. "If another one of those big waves comes down the ravine, we could get washed on out to sea."

"The Dhralls know a lot more about these spring floods than we do," Rabbit replied, nimbly climbing the ladder, "and they've got a lot at stake here. Longbow's not going to take any chances. You might want to hear this, too."

"All right," Ham-Hand agreed as they started aft. They went on into Sorgan's cluttered cabin, and Ham-Hand touched the sleeping captain's shoulder. "Rabbit's here, Cap'n. He's got some news for you."

Sorgan sat up yawning. "What's afoot?" he asked Rabbit.

"Longbow came back from up on the rim, Cap'n," Rabbit replied. "He says that the water's going down, and the benches on both sides are clear now, so it'll be safe for us to start up the ravine. We'll need to pick up our swords and spears before we go on upriver, but the Dhralls have dipped them all in that poison, so they're ready to go now."

"That still makes me go cold all over, Rabbit," Ham-Hand complained. "I didn't hire on to fight no wars with poison."

"That wasn't our idea to begin with, Ham-Hand," Sorgan told him, "but if our enemy wants to play that way, we just about have to play along." He looked over at Rabbit. "Has the river gone down enough for Skell's people to get back into their fortifications?"

"Longbow said it'll be another day or so before the river goes back to where it belongs, but he wants us to be in place on those benches on the off chance that the invaders realize that the benches would be the easiest way to come downriver. Zelana doesn't think they're that clever, but Longbow doesn't want to risk it."

"I'm with him on that," Sorgan agreed, pulling on his boots. "You'd better send word to Narasan, Ham-Hand. Tell him that it's time for us to go upriver."

"Keselo's already taken care of that, Cap'n," Rabbit reported. "He stood on the beach waving a stick with a piece of cloth tied to it. He told me that the Trogites came up with that notion a long time ago. If two Trogites can see each other, no matter how far away they are, they can talk by waving flags at each other. He'll be going up the north bench with us when we start up the ravine. Narasan thinks it might be a good idea if you two can talk to each other even if you're on opposite sides of the ravine."

"Them Trogites are just full of ideas, aren't they?" Ham-Hand said.

"They spend a lot of time fighting wars," Rabbit told him, "so they think about ways to make it easier. We sort of do the same thing by blowing horns, but I think their flag-waving might be quite a bit more complicated."

"Do you and Keselo get along very well?" Hook-Beak asked with a speculative sort of look in his eyes.

"Pretty good, Cap'n. He's sort of young, but he's got a good head on his shoulders. He likes to talk, so I'm learning a lot more about the Trogites than he might realize he's passing on to me."

"Stay close to him, Rabbit," Sorgan suggested. "See if you can learn this flag-waving language. Even if we never use it ourselves, it might be useful later on when we go back to robbing Trogite treasure ships for a living. Ham-Hand, go tell Ox to rouse the crew and get word to the other ships in the fleet. We want to hit the beach by sunup."

"Aye, Cap'n," Ham-Hand replied, turning and leaving the captain's cabin.

"Did Longbow tell you anything about what the enemy's up to, Rabbit?" Sorgan asked.

"From what he says, I guess they're pretty confused, Cap'n. Of course, there aren't too many of them left. They didn't know about these spring floods, so most of them were down by the river when it came boiling down the ravine. Longbow says that it'll take a while for them to replace the army that just got washed out to sea."

"Is he certain that they won't just give up?"

"*He* might not be, but Zelana is. Every now and then she lets something slip. I guess that this Vlagh thing out in the Wasteland has a longstanding grudge against Zelana's family, so it'll keep throwing armies at us until it runs out of people."

"You're just full of good cheer, aren't you, Rabbit? Maybe I should have held out for more gold. Why do they keep calling this Vlagh a 'thing' instead of a chief or a king?"

"I'm not sure, Cap'n. Zelana and her kin never say 'he' or 'she' when they talk about the Vlagh. All they ever say is 'it.' Maybe it hasn't decided what it really is yet. For all I know, it's some kind of animal, or maybe even a bug. Whatever it is, as long as it's still in the Wasteland, the Dhralls won't be safe."

"That's where we come in, I guess," Sorgan said.

THE
RAVINE

1

Keselo of Kaldacin came from a distinguished Trogite family, and he was certain that his choice of a career in Narasan's army had greatly disappointed his parents. His eldest brother was a member of the Palvanum, the ruling body of the Empire, and his next-to-eldest brother was a merchant who was well on his way to becoming the wealthiest man in Kaldacin. Keselo, however, had attended the University of Kaldacin, although he had felt no great longing to spend his time in the pursuit of knowledge. He admitted to himself that his years as a student were really nothing more than a convenient way to put off an unalterable career decision. His brothers, of course, knew exactly what he was doing, and their sneering condescension played no small part in his decision to choose a military career. After some grumbling, his father finally gave in and purchased him a commission in Commander Narasan's army.

His childhood had taught him the value of keeping his thoughts and opinions to himself, and this had served him well during his first few years in Commander Narasan's army. Many junior officers felt the need to assert themselves and to boast about their meager accomplishments. Keselo, however, preferred to do exactly as he was told without comment.

Commander Narasan, he discovered, approved of that. Evidently, a junior officer who knew how to keep his mouth shut was a rarity in the Trogite military.

Keselo had participated in a few military campaigns during his early years, and it was probably through sheer luck that he'd modestly distinguished himself. He seldom took chances, so very few of his men were seriously injured, and even fewer were killed. Commander Narasan approved of that even more than he approved of Keselo's lack of boasting, and Keselo's men became very attached to him.

Then there had come the disastrous campaign in the south of the Empire, when Commander Narasan had seriously underestimated the size of the opposing army, and twelve cohorts had been slaughtered as a result. Commander Narasan, seized by despair, had cast off his uniform and taken to begging. To Keselo's way of looking at things, this was an even greater blunder than that which had cost the army those twelve cohorts. Without Narasan to lead it, the army rapidly began to disintegrate.

And then, almost like a miracle, the Dhrall named Veltan had come to Kaldacin, banished Narasan's guilt and shame, and restored order in the very teeth of chaos.

And so now they were in the Land of Dhrall, inappropriately joined with the pirates of Maag in what promised to be a hopeless war with an enemy the Dhralls called the Vlagh. Keselo determined that he would do whatever duty called upon him to do, but he had little hope that he—or anyone else in Narasan's army—would survive.

As usual, though, he kept that opinion to himself.

Keselo was none too happy about his detachment from Commander Narasan's army to serve as signalman for the pirate Hook-Beak, but he kept his discontent to himself. For some reason, his commander frequently found unusual things for Keselo to do—almost as if he were testing his junior officer to determine the limits of his capabilities. It was flattering, perhaps, but Keselo privately wished that the commander would go find someone else to test.

The weather had turned warm. It wasn't summer by any stretch of the imagination, but it was most unlikely that there'd be any more snow in the mountains to the east of Lattash.

As the Maags began their march up the north bench, Keselo noticed that they weren't really very well organized. Each ship captain commanded his own crew in a rough equivalent of a platoon, but there were no middle-grade officers to form a functioning chain of command. Keselo briefly considered making a few suggestions, but he decided against it. The Maags were temperamentally unsuited to rigid chains of command, apparently, so it would probably be better to just keep his mouth shut.

Keselo found the terrain of this river gorge a bit intimidating. There were mountains in the Empire, of course, but they didn't even approach the size of the mountains here, and the trees growing on the sides of the ravine were enormous. Nothing had prepared Keselo for trees that were thirty feet through at the butt and rose a hundred and fifty feet into the air before sprouting any limbs. He moved through that day in a state of bemused awe.

Just before sunset, Sorgan squinted off to the west. "I think we'd better stop here for the night," he decided. "If any of those snake-men survived the flood, they'll probably be creeping around in the dark, so we're going to have to fort up. Keselo, go signal your commander so that he knows that this is as far as we're going today. I don't think it'd be a good idea for him to get too far ahead of us."

"Yes, sir," Keselo replied, smartly straightening and clashing his fist against his iron breastplate. He was fairly certain that Hook-Beak found his strict adherence to military formality a bit irritating, but since this would probably be his last war, Keselo was determined to do everything strictly by the book.

He went to the edge of the bench, unfurled his red flag, and rapidly signaled to the Trogite force on the other side of the river.

His fellow Trogites halted and began to set up camp for the night, and Keselo rolled up his flag and returned to report to the pirate Sorgan.

"Did they get the message?" Sorgan inquired.

"Yes, sir. They're starting to set up camp."

"Good. Ham-Hand, grab some of the closer ship crews and put them to work setting up a good stout barricade across this bench, and then put out a night watch. We don't want any surprises after the sun goes down."

Rabbit went over to the edge of the rocky bench and looked down at the river. "She's back in her banks, Cap'n," he reported. "I'd say that Skell's most likely back in his fort now."

"We'll see," Sorgan replied. "I want to be absolutely certain sure that Skell and Torl are in those forts before we go too much farther upriver. Longbow thinks that our poisoned spears are going to solve the problem, but I want to have a good safe place to fall back to if he happens to be wrong."

Several crews of Maag sailors threw together a rough sort of barricade, and Sorgan's army settled down for the night around large fires. The night passed quietly, and they were up at dawn to continue their march up the ravine.

By noon of that day, Keselo noticed that the ravine was narrowing significantly, and the sloping walls above the benches were growing steeper.

They rounded a bend late that afternoon, and Sorgan's sour-faced cousin Skell was waiting for them. "What kept you, Sorgan?" he asked.

"Don't try to be funny, Skell," Sorgan told him. "Have you got your ship crews back down in your forts yet? I don't want to go much farther upriver until those forts are finished." He hesitated, but then went on. "There's something you should know, Skell. As it turns out, the enemies we're going to be coming up against aren't quite as helpless as Lady Zelana led us to believe back in Maag. It seems that she somehow forgot to tell us that they're part snake."

"You said what?" Skell replied in a flat, unfriendly tone of voice.

"They don't have swords or axes or bows, since they don't need them. They've got poisoned fangs instead."

"I think I'll go home now, Sorgan."

"Don't get all worked up, cousin," Sorgan told him. "Long-bow gave us an easy way to deal with the problem. He's been hunting them down and killing them for twenty years now. The slick part is that he uses their own poison to kill them. He dips the points of his arrows into the poison sacks of dead ones and then shoots poisoned arrows at any live ones he comes across. We talked it over, and we're fairly sure that poisoned spears will do the job almost as good as poisoned arrows will—*long* spears, if you get my drift."

"Where am I going to find any dead ones to get the poison from?"

Sorgan grinned at his cousin. "I just happen to have a fair supply of the poison, Skell. An awful lot of the snake-men got drowned during the flood, and the Dhralls down in Lattash fished the carcasses out of the river and leeched the poison out of them. We ended up with jugs and jugs full of it. Since you're my cousin, I'll only charge you half-price for a dozen or so jugs."

"Quit trying to be funny, Sorgan. Did Torl manage to get here yet?"

"He hauled in right after the flood came down the ravine. He should be here by midmorning tomorrow."

"Good. I'll put him to work over on the south riverbank. How many more ship crews can you spare us?"

"Thirty, maybe," Sorgan replied. "I don't want to be short-handed if we come up against a major enemy army."

"Thirty should do it. I'd say that the forts down on the river-banks will be pretty much complete by tomorrow evening. Then we'll start expanding up from there to block off the benches. Give us another ten days and we'll have a wall stretching all the way across. If the enemy gets past you, we'll be here to stop him, and you'll have a safe place to hide after the enemy bites half your men to death."

"Very funny, Skell," Sorgan said dryly.

"Just looking out for the family, Sorgan. Once Torl and I finish building this fort, nobody, and I do mean *nobody,* is going to go any farther down the ravine without my permission."

"I'd say that you're earning your pay, then. You're going to be the anchor for this whole campaign, so make your forts as strong as you can and hold them at any cost." Sorgan looked around. "We'll camp here for the night. I need to hammer out a few details with Narasan. Have you bridged the river yet?"

"No, we just swim across," Skell said sarcastically. "It isn't too hard—unless the boulder you're carrying weighs more than a ton or so."

"I wish you'd stop trying to make a joke out of this."

"Stop asking stupid questions, then. Of course we've got a bridge, Sorgan. How do you think Torl and his people are going to get to the Trogite side to build his part of the fort?"

Sorgan let that pass. "We'll probably move on up the ravine at first light tomorrow," he said. "The Trogites and I'll hold back any snake-men until your fortifications are all in place. As soon as you're finished, send word upriver to Narasan and me. If this goes the way I think it's going to, we'll be in total control, so the enemy's going to have to dance to our tune." He turned his head. "Keselo, go signal Narasan. Tell him that we need to talk before we go any farther upriver."

"Yes, sir!" Keselo replied smartly. He was a little surprised at the level of sophistication involved in Hook-Beak's plan. The

Maags *seemed* to be unthinking savages, but evidently they knew exactly what they were doing.

Captain Hook-Beak and Commander Narasan met just upstream from Skell's partially completed fort early the following day. "Nice job," the commander noted, "but won't the river cause some problems on down the line?"

"Not for Skell, they won't," Sorgan replied. "If he and Torl do this right, this'll be part fort and part dam. The snake-men don't swim very well, and if there's ten feet of water standing in front of the fort, they'll have lots of trouble attacking. Torl should get here later today, and then things'll go faster. Right now, there's only about half a fort, but that turned out to be sort of lucky. That flood would have torn it to pieces if Skell's men had finished. When Skell and Torl finish up down here, they're going to extend the walls on both sides to block off the benches. Once that's done, we'll have a safe place to fall back to if things get wormy farther on up the ravine. I think our job's going to involve holding back any enemy forces until Skell and Torl finish building this fort."

Narasan shook his head. "No, Sorgan, our job is getting up to the head of the ravine before the enemy sends people here to replace all the ones that were drowned in the flood. If we can hold our ground at the head of the ravine, no enemies will ever get this far downstream."

"Maybe," Sorgan conceded, "but Longbow says that the enemies are very sneaky, and I don't like surprises. I think we'll all sleep a lot better if we know that we've got a safe place to hole up if things go to pot."

"Would it be all right if I suggested a compromise, sirs?" Keselo asked them.

"We'll listen, Keselo," Commander Narasan agreed.

"Red-Beard's model showed a narrow gap at the very head of the ravine. If we were to send a sizeable advance force up there at a fast march, we should be able to block off that gap within three or four days. In the meantime, we could put a goodly number of men to work building a temporary barricade across the ravine about a mile upstream from these more permanent forts—just in case the enemy's already got people coming down toward Lattash. Of course, if that's the case, our advance force won't have much chance of reaching the gap anyway, and the barricade would give them some cover in an emergency."

"This young fellow spoils a lot of good arguments, doesn't he?" Sorgan suggested. "You and I could have yelled at each other for quite a while, Narasan, and now Keselo just took all the fun out of it."

"Ah, well," Commander Narasan said with mock regret, "nobody's perfect, I guess."

"I'll peel off a fair number of my men to set up the barricade," Sorgan added. "Logs aren't *quite* as solid as boulders, but they'll probably keep the snake-men back—particularly if we line the front with sharp stakes dipped in poison. I noticed down at Lattash that the snake-men that got drowned weren't wearing any shoes or boots, and walking barefoot across a field of poisoned stakes wouldn't be a good way to get any older, would it?"

"I'll make a special point of not doing that, Sorgan," Commander Narasan promised with a perfectly straight face.

About midmorning the following day, Keselo and Rabbit were a short distance in front of the main army, and Rabbit suddenly stopped. "Is that a village over there on the other side of the river?" he asked.

"Where?" Keselo asked his little friend.

"Up near the top of the ravine, under that rock overhang." Rabbit pointed.

Keselo peered across the river. There appeared to be structures of some kind under the overhanging rock. "Ah," he said. "It's abandoned. We come across ancient ruins all the time down in the Empire. They're places where people used to live, but nobody's ever been able to come up with a reason for just exactly why everybody who lived there just packed up and left."

"Maybe they didn't, Keselo. There might have been a war or a pestilence that killed them all off."

"That's possible, I suppose. Those ruins across the river appear to be quite a bit more sophisticated than the houses down in Lattash. If we weren't so busy, it might be sort of interesting to explore that place."

"It doesn't interest me enough to make me want to swim across the river to get there," Rabbit said flatly.

Longbow had been up on the rim of the ravine, but he came down to the north bench late that afternoon. "It seems that the servants of the Vlagh were all washed down the river during the flood," he reported to Sorgan. "We haven't seen a single one yet."

"Maybe they're hiding in the bushes," Sorgan suggested.

Longbow shook his head. "Not from *me,* they aren't. I've been hunting them for many, many years, and if there were any of them in the ravine, I'd have seen them. I've seen a few deer, but no enemies."

"They aren't any too bright, then, are they?" Rabbit said. "Didn't they know how dangerous it was to sit alongside that river when the snow started to melt?"

"They live in a desert, Rabbit," Longbow replied. "Water's very rare in the Wasteland." He turned to Sorgan. "It won't hurt to take a few precautions," he advised, "but I'm fairly sure that the ravine is clear. We'll keep watch from up on the rim of the ravine, and we'll warn you if we see any of the Vlagh's servants. Your army—and Narasan's—should be able to reach the head of the ravine without any problems."

"That was the only shaky part of our whole scheme," Sorgan noted. "If Narasan and I can reach the head of the ravine before that Vlagh thing can get any replacements here, we'll have just won us a war."

"That was sort of what we had in mind," Longbow said mildly.

As evening settled over the scattered, disorganized camp of the Maags, Keselo moved out of the firelight to put some distance between himself and the rowdy pirates.

"What seems to be the problem, Keselo?" Longbow's voice came out of the darkness.

Without even thinking, Keselo reached for his sword hilt.

"Don't do that," Longbow chided him.

"You startled me, that's all," Keselo apologized.

"There's something bothering you, isn't there?"

"This all seems so unnatural," Keselo admitted. "I'm not used to fighting battles in the deep forest like this. There aren't any roads, and the trees make it impossible for me to see anything that's more than five feet away."

"The enemies can't see you either, Keselo. When night falls, *everybody* is invisible. There's something that goes just a little deeper, though, isn't there?"

"I'm afraid," Keselo blurted out the admission. "I've always been afraid of snakes, and now I'm facing the prospect of fighting enemies that are part people and part snake. What sort of weapons can I possibly use to defend myself?"

"You already have the weapon, Keselo. It's called your mind. The servants of the Vlagh have very little in the way of minds. The Vlagh doesn't encourage that. *It* wants to do all of the thinking. I *do* know quite a bit about them, but sometimes their stupidity even surprises me. The only weapons they have are parts of their bodies, so they don't even realize what a sword or a spear or a bow is. I once killed thirteen of them in a single place. I'd have killed more, but I ran out of arrows. The ones who were still living just stood there—wondering why the others were all falling down, probably."

"You're not serious!" Keselo exclaimed.

"Oh, yes. Always remember what One-Who-Heals said back in Zelana's cave: The servants of the Vlagh aren't intelligent enough to be afraid. If the Vlagh tells a thousand of them to attack, the last one that's still alive will continue to attack until you kill it as well. The death of all its fellows will have no meaning for it. The creatures of the Wasteland don't realize that every living thing dies eventually, so they're not aware of the fact that they won't live forever. They always seem to be surprised when death overtakes them."

"They aren't very big, are they?" Keselo asked.

"Very small—even smaller than Rabbit—but they're very quick." Longbow smiled faintly. "Try not to waste the poison on your sword tip. A small jab anyplace on their bodies will kill them almost instantly. You don't have to drive your sword completely through them."

"Now I'll have to learn how to use my sword all over again," Keselo said ruefully.

Longbow reached out and tapped Keselo's iron breastplate with one knuckle. "This should prove quite useful," he observed. "After one of them breaks off its fangs and the spurs on its arms on your iron shirt, it won't be dangerous anymore."

They moved farther and farther up the ravine for the next several days, and the pirate Hook-Beak kept Keselo busy maintaining contact with Commander Narasan. The fact that as yet there had been no contact with enemy forces seemed to make both Sorgan and Narasan more than a little edgy. Keselo noticed that Hook-Beak had started to carry his long spear in both hands rather than resting it on his shoulder, and the rest of the crew of the *Seagull* soon followed his example.

As they moved on up the ravine, Keselo noticed that the trees were thinning out and the underbrush wasn't quite as dense. He definitely approved of that. If the forest thinned out a bit more, things might be more normal. The notion of venomous enemies lurking in thick brush all around him had made him very jumpy. As his nerves settled down, his curiosity began to mount, though. "This doesn't look at all like the lower part of the ravine, Longbow," he said to his friend one afternoon. "What happened to the trees and undergrowth up here?"

"Fire, probably," Longbow replied. "If a dry summer comes along, all it takes to set the forest on fire is a lightning strike. Then, too, we're quite a bit higher up in the mountains now, and the higher you go, the shorter the growing season is. That tends to stunt the trees and bushes."

"I know that you're very fond of the deep woods, my friend," Keselo said, "but I'm much more comfortable with open space around me. Now that I can see more than ten feet, certain anxieties that were bothering me are starting to go away."

"I'm so happy for you," Longbow said with a faint smile.

On the morning of their sixth day out from Lattash, Hook-Beak sent scouts on ahead toward the clearly visible gap at the head of the ravine.

"Maybe the snake-men who got drowned in that flood was their whole army, Cap'n," Ox suggested about noon. "Longbow ain't seen no survivors yet."

"If that's all there were, Lady Zelana wouldn't have gone to all the trouble and expense of hiring us, Ox," Sorgan disagreed. "There's *got* to be more enemies *somewhere*."

Then Keselo looked on up the bench toward the head of the ravine, and he saw Rabbit running toward them as fast as he could. It was easy to see at that point how the little Maag had got his name.

He was gasping for breath when he reached them. "We seen 'em, Cap'n!" he wheezed.

"Where?" Hook-Beak demanded sharply.

"They're still a good ways off," Rabbit replied. "Longbow was up there just on this side of the gap. He told us to keep low, and then we went on up. There's a big, flat plain on the other side, but it's way down below, and there's a slope that leads right up to the gap. The enemy soldiers are gathering at the foot of the slope."

"How many?" Ox demanded, tightening his fist around the handle of his heavy battle-axe.

"I can't count that high, Ox," Rabbit confessed, "but I think we might be in a whole lot of trouble."

2

Hold the men right here, Ox," Sorgan commanded. "We don't want a whole crowd up there just yet."

"Aye, Cap'n," Ox replied.

Then Sorgan and Keselo followed Rabbit on up to the head of the ravine. The river there was a narrow trickle of sparkling water that seemed almost to giggle its way over the stones. The trees were stunted here, and there were still a few patches of dirty snow back under their sheltering limbs. The air was clean, and Keselo could see for miles and miles out over the mountains of Western Dhrall.

Commander Narasan had evidently just reached the head of the ravine. He'd removed his iron helmet, and he and Longbow were quietly talking near the narrow gap that marked the head of the ravine.

"Rabbit tells us that we've finally located some snake-men," Hook-Beak said.

"Just a bit more than 'some,' Sorgan," Narasan replied glumly. "I think we're going to be working for short pay this time out."

"That's what Rabbit told us. Are there really that many?"

"Come and look," Longbow said. He turned and led the way up toward the narrow gap between two tall peaks. Keselo saw that his commander had been right. The gap *would* be a perfect place to erect a fort. No more than a few of their enemies could attack at any one time.

They passed on through the gap, and Keselo stopped and stared in awe at the rock-strewn sea of sand and rock lying a thousand feet below and stretching on out to the eastern horizon. It wasn't just empty desert, however. A horde of tiny figures was coming across the barren land to the east, and the horde stretched across the Wasteland from horizon to horizon.

"It's easy to see why the people who live there would rather find a more pleasant place to set up shop," Commander Narasan observed. "I can't for the life of me see how they manage to survive out there."

"It's a bit bleak," Sorgan agreed. "The next question is how are we going to keep them from resettling in Lady Zelana's part of the country?"

"Don't rush me," the commander said. "I'm working on it."

Keselo had been staring down the slope, and he saw what appeared to be faint ridges that were far too evenly spaced to be the result of ordinary wind and weather. Idly he scuffed at the sand at the top of the slope with his boot. The rock beneath the sand was flat, and there appeared to be a straight edge where that rock butted up against the one beside it. He kicked away more sand. There seemed to be a straight line of squared-off rocks at the front of the gap. He dropped to his knees and pushed the sand away from the front of the flat rocks he'd just exposed. About a foot down, he came to another line of flat rocks. He raised his head and stared down the long slope. "That's impossible!" he exclaimed.

"What's impossible, Keselo?" Commander Narasan asked.

"I don't think this slope is any sort of natural formation, sir," Keselo replied. "It looks to me as if it might just be a stairway."

"You're not serious!" the commander scoffed.

"Look for yourself, sir,"

They all began clearing sand away at that point, and more and more stone steps were exposed. "If this goes all the way down to the desert floor, it would have taken an army *centuries* to build it," Narasan said in an awed voice.

"The Vlagh's very patient," Longbow told him. "This is the lowest place in the wall that separates the Wasteland from the Domain of Zelana, so if the Vlagh was thinking about paying us a call, it needed some way for its army to reach the top of the ravine—a way that wind and weather and time couldn't destroy. I'd say that this invasion's been in the works for a long, long time."

"Well, that's just too bad," Sorgan said with a broad grin. "*They* might have built this silly stairway, but *we'll* tear it apart. Life's going to get very exciting for anybody who tries to come up the stairs when we start rolling blocks down."

"Let's not be too hasty here, Sorgan," Narasan said. He went a short distance down the stairs, kicking dirt off the steps as he went and stopping every so often to turn and look back up at the gap. "It'd be a shame to waste all this perfectly good building material, don't you think? This stairway's at least four or five times wider than the gap, so there'd be enough stone blocks to build an even bigger fort than I'd originally intended. I wasn't really thinking about anything much higher than an ordinary barricade. Now that we've got all these building blocks, though, I should be able to block off the gap completely. That would give the enemies a pretty stone wall to look at while they're charging up the stairway. I rather think they'll get the message, don't you?"

"They should," Sorgan agreed, "particularly if we leave little holes in the wall to poke our spears through if they try to climb up over it. Are your people any good at building? My cousin Skell's got every Maag in the fleet who knows the least bit about that sort of thing working on the forts near the bottom of the ravine."

Narasan came back up the stairs. "Trogite soldiers spend more time building fortifications than they do fighting, Sorgan. If your men tear the stairway apart and carry the blocks up to the gap, my men can put the fort together in short order. Our advance forces should be joining us before the day's out, so we've got time to work out the details."

Something occurred to Keselo. "Excuse me," he said politely. "Wouldn't it be better if the enemies down below can't see what we're doing up here?"

"Do all the work at night, you mean?" Sorgan asked.

"Well, no, not really," Keselo replied. "The prevailing wind comes up the ravine from the west, and smoke goes where the wind takes it. A few bonfires with fresh evergreen boughs piled on top of them would put out enough smoke to conceal us from the enemy down below, wouldn't you say?"

"It would, wouldn't it?" Hook-Beak mused. "This is a very clever young man you've got here, Narasan."

"He earns his pay," Narasan agreed.

"It comes with being a sailor," Rabbit explained the next morning when Keselo noted how smoothly the Maags were taking the top of the stairway apart and passing the stone blocks from man to man. "A ship's crew learns early that they've got to cooperate. We row the ship when the wind's not right, and the ship won't go anywhere if the oars aren't working in unison, and when we raise the sail, we have to pull together." He looked down at the Maags working just below the gap and then over at the steadily growing stacks of building blocks behind the gap. "If every Maag working on this just picked up a block and carried it all the way to those stacks, they'd be falling all over each other."

"They would, wouldn't they?" Keselo agreed.

It was about midafternoon when Ox came up the center portion of the stairway the Maags were leaving intact to facilitate the chore of passing the stone blocks up to the gap. "You want we should put on a fresh crew and work on through the night, Cap'n?" he called up to Hook-Beak. "Those bonfires should put out a fair amount of light, so we'll be able to see what we're doing after it gets dark."

"We might as well, I guess," Hook-Beak agreed. "The sooner we get all those blocks up here, the sooner the Trogites can start building the front wall of the fort."

"Do you people actually work after the sun goes down?" the balding Gunda demanded incredulously.

"When you're out at sea, you almost have to keep working," Sorgan replied. "The tides and wind don't stop just because the sun goes down." He looked over at Narasan. "It's something to think about, you know," he said. "The rest of our people—both yours and mine—should be joining us tomorrow, so we'll have fresh men to take over the chores. If we both put fresh men to work on this even after it gets dark, we'll be able to finish up in half the time it'd take if we only work when the sun's out."

"Good point," Narasan agreed. "About how much longer do you think it'll take your men to finish?"

"If they stick right with it, I'd be willing to bet that they'll have that top fifty feet cleared away by noon tomorrow," Hook-Beak replied. "Then the rest is up to you. My people tear things apart. Your people have to build things."

"You're all heart, Sorgan," Commander Narasan replied sardonically.

Keselo was fairly sure he'd just be in the way if he stood watching the Maags dismantling the top of the stairway, so he went back through the gap to the little glade at the top of the ravine. The bulky Dhrall known as Red-Beard was seated beside a small fire near the sparkling little brook that seemed to be the source of the river that had carved out the ravine.

"Maybe you can explain something for me, Red-Beard," Keselo said.

"If I happen to understand it myself, maybe," Red-Beard said, scratching his hairy cheek.

"Did your tribe live up here in the ravine at some time in the past? When we were coming up the north bench, Rabbit and I saw several abandoned villages over on your side of the river."

"They're not really important. As far as we know, nobody's lived in them since long before our tribe came to this part of Zelana's Domain."

"Is that why you left them out when you were building your map back in Zelana's cave?"

"Not entirely," Red-Beard conceded. "Those places make the old men of the tribe edgy for some reason. Chief White-Braid didn't come right out and tell me not to put them in my model, but I know him well enough to be fairly sure it wouldn't have made him too happy if I had."

"Is there something about them that frightens him?"

"I'm not sure if 'frightened' is the right word, Keselo. Maybe it's just some old superstition. Those of us who live here in the Land of Dhrall take our superstitions very seriously. We avoid graveyards, and we always apologize to any animals we kill during the hunt. I'm not sure if it does any good, but it's the polite thing to do, and it doesn't cost anything. The cliff villages were here when our tribe first came to this part of Dhrall. Whoever built them was obviously not of our tribe. We don't build our lodges out of stone, and we choose places that're more convenient. Why all this sudden interest?"

"Curiosity, I guess," Keselo admitted. "We have many ancient ruins down in the Empire, but they're usually located on land more suitable for farming. Have you ever explored one of those villages?"

Red-Beard laughed. "Why would I want to do that? I'm a hunter, and I'm supposed to chase animals—or fish—to keep the tribe eating regularly. I don't waste my time wandering around in ancient, empty villages or in the caves that crawl off in all directions under these mountains."

"You have caves here as well?" Keselo was a bit startled about that.

"*All* mountains have caves, Keselo," Red-Beard told him with a faint smile. "Everybody knows that. I have a theory, if you want to hear it."

"Of course."

"Mountains could be what happens when Father Earth eats something that doesn't agree with him. When he burps, mountains pop up."

"That's absurd," Keselo said, trying not to laugh.

"If you've got a better theory, I'd be happy to hear it," Red-Beard said mildly. "Anyway, a burp isn't anything but air that boils up out of a man's stomach, so Father Earth's mountains have chunks of empty air in the middle of them—burps that didn't quite manage to make it to the surface, you understand."

"Would you please be serious, Red-Beard?"

" 'Serious' isn't really very much fun, Keselo. All right, then, if you're going to insist, the old men of the tribe tell us that those old villages are cursed and that we're not supposed to go near them or even talk about them. Old men get very peculiar sometimes. Whoever it was that built them or lived in them isn't around anymore. Either they all died or they just packed up and left. If they died, the villages are probably haunted, and if they ran away, something quite awful must have frightened them off. In either case, the old men of our tribe seem to think that staying away from the ruins might not be a bad idea." He shrugged. "There's probably nothing in them that's worth very much anyway, so I don't waste my time exploring. I've got better things to do with my time." He squinted on down the ravine. "Most of us in the tribe more or less go along with what the old men tell us, but every now and then, somebody gets an overpowering urge to snoop around in the ruins, and he almost never comes back again."

"Doesn't that sort of suggest that the old men of your tribe might know what they're talking about?" Keselo suggested.

"Not necessarily," Red-Beard disagreed. "Our tribe's been at Lattash for hundreds of years, and even places made of stone start falling apart after that long. Walls fall down, ceilings collapse, and for all I know, whole villages that used to be there fell down into those burp-holes under the mountains. It's not always ghosts or curses that kill the snoopers, Keselo. It's more likely that it's just natural decay."

"Are the villages only on the south side?" Keselo asked. "Rabbit and I didn't see any of them on the north side as we were coming up here."

"You wouldn't have," Red-Beard told him. "It's always seemed to me that those old villages were built in places where they couldn't be seen from the bench on the same side of the ravine. The people who used to live in the village probably did that on purpose. There were most likely unfriendly people back in those days too. Unfriendliness has been around for a long, long time. The closest one of those villages is only a few miles back down on the north side of the ravine. It wouldn't be hard to find if you were on the north bench. There's an old dead tree snag just above it on the rim of the ravine, and that snag sticks out so much that if you happened to be on the north bench, it should be clearly visible."

"Maybe if there's a lull in this war, I'll go on down and have a look," Keselo mused.

"What for? There won't be anything there but some tumbled-down old buildings, and it might be very dangerous."

"Curiosity again," Keselo confessed. "It's a failing of mine."

Work continued on through the night, and by morning the Maags had quite nearly removed all the stone blocks on either side of the steadily narrowing central stairway.

Keselo and Rabbit were standing unobtrusively off to one side when Narasan joined Sorgan at the front of the gap. "I'd say that's about enough," he said to Hook-Beak. "I think it's time to start building the fort, don't you agree?"

"I'll go along with you there," Sorgan agreed. "If the snake-men down below start charging up the stairway now, we won't be ready for them, so you'd better get your people to work on that fort." He peered through the smoke at the work crews below. "Ho, Ox!" he shouted.

The bullnecked Maag who was supervising the work crews climbed up one of the dozen or more rope ladders Sorgan's men used to stay clear of the increasingly crowded central stairway. "Aye, Cap'n?" he responded when he was about halfway up the ladder.

"The Trogites have all the building blocks they need," Sorgan told him. "Call in the lookouts, and send most of the men on up here. Then tear what's left of the stairway apart. Throw the blocks on down the slope. If the snake-men are trying to sneak up through the smoke, that might just make them a little nervous."

"We'll do 'er that way, Cap'n," Ox called back with an evil grin.

"What do you think?" Hook-Beak asked Commander Narasan. "Should we let those bonfires go out?"

"Why don't we keep them going until the fort's finished?" Commander Narasan replied. He smiled faintly. "It's an old Trogite saying: 'Don't let the customer see the product until it's finished.'"

"I'm hoping that the customer won't care much for the looks of our product, Narasan. Then maybe he'll go shopping someplace else."

"Let's go find Longbow," Rabbit suggested to Keselo. "We should probably let him know that the Maags have finished tearing the stairway apart and that Narasan's people are starting on the fort."

"Good idea," Keselo agreed.

Longbow was coming down from the north rim, and Keselo

and Rabbit went on up to meet him. "The Maags have finished, Longbow," Rabbit told his friend. "Now Narasan's people can start on the fort."

"Good," Longbow said. "Will they let the fires go out now?"

"Not until the fort's finished," Keselo replied. "Commander Narasan wants to hide what we're doing from the enemy."

"It works both ways, Keselo. They can't see us, but we can't see them either."

"We've noticed that too, Longbow," Rabbit agreed, "but the cap'n didn't want to argue with Narasan about it. When you've got Maags and Trogites living together in the same camp, everybody needs to walk softly. Oh, I almost forgot. The cap'n sent word to his cousins, and Skell and Torl should be joining us in a few days."

"That might not be such a good idea, Rabbit," Longbow said dubiously. "If the creatures of the Wasteland find some way to get around us, the Domain of Zelana will lie unprotected."

"You really think a lot of her, don't you?" Keselo suggested.

"This is my home, Keselo, and I live but to serve Zelana. When I was younger, I thought I could avoid her and spend my life in the hunt for the creatures of the Wasteland, but when she called, I found that I couldn't refuse her."

"She seems to have that effect on people," Keselo agreed.

"Some people rule by force, but Zelana rules by love. Love can be crueler than force, but it works better," Longbow observed.

"I've noticed," Rabbit added, "and the little girl's even worse."

Longbow smiled. "Oh, yes," he agreed, "but delightful still, isn't she? How long's the building of the fort likely to take?"

"I can't say for sure, Longbow," Keselo replied, "but I'd guess that they'll probably be finished by late tomorrow afternoon if they work on through the night. Then we can let the fires go out, and come morning on the day after tomorrow, the enemies will be able to see what we've done up here, and I don't think they'll like it very much."

Gunda, Jalkan, and Padan supervised the construction of the fort, and, as was his habit, Jalkan bullied the soldiers under his command outrageously. When he wasn't cursing them, he was slashing at them with a limber switch.

"That one wouldn't last a week on board a Maag ship," Rabbit told Keselo. "The crew would probably band up and feed him to the sharks."

"Unfortunately, sharks are a little hard to find out on dry land," Keselo replied.

"What is it that makes him so unpleasant? His men are working as hard as all the rest are."

"He used to be a priest," Keselo explained, "and the priests of Amar seem to enjoy flogging those who are beneath them."

"If he was having so much fun as a priest, why did he join the army?"

"It's a long story," Keselo said shortly.

"We've got all kinds of time right now, Keselo," Rabbit said. "That Jalkan fellow sort of rubs me the wrong way. If he started switching me the way he's doing to those soldiers under him, he'd get a knife in his belly. Why does your commander let him get away with that?"

"I don't think Jalkan will be with us much longer," Keselo said. "Commander Narasan's reprimanded him a few times already. Jalkan's family was once quite prominent in Kaldacin, but they eventually became very corrupt. Jalkan couldn't bear the idea of doing honest work, so he eventually joined the priesthood of the Amarite faith—the last refuge of the scoundrel. He won't talk about his years in the church, but there are a few rumors floating about. If those rumors come anywhere close to what he was *really* up to, he should have been imprisoned—or even executed. Evidently, he became involved with some professional criminals, and he was making tons of money. When the head of the church found out about his little enterprise—*and* about the fact that Jalkan wasn't sharing his profits with the church—the 'most holy one' expelled him from the church and even went through the Damnation Ceremony. That put Jalkan back out on the street again, and he used the last of his profits to buy himself a commission in Commander Narasan's army. We'd all be much happier if he'd move on, but he doesn't seem to want to leave."

"If it bothers you all that much, why don't you have a little chat with Longbow?" Rabbit suggested. "We've got lots and lots of arrows now, so we wouldn't really miss one all that much. I'd say that your Jalkan fellow would look a whole lot nicer with one of Longbow's arrows sticking out of his forehead."

"Now that you mention it, he probably would," Keselo agreed. "We'd all be terribly sorry, of course, but we could give him a nice funeral—and maybe even wait for a half hour or so before we started to celebrate."

"A half hour sounds about right to me," Rabbit agreed with a wicked little grin.

The fort went up rapidly, and, following Sorgan's example, Commander Narasan's men worked on through the night by the light of the bonfires on either side of the gap.

When the sun rose, Narasan put fresh men to work, and as Keselo had surmised, the Trogites were finishing up as the setting sun painted the western sky.

"Go tell Sorgan that we're finished, Keselo," Narasan said. "He might want to have a look."

"Yes, sir," Keselo replied smartly. He went down the back stairs of the fort and found Sorgan in the Maag encampment at the head of the ravine. "The fort's completed, Captain Hook-Beak," he reported.

"That was quick," Sorgan said. "Where's Narasan?"

"Up on top," Keselo replied. "He seems rather pleased with the way it turned out."

"I suppose I'd better go offer my congratulations."

"I think he'd appreciate that, sir."

"I wish you'd learn to relax, Keselo," Sorgan told him. "You don't have to call me 'sir' every time you walk past."

"Habit, I suppose," Keselo admitted.

The two of them went up the stairs at the back of the fort and joined Commander Narasan at the top of the front wall. The fort was fifty feet high, twenty feet thick, and it fit snugly against the walls of the gap.

"Nice job, Narasan," Sorgan said. "I'm glad I'll be on *this* side of it instead of the front side. I'd hate to have to lead an assault against it."

"Practice, Sorgan," Narasan replied modestly. "My men have built a lot of walls and forts over the years." He surveyed the construction. "We were a little pushed for time on this one, but good or bad, it'll have to do."

"Quit worrying, Narasan. Those little holes your people put in that front wall give us a way to poke the snake-men in the bellies while they're trying to climb up to get at us, and if Longbow's right about how good that poison we've got on our spear points is, we'll see a lot of poke-poke, die-die going on. And if the snake-men are as empty-headed as everybody claims they are, they'll just keep coming, and we'll be able to play poke-poke, die-die all day long for weeks on end."

"I'll have to remember *poke-poke, die-die*," Commander Narasan said with no hint of a smile. "I think we might want to include that in the soldiers' manual—probably someplace near *parry-and-thrust*."

The bonfires had died out by the following morning, and the pall of smoke no longer obscured the view of the desert floor far below. The hordes of the Vlagh were gathering some distance back from the foot of the stairway, waiting, it appeared, for some sort of signal or command.

Keselo, Rabbit, and Longbow stood atop the wall in the

early morning light. "I don't think they like what they see very much," Keselo said. "It must have taken them centuries to build that stairway, but we changed the top of it in about a week. It's a stairway to no-place now. They can run up those stairs as fast as they can, but once they reach the place where the stairs end now, they'll come face to face with a blank wall and they'll be easy targets for the Dhrall archers, won't they?"

"They won't be hard to hit," Longbow agreed, "and our outlander friends can shower rocks on them from up here. I don't think this is going to be one of their pleasant days."

"What a shame," Rabbit said in mock sympathy. "This just about ends the war, doesn't it? We might have to spend the summer here, but come fall, we'll still be here, and what's left of them will still be down there."

"It looks that way to me," Longbow agreed.

From far below there came a thunderous sound, much like the deep-throated roar of an angry bull, and the hordes of the Vlagh shrieked their response. Then, almost like an incoming wave, the enemy force surged forward.

"Enemy to the front!" Keselo reported sharply to alert the Trogite soldiers and Maag pirates stationed atop the fort.

The Maags and Trogites, their ancient enmities laid aside now, came to the front wall of the fort to watch the now futile charge of the enemy.

Longbow watched and waited as the enemy force charged up the broad stairway.

"Shouldn't your archers be alerted, Longbow?" Keselo asked.

"They're watching," Longbow replied. "The enemy isn't quite in range yet. We wouldn't want to waste our new arrows."

"You've got no idea of how much I appreciate that, Longbow," Rabbit said with a tight grin.

The enemy charge continued to swarm up the stairway. Oddly, there were no shouts or war cries. That seemed very unnatural to Keselo.

"That should be close enough," Longbow said. He lifted his horn and blew a long, mournful note.

A cloud of arrows arched out over the stairway from either side of the gap. The arrows seemed almost to hang in the air for an interminable moment, and Keselo saw a certain beauty in the perfect symmetry of that arch.

The enemy charge faltered as the front ranks went tumbling lifelessly back down over the top of the following ranks.

Rabbit chuckled. "I think their day just turned sour," he said, "and the sun's barely over the eastern horizon."

Longbow, however, was frowning with a slightly puzzled expression. "Something isn't right," he said. "They rush toward the foot of the stairs by the thousands, but only hundreds come up. Where are the others going?"

Rabbit peered down toward the foot of the stairway. "It *does* look a bit odd, doesn't it?" he admitted. "It's a little hard to see from way up here, but it almost looks like better than half of that army just vanishes when it reaches the stairway. Where are they going?"

A cold certainty suddenly struck Keselo. "Could the stairway just be a diversion?" he suggested.

"A what?" Rabbit demanded.

"Something that's supposed to attract our attention away from the *real* attack," Keselo explained.

"But where's the real attack going to come from?" Rabbit asked. "They're down there, and we're up here. They *have* to come up that stairway to get to us. As far as I can tell, most of the enemies just vanish when they reach the foot of the stairs. They're kicking up a lot of dust down there, but that shouldn't change the numbers, should it?"

"Burps?" Keselo mused, half to himself as he remembered Red-Beard's humorous description.

"I didn't quite follow that," Rabbit admitted with a puzzled expression.

"It's just something Red-Beard told me a few days ago," Keselo explained. "I was asking him about those ancient ruins we saw up on the sides of the ravine, and he happened to mention the fact that there are quite a few caves running through these mountains. If he was right, isn't it possible that the creatures of the Wasteland have been moving toward Lattash through those caves instead of down the ravine?"

"What's that got to do with what's happening down there at the bottom of the stairway, Keselo?"

"Let's say that there's a cave mouth somewhere on the face of this cliff," Keselo continued, "or maybe even down at the foot of the cliff, for that matter. And just suppose that the cave went through the mountains here to someplace on down the ravine. If the enemies wanted to hide that cave from us, this stairway would be the perfect way to conceal it. First they'd build a kind of corridor that'd lead to the cave, and then they'd cover the corridor by building this stairway right over the top of it."

"Keselo, you're talking about something that would have taken hundreds of years to build," Rabbit scoffed.

"Let him talk, Rabbit," Longbow said. "Time doesn't mean anything to the creatures of the Wasteland, and this notion of his explains what's happening down there. Go ahead, Keselo."

"All right," Keselo continued. "The stairway hides the corridor—or tunnel—that leads to the cave mouth. The next question is where does that cave go?" He snapped his fingers. "Obviously! It goes right straight through the mountain and comes out somewhere on down the ravine—where the enemies could come out between our fort here and Lattash."

"Like maybe right behind those old villages that nobody seems to be living in?" Rabbit suggested.

"Of course!" Keselo exclaimed. "Red-Beard told me that every now and then somebody in his tribe gets curious and tries to explore one of those ruins, but those people almost never come back."

"I think that maybe we'd better go have a look," Longbow said bleakly. "How close is the nearest one of those ruins?"

"Red-Beard said that there's one a few miles down on the north side of the ravine," Keselo replied. "He told me that there's a dead snag on the rim just above it and that the snag sticks out far enough that we'd be able to see it if we were on the north bench. Rabbit and I saw several on the south side while we were coming up the ravine, but they all seemed to have been built in places that wouldn't be visible if you happen to be directly under them."

"We've had some very interesting notions here, but they're just guesswork. Let's see if we can find anything to back those guesses up." Longbow's face was bleak, and his tone of voice seemed tense.

"Did Red-Beard give you any idea of how extensive these caves might be?" Longbow asked Keselo as they started down the north bench in the bright spring sunshine.

"He didn't really go into too much detail," Keselo replied. "I got the feeling that he's not really curious enough about caves to go exploring—or possibly the caves make him sort of nervous. I've heard that some people have problems with enclosed places. I sort of got the impression from what he said that the caves are quite extensive. From what we've seen so far, I'd say that there's a strong possibility that the enemies *are* using the caves to slip behind us so that they can block us off."

"Well, all we know for certain is that a sizeable number of our enemies disappeared when they reached the foot of the stairway," Longbow replied. "These ruins are a possibility. We may have to come up with others, but let's look into this possibility first."

Keselo looked on down the ravine. "I think that might be the dead snag Red-Beard told me about," he told the others, pointing up toward the rim.

"Let's stop here," Longbow said. "If there *are* enemies in that ruin, we don't want to come up right below them."

The wall of the ravine was steep, certainly, but it wasn't a sheer rock face such as the cliff at the edge of the Wasteland. They climbed slowly to avoid making any noise that might alert anyone—or anything—in the ancient stone ruins.

They angled up the side of the ravine until they were a short distance from the overhanging ledge above the village. Longbow stopped, his eyes searching. "There," he whispered, pointing at a grassy protrusion that lay between them and the ancient ruin. "If we move carefully, we can take cover in the tall grass without alerting anyone that we're there."

They climbed carefully up the back side of the knoll, and as they neared the top, Keselo motioned to the others and crawled through the grass until the ruins were in plain sight. Then he crawled back to rejoin Rabbit and Longbow. "We'll be just a bit above and a little to one side," he whispered. "If there's anybody there, we should be able to see them if they come out into the open."

"Let's go watch," Longbow whispered back. "If our suspicions turn out to be right, it won't be long before there'll be too many enemies in the village to hide."

They crawled along through the rustling grass until they could see most of the village lying slightly below them.

"It looks almost like a fort instead of a village, doesn't it?" Rabbit suggested quietly. "That front wall's fairly flat, except for the places where part of it crumbled away and rolled on down the hill. Maybe it really *was* a fort, and part of that front wall got knocked down during a war." He frowned. "But if that flat front wall was solid, how did the people who lived there get down to the river for water?"

"If my suspicion is anywhere close to what that fort *really* is, nobody ever actually lived there," Keselo said. "The only purpose it serves is to conceal the mouth of the cave. Red-Beard said that the Dhralls avoid those ruins because they believe that they're cursed—or maybe haunted. If it was never a real village, there wouldn't have been any need for water or for any level ground for growing food." Then Keselo saw a brief flicker of movement in the ruin below. "There!" he hissed. "Over near the west side of the ruin."

As the three of them watched, more and more furtively moving figures came out of the shadows at the rear of the ancient ruin. The figures were all cloaked and hooded and very small, but many of them moved awkwardly, half bent over, as if standing erect was strange for them. Then one of them barked a command in a raspy voice that sent a chill through Keselo. The hooded figures all stopped, and four of them gathered atop one of the ruined buildings.

The one which had previously spoken reached up and pushed back its hood with a gleaming black appendage that looked much like the claw of a crab. The face of the creature was rounded at the top; it had two waving things protruding from its forehead, and its large eyes bulged.

"It's a *bug!*"

"So it would seem," Longbow replied tensely.

Another of the tiny enemies pushed back its hood to reveal a pale human face, and it spoke at some length with the insect. A third enemy joined them, and that one had a flickering, forked tongue and scaley skin. The last one had a furry face and long, sharp teeth, and it wasn't much bigger than a dog.

"What kind of army is that?" Keselo demanded in a hoarse whisper. "Bugs, snakes, animals, and people all mixed together and talking to each other?"

"Evidently some of the old stories had more truth to them than I'd been ready to believe," Longbow mused. "The only ones I've encountered here in Zelana's Domain have been the ones Sorgan calls snake-men. It would appear that the Vlagh has more than one variety of servants. I always thought that the people who told me about different creatures of the Wasteland were just making things up for the fun of it. It seems that I might have been wrong. This promises to be a very interesting war."

More and more of the hooded creatures emerged from the shadows behind the ruins until the entire village was crawling with them.

"I think you were right, Keselo," Rabbit said sombrely. "Those things almost have to be coming out of a cave back at the rear of that place. There isn't room enough for that many of them in those ruins. Hadn't we better get back up to the head of the ravine to warn Sorgan and Narasan?"

"In a minute," Longbow replied, studying the ruin and the surrounding slope. "It has some possibilities," he said thoughtfully.

"What has?"

"We know that the enemies are here in the ravine, and we know that they're concealed in these imitation towns. We could attack them before they attack us and keep them penned up in the ruins long enough for our friends' armies to get past these ruins—either down in the ravine or up along the rims. Sorgan and Narasan will have to abandon their fort and pull back. If they stay where they are, they're doomed."

3

They carefully climbed back down to the north bench, and then they ran back up to the gap. Keselo and Rabbit were gasping for breath when they reached the Trogite fort at sunset, but Longbow wasn't even breathing hard. Ham-Hand was standing near the back of the fort. "Where have you three been?" he demanded. "I've been looking all over for you. The cap'n wants to see you."

"Where is he?" Longbow asked.

"Up topside," Ham-Hand replied, gesturing toward the fort. "Lady Zelana's brother stopped by, and he wants to talk to you."

"That might make things a bit easier," Rabbit said. "We just saw some things that might be a little hard to explain. Which one of Zelana's brothers is here?"

"The younger one. You'd better get on up there, Rabbit. The cap'n ain't none too happy with you right now."

"I think we just saw something that'll make him even unhappier," Rabbit said as he followed Longbow and Keselo up toward the fort.

Hook-Beak was standing up at the front of the Trogite fort with Narasan and Zelana's brother Veltan.

"Where have you been, Rabbit?" Sorgan demanded.

"Keselo and I saw something that looked a bit peculiar on our way up the ravine, Cap'n," Rabbit explained. "We told Longbow about it, and he wanted to see for himself. We took him back to where we'd seen it, and we all went up the side of the ravine to have a closer look. I don't think you're going to like this one little bit, Cap'n."

"What did you see, Keselo?" Commander Narasan asked.

"There's an enemy army behind us, sir," Keselo replied. "It appears that the ones who've been charging up the stairs are just a ruse to get our attention. The main enemy force is already behind us."

"What are you talking about, Keselo?" Sorgan demanded. "We didn't see a single snake-man on our way up here."

"Ah—may I, Captain?" Zelana's brother Veltan stepped in. "Just what led you to this conclusion, Keselo?"

"When the enemy attacked this morning, Longbow noticed something peculiar," Keselo explained. "It seemed that more than half of the enemy force just vanished when they reached the foot of the stairway. It didn't make any sense at all, and then I remembered something Red-Beard told me a few days ago. He said that there are some fairly extensive caves in these mountains. Longbow, Rabbit, and I put a few things together, and we came up with an answer that none of us liked very much. It appears that the stairway's nothing but a hoax. A fair number of our enemies were charging up the stairway, but most of them went someplace else when they reached the bottom of the stairs. They had to be going *someplace,* and the notion of caves seemed to answer the question."

"Where do those caves go?" Sorgan demanded.

"I was just getting to that, Captain. When we were coming up the ravine, Rabbit and I had seen several very ancient ruins high up on the side of the gorge. Red-Beard told me that the men of Lattash avoid those ruins because of some very old superstitions—which might even have some basis in fact. Anyway, to cut this short, Longbow, Rabbit, and I went a couple miles back down the ravine to the nearest of those ruins. Normally we wouldn't have known where it was, but Red-Beard had told me that there was an old dead snag sticking out from the rim, and that the village was right below the snag."

Veltan suddenly burst out laughing.

"What's so funny?" Narasan asked him.

"Every time I turn around, that snag seems to come popping up," Veltan replied. "When Dahlaine and I were trying to pinpoint the location of this ravine, he mentioned that snag. Evidently, his thunderbolt was what had killed it quite a long time ago, and that irritated Zelana to no end. Sorry, Keselo. Go on with your story."

"Well, anyway," Keselo continued, "we hid in some tall grass near the ruin, and it wasn't very long before our enemies began to come creeping out of the shadows. I'd say that the bulk of the enemy force is behind us already, and they've rather effectively cut us off. We're trapped up here, and if we try to go back down the ravine to Lattash, I'm fairly certain that the enemy forces hidden in those ancient ruins will attack us just about every step of the way."

Hook-Beak started to swear. "We should have known about those caves, Narasan. We spent a lot of time in Lady Zelana's cave down in Lattash while we were waiting for the spring flood. If there are caves under one hill, there are bound to be caves under others as well. I think we've been had. The enemy was there all the time, but he just laid low and let us charge up that ravine until we got all the way up here, and now he's slammed the door behind us."

"Not quite *all* the doors," Longbow disagreed. "The rims of the ravine on both sides are still open, and there aren't any of those old villages up there. We can go around the enemies and leave them sitting in the ravine waiting for us." He scratched his cheek, squinting thoughtfully. "On the other hand," he added, "if this clever game they played irritates you as much as it irritates me, we could probably come up with something to make life unpleasant for them. Red-Beard knows exactly where all those cliff villages are located, so we could conceal bowmen on both sides of each one of them. If we were to send a small force down each bench, the enemy would almost certainly rush out to attack them. As soon as the enemies are out in the open, the bowmen could make life very exciting for them, wouldn't you say?"

"Now, *that* has some interesting possibilities, doesn't it, Sorgan?" Commander Narasan said enthusiastically. "I hate it when an enemy outsmarts me, and Longbow's idea gives us a way to get back at them."

"Anything's better than sitting here starving to death," Sorgan agreed.

"Here, here, here, and here," Red-Beard said, putting his finger on several spots on the representation of the north side of the ravine on Narasan's carefully drawn copy of the sculpture back in Zelana's cave. "The ones on the south side are here, here, here, and here," he added, pointing out the others. "I'm not sure about the one near the place where the river bends. The side of the ravine appears to have collapsed a long time ago, and it took most of the village with it."

"Seven, then—or possibly eight," Commander Narasan said. "Are you absolutely certain that there aren't any more, Red Beard?"

"I've been hunting this ravine for more than twenty years now, Commander, so I'm very familiar with it."

"It's not quite as bad as I thought, then," Hook-Beak said with obvious relief. He looked at Longbow. "You said that you had an idea that might keep our enemies penned up in those ruins so that they won't be able to interfere while we're running away."

"Retreating, Sorgan," Narasan corrected in a pained tone. "It's called retreating."

"It's the same thing, isn't it? What's this idea of yours, Longbow?"

"Your armies came up here along those benches on both sides of the ravine, Hook-Beak," Longbow replied, "and it appears that those imitation villages Red-Beard just pointed out to us were built at about the same time that the stairway at the gap was built, and they were in places where our enemies could watch anyone moving in the ravine. It's all starting to fit together now. The stairway was built to deceive us. The imitation villages were probably intended to be the places where the enemy's main attacks would originate. It would seem that this plan has been in the works for centuries, but it would also seem that the idea of people moving along the rims hadn't occurred to them. The benches are easier and more convenient, but people *can* move along up on the rims if it's necessary."

"You and your people would know more about that than we would, Longbow," Commander Narasan said. "We came up along the benches."

"And I'm certain that the Vlagh had serpent-people hiding in all those imitation towns high up in the sides of the ravine, watching while you did," Longbow added. "Now, if a fair number of your men started to go back down the ravine along those benches, the enemy would believe that your entire armies were returning to Lattash by the same route they used to come up here to the head of the ravine, wouldn't they?"

"That sounds logical," Narasan admitted.

"The imitation towns that conceal the cave mouths are tucked back under overhanging ledges," Longbow continued, "so Commander Narasan's men weren't able to see the ones above them when they came up along the south bench, but Captain Hook-Beak's men on the north bench *could*, isn't that right?"

"I think I see where you're going, Longbow," Commander

Narasan said. "Evidently, the enemies who built those forts didn't realize that eventually we'd develop ways to communicate with each other over long distances. When my people up on the south rim see one of the enemy forts on the north side of the ravine, they can signal Keselo, and when Hook-Beak's people see one on my side, Keselo can signal me. Even though we won't be able to see the forts, we'll know exactly where they are."

"Right," Longbow said. "Now, when Rabbit, Keselo, and I climbed up the north side of the ravine to have a closer look at that first cluster of buildings, we found a spot that was slightly above it and a little way off to one side. We could see almost all of the village from there, and I noticed a similar place over on the other side of the village. If I position well-hidden bowmen on both sides of the ruin, they'll wait until the enemy charges down the slope to attack your decoy army down on the bench, and then they'll shower arrows down on them from behind. A few enemies might roll down as far as the bench, but they'll already be dead, so they won't cause too many problems." He paused, tugging thoughtfully at one earlobe. "I think we might want to position a fair number of your soldiers armed with poison-tipped spears between the bowmen and the enemies," he added. "We wouldn't want our enemies to interfere with the bowmen while they're busy. Then, after the bowmen have eliminated most of the enemies, your soldiers can charge into the village from both sides and kill off the rest. Then we can pull down all the imitation buildings and block off the cave so that any enemies hiding back in there won't be able to come out and cause us any problems."

"Remind me never to get involved in a war when you're on the other side, Longbow," Commander Narasan said.

"It's not really too complicated, Rabbit," Keselo explained early the following morning as the two of them hurried along the north rim of the ravine in advance of Sorgan's army. "There are about twenty signals, and most of them are concerned with dangers of one kind or another. If I wave my flag from side to side over my head, it means danger. Then the next signal tells the one who's reading my signals just exactly where the danger's located. If I wave the flag up and down on my right side, the enemy force is off to the right, and if I wave it to the left, the danger's there."

"That makes sense," Rabbit said.

"Then, if I want my friends to stop right where they are, I wave the flag back and forth at about the level of my knees. You need to exaggerate quite a bit if you're some distance away, because once you get more than a half mile off, your friend's going to have trouble seeing you."

"That might be all right in the daytime, Keselo," Rabbit said, "but after the sun goes down, you're out of business, aren't you?"

Keselo laughed. "Actually, it's easier at night. We use torches when it's dark, and torches are very visible. Stay sort of close, Rabbit. I'm sure we'll be passing a lot of signals back and forth across the ravine, and I'll translate them for you as we go along."

"Isn't it sort of dangerous to use these signals during a war?" Rabbit asked. "I mean, if the signalers in every army know exactly what each signal means, won't you be giving things away that you'd rather they didn't know about?"

"That's no problem, Rabbit. There are only so many signals, but each Trogite army has its own set of meanings. I might see an enemy soldier waving a flag, but I'd have no idea at all about what he's saying, and we usually change the meanings of the signals quite often—particularly during a war."

"You Trogites just love complications, don't you?"

"It makes life more interesting, Rabbit. Doing things the same way over and over gets sort of boring after a while."

A very tall Maag was standing beside the white snag Keselo knew to be just above the enemy's village. "What are you doing up here, Tree-Top?" Rabbit asked the lanky sailor.

"The cap'n told me to run on ahead," Tree-Top replied. "I'm supposed to keep a lookout for Trogite flag-wavers on the other side of the ravine. There's one over there right now, and he's flopping that flag back and forth about something. Maybe your young friend here can figure out what he's trying to tell us."

Keselo shaded his eyes with one hand and peered across the ravine. "He's trying to tell us that the ruins are directly below us," he explained.

"We sort of knew that already," Rabbit said. "That dead tree's right here."

"Yes, I know," Keselo said, still peering across the ravine, "but we need to know where the edges are." He raised his flag and pointed inquiringly to the west with it.

The signalman across the ravine turned to face the west and jabbed a few times with his flag.

Keselo began to pace off some distance to the west, keeping a close eye on his counterpart across the ravine. When the signalman on the south rim sharply struck the ground with his flag, Keselo stopped. "Mark this spot, Rabbit," he instructed. Then he went back to the snag and moved east until the signalman on the other side told him to stop.

"Mark this place too, Rabbit," he instructed. Then he passed his flag back and forth between his hands.

"What's that supposed to mean?" Rabbit asked.

"I was thanking him," Keselo explained. "It's a way to let him know that I've received his message and that I'm ready if he wants to tell me anything else."

"You can say a lot more with that flag than I thought you could," Rabbit observed.

"That sort of depends on who's waving the other flag," Keselo replied. "The man across the ravine was my teacher, Sergeant Grolt. He was a bit rough, but when he teaches, you learn. A few cuffs along the side of your head tend to get your immediate attention."

"I can imagine," Rabbit replied. "Here comes Longbow and the cap'n."

Keselo turned and saw the archer and the pirate coming down the rim of the ravine.

"Is this it?" Hook-Beak called.

"This is the place, sir," Keselo replied. "The eastern edge of the village is directly below this marker, and the western edge is below the marker on past the dead snag."

"You're sure?"

"The man across the river is, and he can see the village from over there."

Sorgan went to the edge of the ravine and peered on down. "I don't think we'll be able to go down right here, Longbow," he said. "It's too steep. We'll have to find a place a bit farther back up the rim."

Longbow nodded. "See what the man on the other side has to say, Keselo," he suggested.

Keselo raised his flag and made several signals. Then he added a sort of circular motion.

"What's that one mean?" Rabbit asked.

"It tells him that I'm asking a question," Keselo replied. "My teacher over there invented the signal himself, and I always try to use it at least once during every conversation. It doesn't cost me anything, and it makes him feel good." Keselo was carefully watching the signals Sergeant Grolt was passing over to him.

"He tells me that there's a place where we can go down the bank about a hundred paces to the east, Captain Hook-Beak," Keselo advised. "He says that we should be able to slip into position without alerting the enemy."

"Why don't you go on down to the west marker and see if he can spot a good place for our people to go down on that side, too?" Hook-Beak suggested.

"Right," Keselo agreed.

"Rabbit," Hook-Beak said then, "go on back up the rim a ways and then drop on down to the bench. Tell Ox to hold up. We don't want him to come into sight until we're all in place. Then get back up here. I think I'll need you with us."

"Aye, Cap'n," Rabbit agreed.

The pirate Hook-Beak led his men down along the narrow creek bed Longbow and his archers were following to reach the position the signalman across the ravine had chosen for them. Keselo stayed close to Hook-Beak and intently watched Sergeant Grolt for further instructions. As he moved along, he realized that the term *pirate* might not really be appropriate in this particular situation, but all throughout his childhood and early years in Commander Narasan's army, he'd heard the word *pirate* in all references to the Maags. Hook-Beak had some rough edges, there was no question about that, but he cared for his men and did all that he could for them. That was the mark of a true leader, as Commander Narasan always said.

"Let's hold up here," Sorgan said quietly. "Let Longbow's

318 ♣ THE ELDER GODS

archers get into place first. Then we'll move into a good position to protect them. Our job here's to keep the enemy soldiers
away from the archers, since they're the ones who'll do most
of the killing—right at first, anyway. Keselo, I want you, Rabbit, and Longbow to stay close to each other. We're going to be
passing messages back and forth between several groups over
here, and probably some from this side of the ravine to
Narasan's flagman over on the other side. So I want you three
all in one place where I can find you in a hurry. Ham-Hand's
in charge on the other side of this enemy fort, and we'll want
the arrows to start flying all at the same time. When everything's ready here, I'll give you the word and you can wave
your flag for our friend across the ravine, and somebody over
there will give Ox a toot. Narasan and I worked that out before
we started. We don't want any toots coming from this side until
we attack. When Ox hears the horn, he'll come marching down
the bench like he didn't have a care in the world. That should
set off the enemy charge. We'll let Longbow decide when to
start shooting arrows, and if your friend over across the ravine
sees any enemies charging in our direction, he can signal you,
and we'll be ready for them. Have you got all that straight?"

"Aye, Cap'n," Keselo said in a fair imitation of Rabbit's usual
response to Hook-Beak's commands.

Sorgan flashed him a quick grin.

They all seemed to have lost most of their fear of the poison-
fanged servants of That-Called-the-Vlagh for some reason.
Their long, poison-tipped spears provided an almost perfect
defense, and their growing realization of the severely limited
intelligence of the venomous creatures of the Wasteland had
given them a growing confidence that this war would turn out
to be one of the easy ones.

Keselo was a bit dubious about that, however. He was almost certain that there might still be a few unpleasant surprises
awaiting them.

*　　*　　*

Keselo and Rabbit moved ahead to join Longbow at the head of the Dhrall archers quietly moving down the dry streambed, and it wasn't too long until the flagman across the ravine made a chopping motion with his flag. "This is the place, Longbow," Keselo whispered.

Longbow signaled for a halt and then moved quietly up the side of the streambed to look. Then he came back down. "Familiar spot," he murmured. "We've been here before."

"You mean it's the place where we went to have a look last time?" Rabbit asked quietly.

Longbow nodded. "I'll move my bowmen up around to the back side of the knoll on the east side of this streambed, where we looked down at the enemy position, and Sorgan and his men can stay hidden here in the streambed. The tall grass up on the knoll should conceal my bowmen, and Sorgan's men can stay hidden here in this dry wash. We'll all be out of sight— until Ox comes down the ravine. Then the enemy will start seeing more of us than he was really ready to see. Let's get into position," he added. "We still have work to do."

A horn sounded from the far side of the ravine to give the burly Ox his marching orders, and Sorgan led his men farther down the dry wash.

"This is the place, Cap'n," Rabbit said quietly. "Longbow's archers are moving around to the backside of this knoll just behind us, and when Ox comes into sight down there on the bench, the enemies are most likely going to charge down the slope to try to kill everybody down there. I don't think they'll go very far before Longbow's arrows start raining down on them, though. Then they'll see all those archers up on the rise, and they'll probably change their minds and try to charge Longbow instead of Ox. That's where we come in. This creek bed's between the enemies and Longbow's archers, so the enemies have to get past us before they can get to Longbow."

Sorgan grunted, squinting down the wash. "This is a good

position," he observed. "Your friend on the other side of the ravine's got a good eye for this sort of thing, Keselo."

"Sergeant Grolt's a veteran, Captain," Keselo replied. "He's been through more wars than he can even count."

Sorgan waved his men on in. "Keep the noise down," he said quietly to one of the bulky ship captains who led the first detachment. "That enemy fort's not too far to the west of us, and we don't want them to know that we're here."

"I know what I'm doing, Hook-Beak," the Maag replied. "You don't have to lead me around by the hand."

"Then go do what you're supposed to do and get out from underfoot," Sorgan told him.

Keselo suppressed a sudden urge to laugh. Military courtesy seemed to be an alien sort of concept to the Maags.

"I think you two need to be someplace where you can see what's happening just a little better," Sorgan suggested. "I want you to be able to see your friend across the ravine, Keselo, and Rabbit needs to watch the enemy charge. I want to know as soon as they change direction, so sing out."

"Aye, Cap'n," Rabbit replied, squinting at Longbow's knoll just behind the streambed. "There, I think," he said, pointing at a rocky outcropping about halfway up the knoll. "What with the tall grass and those boulders, we should be pretty much out of sight, but we'll still be able to see most everything, and it's well within shouting distance."

Sorgan shrugged. "Whatever works best," he said.

Rabbit led Keselo a way back up the creek bed until the rock shelf that loomed out over the enemy fort concealed them, and then they crawled back through the tall grass on the side of the knoll until they reached the rocky outcropping that stood midway between Sorgan and Longbow. "What do you think?" Rabbit whispered to Keselo. "Can you see everything you need to?"

Keselo raised his head slowly up out of the grass. "It looks good," he replied. "If I need to signal, I can slip around the rocks until I'm out of sight of the enemy."

"This is the place, then," Rabbit said. "All we have to do now is wait."

"What else is new and different?" Keselo replied.

There was a bend in the river at the bottom of the ravine just below the enemy fort, which may have had something to do with the positioning of the decoy village. Ox came striding around the bend on the north bench, and Keselo noted that the Maags trooping along behind him were probably the biggest men in Sorgan's army and they were all armed with twenty-foot-long spears. There was a certain logic there, but Keselo wasn't really certain that the servants of the Vlagh would even notice the size of the men they'd been ordered to attack.

He looked quickly at the enemy fort, but there weren't any enemies in sight. He was certain that they were watching, but they weren't making any moves as yet.

"What's keeping them?" Rabbit demanded tensely.

"They're probably holding back until there are more Maags just below them," Keselo replied. "They wouldn't want too many of Hook-Beak's soldiers to escape."

Then Keselo saw some movement back in the shadows under the overhanging rock ledge that concealed the enemy fort. "I think they're coming out," he said.

"Well, it's about time," Rabbit replied.

Then a thunderous roar echoed out from the shadows at the back of the fort, and a mass of small hooded enemies burst out of the shadows, spilled through the ancient ruins, and began to pour through the breaks in the front wall to charge down the steep side of the ravine toward the bench.

"Longbow!" Rabbit shouted.

"I see them," Longbow replied, rising to his feet.

"Shoot!"

"Not quite yet. We want as many of them out in the open as possible."

Rabbit muttered a few curses. "He does that every time," he told Keselo. "Sometimes I think he's got ice water for blood."

Longbow waited, intently watching the charge of the hooded enemies. "That should do," he said, raising his curled horn to his lips.

The single note from his horn seemed to have an almost mellow quality as it echoed back from the far side of the ravine, and then, almost as one man, the archers raised their bows, drew them back, and then waited as the echo from Longbow's horn seemed to fade on down the ravine.

Then Longbow sounded a sharper note, and the bowmen released their arrows in unison. The sheet of arrows rose up to meet the sheet coming from Ham-Hand's position on the other side of the village.

Then the arrows fell down on the enemy force, and a vast sigh rose from the ravine as hundreds of hooded enemies let out their final breath and rolled limply down the steep slope.

Longbow's archers loosed arrows by the hundreds, shooting as fast as they could, even as the Dhralls on Ham-Hand's side of the village matched them arrow for arrow.

The deadly rain falling on the slope swept the enemy force, and so far as Keselo could determine, there were almost no survivors.

The enemies rushing out of the village, however, did not even hesitate but continued their charge down through the rain of arrows.

"That's stupid!" Rabbit exclaimed. "Haven't they got any brains?"

"Evidently not," Keselo replied. "I think this is what that old shaman told us back in the cave, Rabbit. Those enemy soldiers aren't really people, so they have no sense of fear. Even when there's only one of them left, he'll keep on charging."

"That's a quick way to lose a whole army," Rabbit said. "I hope we made enough arrows."

"That's another thing that's a bit puzzling," Keselo continued. "I don't think they really understand how the Dhralls are killing them. They don't seem to know what our weapons are or how dangerous they can be."

Rabbit grinned. "Like the old saying goes, a stupid enemy is a gift from the gods," he said.

The senseless enemy charge continued for almost an hour, but then a hollow-sounding voice thundered from back in the shadows beneath the overhang.

The enemies suddenly veered off in response and charged along the side of the slope toward Longbow's knoll, and, Keselo surmised, toward Ham-Hand's position as well.

"It looks like somebody finally woke up," Rabbit observed.

Longbow's archers turned and sent a fresh arrow storm into the teeth of the enemy charge, and the dead began to pile up in rows much like freshly mown wheat. The servants of the Vlagh, however, continued to charge, and a few of them even reached the dry creek bed where Hook-Beak's Maags were concealed.

The Maags came to their feet and met the charge with long poisoned spears.

The mindless charge continued for perhaps another quarter of an hour, and Keselo observed that fewer and fewer enemy soldiers were coming out of the ruins. "I'd say that he's running out of people," Keselo said to Rabbit with a tight grin.

"What a shame," Rabbit said with a smirk.

"That's not possible!" Longbow exclaimed suddenly.

"There aren't really very many of them left, Longbow," Keselo said. "The Vlagh may have more of them, but they're back in the Wasteland."

"That's not what I meant," Longbow said tersely. "Down there—just above the bench—one of the creatures is moving."

Keselo shaded his eyes and peered down the slope. "I don't see any . . ."

"Just to the left of that uprooted tree," Longbow told him.

Keselo caught a faint flicker of movement, and then he saw one of the hooded creatures crawling very slowly over the limp bodies of the dead.

Rabbit was also staring down the slope. "Oh, *there* he is," the little sailor said. "There must have been a weak dose of the poison on the arrow that dropped him."

"It doesn't work that way, Rabbit," Longbow disagreed.

"Maybe he was just playing dead, then—hiding out among the carcasses so that he could sneak up behind Ox."

Longbow shook his head. "They aren't clever enough to do that."

"There's another one!" Keselo said sharply. "A little to the right of the first one. It seems to be crawling out of some kind of a hole in the side of the hill."

"And another one!" Rabbit hissed. "They're coming up all over down there!"

One of the hooded snake-men suddenly dashed down to the bench, ducked under the overly long spears, and bit one of the tall Maags who were following Ox. The sailor stiffened and fell even as the hooded creature slashed another Maag with the stingers along its forearm. It half turned and then collapsed when another burly Maag split its head with a heavy war axe.

"They're coming up out of the ground all over the slope down there!" Rabbit shouted.

Longbow began loosing arrows as fast as he could, but more and more of the hooded creatures came out of their hidden burrows to rush down the short slope to attack the startled Maags on the bench. The creatures that Hook-Beak called the snake-men did, in fact, behave much like snakes, creeping slowly into positions very close to the north bench and the

Maags, and then striking so fast that their unsuspecting victims had no time to react or defend themselves. The deadly venom brought screams from the dying Maags and hideous convulsions as the snake-men struck again and again.

Ox started to bellow orders, and his men began to regain their senses and to form up—in small clusters at first, fending off the attackers with their long spears, and then in more coherent groups, moving purposefully to kill all of the servants of the Vlagh. By then, however, Ox had lost more than half his men.

Then, even as the bull-shouldered Ox and his men cleared away the last of their attackers, another bellow came from the shadows at the rear of the ancient ruin, and the snake-men who'd been attacking Sorgan's position abruptly turned and ran back to the ruin.

Sorgan, almost inarticulate with rage, came storming up the slope to the knoll, spitting curses with every step. "Why didn't you tell us about those cursed mole holes?" he shouted at Keselo.

"We didn't see them, Captain Hook-Beak," Keselo said. "They're completely hidden, and we were concentrating all of our attention on the village. We thought *that* would be the place where the snake-men would be hiding. The notion of burrows never occurred to us."

"It's my fault, Sorgan," Longbow said tersely. "The signs were there, and I should have seen them."

"This is starting to get real familiar, isn't it?" Rabbit suggested. "First we find a stairway that doesn't really go anyplace, because all it was there for was to hide the caves that led to that imitation village, and now we find out that the village doesn't mean very much either, because the snake-men made their main attack from those mole-holes down by the bench. Every time we turn around, that Vlagh thing seems to outsmart us."

"To make things even worse, they all just stayed in their holes and let us go on up to the head of the ravine," Sorgan added. "Now we're trapped up here, and the snake-men are between us and Lady Zelana's territory. I don't think we're earning our pay. Keselo, why don't you hustle on up to the rim and wave your flag? I have to talk with Narasan. I think we're in a whole lot of trouble here."

"Do you think we should chase them, Cap'n?" Rabbit asked.

"I don't see much point to that," Sorgan replied. "Like you said, that village doesn't really mean anything. Narasan and I've got to come up with some way to get live men back down the ravine, and things don't look very promising right now."

Keselo and Rabbit moved very cautiously as they made their way back up to the rim, shying away from any depression or patch of raw dirt. The speed of the snake-men who'd attacked the Maags down on the bench had been most alarming, and Keselo and his small friend were both quite jumpy.

Sergeant Grolt was standing on the south rim of the ravine, and his first signal was very colorful. It roughly came out as "Why haven't you been watching?" but there were some slight flares and wiggles involved, and they carried a strong suggestion that Grolt was inventing swearwords as he went along. The fact that Commander Narasan was standing by his side might have restrained the sergeant's eloquence to some degree.

Keselo signaled *emergency* and then *conference.* Then he pointed his flag at the bottom of the ravine. It probably hadn't been necessary, since Commander Narasan had almost certainly seen what had happened on the north bench, and most likely he'd ordered Sergeant Grolt to make the same suggestion. Grolt signaled *immediately* several times and then furled his flag to cut off any further discussion.

"Well?" Rabbit asked.

"The commander was way ahead of us," Keselo replied. "Grolt was signaling for a conference almost before I was. Let's get back to Captain Sorgan. Commander Narasan wants to confer with him right now."

"I hope they can come up with some sort of solution," Rabbit said as they started on back down the slope. "The way things stand right now, we're in deep trouble."

"You noticed," Keselo replied dryly.

5

Sorgan's Maags were busily erecting a barricade along the front ledge of the dry creek bed where they'd concealed themselves to protect Longbow's archers.

"It keeps them busy," Sorgan said a bit deprecatingly. "I don't know that it'll do much good, though. I've never come up against an enemy who charges my position from under the ground before. What did Narasan have to say?"

"Sergeant Grolt was signaling *conference* almost before I'd shaken the wrinkles out of my flag, Captain," Keselo replied. "Commander Narasan agrees that it's time to talk."

"I was fairly sure he'd see things that way. Let's go on down and find out if he can come up with some way to get us out of this mess."

"Carefully, though," Longbow added. "Try not to step into any hidden burrows."

"I'll make a special point of that," Sorgan replied.

The need for extreme caution made for slow going, and it was late afternoon before they reached the bench where Ox had put his men to work draining more venom from the numerous dead enemies piled in heaps there. "I sort of stole an idea from you, Cap'n," Ox confessed. "That notion you had down near Skell's fort about sharp stakes dipped in poison come poppin' back to me when I saw that my people are right out in the open here and they ain't got enough time to build no fancy forts. I figured that stakes might slow 'em down just a bit."

"Poisoned stakes are probably a good way to even things up," Sorgan agreed. "Tell your men to keep at it, and then you'd better come along with us. Narasan and I've set up a meet, and you were a lot closer to those mole holes than anybody else. I'm sort of hoping that you might be able to tell the rest of us what we should be looking for. We're not going to be able to move very fast if we've got to probe every inch of ground with our spears."

"That's for certain, Cap'n," Ox agreed.

They crossed the rock-strewn bench to the brushy slope that led down to the narrow stream that was the headwaters of the sizeable river farther on down the ravine.

Just then, from deep within the earth there came a deep booming sound such as Keselo had never heard before, and it was followed by a sharp crack. Then the ground beneath their feet seemed to shudder.

"What was that?" Rabbit demanded, his voice a bit shrill.

Longbow dropped to his knees and put his ear to the ground. When he rose again, he had a broad grin on his face. "I think life for our enemies just got very exciting," he said. "I'd say that we're getting some help."

"I don't quite follow you, Longbow," Keselo said.

"That was an earthquake," Longbow explained. "Not a very big one, but it was probably just the beginning. I'd imagine that there'll be more of them as time goes by. They won't bother *us* very much, but we're out in the open air. The creatures of the Wasteland are down below in caves and tunnels and burrows, and being down under the ground isn't a good idea when the earth starts to rattle and shake."

"Do you think it might be Eleria again?" Keselo suggested.

Longbow shook his head. "Eleria and Lillabeth are more closely associated with the weather. This has to do with the earth, so it's probably Yaltar or Ashad."

"What are you two talking about?" Hook-Beak demanded suspiciously.

"We seem to be getting some help, Captain," Longbow replied just a bit evasively.

"I'll take all the help I can get," Sorgan declared. "Let's get on down to that little brook. Narasan and I need to talk, and it won't be long before the daylight fades. Snakes are bad enough in the daytime, but the notion of coming up against them at night sends chills up my back."

They chose a fairly clear stretch of the slope to follow on down to the small stream, and they moved cautiously, shaking every bush they came across with their spears or swords. They didn't flush out any enemies, however.

"That's a big relief, Cap'n," Ox declared when they reached the brook. "Them snake-men are starting to make me real jumpy."

"Sorgan," Commander Narasan called from the other side of the narrow stream, "what's all the delay here?"

"Just taking a few precautions, Narasan," Sorgan replied. He turned to Longbow. "Do the snake-men ever try to swim or lay quiet underwater?"

Longbow shook his head. "They're snakes, Sorgan, not fish."

"Good. Let's get across while we've still got some daylight." Then he raised his head. "You'd better have your people get a fire going, Narasan—a nice big one. We'll want lots of light after the sun goes down." Then he started wading across the brook, kicking up large splashes as he went.

*　　*　　*

"We couldn't really see very clearly from up on the rim, Sorgan," Commander Narasan said as they gathered near the large fire Red-Beard, Gunda, and Jalkan had built. "As closely as we could tell, a fair number of the enemies who were running downhill toward the bench just fell down and played dead once Longbow and his Dhralls showered them with arrows."

"Longbow says that they aren't clever enough to do that," Hook-Beak said. "Ox here was the closest to them. Tell him what you saw, Ox."

"Aye, Cap'n," Ox replied. "Well, me and my men was all pretty happy when Longbow and his people showered arrows down on them as was charging down the hill at us, and we pretty much figured that we'd just won the day. Then a whole lot of *other* snake-men started creeping up out of mole holes that weren't no more than a few feet from where we was all standing around celebrating, and they was right on top of us, biting and stinging my people afore we could blink twice. I lost more than half of my men afore I could get my wits together and start shouting orders. We managed to clean out the snake-men, but it really cost us a lot of good men."

"They crawl around under the ground?" Gunda demanded incredulously. "That's no way to fight a war. I've never heard of any soldiers that do that."

"We've made a serious mistake by thinking of them as soldiers," Longbow said. "Soldiers, or warriors, function in groups, but the creatures of the Wasteland don't think that way. They attack as individuals. They aren't really strong enough to fight a well-armed soldier, but they don't have to be strong—just fast. Most importantly, though, they have to be close to those they intend to kill. They have to surprise those they've chosen as victims. Without surprise, they stand no chance of winning."

"You know the country around here better than any of the rest of us do, Red-Beard," Sorgan said. "Are there any passes back a ways in the mountains that'd get us back to Lattash without going down this cursed ravine?"

Red-Beard squinted at the nearby peaks. "I don't think so, Hook-Beak," he said a bit dubiously. "It's too early in the year. There are a few passes higher up in the mountains, but they're still clogged with snow."

"That answers that, then," Sorgan said glumly. "It looks like we're going to have to wade through snakes all the way back down to Lattash."

"Everything the snake-men have done so far seems to be based on deception," Narasan mused. "First there was that stairway that was only there to hide those tunnels, and now we come across those imitation villages that don't really mean anything either. I'd say that it's entirely possible that both sides of the ravine are honeycombed with those burrows. We could very well have one of those snake-men lurking within five feet of every one of us no matter where we go in this ravine. This whole thing's nothing but a death trap."

"Burrowing *is* natural behavior for serpents," Longbow explained. "The burrow is both a shelter from the weather and a hidden place from which to strike. It's instinctive—which is about as far as the intelligence of a serpent will go."

"If they're that simpleminded, how did they manage to come up with the ideas of the stairway and these ruined villages?" Narasan demanded.

"I'd imagine that the idea of stairways and villages originated with That-Called-the-Vlagh," Red-Beard suggested. "In a peculiar sort of way, it's been behaving much like a fisherman. It baits its hooks with stairways and villages."

"And we're the ones who took the bait," Rabbit added. "Now we've got to find some way to break that thing's line."

"Can anybody think of some way we might be able to flush those snake-men out of those burrows?" Gunda asked. "Water, maybe, or possibly smoke?"

"That might be a possibility," Narasan agreed. "Smoke would probably be better. Even if it doesn't kill them, it'll reveal the locations of their burrows."

Just then there was another of those deep booming sounds coming from deep within the earth, and the shuddering of the ground this time was more violent than it had been the previous time, and large boulders, unseated by the earthquake, came rolling down the sides of the ravine.

There was a sudden, deafening crash of thunder and a brief, blinding light. Then Veltan was there. His eyes were wild, and his face was deathly pale. "Get up out of this ravine!" he shouted. "Your lives are in danger!"

"What's the matter?" Commander Narasan demanded.

"Move, Narasan!" Veltan shouted. "If you stay here, you'll die! Run! And when you get up to the rim of the ravine, pull your people back until you're at least five miles back up into the mountains! You're standing right in the middle of the most dangerous place in the world! Get out of here just as fast as you can!"

From deep within the earth there came another series of sharp cracking sounds, and the ground beneath their feet began to shake again, but this time it convulsed so violently that it was almost impossible to remain standing.

Then, from off to the east there came a sound that went beyond sound, and a vast pillar of smoke and debris shot miles up into the sky.

"Fire mountain!" Red-Beard exclaimed. "Run!" He spun and ran up the riverbank.

"Now!" Longbow said sharply as the shuddering of the earth beneath their feet subsided. "Run before it starts again."

With Hook-Beak in the lead they splashed through the shallow stream to the other side of the river, even as Commander Narasan and Red-Beard scrambled up the riverbank toward the south bench.

"Rabbit!" Sorgan said sharply when they reached the north riverbank. "Scamper up to the bench just as fast as you can and tell all those men who were following Ox to get up to the rim of the ravine before the sides collapse and bury them alive!"

"Aye, Cap'n," Rabbit replied, already running.

Hook-Beak, Keselo, and Longbow had just reached the north bench when the ground began to shudder violently again.

Longbow looked up the slope. "This way!" he told Hook-Beak and Keselo, already running toward a large boulder jutting up out of the center of the bench.

Rocks were rolling and bouncing down the north side of the ravine to spill across the bench in a thunderous landslide. The three men huddled behind their protective boulder, listening to the sharp crashing sound of large rocks slamming into the other side of their shelter.

"What were Veltan and Red-Beard talking about, Longbow?" Hook-Beak demanded. "What's a fire mountain?"

"It's a mountain that spews out melted rock," Longbow explained. "I've seen a couple of them up in the lands of Old-Bear's tribe."

"Rocks don't melt, Longbow," Sorgan scoffed.

"They will if the fire under them's hot enough," Longbow disagreed, "and melted rock will run downhill just like melted ice will."

The trek up to the rim of the ravine involved a series of short dashes from one slightly protected spot to another, with short pauses during the recurring earthquakes to permit the accompanying landslides to rush past.

Keselo was winded by the time they reached the rim, and he paused to catch his breath.

"Great gods!" Sorgan gasped, staring toward the east in stunned disbelief.

Keselo turned and saw dark smoke boiling up out of the twin mountains that formed the gap. Then there came another earthshaking explosion, and sheets of flame came spewing out of the two peaks in twin geysers of liquid fire, reaching up and up toward the sky and spattering the sides of nearby peaks with globs of molten rock.

"Run!" Sorgan bellowed to his men. "Get back away from the edge!"

The Maags were all gaping at the explosion at the head of the ravine.

"I said *run!*" Sorgan roared. "Run or die!"

Keselo leaned out over the edge to look briefly at the ancient ruin just below. A fountain of fire came spurting out of the hidden cave mouth, and it blasted the walls and towers far out over the river. The molten rock poured down the steep slope, and a vast cloud of steam boiled up into the air when the liquid rock reached the brook.

Keselo bolted, running as hard as he could toward the nearby mountains.

The twin eruptions continued for the rest of the day and on through the night. Hook-Beak's forces gradually gathered together on the steep north slope of a nearby mountain, quite obviously in the hope that the mountain might shield them from the molten rock still spewing out of the twin mountains at the head of the ravine. Along toward morning, Ox, who'd been out gathering the straying Maags who'd survived the encounter with the snake-men and the sudden violent eruption, came wearily up the slope. "This was about as many as I could find, Cap'n," he reported. "I'm pretty sure there's more of them, but they're probably *way* back in the mountains by now."

"Did you come across any of the snake-men?" Sorgan demanded.

"Not so much as a single one, Cap'n," Ox replied. "Since they ain't none too smart in the first place, I'd say they probably tried to hide out in them nice safe caves and tunnels and burrows, and those are the *last* places anybody with any brains wants to be along about now. I'd say that the war's over, Cap'n.

All our enemies just got theirselves tossed into the cooking pot." He frowned slightly. "I really hate to see all that fresh-cooked meat go to waste, but I don't think I'd care much for fried snake."

"I could probably get along without it myself," Sorgan agreed with a grin. "Look on the bright side, though, Ox. As hot as rock has to be to start melting, all those dead snakes are probably way overcooked."

"There is that, I suppose," Ox conceded.

Longbow was standing off to one side, and he motioned to Keselo and Rabbit and led them some distance away from Sorgan and Ox. "Zelana wants to speak with us," he told them quietly.

"It's quite a long way back to Lattash," Rabbit protested.

"She came up here," Longbow explained. "She's waiting back in the forest just a little ways."

"How did she get word to you?" Keselo asked. "You've been right out in plain sight ever since we came up out of the ravine, and I didn't see a sign of her."

"Longbow and Lady Zelana can talk to each other without anybody else hearing them," Rabbit explained. "A lot of that was going on in the harbor at Kweta when Longbow and I killed off some Maags who were trying to steal the cap'n's gold blocks. That was a wild night, let me tell you." Then Rabbit looked sharply at Longbow. "How far down the mountains will that melted rock go?" he demanded.

"Probably all the way down to Mother Sea. Why?"

"Won't that destroy Lattash?"

"Probably, yes. I think Chief White-Braid's tribe might have to find someplace else to live."

"Probably so, but Lady Zelana has her gold stacked up in that cave just outside of town, and if this liquid rock happens to run into her cave, the gold will melt and get all mixed up with the rock, and the cap'n won't get paid, will he?"

"Quit worrying so much, Rabbit," Longbow said. "Zelana's

probably already moved her gold," He looked around. "She's right over there in that clump of trees. Let's go see what she has to say."

Zelana and Eleria sat side by side on a moss-covered log in the center of a clearing in the middle of the grove. "Is everybody all right?" Zelana asked as Keselo and Rabbit followed Longbow into the clearing.

"As far as we know, they are," Longbow replied. "Did your younger brother happen to remember to warn Sorgan's cousin Skell? Sorgan's been worrying about that since yesterday."

"Veltan warned Skell on his way up here, Longbow," Zelana said. "Tell Sorgan that he worries too much."

"Your younger brother cut things a little fine, Zelana," Longbow declared. "He should have warned us earlier."

"That was Yaltar's fault," Eleria told him. "I think his volcano got away from him. Vash tends to overdo things now and then."

"Who's Vash, baby sister?" Rabbit asked.

"Did I say Vash?" Eleria asked. "I meant Yaltar, of course."

"Yaltar was angry, Eleria." Zelana excused Veltan's little boy. "Those caves and burrows took us all by surprise, and Yaltar doesn't like surprises, so he overreacted."

"Then the earthquakes and all of that melted rock were sort of like Eleria's warm wind?" Rabbit suggested.

"My wind wasn't nearly as nasty as Yaltar's volcano, Bunny," Eleria sniffed. "Boys are so noisy. They just have to show off when they do something."

"His liquid rock did seal up the Vlagh's caves and burn up all the snake-men in the burrows, baby sister," Rabbit reminded her. "We were in a lot of trouble before those twin peaks up at the gap exploded."

"There's something I don't quite understand, ma'am," Keselo said to Zelana. "If you and your family are able to unleash these catastrophes, why did you go to all the trouble and expense of hiring armies to fight this war for you? Why didn't you just go ahead and deal with your enemies by yourselves?"

"It's just a little complicated, Keselo," Zelana replied. "That-Called-the-Vlagh created its servants by the thousands, so they vastly outnumber the people of the four Domains, and they're very savage. Our people aren't nearly as numerous as the creatures of the Wasteland. When we learned that the Vlagh was about to unleash the monsters of the Wasteland on our Domains, we knew we were going to need help, so my brothers, my sister, and I went out to other lands to buy that help with gold. We didn't really understand at that time just how far the Dreamers could go. My family and I are limited by certain constraints. I'm sure that none of *us* could have unleashed that volcano the way Yaltar's dream did, or caused the flood Eleria's dream set in motion. Our minds don't work that way. The dreams don't *have* limitations, though. They're based on imagination—or possibly inspiration—not reality." She paused. "Is this making any sense to you at all, Keselo?" she asked him.

"Not really, ma'am," he admitted.

"I'm sure it'll come to you in time," she said with a faint smile.

"Things got a little exciting there for a while," Rabbit was saying to Zelana. "We were all fairly certain that we were up against a bone-stupid enemy, but they're not nearly as ignorant as we'd thought. If it hadn't been for that fire mountain, we'd have been in some real trouble."

"It's easy to underestimate the intelligence of the creatures of the Wasteland, little man," Zelana replied. "As individuals, they're stupid beyond belief, but as a group, they have a surprising intelligence. They have many ways to communicate with each other. Some of them speak, but others are more elemental. Unlike you man-creatures, they tell each other everything they've encountered, and those who receive that information share it with still others. Everything that any one of them has seen or experienced becomes the possession of all members of the group, and the group is wiser by far than the individual members. The ultimate decisions are made by That-Called-the-Vlagh, but I think that the Vlagh itself is to some degree susceptible to the dictates of that overmind. They will most probably surprise you many times. I know they've surprised *me* quite a few times already, and that hasn't made me very happy."

"What we really need, then, is some way to disrupt their communication with each other, wouldn't you say?" Keselo suggested. "Loud noise, maybe, or dense smoke, or possibly odors of some kind."

"Odors is something we should really investigate," Zelana agreed. "If something smells bad enough, it might very well interfere with their ability to communicate with each other. I'll speak with my brothers and my sister about it." She paused and then moved on. "The servants of the Vlagh have been blocked in my Domain, but there are still three more Domains that need protecting. I'm almost positive that Dahlaine and Aracia will need help as much or more than Veltan and I. What I'm getting at, gentlemen, is that I'm sure that we'll need Hook-Beak and Narasan for much longer than we'd originally anticipated."

"I'm not too sure that the cap'n will buy into a long war," Rabbit said dubiously. "He'll help Commander Narasan because the Trogites helped us, but that might be about as far as he'll be willing to go. Once we win Narasan's war, the cap'n might just decide to take his gold and go on back home." The little fellow paused reflectively. "We Maags aren't really all that good at land wars," he admitted. "All this slogging around in the mud, sleeping on the ground, and eating cold food sort of goes against our grain. We like short, noisy wars that're over by suppertime."

Zelana shrugged. "The offer of more gold will probably persuade Hook-Beak that land war's not really all that bad."

"Gold's nice," Rabbit countered, "but you've got to live long enough to spend it. I'm not sure how Keselo felt about what happened in the ravine, but it scared me silly."

"It sort of made my hair stand on end as well," Keselo admitted. "I've been on the opposite side of the ravine from Commander Narasan for quite some time now, so I'm not exactly sure how he feels about what happened here, but he might be starting to have second thoughts. Those serpent-men who were trying to kill us aren't intelligent enough to be afraid. Usually, we Trogites feel that a stupid enemy is a gift from the gods, but if the stupidity goes far enough to eliminate fear, it might have caused the commander to have second thoughts about this whole arrangement. A key element in any war strategy is undermining the enemy's morale. A frightened man will usually just give up and run away. An insect or a serpent doesn't know *how* to be afraid, though, so many standard Trogite tactics just won't work."

"I want you gentlemen to think very hard about this," Zelana said firmly. "You need to come up with some way to persuade your leaders to stay here and help us. If you can't, I might just have to burn all their ships to keep them here, whether they like it or not."

"We should get back," Longbow told Keselo and Rabbit. "Hook-Beak might miss us, and I don't think we want any Maags to come looking for us. They don't really need to know anything about this discussion, do they?"

"Not if we're going to keep talking about burning ships, they don't," Rabbit agreed.

Keselo was profoundly troubled as he lay wrapped in his blankets some distance from the fires in the encampment of the Maags. The thunderous eruption of the twin volcanos at the head of the ravine was subsiding, and there was much cheer in the ranks of Hook-Beak's army. The Maags continued to marvel about "the greatest stroke of good luck in history" as if the eruption had been nothing more than sheer coincidence.

Keselo, however, knew better, and he profoundly wished that he didn't. Zelana's coldly brutal evaluation of the situation here in the Land of Dhrall chilled Keselo to the bone. Although she was beautiful beyond belief, there was a rock-hard practicality at her center, which only Eleria could soften, and Eleria, when the situation required it, was even worse.

The Dreamers could unleash natural disasters far worse than the ordering of armies into hopeless struggles and threatening to burn the ships that were the only hope of escape those armies had.

Worse yet, the soldiers, ignorant of what was truly happening, were cheering.

Keselo, however, had gradually come to perceive the true nature of That-Called-the-Vlagh. Driven by an uncontrollable need to possess the entirety of the Land of Dhrall and surrounded by countless nonhuman servants, the Vlagh would pursue its need despite defeat after defeat after defeat, giving no thought to the vast number of servants it would inevitably lose. Even worse, perhaps, was the fact that the Vlagh did not function solely on instinct. There was an evil cunning there, which in the end might very well overcome them all—human or divine.

And now the Maags and Trogites were effectively trapped here in the Land of Dhrall, doomed to fight a dreadful war that they could not possibly win, given the overwhelming numbers of their enemies.

THE PINK GROTTO

1

Eternal Zelana was filled with unspeakable horror and an overwhelming sense of guilt at the chaos unleashed by the Dreamers. It had seemed at first that her elder brother's solution to the current crisis had been the perfect answer. Eleria's flood and Yaltar's volcanos were natural disasters, after all, and nobody was *really* to blame for them, were they?

It had seemed so to Zelana at first. Her Domain had been threatened by the creatures of the Wasteland, and now the threat was gone. None of the events in the ravine had been the result of anything she had *personally* done, so why was she now filled with this wrenching sense of guilt? No matter how many times she said to herself, "*I* didn't do any of this," the accusing finger at the back of her awareness continued to point directly at her.

Slowly, reluctantly, she was finally forced to face a dreadful reality. The disasters unleashed by the innocent Dreamers had been a response to *her* needs. It was becoming increasingly clear that the children could somehow sense what she wanted, and their dreams provided it. The dreams were gifts, in a certain sense, but they carried with them a dreadful burden of responsibility, and try though she might, Zelana could not shrug off that burden.

And so it was that finally, without so much as saying a word to her brothers or sister, Zelana of the West took her beloved Dreamer Eleria in her arms and fled.

"What are we doing, Beloved?" Eleria cried, clinging to Zelana in fright as they rose up and up through the smoky midnight air toward the pale moon.

"Hush," Zelana told her as she searched with her mind and senses for an eastward-flowing wind.

Far below them Zelana could see Yaltar's cursed volcano spewing molten lava high into the air, and the glowing river of liquid rock surging down the ravine toward the village of Lattash. "Idiocy!" Zelana fumed, still rising and searching.

"Please, Beloved!" Eleria cried. "I'm afraid!"

"Everything's all right, dear," Zelana told the child, trying her best to sound calm.

"Where are we going?"

"Home," Zelana replied. "I've had about enough of all this, haven't you?"

"Do we have to go up so high?" Eleria cried, clinging desperately to Zelana.

"Hush, Eleria. I'm trying to concentrate."

It was hardly more than a fitful breeze, but it was moving in the right direction, so Zelana seized it, and they moved haltingly through the spring night, away from the horror below them.

Once they had moved out beyond the west coast of the mainland, the breeze grew stronger, and it carried them across the straits to the coast of the Isle of Thurn. Zelana thanked the breeze, and she and Eleria drifted south through the moonlit air toward the stark cliffs on the southern margin of the Isle.

"The world looks different from up here, doesn't it, Beloved?" Eleria said. She seemed a bit calmer now, and she relaxed her desperate grip somewhat. "This is quite a bit like swimming, isn't it?"

"A little bit, yes," Zelana agreed. "You do know why we absolutely *had* to come away, don't you?"

"Well, not entirely, Beloved," Eleria admitted. "Is something wrong?"

"Everything was wrong, Eleria. Things weren't supposed to happen the way they did."

"We won, didn't we? Isn't that all that really matters?"

"No, dear, dear Eleria," Zelana replied, tightening her embrace about the child. "We lost much more than we won. The Vlagh stole our innocence. We did things we weren't supposed to do, and nothing will ever be the same again." She peered down at the south coast of Thurn. "There it is," she said when her eyes found a familiar beach glowing in the moonlight. "Let's go home."

They settled quietly through the cool night air to the calm surface of Mother Sea, and then, as one, they dove deep into the dark water to the hidden mouth of their grotto.

The pink light of the grotto seemed pale and soft under the gentle touch of the moon, and Zelana clung to that light, pushing the horrid memories away.

"It's nice to be home again, Beloved," Eleria said. "I think I've had about enough excitement for a while, haven't you?"

"More than enough, dear," Zelana agreed. "Are you hungry?"

"Not really," Eleria said. "I think I'd like to sleep now. I wasn't sleeping very well back there, and it seems to be catching up with me now."

"Go to bed, child," Zelana told her fondly. "We're back where we're supposed to be, and the world can't hurt us here."

"Kiss-kiss," Eleria said, holding her arms out.

Zelana took the child in her arms and kissed her. "Go to bed, Eleria. Nothing can bother you here, and I'll watch over you."

Eleria sighed contentedly and went to her bed, nestling down with her pink pearl in her hand. She drifted off to sleep, and Zelana of the West envied her, even though she could scarcely remember sleep. Idly she wondered what it might be like to sleep away a part of every day and then to rise and eat food rather than light. Because of their unique situation, the Dreamers were experiencing things Zelana and her family had never experienced, nor would they ever.

Zelana's thoughts wandered and circled almost like hungry birds as she sat lost in contemplation in the glowing pink light of her grotto, but inevitably they returned once more to the horror of what had taken place in the ravine above the village of Lattash.

Why had Veltan's Dreamer gone to such extremes? Yaltar had seemed to be a solid, sensible little boy, but at the first hint of a threat to Zelana's Domain, he'd gone absolutely wild.

Except, she reminded herself, it wasn't *her* Domain Yaltar had sought to defend. It was the Domain of his sister, Bala-cenia.

That thought jerked Zelana sharply around. Dahlaine had assured them all that the Dreamers would have no memories of their previous existence, but both Yaltar and Eleria had occasionally referred to each other by their real names. Could it be that Dahlaine's assurances had been nothing more than bald-faced lies designed to gain their approval? Dahlaine was obviously capable of lying. Zelana had caught him lying to her innumerable times herself, and she was fairly certain that Veltan and Aracia had also seen their elder brother wandering away from the truth.

That thought raised a very disturbing possibility. If Yaltar knew that Eleria was really Balacenia, did he also know that he was Vash? Had all four of the Dreamers been quietly deceiving their elders? If Vash and Balacenia had been engaged in this deception, wasn't it entirely possible that . . .

What *were* their names? Zelana should know the real names

of Lillabeth and Ashad, but when she searched her memories of the countless eons that lay behind, she could not for the life of her bring the other two names to the surface. It was maddening! The names were right on the tip of her tongue, but they absolutely refused to come out.

She pushed that away. The names would probably surface as soon as she stopped worrying at the problem.

Longbow had definitely been the proper choice as the man to lead the Dhralls of her Domain. The outlanders had stood in awe of him, not only because of his unerring accuracy with his bow, but also because he seemed able to come up with answers to impossible problems. Had it not been for Longbow, Zelana was certain that the outlanders might very well have viewed the Dhralls as ignorant savages ripe for plundering, or even for enslavement.

That notion brought Zelana up short. Her encounters with the outlanders hadn't been very extensive, but she'd occasionally caught hints that the more advanced cultures of the world beyond the shores of the Land of Dhrall routinely gathered up the people of more primitive societies and sold them as slaves. Zelana's eyes narrowed. *Let* them try that here. There were all sorts of things—short of killing—Zelana could do to them to persuade them to give up that particular notion.

Not all of the outlanders were evil, however, she realized. Eleria herself had unerringly found two, at least, who could be trusted. The child had chosen the Maag known as Rabbit and the earnest young Trogite Keselo, and had somehow managed to persuade Dahlaine that those two were the ones who should be made aware of the *real* situation here in the Land of Dhrall. There were times when Eleria went far beyond what Dahlaine had assured them would be the limitations of the Dreamers. Child Eleria *pretended* to be simple and sweet, but the more Zelana thought about it, the more it seemed that the kissing and lap-sitting were means to an end far more serious than demonstrations of childish affection. Could it be that the volcanic eruption that had so effectively destroyed the servants of the Vlagh in the ravine above Lattash had *not* been the desperate response of Yaltar? Could the eruption possibly have been Eleria's idea?

Zelana shuddered back from that unthinkable notion.

Hideous though it was, however, Zelana was forced to admit that pouring molten rock into the caves of the servants of the Vlagh had been far and away the most effective solution to an otherwise unsolvable problem. Earthquakes might have killed all the invaders, but the possibility that a few of the caves could have remained intact would have left doubts. Molten lava, however, left no doubts. The servants of the Vlagh were gone, and Zelana's Domain was safe.

Zelana corrected that notion. It had not been *her* Domain Yaltar's dream had saved; it was the Domain of Balacenia.

She was almost certain that the Maags and Trogites had taken ship, or would very soon, to sail down along the coast to Veltan's Domain. There was no absolute certainty that the servants of the Vlagh would attack Veltan's domain in the foreseeable future. It might well be that Yaltar's volcano had so decimated the creatures of the Wasteland that it would take many generations for them to propagate replacements. Then again, perhaps not. That-Called-the-Vlagh could produce countless offspring in virtually no time at all, and Zelana's brother Veltan knew that as well as anybody. The servants of the Vlagh would almost certainly attack each of the four Domains in their mindless quest for more land. The Vlagh wanted—or needed— the entire continent if it was to have any chance at all to expand its swarm.

What *were* their names? It was infuriating! The names were right there. Why couldn't she remember them?

Zelana yearned for sleep. The endless eons of her cycle weighed down upon her, and she was glad that the cycle was almost over.

But Eleria wasn't ready to take up the burden of Dominion

yet. There were so many things she had to know, and there was so little time left to teach her. The changing of the cycles had posed no real problems in times past. The man-things had been little more than animals during Balacenia's previous cycle, but they had come so far now, and it seemed that they were growing and developing faster and faster with each passing year. Zelana shuddered back from the thought of what they might be when Balacenia's cycle had run its course and Zelana awakened once more to begin her next cycle.

She smiled faintly. Maybe Veltan had come up with the best solution after all, and the moon was still there.

Zelana pushed that thought away.

The lovely village of Lattash was doomed, of course. Yaltar's idiocy had seen to that. Even now the lava from the twin peaks was flowing inexorably down the ravine, consuming all in its path. The people of White-Braid's tribe would have to leave their homes and find some new place and build a new village. The loss of Lattash caused Zelana an almost physical pain.

"The gold!" she suddenly exclaimed. "I forgot all about the gold in that cave! I'll have to go back and move it to a safer place. How could I possibly have forgotten that? I must be even older than I'd thought. First I forget my gold, and now I can't remember names." She looked at the sleeping child. "Please wake up, Balacenia," she pleaded softly. "I just can't carry all of this anymore. I'm so tired, so very, very tired."

If Yaltar was aware of Eleria's true identity, and Eleria was aware of Yaltar's, could it be possible that they knew other things as well? Zelana searched back through her memories to see if she could find any evidence whatsoever that the children had, no matter how briefly, used their dormant abilities to alter reality in any small way. Their dreams were one thing, but if they'd been using their gifts consciously, the fabric of reality could very well be in danger.

There seemed to be nothing overt. The only peculiarity Eleria had shown was her overwhelming need for the affection of the mortals. Her "kiss-kiss" game with Longbow, Rabbit, and finally even the stuffy young Trogite Keselo had seemed on the surface to be no more than some childish game, but what if it went much further? For obvious reasons, Zelana had never actually witnessed Balacenia's methods to control the man-things of the Western Domain. Could it possibly be that she'd just kissed them all into submission? It had certainly worked with the pink dolphins when Eleria had been no more than a baby. Zelana almost laughed. What a clever way to rule that would be, and, by extension, it might just explain why Yaltar had gone to such extremes to protect Balacenia's Domain. A few of those "kiss-kiss" encounters would have rendered poor Vash helpless. Then, with Vash wrapped around her finger, Balacenia could have turned to . . .

What *were* their names? It was maddening! Why *couldn't* Zelana remember their names?

THE
TIME
OF
SORROW

1

It was early summer now in the Domain of Zelana of the West, but this summer was unlike any other Red-Beard had ever seen. Summer is usually a time of beauty, but this one was haunted by the twin fire mountains at the head of the ravine. Each sunrise seemed to be smeared with blood as the fire mountains continued to belch forth smoke and ash, and a perpetual gloom hung over the village of Lattash.

A few of the women of the tribe had gone through the motions of planting the customary gardens, but what was the use of that? The village was almost certainly doomed, and in all probability it wouldn't even be here by next autumn at harvesttime.

Lattash still looked much the same as it had for years. The bay was still blue, the sandy beach was still white, and the forest to the east was still dark green as it mounted up the foothills toward the snow-covered peaks. The tides continued to rise and fall as they had since the beginning of time. The only noticeable difference lay in the river that had always come joyously down the ravine to join the waters of the bay. It was no longer a river, though. It was hardly even a brook. The cursed fire mountains had obviously sealed off the source of the river, and it was now no more than a scant trickle that would almost certainly dry up by midsummer.

That, of course, would mark the end of Lattash. Without fresh water, the gardens of the women of the tribe would die out, and there would be no food to eat next winter. The mood in the village was somber, and a cloud of melancholy seemed to hang over Lattash.

Red-Beard sighed. There was no getting around the fact that it was time to seek out another home for the people of White-Braid's tribe. That was where the problem lay. Red-Beard's uncle, Chief White-Braid, was so overwhelmed with sorrow by the inevitable loss of the village that had been the home of the tribe for many centuries that he couldn't function anymore. The tribe had to find a suitable new location, build new lodges, and grow food before winter came again, but Chief White-Braid refused to even talk about it. No matter how much Red-Beard cudgeled his brain, he couldn't for the life of him come up with a way to bring his uncle back to his senses.

Muttering curses under his breath, Red-Beard went looking for Longbow.

"I don't see that you've got much choice, Red-Beard," his friend said gravely as the two of them stood on the protective berm looking down at the tiny trickle of muddy water that was all there was left of the river. "The fire mountains killed the servants of the Vlagh, certainly, but it looks to me like they've *also* killed the village of Lattash. Without water, your tribe will either have to find a new place to live or stay here and die."

"I know that, Longbow," Red-Beard replied. "I can see it as well as you can, but how am I going to be able to pound the idea down Uncle White-Braid's throat? Every time I even so much as hint at the notion, his eyes go blank and he starts talking about something else. He refuses to even *think* about relocating the tribe. Lattash is so much a part of him that he won't even consider moving."

"You'll probably have to step around him and take charge of the tribe yourself, then."

"I can't do that!" Red-Beard exclaimed. "He's the chief. If I start showing that kind of disrespect, the whole tribe will turn their backs on me. They won't follow any orders I might give them."

"They will if your uncle tells them to." Longbow looked at the clustered lodges of the village and the fishnets hanging from poles along the beach. "I'm sure this was a good place to live in the past, my friend, but the past is over, and *now* came along just as soon as the river started to dry up. *Then* went away, and your tribe's living in the world of *now*. If they don't move very soon, they'll die for lack of food and water. If you put it to them in those terms, I'm sure they'll listen to you. If your chief isn't willing to give the necessary commands because of his sorrow, he'll have to step aside and hand the authority off to someone else—you, most likely." Longbow smiled faintly. "'Chief Red-Beard' has a rather pleasant sound to it, don't you think?"

"Not to me, it doesn't," Red-Beard objected. "Do you have any idea of how stuffy and tedious the life of a chief must be? I don't think I could stand that."

"Be brave, Chief Red-Beard," Longbow said with mock sententiousness. "If something is for the good of your tribe, you can't just turn your back on it, can you?"

"You had to go and say that, didn't you?" Red-Beard grumbled sourly.

Longbow shrugged. "It's time for you to face reality, my friend. Sooner or later you *will* have to assume the authority in your tribe if your uncle can no longer function. This might give you some practice in the fine art of being stuffy. Right now, though, we've got a more pressing problem to deal with."

"The sky is falling, maybe?"

"Well, not today, probably, but we've got a goodly number of unhappy people in those ships out in the bay. In her infinite wisdom, Zelana of the West saw fit to leave the village without bothering to pay Sorgan Hook-Beak and the other Maags for their services during the recent unpleasantness."

"The gold's stacked up in that cave of hers just outside the village," Red-Beard reminded his friend. "Why don't they just walk into the cave and pay themselves?"

"They've already tried that, but they can't get into the tunnel where the gold's piled up."

"What did Zelana do?—make the ceiling fall down or something?"

"No, it's completely intact, but there's a solid wall blocking off the tunnel that's filled with all those pretty yellow blocks. It's a very unusual sort of wall. The Maags can see through it, but it's harder than any stone. That means that they can look at the gold as much as they want, but they can't reach it. Ox took his axe into the cave and chopped at the wall for the better part of a day, but he didn't so much as knock a chip out of it. He did manage to destroy his axe, though. Now Sorgan's absolutely positive that our Zelana's trying to cheat him."

"She wouldn't do that."

"You and I know that, but Hook-Beak doesn't know her as well as we do. Lying, cheating, and stealing are part of the Maag culture, so honesty's an alien concept for them. If Zelana doesn't come back here fairly soon, we might just have another war on our hands before long."

"Now I've got something *else* to worry about." Then Red-Beard remembered something. "Rabbit told me that you and Zelana can speak with each other without making a sound. He said you two did that back in the Land of Maag when trouble broke out in the harbor at Kweta. Could you possibly reach out to her from here?"

"I've already tried it a few times. Either she's too far away, or she refuses to listen to me."

"Do you think that maybe Eleria could hear you? If anybody could bring Zelana to her senses, it'd be Eleria. If nothing else, the little girl could probably kiss Zelana into submission. She had you and Rabbit and that young Trogite, Keselo, wrapped around her little finger in no time at all."

"Tell me about it," Longbow said. Then he squinted at his friend. "She never tried that on you, did she?"

Red-Beard shrugged. "I probably don't have anything she wants," he replied.

"Why don't we go out to the *Seagull* and have a talk with Sorgan?" Longbow suggested. "If he realizes that we're trying to get word to Zelana that it's time to come back and give him the gold she promised him, maybe he won't come ashore and burn the village of Lattash right down to the ground."

"Let's not rush into anything here, Longbow," Red-Beard said in mock seriousness. "If the Maags come ashore and burn Lattash to the ground, it might just persuade my uncle that it's time to pack up and move on. Then I won't have to do anything except obey his orders—or sneak off to someplace where he can't find me. He'll go back to being the chief, and I won't have to grow up."

"Don't hold your breath, Red-Beard. Let's go see Sorgan Hook-Beak."

The sun seemed very bright as Red-Beard deftly drove his canoe toward the *Seagull* with long, smooth strokes of his paddle. It was early summer now, and Red-Beard was sure that the fishing would be very good. He pushed that thought aside. Despite the bright sun and sparkling water, there wouldn't be any fishing today. He was almost positive that he and Longbow would have to waste a perfect day listening to Hook-Beak's complaints.

"Your canoe moves smoothly," Longbow noted.

"I got lucky when I put this one together," Red-Beard replied modestly. "I finally managed to get the right curve on the ribs. The one I built before was sort of skittish. Every time I sneezed, she'd roll over and dump me into the bay."

"I've had the same thing happen to me a few times," Longbow admitted. "Sometimes I think canoes have a warped sense of humor."

Red-Beard tried to avoid looking at the towering cloud of smoke and ash spouting up out of the twin volcanos that blotted out most of the eastern sky, but he ruefully realized that he wasn't going to make it go away by not looking at it. "Have you managed to come up with a way to pacify Sorgan yet?" he asked.

"Let's try 'emergency.' "

"You missed me there, I'm afraid."

Longbow shrugged. "Zelana left in a hurry. Doesn't that sort of hint that there might be a crisis somewhere that needed her immediate attention?"

"We can try it, I suppose," Red-Beard said a bit dubiously. "Trying to persuade Hook-Beak that there's something in the world more important than he is might be a bit difficult, though."

"We'll see," Longbow replied as Red-Beard eased his canoe in against the *Seagull.*

"Did she finally decide to come home?" Rabbit called down to them from the *Seagull*'s deck. "If the cap'n doesn't get the gold she promised him pretty soon, he might just start a whole new war."

"We'd really rather that he didn't, Rabbit," Longbow called back. "Red-Beard and I've come to see if we can calm him down a bit."

Rabbit pushed the rolled-up ladder off the rail, and it unwound its way down to the canoe.

Longbow took hold of the ladder. "It's time to go to work, Chief Red-Beard," he said with a faint smile.

"I *wish* you'd stop that, Longbow."

"Just trying to help you get used to it, friend Red-Beard," Longbow replied with feigned innocence.

Sorgan Hook-Beak of the Land of Maag was in a foul temper when Red-Beard and Longbow entered his cluttered cabin at the stern of the *Seagull*. "Where *is* she?" he demanded in a harsh voice. "If I don't start handing out the gold I promised all these people back in Maag, things are going to start getting ugly around here. We did what she wanted us to do, and now it's time to settle up."

"We really can't be certain just *where* she went, Sorgan," Longbow replied. "Her Domain's very large, and there might just be an emergency somewhere off to the north of here. When a fire breaks out somewhere, you don't really have time to be polite before you rush off to put it out. I'm sure that as soon as she gets things under control, she'll come right back."

"I guess that sort of makes sense," Sorgan grudgingly conceded. "Have you got any idea at all of where this new trouble might be?"

Longbow shrugged. "She didn't bother to tell me. You know how that goes."

"Oh, yes," Sorgan said sourly. "She's an expert when it comes to *not* telling people things they should know, I've noticed."

"How very perceptive of you," Longbow murmured. "I'm sure she'll be back as soon as she's dealt with whatever it was that pulled her away from here, but we've got another problem that's a bit more pressing."

"Oh?"

"The fire mountains up at the head of the ravine are still spouting, and I don't think Lattash will be a safe place for anybody when the liquid rock comes boiling down the ravine. A flood of water's bad enough, but a flood of liquid rock might be a lot worse, wouldn't you say?"

"I'd say that it'll go a long way past 'might,' Longbow. What should we do about it?"

"How does 'run away' sound to you?"

"Narasan tells me that the proper term is 'retreat,' but 'run away' sounds close enough to me."

"We *do* have a bit of a problem, though," Longbow continued. "Red-Beard's uncle, Chief White-Braid, can't quite accept the idea that the tribe will have to move away from Lattash. Red-Beard and I are sort of sneaking around behind his back right now, so we'd appreciate it if you didn't mention what we're doing if you happen to speak with him."

"Old men get strange sometimes, don't they?" Sorgan observed. "Don't worry, Red-Beard. Your secret's safe with me. When are you planning to pull off your mutiny?"

"Mutiny? I don't think I've ever heard that term."

"It's something that happens on a ship when the crew gets unhappy with the captain. They either kill him or set him adrift in a small skiff. Then the leader of the mutiny takes command of the ship."

"We don't do that sort of thing here, Hook-Beak," Red-Beard said firmly.

"Maybe you should give it some thought, Red-Beard," Sorgan suggested. "If your chief is starting to lose his grip, *somebody's* going to have to take charge before that boiling rock comes rushing down the ravine."

"We can hope it doesn't come to that," Longbow stepped in. "Right now, Red-Beard and I need to find a suitable place for a new village. Most likely, it'll be somewhere on down the bay—or even out beyond the inlet. It'll have to have fresh water, open land for farming, and some protection from the wind and tides."

"I gather that once you find it, you'd like to borrow my fleet to move the tribe to their new home?"

"If it's not too much trouble," Red-Beard agreed.

Sorgan shrugged. "It'll give the other ship captains something to do beside coming here to the *Seagull* to complain about not getting paid. Besides, your people and their bows helped us a great deal in the ravine, so we're more or less obliged to lend you a hand when you . . ." Sorgan stopped suddenly. "The gold!" he exclaimed. "Lady Zelana's gold's still in that cave! If that melted rock pours down over Lattash, it'll fill up the cave, won't it?"

"That's not very likely, Sorgan," Longbow disagreed. "Didn't Ox shatter his ax when he tried to chop down that wall Zelana put up to protect the gold?"

"So *that's* why she put that wall there," Sorgan said. "We thought she'd put it up to keep us away from her gold, but it's really there to keep the melted rock from oozing in and swallowing it, isn't it?"

"It seems to be the sort of thing she'd do," Red-Beard agreed. "Don't worry so much, Hook-Beak. The gold's perfectly safe, and I'm sure you'll get paid just as soon as Zelana comes back. You might want to pass the word to the ship captains who spend all their time complaining. They *will* get paid, but right now Zelana's off someplace in her Domain dealing with some new emergency."

"That might just be the answer to *your* problem right there, Red-Beard," Sorgan suggested. "When she comes back, you can tell her that your uncle's not quite right in the head, and then *she* can set him aside and put you in charge. That'd be a lot better than a mutiny, wouldn't you say?"

"It's something to consider, Chief Red-Beard," Longbow agreed.

Red-Beard scowled at him.

"What's the problem, Red-Beard?" Sorgan asked. "The word 'chief's' a lot like the word 'captain,' and I've always thought that had a pleasant sort of sound to it."

"Not to *me* it doesn't," Red-Beard declared.

2

The wind coming in from Mother Sea was quite gusty, and that didn't bode too well for Red-Beard's plans to relocate the tribe. The village of Lattash was well sheltered from foul weather, and Red-Beard could almost hear the steady chorus of complaints he was certain the villagers would hurl at him every time he passed by if they were obliged to move out here.

The sun was already low over the western horizon, but due to the prevailing wind, Red-Beard and Longbow were only about halfway along the north side of the bay.

Longbow squinted toward the west. "We're about to run out of daylight," he noted. Then he looked at the shoreline. "Isn't that a river just ahead?" he asked.

Red-Beard looked at the beach. "I think you're right, Longbow. The brush sort of hides it, but brush usually means fresh water. Let's go have a look." He turned his agile canoe toward the beach with a single backstroke.

"Are you at all familiar with the coast on this side of the bay?" Longbow asked as they smoothly paddled the canoe toward the beach.

"No. The fishing's so good off the beach at Lattash that I've never had any reason to come this far out. Besides, I didn't want to offend the local fish at Lattash by trying my hand somewhere else. Fish are very sensitive about that sort of thing, you know. They get miffed if you ignore them, and sulky fish don't bite. Everybody knows that."

"You've got a very warped sense of humor, friend Red-Beard."

"How can you *say* that, friend Longbow? I'm shocked at you! Shocked!"

"Oh, quit." Longbow peered at the brushy beach. "The river's a bit larger than I thought. We might want to explore this area."

"I don't think the people of the tribe would care for the wind very much," Red-Beard said dubiously. "Lattash is sheltered, but this area's right out in the open."

"Wind isn't as bad as melted rock," Longbow reminded him as they drove the canoe up onto the beach. "Let's have a look at this river. If the water's brackish, this wouldn't be a good place for the new village, and we'll have to move on. If it's fresh, though, we might want to explore the surrounding countryside."

"Lead the way," Red-Beard agreed, and they fought their way through the wind-whipped brush toward the slow-moving river. "Isn't it odd that the sun was going down just as we reached this place?"

Longbow shrugged. "Coincidence, probably."

"There's no such thing as coincidence, friend Longbow. That's why we have gods. They make *everything* happen. If you happen to stub your toe, it's because some god knew that you'd be following that trail someday, so just as a joke he put a rock in the middle of that trail along about the beginning of time. Gods are like that. They play tricks on us all the time."

"Will you stop that, Red-Beard?"

"Probably not. I like absurdity. It makes life a lot more fun." Red-Beard ducked under a stout limb that jutted out from a substantial bush. "All this clutter's going to have to go if we move here," he grumbled. "The women of the tribe will get very grouchy if they have to fight their way through this every time they go to the river for water."

They reached the bank of the slow-moving river, and Long-bow bent and scooped up a handful of water and tasted it. "Not as bad as it looks," he said. "It's a little muddy, but it should clear up later in the summer. When morning comes, we might want to explore the ground upstream. If there happens to be a meadow nearby, we should give this place some serious consideration."

"Maybe so," Red-Beard agreed, "but we should probably see if we can find some other places as well. That way, the tribe will be able to choose—and to argue. Arguments are good for people, did you know that? They stir up the blood, and lazy blood isn't good for people." He looked around. "I'll put out some setlines," he said. "If we're going to dawdle around here on dear old windy beach, we'll need something to eat."

"Sound thinking," Longbow agreed.

As the sun came up the next morning, it turned the cloud of smoke hovering over Lattash a bleary sort of red, almost as if reminding Red-Beard that Lattash wouldn't be there much longer. That had been happening every morning since the twin mountains at the head of the ravine had ended the war, but Red-Beard was still unhappy about the whole thing.

He fought his way back through the brush to the river and pulled in the setlines he'd put out the previous evening. He was just a bit surprised at the size of the fish the untended lines had hooked.

"Not bad at all, friend Red-Beard," Longbow said when Red-Beard carried his catch back to the campfire. "We might want to mention that when we get back to Lattash. If the fishing's good around here, it might take some of the sting out of leaving the old village."

"We'll see. Why don't you build up the fire while I clean these? Then we'll have fish for breakfast."

"Sounds good to me," Longbow agreed, piling more limbs on the fire. "The wind seems to have backed off," he observed.

"What a shame," Red-Beard said. He held up the iron knife Rabbit had made for him. "This makes cleaning fish go a lot faster," he observed. "Iron makes good tools. Let's hope that Zelana will let us keep them after we've won all these wars and the Maags go home."

"Why would she tell us to throw them away?"

"I don't know—maintain the purity of our culture, maybe. She might not like the idea of contamination. Gods are strange sometimes."

"You know, I've noticed that myself," Longbow replied with no hint of a smile.

The fish were of a different variety than the ones that were common out in the bay, and they tasted very good. Red-Beard hoped that might help to persuade the members of the tribe that this would be a good place to live despite a fair number of drawbacks. It would never be as pretty as Lattash, and the constant wind would irritate the tribe almost as much as the thick brush and muddy river would.

After they'd eaten, Longbow stood. "Let's have a look around," he suggested. "So far we've found fresh water and good fishing. Let's see what else this place has to offer."

The morning light had a bluish tint to it as the two of them entered the forest that lined the upper side of the sandy beach. The trees were large, and they blocked off the perpetual wind that had made the beach so unpleasant.

"Deer," Longbow said very quietly, pointing off to the right.

Red-Beard turned slowly. Quick movements usually startle deer.

It seemed to be a fairly large herd—two dozen or so at least—and there were quite a few spotted fawns grazing with the adult deer. "They look to be in fairly good shape," Red-Beard noted.

"I'd say so, yes. Let's ease on past them. There's no point in disturbing them while they're busy eating."

The two of them moved on quietly through the damp forest. After about a half mile the light ahead seemed to grow brighter, a fair indication that there was a clearing in that direction.

When they reached the edge of the trees, Red-Beard saw that "clearing" was a gross understatement. The meadow beyond the trees extended for miles, and the stream they'd seen on the beach the previous day seemed to wander aimlessly through that meadow. The grass was very tall, and there was a sizeable herd of bison out there grazing in the gentle light of the morning sun.

"That answers that question, doesn't it?" Longbow said. "It looks to me like there might be about five times as much land for farming as the women of your tribe will need right here."

"At *least* five times," Red-Beard agreed. "Those bison might be a bit of a problem, but we should be able to come up with a way to keep them out of the gardens." He looked around with a certain satisfaction. "We might as well go on back to Lattash, friend Longbow. I don't think we'll find any place that's better than this one."

"Except for the wind," Longbow added.

"The tribe can learn to live with the wind, I think. Good fishing, good hunting, and good farmland are the important things. This is the place."

"You never know, friend Red-Beard. Perfection might lie just a few miles farther ahead."

"I'm not really in the mood for perfection right now, friend Longbow. This place is good enough for me."

"Spoilsport," Longbow accused mildly.

*　　*　　*

It was about midmorning when they put Red-Beard's canoe back in the choppy water of the bay, and the wind, which had slowed them on the previous day, was behind them now, so they made very good time.

Red-Beard felt a certain satisfaction. The constant wind and the thick brush along the riverbank were drawbacks certainly, but the advantages of the location far outweighed them. The one thing that might help Chief White-Braid get over his sorrow was the lack of any serious mountains in the general vicinity. From what Red-Beard had seen, there was nothing that could really be called a mountain anywhere near the beach. There were rounded hills, but hills usually don't catch on fire, and their gentle slopes wouldn't encourage the spring floods which were such a nuisance in Lattash. All in all, it was a very good location, and if he could persuade his uncle that the tribe should move here, Chief White-Braid might set his sorrow aside and start making decisions again. That was Red-Beard's main concern right now. Just the thought of being forced to accept the tedious responsibilities of chieftainship made him go cold all over. He enjoyed his freedom far too much to find much pleasure in the possibility of leadership.

It was late in the afternoon when they reached the harbor of Lattash, and Longbow looked back over his shoulder from his place in the bow of the canoe. "As long as we're here anyway, let's swing south a ways. I think we might want to have a word with Narasan."

"We might as well, I guess," Red-Beard agreed, veering his canoe toward the anchored Trogite fleet.

The sun was low over the western horizon, and it was turning the sky a rosy pink when they reached Commander Narasan's wide-beamed ship. The young Trogite Keselo was standing at the rail with a worried sort of expression on his face. Keselo was very bright, Red-Beard had noticed, but he always seemed to take everything much too seriously. "Is there some sort of problem?" he called down to them as Red-Beard pulled his canoe in alongside the Trogite ship.

"Oh, nothing really all that serious," Red-Beard replied, trying to sound casual. "The fire mountains are still belching, the village of Lattash is doomed, and it hasn't rained for ten days. Aside from that, everything seems to be all right."

"I really wish you wouldn't do that, Red-Beard," Keselo said with a pained expression.

"I think we should talk with your commander, Keselo," Longbow said. "We seem to have a problem, and he might be able to come up with a solution."

"More trouble up there in the ravine?" Keselo asked in a tense tone of voice.

"Everything's fine up there," Red-Beard replied. "Our problem's quite a bit closer—right out here in the bay, actually."

"Sorgan Hook-Beak and the other Maags haven't been paid yet," Longbow explained, "and they're not really very happy about it. We're sort of hoping that your commander can come up with a way to pacify them."

"Have you considered beer?" Keselo asked with a faint smile. "Lots and lots of beer."

"Interesting notion," Red-Beard said, "but eventually they'd sober up, and trying to argue with a Maag who has a screaming headache wouldn't be all that much fun, I'm afraid."

"It was just a thought," the young Trogite said. "Come on board, gentlemen. I'll take you back to the commander's quarters."

Red-Beard led the way up the ladder to the broad deck of the Trogite ship with Longbow close behind, and they followed Keselo on back toward the stern of the ship.

"Yes?" Narasan replied when Keselo politely rapped on the door. Red-Beard had noticed during the war up in the ravine that the Trogites had a tedious sort of formality about them and that very few of them had anything even remotely resembling a sense of humor.

"You have visitors, Commander," Keselo reported.

Narasan opened the door to his rather spacious quarters. "Good evening, gentlemen," he greeted Red-Beard and Longbow. "Is there something I can do for you?"

"Perhaps," Longbow replied. "You and Sorgan Hook-Beak get along with each other fairly well, don't you?"

"He doesn't automatically reach for his sword every time he sees me," Narasan replied. "Is he giving you trouble of some kind?"

"He's been spending a lot of his time complaining lately," Red-Beard said. "Zelana left here without giving him the gold she promised him, and he doesn't like that one little bit."

"He's mentioned that to me a time or twelve, too," Narasan replied with a slight smile. "Actually, it's just about the only thing he ever discusses. He seems to believe that Lady Zelana's trying to cheat him out of the gold she's supposed to pay him."

"She wouldn't do that," Longbow declared firmly.

"Where is she, then?"

"We don't really know for sure," Red-Beard admitted. "I'm just guessing here, but I don't think she fully understood what's involved in a war. The killing part of war seems to have disturbed her quite a bit. 'Kill' is just a word. Seeing it happen was probably more than she was prepared for."

"Is she really that innocent?" Narasan asked with some surprise.

"She's been somewhat isolated for a long time," Longbow replied, glossing over a few realities that Red-Beard was sure Narasan wasn't ready to accept just yet.

"We've got a problem, gentlemen," Narasan said with a slightly worried frown. "Sorgan gave me his word that he'd bring his people down to the southern part of Dhrall to help me in the war that *I'm* getting paid to fight, but he won't leave Lady Zelana's Domain until she pays him. I think I'm going to need him down there, but the way things stand right now, he won't move until he gets paid for *this* war."

Longbow scratched thoughtfully at his cheek. "Why don't you just sit here and wait, then?" he suggested.

"I didn't quite follow you, Longbow," Narasan admitted.

"We need somebody who can persuade Zelana to come back here and pay Sorgan, right?"

"That gets right to the bottom of things, yes."

"Zelana's brother needs you to go fight the war down in his Domain, doesn't he?"

"That's what he's paying me for," Narasan conceded.

"If you don't arrive there when he expects you, he'll most likely come here to find out what's delaying you, won't he?"

"Almost certainly."

"Veltan's probably the only one who'll be able to persuade his sister to do what she's supposed to do, and if we all just sit here and refuse to move, he'll have to go find Zelana and drag her back here. Then she'll pay Sorgan, and the Maags will celebrate a bit. Then, when they sober up, they'll join your fleet and you can all sail south to fight Veltan's war for him. That should just about solve all of our problems, wouldn't you say?"

"You can be a very devious fellow when you set your mind to it, Longbow," Narasan observed.

Longbow shrugged. "Whatever works," he replied.

"Then all we really have to do now is practice sitting still," Red-Beard said.

"Only after we've moved your tribe to their new home, friend Red-Beard," Longbow reminded him. "We'd better go back to Lattash and see if your uncle's come to his senses yet. If he hasn't, we might have to rearrange a few things."

"Is Chief White-Braid sick or something?" Narasan asked.

"I don't know if 'sick' is the right word," Red-Beard replied. "Those fire mountains have dried up the river that comes down through the ravine, and if they happen to spout out more of that melted rock, Lattash—and the whole tribe—will get cooked in the same way the snake-men did. Longbow and I found a safer place for the tribe to live, but we'll have to get my uncle's permission before we can start moving people, and I'm not sure that he'll agree."

"Is there any way that I can help?" Commander Narasan asked.

"No, thanks all the same," Longbow said. "I think Chief Red-Beard here can take care of it."

"Will you *please* stop that?" Red-Beard growled.

"Probably not," Longbow said. "You'd better start getting used to it, my friend. I think 'Chief Red-Beard' is something you won't be able to dodge much longer."

3

One-Who-Heals was the shaman of Longbow's tribe, and
he'd always made Red-Beard a little nervous. An ordinary
shaman could deal with broken bones and treat minor ailments
with assorted herbal concoctions, but One-Who-Heals appeared to have a much greater knowledge than the average
shaman, and he was not above a certain amount of experimentation.

Darkness had fallen over the village of Lattash when Red-
Beard beached his canoe, and then he and Longbow went up
through the quiet village to the lodge of Chief White-Braid.
One-Who-Heals was there, and he was sitting beside the fire pit
in the center of the lodge, carefully watching the sleeping chief.
He touched one finger to his lips when Red-Beard and Longbow entered. "Don't wake him," he whispered.

"Is he sick?" Red-Beard asked quietly.

"Not exactly," the old shaman replied. He rose to his feet.
"Let's go outside," he suggested. "There are some things you
should know."

They all went on out of the lodge and walked a few yards

away. "Your chief's been having some problems, Red-Beard," One-Who-Heals said gravely.

"I've noticed that. Can you make him well again?"

"In time, perhaps, but not immediately. Some things happened during the recent war that your chief can't accept. The village of Lattash is a part of him—so much a part that its loss is more than he can comprehend."

"I know. Is there any way . . . ?" Red-Beard left it up in the air.

"There's a powerful potion—a mixture of certain roots, leaves, and a rare mushroom—that dulls the awareness and quiets the more powerful emotions. I seldom use this potion, but it seemed necessary this time. I made certain suggestions to him before he went to sleep—and several others *after* he dozed off. The burden of leadership will be most unpleasant for him when he awakens, and he'll willingly hand over his authority to someone he knows that he can trust—you, most likely. He trusts you, so you're the obvious choice."

"You planned this all along, didn't you, Longbow?" Red-Beard demanded accusingly. "That's why you kept throwing 'Chief Red-Beard' in my teeth, wasn't it?"

"The choice was fairly obvious, friend Red-Beard. It's time that you grew up anyway. You have talent, but you've been trying to conceal it in order to avoid responsibility. Your tribe needs you, and you can't turn your back on that need."

"That's a rotten thing to say, Longbow," Red-Beard flared. "You're jamming duty right down my throat."

"You might as well swallow it, my friend," Longbow replied, "because I'll pick it up, dust it off, and stuff it back down your throat every time you spit it out."

"I hate you!"

"No, you don't. You're just a bit grouchy because your childhood's over now and you've grown up. It might take you a while to get used to it, but you'll probably do all right. If it'll make you feel better, I can stand behind you and cuff you across the back of the head when you do something wrong."

"What if I make mistakes?"

"Everybody makes mistakes, Chief Red-Beard," the old shaman told him. "That's one of the ways we learn things—not the best way, perhaps, but it's there if you need it."

Chief White-Braid's lodge was a bit rickety, but it had been there for a long time. Like all the lodges in the village of Lat-tash, it had been built with limber willow branches interlaced with limbs taken from evergreen trees. It had originally been constructed in the shape of a dome, but it was sagging quite noticeably now, and the limber willow branches were now brittle. Red-Beard saw some correspondences there. His uncle White-Braid sagged now and then, and he also seemed quite brittle. Red-Beard sighed. The thought of getting old was very depressing.

It was quite late, and Red-Beard was tired, but he forced himself to remain awake as he sat cross-legged beside his uncle's pallet. Chief White-Braid appeared to be sleeping soundly, so Red-Beard's vigil didn't really seem to make much sense, but the presence of the elders of the tribe in White-Braid's lodge obliged him to stay awake.

His mind seemed to wander, though, and he had to keep jerking it back to the business at hand. His eyes seemed sandy, and he really wanted to get some sleep.

The vigil in his uncle's lodge was quite peculiar. It wasn't as if White-Braid were dying, but the elders, one by one, had come unsummoned and had quietly seated themselves in the lodge without so much as saying a word.

Red-Beard was catching a strong odor of collusion here.

Then Chief White-Braid's eyes opened.

"Did you sleep well, uncle?" Red-Beard asked him.

"Not really, my son. No matter how much I sleep, I seem to be tired all the time now. Things here in Lattash are not as they should be, and my sleep is much troubled. I am burdened with cares now, and it seems that I am no longer able to bear those cares." He sat up, smiling faintly. "It had been my thought that sleep might allow me to set those cares aside and return to Lattash when it was a good and pleasant place in which to live, but it has not been so. The fire mountains hover always at the edge of my mind, even when I sleep." He sighed and shook his head.

Then he straightened, and his voice became stronger and his eyes more alert. "I think it is time for a change, my son. What is old is going away, and what is new approaches fast, and I do not like what is new. Lattash is old, and I am old. It is my thought that *you* should be the new, and you should find some new place for the tribe to call its home."

Red-Beard winced. He'd been hoping that this wouldn't happen. "Longbow and I looked at a new place yesterday, uncle," he ventured. "It's not as pretty as Lattash, but I think it might be safer. There's a stream there, but it moves sluggishly, since it comes down to the bay through rounded hills rather than tumbling down out of mountains. Longbow and I saw no signs of spring floods, which isn't a bad thing. Some years the river that comes down out of the mountains here at Lattash is just a little too frisky. It's a nice enough river I guess, but spring excites it too much. The hunting and fishing in the place Long-bow and I found should be very good, and there's much open land for planting."

"It would seem that you have chosen wisely, my son. In time, the memories of Lattash will fade, I think, and the new village will make the tribe content."

"There's much promise there, uncle," Red-Beard replied, glossing over the stiff winds that were likely to cause a few problems. "The best thing about it is probably those rounded hills. Mountains are pretty to look at, but they seem to get excited every so often, and they start belching fire."

"I've noticed that myself, my son. Mountains are young, and

they sometimes feel the need to show off. Rounded hills are older, and they have more sense." Chief White-Braid rose to his feet. "It would seem that *old* is not as good as it was once," he said to the tribal elders. "It is my thought that it might be best for the tribe if we were to look to *young* for leadership."

The elders all nodded gravely.

"It is good that we all agree," Chief White-Braid declared. "I will make one last suggestion, and then I will speak no more of this matter. Red-Beard is the son of my younger brother, who died many years ago. You all may have noticed that Red-Beard laughs often and finds life most enjoyable. It is my thought that he will laugh less often if we lay the burden of leadership on him." There was not the slightest hint of a smile on the old chief's face.

The tribal elders, however, were all grinning broadly.

Red-Beard wasn't amused, though. No matter which way he'd turned, Longbow had been ahead of him.

Red-Beard moved about the village of Lattash the next morning, advising the men of the tribe that he and Longbow had found a suitable location for a new village. His status in the tribe had changed, of course, but he didn't want to strut around waving it in everybody's face. Most of the men of the tribe seemed to be very interested when he described the place, but there were those who voiced certain objections when he admitted that the new place would not be identical to the place where the tribe now dwelt. The notion of change seems very disturbing to some men. Red-Beard patiently kept reminding them about the distinct possibility that the fire mountains would spew forth more molten rock and engulf the village and everybody in it. The ones who objected responded with maybes: "Maybe the fire mountains will go back to sleep," or "Maybe Zelana will come back and put out the fires," or—the most absurd of all—"Maybe a good rainstorm will blow in and put out the fire." The dimwits seemed to feel that if they talked about something long enough, the problem would go away.

Sometimes the objectors made Red-Beard want to scream.

"I think you might be going at it the wrong way, friend Red-Beard," Longbow suggested along about noon. "Don't ask; tell."

"You lost me there, Longbow."

"You never want to ask a fool for his opinion about a decision that's already been made, because he'll *give* you his opinion, and that usually takes the rest of the day."

"I'm just a little new at this, friend Longbow," Red-Beard reminded him. "I'm sort of feeling my way along right now. It doesn't seem that it'd be polite to just bull my way around, giving everybody orders."

"It doesn't work that way, friend Red-Beard. You don't have time to be polite. The growing season's already started, so the women of your tribe should be planting. If the women don't plant, nobody will eat when winter comes."

Red-Beard blinked. "I'd forgotten about that, I guess," he admitted a bit sheepishly.

"Meat and fish are only a part of the food that keeps the people of the tribe alive, Red-Beard. Hunters forget that sometimes. If *I* happened to be the one who was doing this, I'd be talking with the women instead of the men. Never offend the ones who cook the food. If you do, you might get boiled dirt for supper."

"I'll have to see the meadow," the stout middle-aged woman named Planter told Red-Beard that afternoon. Red-Beard had asked around, and almost everybody in the tribe had told him that the women of Lattash took all their problems to Planter, and she usually solved them. In an odd sort of way Planter was the actual chief of the women of the tribe, largely because she knew more about growing food than anyone else.

She also had a bad temper when things didn't go the way she wanted them to go, so Red-Beard stepped around her rather carefully. "We'll talk with my friend Longbow," he said. "He might have noticed some things I didn't. I'll be honest with you, Planter. This new place isn't nearly as pretty as Lattash, but *safe* is way ahead of *pretty*. The tribe *must* move away from here, or we'll be drinking melted rock instead of water before long."

"You speak plainly, Red-Beard," Planter observed. "That's a rare thing for a chief."

"I'm still a little new at it," Red-Beard confessed.

"You'll do," Planter said a bit cryptically. "Let's go speak with this friend of yours. If time's as crucial as you seem to think, we'd better hurry."

Red-Beard and Planter found Longbow in the lodge of his chief, Old-Bear, and Planter cut across the usual courtesies rather abruptly. "Has this meadow ever been worked?" she asked.

"I don't think so," Longbow replied. "Red-Beard and I didn't see any signs that any tribe had ever lived there."

"How high was the grass?"

"Waist-high or so, wasn't it, Red-Beard?"

"At least that high," Red-Beard agreed.

"You'd better find someplace else, then," Planter declared.

"What's wrong with that one?" Red-Beard asked her.

"Tall grass means thick sod," Planter explained, "and we'll have to clear the sod away before we can plant. That'll take too long. Summer's almost here, and we should have planted already. If the women of the tribe have to spend half the summer clearing the sod away before they plant, the crop won't have time enough to grow before the first frost, and there won't be anything to eat this coming winter."

Old-Bear squinted at her thoughtfully. "It is my thought that we should find some way around certain traditions," he said gravely. "If the tribe of White-Braid is to have food to eat after the seasons turn, we will need many hands to remove the sod so that the women of the tribe can plant."

"There aren't really that many women in our tribe, Chief Old-Bear," Red-Beard reminded him.

"Then perhaps those who are *not* women should help."

Red-Beard laughed. "That might just be the quickest way for me to get out from under something I didn't want in the first place," he said. "If I order the men of the tribe to do women's work, they'll find themselves a different chief almost immediately."

"I am not familiar with the customs of your tribe, Chief Red-Beard," Old-Bear admitted, "but in my tribe, the building of lodges is men's work. Is it also men's work in your tribe?"

"It's customary," Red-Beard conceded. "Where are we going with this?"

"When I was much younger and adventurous, I traveled far to the north into the Domain of Zelana's older brother Dahlaine, and I came upon a place where there were no trees. It was a land of grass only. The region had much game—large deer and wild cows—for there was much grass for them to eat. The hunting was very good, but the absence of trees made the building of lodges very hard. The people of the place with no trees gave the matter much consideration, and a very clever young man had a thought. Since there were no trees, the tribe would be obliged to build the lodges from something that was *not* trees."

"I don't think a lodge made of grass would be very good in the wintertime," Red-Beard said dubiously.

"It seemed that way to me also," Old-Bear said, "but I was wrong. The clever young man saw that grass is not stems only, but it is also roots, and the roots of grass cling quite firmly to the dirt from which the grass grows. The result is that which we call sod, and it was sod which the clever young man used to build his lodge. The other men of his tribe saw the wisdom of what he had done, and they also built their lodges of sod. I visited several of those lodges and found that no wind, however strong, can blow into a lodge made of sod, and the winter cold cannot penetrate such a wall. The lodges were strong and warm in the coldest of winters, and the people of the tribe were content. It is my thought that if the men of your tribe were told to build their lodges of sod, they would clear much ground for planting without feeling shame that they were doing women's work."

"You are fortunate to have so wise a chief, Longbow," Planter said with a broad smile.

"The next problem is how to persuade the men of the tribe that sod will make better lodges than tree limbs and bushes," Red-Beard said a bit dubiously.

"As I remember, the beach near that river was very windy," Longbow mused.

"It seemed that way to me, too," Red-Beard agreed.

"A lodge made of tree limbs might not be a good idea in such a windy place. It would be very embarrassing to have one's lodge blown down in the middle of winter, wouldn't you say?"

"'Embarrassing' might not be the right word, Longbow," Red-Beard said. "I think it might go quite a bit past that. Winter winds are much stronger than summer winds, though. If we want the men of the tribe to start cutting sod now to clear the meadow for planting, I don't think we should depend on the summer wind to persuade them that it's the best thing to do."

"You and I might need to help the summer wind just a bit, friend Red-Beard," Longbow replied. "I'm sure she'd appreciate that. If every lodge the men of your tribe have built collapses some breezy night, sod should start to look very attractive, wouldn't you say?"

"You people of Old-Bear's tribe are very devious, aren't you?" Planter suggested.

"Indeed they are, Planter," Old-Bear said with a broad grin, "and that makes life much, much easier for me."

"There's something I've been meaning to ask you, Chief

Old-Bear," Red-Beard said a bit hesitantly, after Planter had left the lodge.

"I will answer you as best I can, Chief Red-Beard."

"Is it really necessary for a chief to speak so formally?"

"It's a part of the pose that goes with the position, Chief Red-Beard," Old-Bear responded in a somewhat more relaxed manner. "Formal speech makes a chief sound as if he knows what he's doing. When you speak formally, the men of your tribe will usually do what you tell them to do. Formal speech will make you sound wiser."

"But it's so tedious to talk like that," Red-Beard complained.

"Tell me about it," Old-Bear replied sardonically. "It's tiresome and pompous, and about half the time you'll forget what you're trying to tell them before you finish talking. The important thing's that it makes you sound wise—even when you're telling them to do something that's foolish." The old chief paused. "If I were you, Red-Beard, I'd sort of keep that to myself. It's one of the secrets of the trade. If you pay close attention to the outlander chieftains, you'll notice that they do things in more or less the same way. If you *sound* like you know what you're doing, the men of your tribe will believe that you *do,* even when you don't."

"It's all just a deception, then?" Red-Beard demanded.

"I thought I just said that," Old-Bear replied.

"It's not nearly as well protected as the old village was," Sorgan Hook-Beak observed as the *Seagull* approached the beach at the new village site a week or so later.

"There aren't any fire mountains nearby, though," Longbow reminded him. "White-Braid's tribe can stand a bit of wind and weather. It's much better than trying to wade through melted rock."

"That's true, I suppose," Sorgan conceded. "What have the people we brought here last week been doing? They haven't even started building huts yet."

"They're back a short way from the beach," Red-Beard explained. "The men are gathering sod, and the women are planting beans."

"What do you need with sod?"

"We're going to build our lodges with it."

"Why not use tree limbs, like you did back in Lattash?"

"Several of the young men tried that when they first arrived," Red-Beard said. "A wind came up one night, though, and their lodges fell down."

"That must have been *some* wind," Rabbit said.

"Longbow and I helped it just a bit," Red-Beard admitted. "If you know where to push, it isn't too hard to make a lodge collapse."

"What did you do that for?" Rabbit asked curiously.

"We needed to persuade the young men that sod would be much stronger than tree limbs." Red-Beard made a sour face. "Actually, it was just a deception. The young men *think* they're digging up sod for building lodges, but all they're really doing is opening up the dirt below the sod so that the women can plant beans and yams. We'll need that food when winter comes, so it's important to get the seeds into the ground."

"Why did you have to lie to them?" Rabbit sounded a little baffled.

"Planting is women's work. Young men feel insulted if you tell them to plant. Building lodges is men's work, though, so when all the lodges the first ones who came here built just 'happened' to fall down one gusty night, Longbow and I suggested sod houses instead. Now they're out in the meadow doing what they *think* is men's work. Everybody's happy, and the tribe will have plenty to eat when winter comes along."

"You people have a very complicated set of rules," Sorgan observed.

"It makes life more interesting, Sorgan," Longbow said. "Dancing around the rules gives us something to do when the fish aren't biting."

4

Veltan's little sloop came through the inlet a few days later, and Zelana's younger brother seemed to be just a bit upset. "What are you people *doing?*" he shouted as he beached his sloop near the new village.

"Moving," Red-Beard explained. "We didn't think Lattash would be safe anymore, so we're setting up a new village."

"Where's Narasan?"

"Probably on his boat out there in the bay."

"He's supposed to be on his way down to my Domain," Veltan fumed.

"I think he might be waiting," Red-Beard replied. "Something that was *supposed* to happen hasn't happened yet, and I think Narasan's going to stay here until it does."

"What's this all about, Red-Beard?"

"Your sister promised to give Sorgan a big pile of those yellow blocks for helping us up there in the ravine. She hasn't done it yet, and I think Narasan wants to find out if your family keeps its promises."

"Well, of *course* we do!"

"You'd better find your sister and remind her about it,

then," Red-Beard advised. "I don't think Narasan will move until he sees Sorgan getting paid. That's up to you, though. I've got enough problems of my own to keep me busy."

"Where's Longbow right now?" Veltan asked with a slightly worried look.

"The last time I saw him, he was showing the young men of my tribe how to cut sod. The sod blocks need to be all the same size, and the young men weren't cutting them right."

"What do your people need sod for?"

"It'd take much too long to explain," Red-Beard said with a weary sigh.

"Just exactly where *is* this place?" Red-Beard asked Veltan as the sloop sailed out through the inlet that led into the bay of Lattash.

"Not too far from here," Veltan replied a bit evasively.

"We've both seen the sort of things the members of your family can do when it's necessary, Veltan," Longbow said. "I think we might be just a little pressed for time, so Red-Beard and I won't be particularly upset if you cheat."

"We don't really look upon it as cheating, Longbow," Veltan replied almost apologetically. "We try to avoid waving certain capabilities in the faces of the outlanders, that's all. It gets to be a habit, I guess. You and Red-Beard are both natives of the Land of Dhrall, though, so I don't really need to be secretive. We'll go around the southern end of the Isle of Thurn. Zelana's grotto's not too far up on the west side." He gave the two of them a sly look. "If you think that speed's really essential, I suppose I *could* call my pet. She could take us there in the blink of an eye. She's terribly noisy, though."

"So *that* was how you came popping out of nowhere up in the ravine when you came to warn us about the fire mountains, wasn't it?" Red-Beard suggested.

Veltan nodded. "I didn't really have much in the way of

alternatives. Yaltar's dream took us all by surprise, and we had to get our friends out of that ravine in a hurry."

"What causes mountains to do that?" Red-Beard asked curiously.

"That particular eruption was the result of Yaltar's dream," Veltan replied. "The Dreamers can break all sorts of rules when they think it's necessary."

"But sometimes that sort of thing happens even when there isn't a Dreamer around to make it happen, doesn't it?"

Veltan nodded. "It's a natural phenomenon," he said. "The core of the world is molten rock, and it's under enormous pressure. Every so often, it breaks through the crust, and the pressure sends it spurting up into the sky for miles." He pointed toward the west. "There's the coast of Zelana's isle," he told them.

"How far have we *really* come from the inlet?" Longbow asked.

"Oh," Veltan replied, squinting thoughtfully, "about half as far as it is from Lattash to the head of the ravine. It won't take us too much longer to reach Zelana's grotto." He scratched his chin thoughtfully. "I think that maybe the best way for us to do this would be to speak with Eleria first. She knows Zelana even better than I do, and she can manipulate my sister in ways I couldn't even imagine. Balacenia's always been the most devious of the younger ones."

"Who's Balacenia?" Red-Beard asked curiously.

"That's Eleria's real name." Veltan paused. "I wouldn't spread that around if I were you," he told them. "Our big brother Dahlaine came up with the idea when we realized that the Vlagh had decided to annex our Domains. The Dreamers *look* like children, but they really aren't children. They're our alternates, and they'll take over when our cycle reaches its end. That's something else you don't need to mention to the outlanders. They don't really need to know about the cycles. Actually, the less they know about what's *really* happening, the better. If they find out who and what we're facing here, they'll probably turn and run."

"I've heard a few of the old stories," Red-Beard said, "but they've never really made very much sense to me. Every now and then somebody mentions something called the overmind. Just exactly what *is* that?"

"Red-Beard's the chief of his tribe now," Longbow reminded Veltan. "It might not be a bad thing for him to know a bit more about the thing out in the Wasteland."

"You could be right, Longbow," Veltan agreed. Then he looked at Red-Beard. "How much do you know about bugs?" he asked.

"They have more legs than we have, and some of them can fly. That's about all I've managed to pick up. I've always concentrated on things that I can eat, and I don't think I'd really care to eat a bug."

"This may take a while," Veltan mused. "All right, then. Some bugs are solitary. They have very little contact with others of their species, except at mating time. Spiders are about the best example of those particular bugs. There are other kinds, though—various bees and ants, for the most part. As individuals, they're almost totally mindless. They're too stupid to even be afraid. You probably noticed that up in the ravine."

"They didn't really seem very clever," Red-Beard agreed.

"They don't *need* to be clever, Red-Beard. It's that overmind you've heard about that does the thinking."

"The Vlagh, you mean? I've always sort of wondered how anybody ever managed to find out what that thing's name was. Bugs don't usually have names, do they?"

"Vlagh isn't exactly a name, Red-beard," Veltan explained. "It's more in the nature of a title. The creatures of the Wasteland refer to it as '*the* Vlagh,' sort of in the same way that the people of your tribe call you 'the chief.' The Vlagh has certain advantages, though. The creatures that serve it know exactly what it's thinking all the time, because they all share the awareness of what's called the overmind. Every one of them is aware of what any of the others has seen or heard, and all of that information lies in the mind of the Vlagh."

"That *would* be sort of useful, I suppose," Red-Beard conceded. "That Vlagh thing doesn't *have* to give orders, because everybody in the tribe knows exactly what he's thinking every minute of the day."

"The Vlagh isn't a 'he,' Red-Beard," Veltan corrected. "Actually, it's a 'she.' It lays eggs, and anything called a 'he' doesn't do that."

"We're at war with a *woman?*" Red-Beard exclaimed.

"I wouldn't really think of the Vlagh as a woman, Red-Beard. Laying eggs is only part of what the Vlagh does. What it's doing right now is attempting to expand its territory. It wants more food for its servants. The more food that's available, the more eggs it can produce, and the more servants it has, the more complex the overmind becomes. For now, it wants the entire Land of Dhrall, but that's only a start. The ultimate goal of the Vlagh is the entire world. If it has the world, there won't be any limits on the overmind."

"Are you saying that it wants to rule people as well as bugs?" Red-Beard demanded incredulously.

"Probably not," Veltan replied. "Most likely, people will just be something to eat. More food; more eggs. That's the way the overmind works."

"We *have* to kill that thing!" Red-Beard exploded.

"I rather thought you might see it that way," Veltan agreed. "The outlanders think that they're working for gold, but what they're really working for is survival. If we don't win, the servants of the Vlagh will have us all for lunch."

It was about midmorning when Veltan's sloop rounded the southern tip of the Isle of Thurn. Red-Beard had been keeping a close eye on the coast of the Isle, and it didn't seem that the sloop was moving all that fast.

"Don't think about it, Red-Beard," Veltan told him. "I'm tampering just a bit. If you happened to see what's really happening, it might disturb you. Time and distance aren't quite as rigid as they might seem to be."

"I think I'd be more comfortable if you didn't tell me what you're really doing, Veltan," Red-Beard agreed.

"We'll do it that way, then. Zelana's grotto's just ahead. Excuse me for a moment, gentlemen. I want to let Eleria know that we're here." He frowned slightly, and then he smiled. "She's coming out," he advised.

"Out of where?" Red-Beard asked, looking around.

"The grotto." Veltan pointed at the surface of the water. "The entrance is down there."

"*Under* the water?" Red-Beard demanded incredulously.

"Actually, it's a cave, but it's not much like those caves we came across up in the ravine to the east of Lattash." Veltan laughed. "Dahlaine went wild when Zelana told him that Eleria was swimming up out of the grotto to play with the pink dolphins when she was only about five years old."

Just then the beautiful child Eleria rose to the surface and swam to Veltan's sloop. "Is there something wrong?" she asked.

"Well, sort of," Veltan replied. "Is my sister all right?"

"Not really," Eleria replied. "The Beloved's having a lot of trouble with some of the things that happened up there in the ravine. I don't think she realized exactly what the word *war* really means. Killing things and people by the thousands seems to be something she didn't completely understand."

"It was sort of necessary, little one," Longbow reminded her.

"Well, maybe, but the Beloved didn't really expect it to go quite so far. She absolutely *had* to get away and come back home."

"Is she settling down at all?"

"Well, a little bit, maybe. Just being back home in the grotto helps her."

"She shouldn't have left quite so fast," Veltan said. "She forgot something that was fairly important."

"Oh?"

"She didn't give Sorgan the gold she'd promised him, and he's *very* unhappy about that. She can stay here in her grotto if she really thinks it's necessary, but she's going to have to come back to Lattash for a little while and pay the pirates what she owes them. The delay's making Narasan very suspicious, and he won't move until he knows that my sister kept her promise. If Sorgan doesn't get paid, Narasan won't come south to my Domain, and I think I'm going to need him there before too much longer."

"I'll go back down to the grotto and tell the Beloved that you're here, uncle Veltan. I *might* be able to persuade her to come out, but I'm not making any promises." Then the little girl arched gracefully over and plunged on back down through the water.

It seemed almost like forever as the three of them sat in Veltan's gently bobbing sloop, but it was probably only about a quarter of an hour before Eleria and Zelana came to the surface no more than a few yards from the sloop.

"What's this all about, Veltan?" Zelana demanded, smoothly treading water.

"You seem to have neglected something, dear sister," Veltan suggested. "I know that you've got a lot on your mind right now, but you seem to have overlooked certain obligations."

"Get to the point, Veltan," she said irritably.

"You neglected to pay the Maags for their services during the recent unpleasantness," Veltan reminded her.

"I'll get around to it one of these days."

" 'One of these days' is just a little vague, wouldn't you say, dear sister?"

"Sorgan doesn't need the gold right now. There's no place here in the Land of Dhrall where he could spend it."

"He may not *need* it, Zelana, but he *wants* it."

"That's just too bad."

"And it's getting worse every day. Sorgan's discontent's starting to spread. Narasan's starting to have some doubts about the honesty of our family. I hired him with promises, just like you hired Sorgan. If you don't pay Sorgan, Narasan won't believe that I'll pay *him*. He's sitting on board his ship in the bay of Lattash waiting for a demonstration of good faith. You gave Sorgan your word, sister of mine, and if you don't make good on your word, the outlanders will probably steal everything they can lay their hands on and then set sail for home. Without Narasan's assistance, there's no way that I can defend my Domain, and if I lose, we'll all lose, and the Vlagh will win dominion over the entire Land of Dhrall. Was there any part of that you didn't understand?"

"You're hateful, Veltan."

"I do my best, dear sister. Are you going to keep your word or not?"

"Oh, all right!" She almost spat her response at him. "I'll go back to Lattash and pay that greedy pirate, but that's as far as I'll go. I will *not* get involved in any more of this savagery!"

The face of the child Eleria hardened. "That's all right, Beloved," she said in a sugary sweet tone. "You can stay here and play with your pink dolphins, strum your harp, and compose bad poetry, if that's what it takes to make you happy. I'll go in your place. I may not be as skilled as you are, and I might make a lot of mistakes, but at least I'll be there when my people need me."

Zelana's eyes went very wide. "You can't do that, Eleria," she exclaimed. "I won't permit it."

"Then I'll just have to go without your permission, won't I, Beloved? Either you go or I go, and that's all there is to say. The choice is yours, Beloved. It's either you or me. Make up your mind, Zelana. We don't have all day, you know."

Red-Beard was stunned. The sweet child suddenly wasn't

sweet anymore. Red-Beard glanced at Longbow to see if his friend was as shocked as he was.

Longbow's expression, however, showed no signs of shock. He placidly returned Red-Beard's gaze.

And then he slyly winked.

5

They moved smoothly down the west coast of the Isle of Thurn, and Red-Beard carefully watched Zelana and Eleria, trying his best not to be too obvious about it.

Now that she'd jerked Zelana back to normalcy, however, Eleria had reverted back to her previous sweetness, and Zelana seemed to be her old self again. She spoke at some length with Veltan back at the stern of the sloop, and then she joined Red-Beard and Longbow near the bow. "My brother tells me that Chief White-Braid's having some problems," she said. "What seems to be the trouble?"

"The fire mountains at the head of the ravine seem to have blocked off the river," Longbow replied, "and without that river, Lattash isn't a good place for Chief White-Braid's tribe to live anymore. The notion of leaving Lattash disturbs White-Braid so much that he can't seem to make decisions anymore. Our shaman, One-Who-Heals, tells us that things like that aren't uncommon in older men. Red-Beard here has been taking care of things, and he hasn't made *too* many mistakes yet."

"Thanks, Longbow," Red-Beard said in a flat, unfriendly tone.

"Don't mention it," Longbow replied blandly. "Anyway," he continued, "Red-Beard and I found a suitable place for the tribe to live on down the north side of the bay, and Sorgan's fleet's been moving the members of the tribe there."

"That was nice of him," Zelana observed, "and 'nice' is something I wouldn't really have expected from somebody like Sorgan."

"He's not really all that bad, Zelana," Red-Beard disagreed. "It seems that sometimes wars bring out the best in people. We helped him quite a bit up there in the ravine, so now he's helping us. He'll be going south with Narasan to help out during the war in your brother's Domain, too."

"Isn't that sweet, Beloved?" Eleria said.

"Maybe I underestimated him," Zelana confessed. "He hides it very well, but there might just be a certain amount of decency lurking behind that rough exterior. Are those fire mountains still belching smoke?"

"They were when we left," Red-Beard replied. "We were hoping that they'd just roll over and go back to sleep, but they're still grumbling up there."

"It was probably a wise decision to move your tribe, Red-Beard," she said gravely. "Once a mountain starts spitting fire, it can go on for years and years, and you don't really want to be downhill from one of them while that's happening." She turned. "I think we'd better hurry, little brother. Let's get all of our friends away from that ravine. That might be a very dangerous place for the next several years."

"I sort of thought so myself, dear sister," Veltan agreed.

Red-Beard braced himself. "There's something you should probably know about, Zelana," he said. "My uncle's always been very attached to the village at the bottom of the ravine, but the fire mountains stopped our river, and if they don't go back to sleep, there's a good chance that Lattash will be buried in melted rock. Longbow and I found a place to set up a new village, but I didn't want to just jam the notion down uncle White-Braid's throat."

"Get to the point, Red-Beard," Zelana told him.

"This isn't too easy," he replied. "When Longbow and I went back to Lattash, my uncle seemed to have realized that he couldn't really make decisions for the tribe anymore, so he told the elders that he wanted to step aside, and he suggested that I might be the best one to replace him. It wasn't my idea, and I don't really like it very much, but I guess I'm the chief of the tribe now."

"Your uncle's very wise, Red-Beard," Zelana assured him. "You were the proper choice. Sometimes old ones become confused when things start moving too fast for them." She smiled faintly at Eleria. "That's when younger ones have to step over them."

"Would *I* do something like that, Beloved?" Eleria asked with wide-eyed innocence.

"Why don't we talk about that some other time, little one?" Zelana replied. "Right now, I've got more important things to consider."

Red-Beard's heart sank when Veltan's sloop reached the inlet that led back into the bay of Lattash. The fire mountains were spouting red-hot liquid miles up into the air again. He'd been hoping against hope that somehow his boyhood home might still be there to look at, but now that was obviously out of the question.

"I'm sorry, friend Red-Beard," Longbow said.

"It wasn't your fault, friend Longbow," Red-Beard replied. "Nothing we hope for comes to us without a cost, I guess. We won this war, but the winning cost us our home. It used to be a nice place, but nothing lasts forever, I suppose."

Sorgan Hook-Beak appeared to be in a state of near-panic when Veltan pulled his sloop up alongside the *Seagull* a bit later. "Where have you *been?*" he demanded of Zelana in a shrill voice. "That molten rock's coming down the ravine faster than any man could run. It'll probably swallow up the village before the sun goes down, and we'll never be able to save all the gold in that blasted cave."

"Calm yourself, Hook-Beak," she told him. "Rabbit, why don't you hop into that skiff of yours and go fetch Sorgan's cousins—Skell, Torl, and the rest of them? If we try to load all the gold in the cave on the *Seagull,* we'll sink her."

"Yes, ma'am," Rabbit agreed, hurrying forward toward the bow of the *Seagull.*

"We'll go on ahead, Sorgan," Zelana continued. "I'll need to remove the barriers I set up earlier before your men can start carrying the gold out."

"Do you think maybe you could widen that tunnel where the gold is just a bit, Lady Zelana?" Hook-Beak asked her. "It's awfully narrow, and things would go a lot faster if I could put more than two lines of men to work in there."

"That wouldn't be a good idea, Sorgan," she told him. "The walls of that tunnel support the roof, and if I push them out much farther, the ceiling could collapse. Just tell your men not to spend so much time fondling the gold bricks and move faster. Let's clear out the cave before the lava hits the bay."

"It can slop down into the bay all it wants to," Sorgan said. "I want to keep it out of the cave, is all."

"Once it hits the water, you and your men won't be able to see what you're doing, Sorgan. The clouds of steam will be thicker than any fog you've ever encountered."

"I guess I hadn't thought of that, Lady Zelana," he conceded.

The Maags followed the procedure that had been so successful when they'd dismantled the top of the stairway at the head of the ravine during the recent war, passing the gold bricks from man to man along twin lines of sailors. The rocky passageway that led back to the gold from the large chamber near the mouth of the cave was narrow, so there wasn't really enough room for more than two lines, but the sailors moved rapidly, so things seemed to be going quite well.

Red-Beard drifted on back into the side chamber to take one last look at the imitation ravine he'd constructed before the war in the real ravine had started, and for some reason Eleria followed along behind him. "Oops," she said. "We forgot something, didn't we?"

"I didn't quite follow that," Red-Beard admitted.

"There are quite a few of those yellow blocks buried under the clay, remember?"

Red-Beard suddenly burst out laughing. "I'd forgotten about that," he admitted. "Maybe we should remind Sorgan that there's gold here as well as in the back of the cave." He squinted at the model of the ravine. "It might take a while to dig it out, though. The clay we piled on top of those blocks has had enough time to dry by now, so the Maags are going to have to dig if they want this gold, too."

"It'll be good for them. I've noticed that sailors are sort of lazy when there's nothing exciting going on."

Red-Beard left the cave to the sweating Maags and began to climb up the steep slope behind the village, but he met Longbow coming down. "How much time do we have left?" he asked his friend.

"A few hours at least," Longbow replied. "The flow isn't moving quite as fast as it was before. That narrow place in the ravine where Skell built his fort seems to have slowed it somewhat. I think we'd still better get Sorgan's people off the beach as quickly as possible, though. In a peculiar sort of way the lava flow's behaving very much like Eleria's flood did."

"Do you think the berm might hold it back?"

"I doubt it. It kept the water from flooding the village, but water isn't as heavy as molten rock, and it follows the course of least resistance. The berm was built to hold back water, not liquid rock."

Red-Beard sighed. "Maybe it's for the best," he said. "If even a little bit of the village was still here, just the sight of it would keep bringing back memories—particularly in the minds of the old men of the tribe. I think it'll be better if there's no trace of Lattash left here. The tribe needs to move on, and memories of the past would only be a burden."

"You're getting better, Chief Red-Beard," Longbow noted. "You seem to be able to think past tomorrow now."

"I didn't ask for this, Longbow," Red-Beard complained.

"I know, my friend," Longbow said, "and that's what's going to make you a very good chief. Your tribe's lucky, you know. You just happened to be in the right place at the right time."

"I'd still much prefer to spend my time fishing or hunting."

"Wouldn't we all?"

"If it hadn't been for those cursed fire mountains, I'd have left that gold right where it was," Sorgan told Commander Narasan the following morning in the cabin at the stern of the *Seagull*. "If I pay the other ship captains now, they'll sail for home on the afternoon tide. I think we're going to need them when we fight your war off to the south, but I don't think they'll be very interested after they've got their hands on all that gold."

"You're probably right, Sorgan," the Trogite commander agreed. He smiled faintly. "Sometimes gold can be an enormous inconvenience, can't it?"

"Bite your tongue," Sorgan suggested. "The real problem's going to be that there's no possible way for me to keep the fact that the *Seagull* and the ships of several of my relatives are loaded with gold a secret. Ordinary sailors talk too much—particularly after they've had a gallon or so of beer to loosen their tongues. Sooner or later I'll be looking another one of those

'Kajak affairs' right in the face." He looked at Longbow. "How are your arrows holding out?" he asked wryly.

"There aren't quite that many, Hook-Beak," Longbow replied.

"What it all boils down to is that I need a safe place to hide all this gold, but no matter where I try to hide it, sooner or later somebody on one of these ships will get drunk and start bragging."

"Why don't you let me take care of it, Sorgan?" Zelana suggested.

"Shouldn't you give the various sea captains in your fleet a part of the gold you promised them, Captain Hook-Beak?" the young Trogite, Keselo, suggested. "If you don't pay them anything at all, they're likely to be very unhappy. If you give each one a quarter of what you promised him and tell him that the war isn't over yet, he may not be wildly happy, but at least he won't try to set fire to the *Seagull*."

"That's something you might want to consider, Sorgan," Narasan agreed with the young Trogite. "The war you hired the Maags to fight isn't really over yet. Our campaign up in the ravine was really only the first battle in a war that's still going on, wasn't it? We won that battle, but I'm fairly certain that there'll be three more. So far, they've only earned a quarter of what you promised to pay them. Give them quarter payment, and tell them that they still have to earn the rest."

"That might just work, Cap'n," the small Maag, Rabbit, agreed. "Part pay's better than no pay, and they'll probably decide to stay here so they can earn the other three parts."

"It might work," Sorgan conceded a bit dubiously. "Some of them might think that I tricked them, though, and they'll just take their quarter pay and set sail for home."

"Let them," Zelana suggested. "The ones who turn and run won't be of much use anyway, will they? The good ones will probably stay, and those are the ones we want anyway."

"Where are you going to hide the rest of my gold, Lady Ze-lana?" Sorgan asked.

"You don't really need to know that right now, dear Sor-gan," Zelana replied sweetly. "I *might* consider telling you, but only if you give me a firm promise that you won't touch a sin-gle drop of beer until this is all over."

"That's not fair at all!" Sorgan objected.

"You didn't really expect life to be fair, did you, dear Sor-gan?" she replied with a sly smile.

Red-Beard carefully covered his mouth until he managed to get his broad grin under control. Zelana was still as sharp as any knife when she put her mind to it. He'd been very worried when she'd fled back to her hiding place on the Isle of Thurn, but now that she'd regained her senses, things were looking better and better.

"How in the world did you come up with this idea?" Zelana asked Red-Beard when he showed her the sod lodges in the new village.

"Longbow's Chief, Old-Bear, told us that the tribes of the far north in your brother's Domain build their lodges out of sod because there aren't that many trees up there. It's windy here, so sod lodges give the people more protection. That's not re-ally why we decided to do it this way, though." Red-Beard quickly described the scheme he and Longbow had used to trick the men of the tribe into clearing the ground for planting.

"You're a very devious man, Red-Beard," she observed with a faint smile.

"I'm glad you approve," he replied with a sly smirk. "It all worked out quite well. Everybody got what they needed, and nobody was offended. Old customs and ideas can get in the way sometimes, but if you're quick on your feet, you can usu-ally come up with a way to step around them." He looked around at the blocky sod lodges. "It's not as pretty as Lattash was," he observed rather sadly, "but Lattash is gone now, so this village will have to do, I suppose."

"Nothing lasts forever, Red-Beard," Zelana said rather sadly. "After a while you learn to accept your losses and move on."

"I don't particularly like that very much, Zelana," Red-Beard admitted.

"You don't have to *like* it, Red-Beard," she said sweetly. "You just have to *do* it."

"Let's talk about gold, gentlemen," Zelana suggested to the gathering of Maags and Trogites later that day in the large cabin at the stern of the Trogite ship that served as Commander Narasan's headquarters.

"I could talk about gold all day long," Sorgan Hook-Beak said with a broad smile.

"We've noticed," Longbow observed.

"As you may have realized," Zelana continued, "our war here in the Land of Dhrall isn't over yet. Actually, it's only just begun. As you gentlemen have probably noticed, Veltan and I didn't provide too many specific details when we offered to give you gold for your help. Now that we've all come to know each other a little better, I think we might want to reconsider some of the terms of our original agreement."

"You're going to cut our pay in half?" Sorgan asked, his eyes narrowing.

"No. I thought we might double it instead. You people turned out to be about twice as useful as we'd originally thought you'd be, so twice as much gold would only be fair, wouldn't it?"

"I like the way Lady Zelana thinks," Ox said with a broad grin.

"I'll go along with you there, Ox," Gunda agreed.

"Are you going to follow your sister's example, Veltan?" the Trogite Narasan asked with a certain enthusiasm.

"I never argue with my sister," Veltan replied blandly. "Now that you've gotten to know her, I'm sure you can see why."

"Why, yes," Narasan said. "Now that you mention it, that does seem to be the wisest course."

"Is there really all that much gold here in the Land of Dhrall?" the bone-thin Trogite, Jalkan, asked in a tense voice.

"Mountains of it," Veltan said with an indifferent shrug. "Our older sister Aracia will quite probably have her next temple made out of the silly stuff. It's sort of pretty, I guess, but it's too soft to be of much use. Iron's not as pretty, but it's much more useful."

A strange, almost hungry expression came over Jalkan's face. Red-Beard didn't particularly like the Trogite Jalkan. He seemed to spend most of his time trying to impress Narasan, and he didn't treat the men under him very well.

Narasan looked at Sorgan. "I take it that you'll be coming south with us then?" he asked.

"I might even get there before you do, Narasan," Sorgan boasted. "We could make a wager on that, if you'd like."

"I'm not really a betting man, Sorgan." Narasan looked at Veltan. "How much time do you think Sorgan and I have before trouble breaks out in your part of this land?"

Veltan squinted. "I couldn't really say for certain, Commander. The servants of the Vlagh are probably a bit confused right now. It'll take them a while to change direction. The ravine was the only possible route for an invasion, and now it's totally blocked off. From what the people of my Domain have told me, it's obvious that the servants of the Vlagh will be paying me a call before too long."

"I don't think you should delay," Longbow told him. "Those Trogite ships will have to come back here after they've delivered your armies down there."

"Why's that, Longbow?" Sorgan asked.

"You didn't really expect the tribes of Zelana's Domain to walk, did you?"

"Are you saying that you and the other archers plan to join us, Longbow?" Narasan asked with a certain amount of surprise.

"Of course. Zelana owes her brother for bringing you and your men here, and *we're* the ones who take care of those responsibilities. You helped Sorgan, so Sorgan's going to help you. Veltan helped Zelana, so it's only right for her to help him. There's more, though."

"Oh?" Narasan said. "What's that?"

Longbow grinned at the Trogite. "You didn't *really* think that we were going to let you two have all the fun, did you?" he demanded.